S
Paxson

Paxson, Diana L.

Marion Zimmer
Bradley's Sword of
Avalon.

DATE			

MARION ZIMMER BRADLEY'S

SWORD OF
AVALON

OTHER BOOKS IN THIS SERIES

Marion Zimmer Bradley's Ravens of Avalon

Marion Zimmer Bradley's Ancestors of Avalon

Priestess of Avalon

Lady of Avalon

The Forest House

The Mists of Avalon

MARION ZIMMER BRADLEY'S

SWORD OF
AVALON

Diana L. Paxson

A ROC BOOK

ROC
Published by New American Library, a division of
Penguin Group (USA) Inc., 375 Hudson Street,
New York, New York 10014, USA
Penguin Group (Canada), 90 Eglinton Avenue East, Suite 700, Toronto,
Ontario M4P 2Y3, Canada (a division of Pearson Penguin Canada Inc.)
Penguin Books Ltd., 80 Strand, London WC2R 0RL, England
Penguin Ireland, 25 St. Stephen's Green, Dublin 2,
Ireland (a division of Penguin Books Ltd.)
Penguin Group (Australia), 250 Camberwell Road, Camberwell, Victoria 3124,
Australia (a division of Pearson Australia Group Pty. Ltd.)
Penguin Books India Pvt. Ltd., 11 Community Centre, Panchsheel Park,
New Delhi - 110 017, India
Penguin Group (NZ), 67 Apollo Drive, Rosedale, North Shore 0632,
New Zealand (a division of Pearson New Zealand Ltd.)
Penguin Books (South Africa) (Pty.) Ltd., 24 Sturdee Avenue,
Rosebank, Johannesburg 2196, South Africa

Penguin Books Ltd., Registered Offices:
80 Strand, London WC2R 0RL, England

First published by Roc, an imprint of New American Library, a division of Penguin Group (USA) Inc.

First Printing, December 2009
1   3   5   7   9   10   8   6   4   2

ROC REGISTERED TRADEMARK—MARCA REGISTRADA

Library of Congress Cataloging-in-Publication Data:
Paxson, Diana L.
Marion Zimmer Bradley's Sword of Avalon/Diana L. Paxson.
p.   cm.
ISBN 978-0-451-46292-3
1. Avalon (Legendary place)—Fiction.   I. Bradley, Marion Zimmer.   II. Title.
PS3566.A897M345   2009
813'.54—dc22   2009024978

Set in Bembo RegularInD
Designed by Ginger Legato

Printed in the United States of America

To Steve,
fellow forger of words.

NAMES IN THE STORY

PEOPLE

PEOPLE OF THE ISLAND OF THE MIGHTY

(Names in parenthesis are people dead before the story begins. Names in capital letters indicate main characters. A + marks figures known from legend.)

Acaimor—an Ai-Utu boy, one of Mikantor's Companions

Adjonar—Ai-Zir, one of Mikantor's Companions

Agraw—Cimara's bridegroom

Alder—a girl of the Lake Village

Analina—a student at Avalon

Anaterve—a trader of Belerion, father of Analina

ANDERLE—Lady of Avalon

Badger—headman of the Lake Village

Beaver—a Lake Village boy, one of Mikantor's Companions

Belkacem—priest and lore master at Avalon

Beniharen—an Ai-Ilf boy, one of Mikantor's Companions

Chaoud—an Ai-Zir farmer

Cimara—princess and later queen of the Ai-Zir, Mikantor's cousin

Curlew—a hunter, one of the moor folk of Belerion

Durrin—a priest and bard of Avalon, father of Tirilan

(Eilantha—temple name of Tiriki)

Ellet—a young priestess from the Ai-Giru

Eltan—king of the Ai-Ushen, brother of Ketaneket

Eltanor—a senior priest of Avalon

Eran—the smith at Avalon

GALID—a chieftain of the Amanhead clan of the Ai-Zir

Ganath—an Ai-Giru boy studying on Avalon and later a healer

Goosey and Gander—twin children of the Lake Village

Grebe—Mikantor's foster brother, one of his Companions

Hino—Galid's fool

Iftiken—king of the Ai-Giru

Irnana—cousin of Anderle, wife of Uldan and mother of Mikantor

Izri—one of Galid's men

Kaisa-Zan—High Priestess of the Ai-Utu

Keddam—one of Galid's warriors

Ketaneket—queen of the Ai-Ushen, sister of Eltan

Kiri—an old priestess

Larel—a priest of Avalon

Leka—High Priestess of the Ai-Akhsi

Linne—High Priestess of the Ai-Giru

Lycoren—a chieftain of the Ai-Akhsi

Lysandros—of Troian descent, one of Mikantor's Companions

Menguellet—queen of the Ai-Akhsi

(Micail—Prince of Ahtarrath in the Sea Kingdoms, high priest of the Temple of Light, and later, of Avalon)

MIKANTOR (Woodpecker)—dispossessed prince of the Ai-Zir

Muddazakh—Galid's champion

Nuya—High Priestess of the Ai-Zir

Olavi—High Priestess of the Ai-Siwanet

Orlai—a farmer of Azan

(Osinarmen—temple name of Micail)

Pelicar—Ai-Ilf, one of Mikantor's Companions

Ramdane—one of Galid's men

Redfern—Miko's foster mother

Romen—Ai-Utu, one of Mikantor's Companions

Rouikhed—an Ai-Akhsi boy trained at Avalon, one of Mikantor's Companions

Saarin—High Priestess of the Ai-Ushen

Sakanor—King of the Ai-Utu

Shizuret—High Priestess of the Ai-Ilif

Soumer—one of Galid's warriors

Squirrel—an old man of the elder folk of the Vale

Tanecar—son of Queen Ketaneket of the Ai-Ushen

Tegues—Ai-Giru, one of Mikantor's Companions

(Tiriki—Princess of Ahtarrath, high priestess of Avalon)

TIRILAN—Anderle's daughter and heir

Ulansi—Ai-Zir, one of Mikantor's Companions

Uldan—war leader of the Ai-Zir

Urtaya—queen of the Ai-Utu

Vole—a Lake Village boy studying on Avalon

Willow Woman—Badger's mother, headwoman of the Lake Village

Zamara—queen of the Ai-Zir, sister of Uldan

People of the Middle Sea and Northern Lands

Aelfrix—a boy from the City of Circles

+(Agamemnon—King of Mycenae, victor of Troia)

Aiaison—eldest son of the King of Tiryns

+Aletes—great-grandson of Heracles and of Iolaos, leader of the Eraklidae attacking Korinthos

Bodovos the Bear—commander of the guard at the City of Circles

+(Brutus—a prince of Troia who emigrated with his followers to the Isle of the Mighty)

Buda—sister of Bodovos, mother of Aelfrix

+Doridas and Hyanthidas—Kings of Korinthos

+(Erakles [Heracles]—disinherited prince of Argos, hero, ancestor of the Eraklidae)

Katuerix—smith at Bhagodheunon

+(Klytemnaestra—wife, and murderer, of Agamemnon)

+Kresfontes—son of Aristomakhos, brother of Temenos and Aristo-demos, great-great-grandson of Erakles, leader of the attack on Tiryns and Mykenae

Leta—daughter of Aletes

Lord Loutronix—Master of Dikes and Locks, City of Circles

Maglocunos—King of the Tuathadhoni

Melandros—chariot driver and lover of Aiaison

+(Menelaos [Menelaus]—King of Sparta, husband of Helena)

Naxomene—Queen of Tiryns

+(Odikeos [Odysseus]—king of the Ionian Isles, hero of Troia)

+(Orestes—son and avenger of Agamemnon, father of Tisamenos)

+(Persaios [Perseus]—heir of Tiryns and founder of Mykenae)

Phorkaon—King of Tiryns

Tanit—a slave girl in the service of Queen Naxomene

Thersander—a trader from Korinthos

+Tisamenos—King of Mycenae

Tuistos, Mannos and Sowela—priest-kings and -queen of the City of Circles

VELANTOS—bastard son of the King of Tiryns, a smith

POWERS

Honored at Avalon

Banur—the four-faced god, destroyer/preserver; ruler of Winter

Caratra—daughter or nurturing aspect of Ni-Terat, the Great Mother. Venus is Her star

Manoah—the Great Maker, Lord of the Day, identified with the Sun; ruler of Summer

Nar-Inabi—"Star-Shaper," god of the night, the stars and the sea; ruler of Harvest time

Ni-Terat—Dark Mother of All, Veiled aspect of the Great Mother, goddess of the Earth; ruler of Planting time

Honored by the Tribes

"Achi"—Exalted or Enduring One, used as a title of respect or a name for the goddess of upwelling power

Achimaiek—"Grandmother," Crone Face of the Goddess

The Chiding One—proto-goddess later called Ceridwen

Guayota—the Evil One, appears as a dog

Magek—the Sun god

Honored in the Lands of the Middle Sea

Apollon—Apollo

Arei—Ares

Athana—Athena

Castor and Pollux—twin demigods, sons of Zeus (also the names given by Velantos to his war axes)

Diwaz—Zeus

Epaitios—Hephaestus

E-ra—Hera

Ereias—Hermes

Keraunos—Thunderer (Zeus)

Lady of the Doves—Aphrodite

Lady of the Forge—an aspect of Athena

Paion—Apollo

Posedaon Enesidaone (Earthshaker)—Poseidon

Potnia—"the Lady," a general goddess-title

Potnia Theron—Lady of the Beasts, or Nature

PEOPLES

Ai-Akhsi—People of the Ram

Ai-Giru—People of the Frog

Ai-Ilf—People of the Boar

Ai-Siwanet—People of the Hawk

Ai-Ushen—People of the Wolf

Ai-Utu—People of the Hare

Ai-Zir—People of the Bull

Akhaeans—the people of the Peloponnese

Danaans—peoples of southern Greece

Dorians—peoples of northern Greece

Elder Folk—people of the oldest blood of the Island of the Mighty, now living on the edges of the arable land; includes the people of the Lake Village and the moors of Belerion

Eraklidae, Children of Erakles—the Dorians, said to be descended from the offspring of Heracles

The Tribes—dominant culture of the Island of the Mighty

Ti-Sahharin—the Sacred Sisters, priestesses to the tribes

Tuathadhoni—proto-Celtic people north of Danube Plain

PLACES

Aman river—the Avon that flows through Wiltshire and Dorset

Amanhead clanhold—Galid's home

Akhaea—the Peloponnese and Central Greece

Akhsian—territory of the Ai-Akhsi—the Dales, Lancashire, Yorkshire, Cumbria

Argolid—the plain below Argos, including Mykenae and Tiryns

Azan—the "Bull-Pen," territory of the five clans of the Ai-Zir—Dorset, Wiltshire, Gloucester, Oxfordshire

Azan-Ylir—Center of Azan, hold of the Henge Plain clan—modern Amesbury

Barrow of the Three Queens—Three Spinsters' dolmen, Devon

Belerion—an area in Utun—southern end of Cornwall

Bhagodheunon—Dun of the Beeches, near Wurzberg, Germany

Carn Ava clanhold—Avebury

City of Circles (old Zaiadan)—located between modern Heligoland and Eiderstedt on the Jutland coast

Girun—territory of the Ai-Giru—Essex, Norfolk, Suffolk (Anglia)

Gorsefield—Shovel Down, near Chagford, Devon

The Henge—Stonehenge

Hidden Realm—Faerie

Hyperborea—Britain and Scandinavia, the country beyond the north wind.

Ilifen—territory of the Ai-Ilf, the Midlands, Warwick-, Derby-, Lincoln-, Leicestershires

Isle of the Mighty, Isle of Tin, Hesperides—Great Britain

Khem—Egypt

Korinthos—Corinth, Greece

Maiden Circle—Merry Maidens, near Penzance, Cornwall

Maidenhills—near Five Knolls tumulus, on the Ridgeway

Mykenae—Mycenes, Peloponnese, Greece

Nemea—northern Peloponnese, Greece

New Troia—lands held by descendants of Brutus of Troia, Kent, Sussex, Hampshire

Sabren river—Severn

Siwan—territory of the Ai-Siwanet, lands north of the Cheviot Hills

Springs of Sulis—Bath

The Summer Country—the Vale of Avalon

Three Alders—Tewkesbury

The Lead Hills—the Mendips, Somerset

Tiryns—ancient citadel outside of Nafplion, Greece

The Tor—Glastonbury Tor, Somerset

Troia—Troy

Ushan—Ai-Ushen territory, Wales

Utun—territory of the Ai-Utu, Devon and Cornwall

The Wombhill—Silbury Hill, Avebury

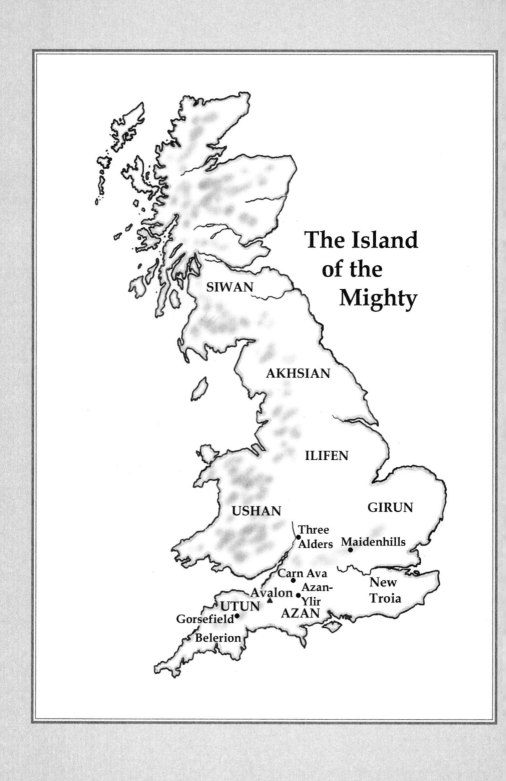

The Island
of the
Mighty

SIWAN

AKHSIAN

ILIFEN

USHAN

GIRUN

Three
Alders

Maidenhills

Carn Ava

New
Troia

Avalon

Azan-
Ylir

UTUN

AZAN

Gorsefield

Belerion

MARION ZIMMER BRADLEY'S

SWORD OF
AVALON

PROLOGUE

Morgaine speaks:

*T*hey say that the old sleep little, as if they have no need of rest with the body's last sleep so near. Whether it is age or the weight of memory that keeps me restless, at night my sleep is broken, and I rise early. This morning I left my bed without waking my maidens to walk by the Lake just at that misty hour between the dark and the dawning, when the birds sing forth their promise that the light will return. As the first rays of the sun glimmered through the clouds, a gleam of light pierced the waters, and for a moment I saw the blazing length of the Sword.

Time converged around me, and once more I was in the Sacred Barge of Avalon, and Arthur lay dying in my arms. Lancelet cast Excalibur into the Lake and saw it received by the Lady. My breath stopped as I waited to see if Her hand would reappear, returning the Sword from the depths to choose a new King to save Britannia.

Vision followed vision, but what I saw was fire—the metal first forged in the fires of heaven, hailed as a thing of power by the folk who dwelled on the chalk before ever a Druid or Adept from the drowned islands came to these shores. I saw the fires of the forge in which a master smith, fleeing his people's doom, had made it into a sword to fit the hand of a king. Hidden and renewed, broken and reforged, in the time of Britannia's greatest need it had returned to bring victory.

I stared, and clearing vision showed me the surface of the Lake gray and still once more. Then I wept, and even that image blurred. The dark people of the hills who had been the Sword's keepers were gone. Water, not fire, hid the blade Arthur wielded, and there was no king of the ancient line to call it forth again. The gleam that I had seen had been the leap of a fish, no more.

And yet as I began to walk again I realized that the tears in my eyes were not from despair. When Excalibur went into the Lake, I knew it for the end of an Age, *the loss of all that I had loved. And yet behind its veil of mist, Avalon endures. The star-steel was only metal until the skill of a smith and the passion of a priestess ensouled it. What they did in those days, when the world they knew seemed doomed, may be done again if the Lady of the Forge takes up her hammer once more.*

The Sword is gone, but hope does not die.

ONE

ire.

The acrid reek of burning thatch catches in her throat; then smoke sets her coughing, panic flaring along her limbs as red light flickers across the floor. She snatches up the wailing child. The hide across the door is wrenched away. Beyond, she glimpses figures and the gleam of blades.

A woman screams with a shrill intensity that cuts across the clash of bronze weapons and the battle cries. The scream is her own, and yet the self that knows this is somehow detached from the hot breath of the flames. The baby coughs and struggles, strong limbs, strong spirit fighting to survive. A roof beam crashes across the doorway and she whimpers, wracked by an anguish beyond her body's pain. She stares through the flames, seeking an escape, and enemy faces leer back at her. She recoils and sinks to the floor, smoke stealing her breath as a cry severs soul from sense—"So dies the Son of a Hundred Kings!"

And awareness whirls outward—she sees the thatched roofs of the royal enclosure collapsing as the fire spreads; the bull horns mounted above the great gate crash down. The bodies of warriors, startled naked from sleep, lie scattered on the bloody ground as enemies pile up the looted cauldrons of bronze, the fine weavings, the cups and ornaments of gold.

Time speeds, and the charred timbers of Azan-Ylir become sodden lumps that are soon covered by green. But the flames spread, and the Ai-Giru, the Ai-Ilf, the Ai-Utu, and then the Ai-Akhsi and the Ai-Ushen and even the Ai-Siwanet far to the north are engulfed in turn. The tribes of the Island of the Mighty tear at each other's throats like starving dogs as generations pass. And when ships with painted sails approach the white cliffs of the island, there is no one to face the fair-haired warriors who leap onto the sand, their striped and chequered garments swirling about their knees. They rampage across the countryside, burning whatever the earlier wars have left, and the songs, the arts, the wisdom of the Seven Tribes are as if they had never been.

"Goddess, what can save us?" her spirit cries.

And in answer she hears a call, "From the stars will come the Sword of the King!"

"LADY, ARE YOU ILL? What's wrong?"

Shuddering, Anderle opened her eyes. Kiri was bending over her, her old face creased in concern. Smoke hung in the air, but it carried the sharp scent of burning charcoal, not thatch . . . not the smell of roasting flesh. She caught her breath, fixing her gaze on the soot-blackened ceiling of the smithy on the Maiden's Isle, and trees and sunlight on the green peak of the Tor.

Summer had come at last to the marshlands. For the moment, the clouds had retreated, and everything living made the most of Manoah's light. An exultant tide of greenery choked the watercourses and hung above the pools; insects hummed in the humid air.

"Sit you down, my lady—" scolded Kiri, helping her to the bench by the open side of the shed, where a light breeze wafted from the direction of the sea. "You came over faint, what with the heat of the day and the forge." Kiri looked accusingly at the smith.

"Do not blame me—" He frowned. "She knows better than to lean over the fire." The smith-priest wore only a loincloth beneath the heavy hide apron. Anderle wished she could do the same, but the blue draperies of the High Priestess were a symbol of her dignity, and old Kiri, who had attended her since she was small, would not have let her leave the Tor without the fine linen veil.

"You screamed—" said little Ellet, fanning her. "I thought you were burned."

"I'm all right! I was seeing . . . pictures . . . in the flames."

"Was it a vision, Lady?" Ellet's blue eyes grew round. Her brown hair was fine and inclined to escape its braid, fluffing around her face like the feathers of a young bird.

"Goddess, I hope not!" Anderle exclaimed. "Azan-Ylir was burning—they were all killed, even Irnana's child."

She brushed back a strand of heavy dark hair and sighed. She and Irnana were both descended from the old line that had provided so many priests and priestesses to rule Avalon, but her cousin had inherited their height and the family's red hair, while Anderle took after the slender, dark folk of the Lake Village, or perhaps, as legend had it, after the folk of that Otherworld that was only a heartbeat from their own.

Kiri's lips thinned. There had always been raiding back and forth among the tribes and clans of the Island of the Mighty, but in the past year the situation had gotten worse. The older priestesses spoke of a time when the weather was warmer, but the rains came more often with each year and the floods remained longer, turning every piece of high ground in the Vale into an island. Men muttered that one day there might be no summer at all. And the Bull of Azan who led the warriors of the tribe was old, his grown sons killed in the battle in which the sister's son who should have been his heir had died as well. He had taken Irnana to wife three years before. Mikantor was their only child.

"We've had no word . . ." said Eran, frowning.

"The fields were stubble . . ." Anderle said slowly. "This was later in the summer, when the hay harvest is done . . ."

"It was a heat-born fancy!" Kiri proclaimed. Anderle sighed. She was surrounded by people who had known her since she was an infant, already designated as heir by the word of her grandmother and the will of the stars. She had first put on the ornaments of the high priestess when her breasts were barely grown. It was only to be expected that they should treat her as an icon and not as an adult with a mind of her own. But she was eighteen now, and expecting a child. She laid a palm upon the swell of her belly. Perhaps when they saw her with a babe at the breast, they would realize that she was a woman grown.

"Drink this water now, my love, and let the fear fade. To dwell on such things does no good to you or the child!"

Perhaps, thought Anderle, sipping from the elm wood cup. Or perhaps it was a warning. Terrifying as the vision had been, it was the cry that haunted her. The loss of any child was a tragedy; the death of her cousin's child would be a personal sorrow. But the Voice had lamented Mikantor as something greater, as the heir to the royal line that had come to the Island of the Mighty from the Drowned Lands across the sea. She could not prevent tribal raids, even when they threatened those dear to her, but to safeguard that heritage was most certainly a part of her duty as Lady of Avalon.

"Rest now, my little one, and we'll send for a litter to bear you back to the Tor . . ."

Anderle nodded and drew down the veil, grateful now for its protection. Better that Kiri should believe her tired than to start asking why Anderle still frowned.

ANDERLE FLINCHED AS THE landscape of her vision came into view. They were passing through the opening in the stone fence that wound along the edge of the down. Before her, the fields of Azan were bright with the stubbled gold of harvest. To her right a line of grave mounds paralleled the road. To the left rose the stark stones of the great henge. The track descended to cross the shallow bed the Aman had carved through the plain, with the clanhold beyond. She had forgotten that crops on the plain ripened faster than they did in the marshes around Avalon.

Durrin came up beside her, fair brows creasing in concern.

"It's nothing. The child kicked me—" she said quickly.

"You should not have walked so far," he said repressively.

When priests and priestesses lay together in the Great Rite, they were not supposed to remember who the mortals carrying the power of the gods had been, but everyone knew that Durrin had begotten the babe now stirring in her womb, and he was inclined to behave as if he were her husband as well as the father of the child.

"Would you have me swaying in a litter for all those miles? Or bouncing in one of King Uldan's chariots? Walking is easier, I assure you." Anderle suppressed her urge to snap at him. He would have forgiven her—everyone said that pregnant women were often short-tempered. But she was the Lady of Avalon, and ought to be beyond such frailty.

"In your condition, I would have had you stay at the Tor," he replied, his fair skin reddening, "and not make this journey at all."

He was not alone in that, she thought with a sigh. When she announced her intention to visit her cousin in Azan, everyone from old Kiri on down had yammered objections. Kiri was too old to travel so far, but she had sent Ellet, who was utterly devoted, if a little naive, along as her deputy. Anderle set herself to endure their solicitude. She knew Irnana, and she knew the old king. They would not have listened to a messenger. Would they listen to *her*? If they did not, perhaps she could persuade Uldan's sister, the queen. War was men's business, but the queen was the final authority.

"Well, we will be there soon—" Durrin mastered his own irritation and gave her the smile that always lifted her heart. The gods had blessed him with beauty beyond the ordinary. She hoped their child would take after him.

Sweet with distance, they heard the calling of a horn. They had been seen, and soon her cousin's people would welcome her with something cool to drink and a soft place to lie down. Despite her proud words to Durrin the ache in her back was constant now. The track led toward the royal clan-hold, a ditched enclosure with a bank and palisade. Men came running along the paths that led in from the fields to the smaller gateways. The thatched cones of several roundhouses showed above the fencing, and the crosspiece above the main gate was crowned by a pair of aurochs horns and a sun disk of gilded bronze. The shaggy red cattle grazing in the home pasture lifted their heads in momentary curiosity as the party from Avalon passed. As they drew nearer, the warriors of the king's household formed two lines. They were big men in woolen kilts cinched by broad leather belts, holding round shields of painted leather and broadbladed ceremonial spears. From inside the compound she heard the deep boom of a drum.

Anderle lifted her hand in blessing as they passed. "Achi! Achi!" came the murmur from either side. As the warriors raised their spears in salutation, the setting sun flashed on golden armrings and spearpoints of polished

bronze. The display went far to explain why King Uldan's neighbors envied
him. She suppressed a shiver of apprehension as they passed beneath the
shadow of the horns.

"YOU CAN SEE THAT we are well defended." The king set down his golden
beaker of barley beer. He was a big man and still strong, though the muscle
was beginning to sag on the strong bones and gray frosted his brown hair.
He gestured at the circle of stout pillars that supported the roof of the feasting hall, carved and painted in chevrons and spirals that glowed and faded
as the firelight rose and fell. Strong they might be, but the walls, white-
washed on the outside and hung with fine weavings within, were no more
than plastered wicker. An enemy that breached the palisade would have no
trouble getting through.

"The wolves may howl around my gates, but none will pull me down,"
he continued, "whether they go on two legs or on four."

Anderle sighed. This last season, both kinds had grown bolder. A wolf
pack roamed the hills above the plain, but it was the Ai-Ushen, whose lands
lay beyond the estuary to the north, whose raids had decimated the herds
of the Amanhead clan. The mutton that had been simmered with herbs and
barley for the feasting lay like a lump in her belly. This was not going well.

"That is what the body's eyes see," she said patiently. "But I have been
trained to see with the spirit, and vision showed me these roofs in flames…"
The sight of the hearth fire brought it back again.

Irnana sniffed. "Such talk of visions may impress the common folk,
cousin, but I grew up on Avalon too. Did our teachers not tell us that time
is always the hardest thing to pin down in prophecy?" She patted Anderle's
arm. "I remember how I fretted when I was carrying Mikantor. You have
said yourself that the day was warm. Is it not more likely that this is some
fancy born of your own fears?"

Anderle bit back her first retort. Irnana might be married to the most
powerful king in the Island of the Mighty, but she must always defer to
Uldan's sister Zamara, who was the queen. The priestess suspected her

cousin had always resented that it was Anderle, not she, who had been chosen to rule in Avalon.

"Surely my own fears would have shown me danger to the babe in my womb . . ." She laid her hand protectively on the hard curve of her belly, where the growing infant stretched and turned. "The child I am trying to save is yours!"

"Anderle," said the king, "we do appreciate your care. But the responsibility and the right to protect my son belong to me, not to the Lady of Avalon!" He drained his beaker, and held it out to be refilled by the girl who was carrying the ale bucket around the hall.

Anderle held her hand across the opening to her own cup. She had drunk enough, and did not need to add ale-sickness to the other discomforts of pregnancy. She shifted on the cushioned bench, but she suspected that for her there would be no comfortable position until the child was born.

"And who do you think would attack us?" asked Irnana. "The Ai-Ushen worry our northern border, but their war leader is Eltan, a boy without the prestige to mount a serious campaign, and the Ai-Utu to the southwest have always been our friends."

"Not all enemies are outside borders," Anderle said in a neutral tone. "Are the chieftains of all your clans content with your rule?"

Uldan's face darkened. "Priestess, you go too far! Do you think I do not know my men, warriors with whom I have shed blood, who have guarded my back when we faced our foes?"

He gestured toward the benches that circled the fire. Anderle recognized the clan chiefs from Amanhead and Oakhill, Carn Ava and Belsaira and the rest, and wondered. She knew that Galid of Amanhead, for instance, had recently lost his family to one of the illnesses that periodically swept the land, and floods had drowned their fields. Did their chieftains still believe in the luck of the old bull?

They see you growing old, and your sister without a son. . . . Anderle lowered her eyes. She felt Durrin stiffen protectively beside her and laid a hand on his arm. *There's none so deaf as the man who refuses to hear.*

"They have been content to follow me for twenty winters and more,"

Uldan went on. "The plain is the heart of our land. How could it be ruled from Amanhead or Carn Ava or Oakhill?"

"We guard the great henge and the ancestral mounds," Irnana said proudly. "This is the sacred center of Azan."

"Does anybody still care?" Anderle asked bitterly. "You and I are descended from the People of Wisdom who raised the Henge, and we were brought up on tales of its power, but what does it mean to the clanmothers of the Ai-Zir? Who cares about grave mounds when our people bury the ashes of their dead in pots in the soil? If they did, Carn Ava might challenge you—their circle of stones is just as holy as the Henge. But from them I believe you safe. I only hope that you know the other four clans as well as you think you do."

"Peace—" Durrin's soft voice took the sting from his reproof. He smiled at Irnana, and the other woman sat back with a sigh.

Durrin had that effect on most women, Anderle reflected, trying to suppress bitterness. When they came together in the ritual, she had carried the power of the Goddess as he did that of the God, and now she carried his child. But would he have even looked at her if she had not been the Lady of Avalon?

"Surely you know your own people best. . . ." he went on, and the tension faded from the air.

Perhaps, Anderle thought grimly. *I must speak with Zamara.* It did not bode well that the queen had not come to the welcome feast. She was older than her brother and would bear no more sons. To continue the royal line, Uldan had to hold on to power until Mikantor was old enough to lead the warriors for Zamara's daughter. To keep track of the shifting stresses and alliances within the tribe was the job of the queen. Unless grief for her son had completely overwhelmed her, Zamara would know where any danger might be.

"Enough of such talk." Irnana spoke into the silence. "I refuse to be frightened by such vapors when it is clear that the plain has been blessed by the gods. You must walk out with me tomorrow and see how this year's heifers have grown!"

As if in agreement, the child in Anderle's belly kicked strongly. Irnana noted Anderle's flinch and laughed. "Do you have another warrior in there who will spar with my Mikantor?"

Anderle shook her head. The priestesses had assured her that the child was a girl, a daughter to inherit the leadership of Avalon, though what use would that be if the tribes destroyed each other? *We should strive to leave our children a better world,* she thought unhappily as her cousin rattled on.

"You have spent too much time at your prayers, Lady of Avalon. No doubt the babe will appreciate the motion if you take some exercise."

She gestured to the girl who had brought the ale to continue onward, and Anderle did the same, but Durrin and Uldan both held out their beakers to be refilled. Perhaps that was just as well. If they drank together, Durrin's charm might accomplish what Anderle's authority could not.

"Shall we go, cousin? Let the men drown their wits if they will. They will regret it when morning comes." Irnana rose.

"Indeed, if you mean to drag me all over the plain tomorrow I had better get what rest I may." Anderle managed a smile.

THE BED WAS TOO soft. In the house of the Lady of Avalon, even the high priestess slept on a pallet of straw on the floor. At Azan, the bedplace reserved for honored guests was of a different order entirely, a yielding mattress of goose down laid atop one of straw supported by a web of rope strung across a frame. Each time Anderle or Ellet turned, it creaked and swung. She had expected to fall asleep quickly. The younger priestess had nodded off as soon as they retired, but Anderle lay wakeful, listening to the snorts and whistles coming from the other sections. The partitions of wicker or woven wool between the posts and the wall did little to muffle the sound.

Even the disciplines that were a part of the training of a priestess had brought her no more than a few hours of rest. True sleep eluded her, and at length she sighed and carefully levered herself upright. Ellet stirred with a mumbled query.

"Sleep, child," she whispered. "I am only going to relieve myself. There's no need for you to get up too." It was true enough that with the baby sitting on her bladder it had been months since she had been able to sleep the night through, but whether the reason was discomfort or anxiety, Anderle could no longer bear to lie still.

She parted the hangings that defined their sleeping place and carefully stepped over Durrin, who lay snoring on a straw pallet just outside. The dim glow of the coals gave enough light for her to thread her way between the warriors who lay by the fire, and ease out past the hide that curtained the main door.

It was the still hour just before dawn, dank and chill. Ground fog curled among the buildings. Anderle took a deep breath as she emerged from behind the wicker screen and coughed as an acrid reek caught in her lungs. Shock pebbled the skin of her arms. That was no fog! She was smelling smoke, illuminated by the first faint glow of a fire. The thatch of one of the smaller roundhouses was burning. For a moment despair paralyzed her limbs. It was the scene of her vision. But in her vision *she* had not been here.

She swallowed a shout as she lumbered back across the yard. What good was a warning if she could not use it to change the outcome? Swiftly she slipped through the door, bending to shake the shoulder of the first sleeping warrior.

"Up, man! There are foes within the ward. But quietly, and you may take them by surprise before they know you are warned."

She felt rather than saw the ripple of motion as the word was passed. Men leaped to their feet, scrambling to snatch swords from their pegs on the posts and shields from the wall. Anderle clung to one of the uprights. Indoors, she risked being trapped in a burning building, but would she be safer outside? No man of the tribes would knowingly harm the Lady of Avalon, but even if she had been wearing the blue robes of her calling instead of a shift and a shawl, they might not have recognized her in the dark. She tried to convince herself that she was safest here.

Metal clanked and someone swore. She heard Uldan's voice, low but firm, and felt her galloping heartbeat slow. The lack of imagination that had made him ignore her warning kept him from panic now. Tall forms shoved past her, gathering in front of the doorway. Then a curt command sent them pounding forward. There was a cry, a clash of bronze. "Ai-Zir! 'Ware the horns of the Bull!" came the full-throated roar, and "Fear the Fang! Ai-Ushen!" drawn out in a wolf's shrill howl in reply.

She should have expected it. The tribe to the north was under constant pressure from mountain dwellers who had suffered worse still. No doubt the heifers of which Irnana had boasted were already on their way to the Ai-Ushen fields. Productive land was the greatest treasure, but gold and bronze could buy food from those who still had fields in which grain would grow.

Someone stirred up the hearth fire and she met Ellet's horrified gaze. Durrin was struggling to his feet, blinking at the commotion around him.

"Get our cloaks! Irnana, are you here?"

But the king's wife was already pushing toward her. Red hair streaming wildly, she clutched at Anderle's arm. Outside the shouting was louder, the scent of smoke stronger now.

"Help me get to Mikantor!'

For a heartbeat the priestess stared. Then she remembered that the child slept with his nurse in one of the other roundhouses. Anderle quailed at the turmoil she could hear outside. Her spirit, if not her body, had been weakened by Kiri's cosseting. No use to protest she was unable to help—Uldan's men were fighting; Ellet and Durrin looked to her for direction. Pregnant or not, she would have to use whatever power she had. *And if the Lady of Avalon cannot find a few spells for protection,* she thought then, *our line deserves to fail.*

"We will go together. Be still, and remember your training!" she said aloud. "Take a deep breath, blur the air around you. If we rush out in a panic, they will cut us down!" She hoped Zamara had the sense to stay inside. Her house was in the center of the enclosure, marked by the standard on its pole. Even the Ai-Ushen wolves would not dare to kill a queen.

We must be shadows . . . She drew power from the earth and wrapped it around them, extending her inner awareness to sense the flow of energies outside. There was no one near. She squeezed Irnana's arm and drew her through the door.

The body of one of the house guards lay before it, other forms littered the ground nearby, but near the main gate bronze flared as struggling figures moved in and out of the fitful glow. A woman screamed as a warrior forced her down, tearing at her clothes. Anderle's gut twisted as a child's wail went on and on.

"Which house?" she whispered as they edged forward, and Irnana pointed toward a smaller building behind the house of the queen.

Behind them light flared as someone set a torch to the thatch of Uldan's feasting hall. Men were running in and out of the building, bundling goods and gear into the woolen hangings that had insulated the walls. If Irnana had not begged her help she would have been inside. Could either rank or magic have protected her against men maddened by battle lust and greed?

They had nearly reached the house where Mikantor slept with the other children. Anderle recoiled, hands flashing a gesture of warding as a slight figure darted toward them, then recognized her as one of the maids who had served in the hall.

"My lady, you're safe—" The girl clutched at Irnana's arm.

"Be quiet, you fool—" hissed Anderle. But it was already too late. The maid's movement had caught the attention of one of the warriors as the scurry of a mouse will bring an owl. As the man leaped toward them Anderle tensed, then recognized the bulky figure as the chieftain from Oakhill who had been in the feasting hall.

"Galid!" cried Irnana. "Guard us—I must get to my son!"

The man shook his head, lips curling in a mirthless grin. "Let Uldan's spawn die as my sons died. Uldan has lost the favor of the gods!"

For a moment Irnana stood staring. "Was it you? Are you the traitor who let in the wolves?"

Galid's gaze kindled as he looked her up and down, firelight glinting on the bands that confined the many braids of his hair. "Indeed, and you are a bleating ewe, but a pretty one. I'll spare you to warm my bed if you behave."

Fury blazed in her face—no, Anderle could see it so clearly because the Children's House was on fire. As Galid reached for her, Irnana ducked under his arm and dove through the doorway.

As the man turned back Anderle drew herself up, rage and terror beating in her veins. "Do you dare to oppose the power of Avalon!"

His eyes widened. What was he seeing? This was the first time Anderle had put on the glamour of the Dark Mother in earnest. She had not known if she could, especially now. It was need that had unleashed the power, observed that part of her mind that was not gibbering, need channeled by the disciplines of Avalon. She had never truly *needed* that power before.

"You will stand aside," she said in a compelling voice. "We are not your enemies. . . ."

Her heart leaped as she realized that the cruel triumph in his face was giving way to fear. She turned to follow Irnana through the door.

"Anderle, it's too late!" Durrin grabbed her arm. Heat seared her face, and she realized that not only the thatching but the walls were aflame. Had smoke already overwhelmed those within? She reached out with her spirit, and heard a child's wailing cry.

So dies the Son of a Hundred Kings!

"No!" Anderle denied the words that reverberated in memory. The smoldering hide that curtained the door was pulled aside. Through a swirl of smoke she glimpsed Irnana with her son clasped to her breast.

"Save him!"

Anderle jerked free of Durrin's grasp and leaned into a blast of heat like a demon's forge, staggering as Irnana thrust the child into her arms and swayed back, robed and crowned in flame. In the next moment her triumphant smile contorted. Anderle reeled away, shutting her eyes as the vision of splendor turned to a horror of blazing hair and crisping skin.

Her scream broke Galid's trance. Seeing the child in her arms, the warrior grinned and swung up his sword.

"Anderle!" yelled Durrin, thrusting past her to grab Galid's arm. "Run!"

Ellet shoved her away from the struggling men. Anderle saw Durrin break loose. His anguished gaze sought hers. Galid turned as well. Durrin shouted his name, and threw himself into the swing of Galid's sword.

"Run!" The plea came to her heart, not her ears. Weeping, she allowed Ellet to drag her away.

TWO

*M*y lady, we can't stop here!" Ellet stared at the dim bulk of the barrow. "This is a place of ghosts!" She clutched at Mikantor, who began to cry. Despite her words the younger priestess was reeling where she stood. Ellet had carried the baby most of the way across the ford of the Aman and up the rise, and even her youthful energy had come to an end.

"The ancestors will not hurt us. But if we exhaust ourselves now, we will join them." Anderle got her own breathing under control. *I am carrying a child too,* she thought grimly, *though she weighs less than Irnana's boy.* She looked back the way they had come.

The scene below was the reverse of the one on which she had gazed when they arrived. The reek of burning thatch had replaced the scent of hay. The beasts that grazed in the fields had been driven off, the roundhouses that had seemed so snug behind their palisade were now cones of flame in whose light black figures capered. Thank the gods she could not hear the screaming anymore.

But on the track behind them nothing moved.

Were the Ai-Ushen wolves simply too busy looting to go after fugitives now? Images of those last moments in the clanhold wrenched Anderle's heart. She had seen Galid's blow bring Durrin down. *He died to save us. When we are safe I will mourn him.* . . . That litany kept her moving down the road.

Galid would come after them. Durrin's sacrifice had bought them time, not safety, and it was up to Anderle to use it well. When pursuit did come, they would expect to find the fugitives on the road to Avalon. It was only a matter of time.

A dog howled and Ellet began to tremble once more, obviously remembering stories of the demon Guayota who haunted lonely places and was said to take the form of a hound.

"You are right—I think we must leave the road."

"But where can we go?" Ellet gazed at the gently rolling landscape around them, lumped with the barrows built by men whose names had faded from memory but whose power dwelt here still.

"Let me take Mikantor—" The priestess drew the whimpering child from the girl's arms. The boy was barely three months old, but big for his age.

After a few moments, Ellet's breathing began to ease. Anderle's gaze moved to the Henge, its uprights blocks of shadow beneath the stars. Even from here, she could feel the energy it focused as a faint buzz along her nerves. At Avalon it was said that it had been built by a priest from beyond the seas who was an ancestor both to her and to the babe in her arms. She had been taught the disciplines to wake its powers, but to do so might be dangerous to her own unborn child. Their situation was not so desperate. Not yet. But Mikantor was descended from the men who had built the barrows as well as those who had built Avalon. Perhaps they would be willing to help him.

"Old Ones!" she called softly. "Grandmothers, grandfathers of Azan, hear me! Behold your heir!" She held the squirming baby high and slowly turned. He ceased to whimper and stared. Ellet's eyes were huge in her pale face as she too felt the change in the air. *Something* was listening. Anderle took a deep breath and went on. "The clanhold has fallen and enemies pursue him. Only you can help us now! Come forth to guard the way. Confuse those who come after us." Her grip tightened on the boy's strong limbs. "By blood of your blood and bone of your bone, I adjure you! Lead them astray, and guide us safely home!"

Anderle staggered and clutched at the child as a sudden wind whispered around her. When she could see again, the grass was still. But her awakened

Sight showed a glimmer of radiance above the barrow. The same light glowed above the other mounds scattered across the plain. It blazed from the mighty stones of the Henge.

"Can you see?" She turned to Ellet, fear giving way to wonder. She touched the girl's forehead, and Ellet gasped. The plain had long held some of the Isle's richest farmlands. Its dead were many, and they were mighty, and they were still here . . . A kingdom of the dead lay all around them, and their peace was giving way to a throbbing anger that raised the gooseflesh along Anderle's arms.

"Come—" she whispered, stepping onto a path that led off from the road. Now she could see many such trails, leading between the rectangular outlines of ancient fields. To surface sight they were invisible, but the earth remembered. All times were present here; the land held the memory of every action for those who had eyes to see.

"But how will we find our way?" Ellet clutched at her arm.

"See how the trail leads us. From one barrow to another, the ancestors will pass us along."

Mikantor had fallen asleep, warm and limp in her arms. She smiled a little, and handed him back to the girl. They continued in this manner while the stars wheeled toward morning, moving easily along the ancient trackways and clambering over the new walls of stone that had been built across the paths. In the gray hour just before the dawn, Mikantor woke again, crying with a fretful intensity.

Anderle looked around her with a sigh. The glimmering light that had guided them was fading with the approach of day. To the north a last glow crowned a large barrow whose sloping sides were obscured by brush and trees. The baby had begun a desolate whimpering.

"He's hungry—" said Ellet.

"We'll stop at the next stream," the priestess replied. "We can drip water into his mouth from a corner of my veil." And indeed, when they did so the baby sucked greedily, but it seemed only moments before he was crying again. The energy that had carried Anderle so far was fading as well. When she tripped for the second time, saved only by a back-wrenching twist from a fall, she knew that they must find not only food but a place of refuge, and soon. But where could they go?

Anderle forced herself to take a deep breath, and let her exhalation carry the pain away. She was still tired, but for a moment at least she could stand in balance upon the earth and remember that she was something more than a stumbling creature of flesh and bone.

The sky was filling with radiance. Old disciplines straightened her back, brought her arms up in salutation to the coming day.

> *"Oh beautiful upon the horizon of the east,*
> *Lift up Thy light unto day, O Eastern star,*
> *Day Star, awaken, arise!"*

Ni-Terat, she added in silent prayer to the Goddess, *You who from the darkness gives birth to day, have mercy upon this little one, hide us from our foes!*

For a moment Manoah's golden arc burned upon the horizon. Dazzled, she shut her eyes, and with the image still imprinted upon her inner eyelids, turned and took a step away. In the moment between the lifting of her foot and its descent, she heard a bleating that did not come from the child.

"What is it?" came Ellet's voice from behind her.

"The Lady's answer . . ." Anderle fought to keep her voice from shaking. "Come—" Together they pushed upward through the tangle of hawthorn, dog rose and bramble that had grown up around the base of the old mound.

Ellet squeaked as something moved behind an elder bush, black and then white—were there two creatures there? Carefully Anderle lifted a trail of bramble, met the baleful glare of the she-goat trapped by her horns among the branches, and stifled a laugh. Sheep, the silly creatures, were always having such mishaps, but it was unusual to find a goat in such a fix.

"Never fear us, nanny!" she said softly as the goat wrenched at the branches and bleated again. "Have you lost your kid?" she asked, seeing the swollen udder swing as the animal moved. "Here's a youngling that has lost his mother, perhaps we can help each other . . ." There was a small clear space beneath the ash trees that grew at the top of the mound.

For a long moment the yellow slit-pupiled eyes held hers in an evaluating stare. Then the she-goat's head drooped, resting in the branches rather than fighting them as the tension left her limbs. Her front half was black, the back white with black spots. No wonder she had been hard to see.

"So . . . so. . . ." Anderle moved forward until she could stroke the goat's ragged flank. Heavier guard hairs hid a soft undercoat. The branches of the elder were festooned with tufts of fleece where the goat had struggled to get free, and all the nearby twigs grazed bare. "Be easy, then, and we will take care of you.

"Ellet," she said in a low voice, "bring the baby and hold him beneath her teats." Humming softly, she stroked down the she-goat's flank with one hand and with the other felt down the udder. The goat stirred a little at the touch, but did not try to kick or jerk away.

"Be still and I will ease you," murmured the priestess, blessing the tradition that required the priestesses to learn the practical skills that maintained the community. She angled the teat toward the child's pursed lips and squeezed. A thin stream of milk hit his mouth and dribbled down his chin. For a moment Mikantor stared in astonishment; then his mouth opened. The second squirt went in before he could decide whether or not to cry. He coughed, swallowed, and opened his mouth again.

About the time the goat's milk began to fail, Mikantor's eyes closed and he subsided into peaceful sleep for the first time since their escape. Anderle sat back with a sigh and held out her arms.

"I can take care of him now. I want you to use your belt for a tether and take the goat back to that rivulet to drink. She must be nearly dry."

"And what about you?"

"I drank when we crossed it. You and I can go without more water until nightfall, and so can Mistress Nanny, once she has drunk her fill. Keep your ears open. You can let her graze a little, but you must both be back here before full day."

"And if the Ai-Ushen wolves find me?" asked the younger woman as she unlaced the branches that had trapped the goat's horns.

"Why, you're naught but a girl from a farmstead nearby who lost yourself seeking this strayed goat and spent the night in the fields. They will be looking for a woman with a baby, and in your present state, if you pull your hair down to hide the crescent moon on your forehead, I assure you that no one will take you for a priestess of Avalon!" With her brown hair and blue eyes, burrs in her shawl, and the hem of her sleeping shift ragged and mud stained, Ellet was a typical, if rather grimy, daughter of this land. "Try to sound stupid and don't lose your nerve, and I think they will leave you alone."

"I'll pretend it's Master Belkacem, quizzing us on the lineage of the High Priestesses," the girl said dryly. "Name lists always turn my brains to wool."

Anderle leaned back against the trunk of the ash tree, as the girl and the goat picked their way lightly down the side of the mound. This sense of safety was an illusion, but at least she was sitting still. She had not known how completely their dash across the countryside had exhausted her. Just at this moment she did not think she could have moved if the entire Ai-Ushen war band had appeared below.

THEY REMAINED ON THE mound throughout the day, sleeping fitfully while the goat, whom they had named Ara, continued to trim the undergrowth beneath the ash trees. She proved a bountiful producer of milk, providing enough to feed Mikantor and the two priestesses as well. With that, berries from among the brambles and some cresses Ellet had brought back from the stream, they felt strong enough to continue, leading the goat, once darkness fell.

The second night's journey was uneventful, and they found another mound on which to shelter when daylight came. They had seen no pursuers, and by the third morning Anderle was beginning to believe they had evaded their enemies. Their wanderings had forced them north of their best route, but if taking a roundabout way home cost them time, it gained them safety.

Old Kiri would have a seizure to see me now, thought Anderle, marching along with her skirts kirtled up beneath her swaying belly and her hair knotted and wound around a thorn. Until this journey had proved her endurance, she had not realized that she herself had doubted it. But she could see the gaunt hollows in Ellet's cheeks and knew her own must be the same. A diet of berries and goat's milk was not sufficient for such an extended use of energy.

"If I remember right, just over that hill is the settlement from which Chrifa came."

"Wasn't she the tall girl who told such good stories? She was just finishing her training when I arrived, and then she went off to serve at Carn Ava."

"She did, and I think her people would be willing to help a priestess who had become separated from her escort."

"Just one priestess?" Ellet looked at her warily.

Anderle nodded. "I believe that we are safe, but there's no need to take foolish chances. I will stay in that wood by the old tomb with Mikantor and Ara while you go and ask for some bread and cheese in the name of Avalon."

"And if they try to keep me there?"

"They will hardly dare object if you declare you must go out to the wood to make an offering!"

The mound was old enough to have lost the earth that covered one end. The denuded stones that had framed the first tomb looked pink in the morning light. A dark opening beyond them suggested another chamber farther within. After a greeting to those whose bodies had lain here, Anderle tied the goat's tether to a hazel trunk, curled up against one of them, and settled Mikantor in the crook of her arm. Thank the gods he was not yet crawling.

For a time it was enough to enjoy the solid support of earth and stone. Somewhere above her, a warbler was greeting the sun with a descending "hoo eet" that ended in a trill. She gazed upward through the canopy of beech leaves until she could see the pale greenish feathers of the bird. Here was peace, she thought drowsily. Both the subtle stresses of life in Avalon and the violence of the attack on Azan seemed far away. Whatever passions had ruled those buried here had faded long ago. She tried to stay awake and watch for Ellet's returning, but the warming air drew her into a sweet embrace.

It was not the light footstep of the girl that woke her, but the hard tread of sandaled feet. And perhaps her sleep had not been so deep as she believed, for without needing to think Anderle found herself pushing Mikantor through the gap between the stones of the tomb and forcing her swollen body through the opening after him.

"I saw somethin' move—" came a man's voice, dulled through earth and stone.

Anderle curled into the dirt. Her heart hammered in her chest—surely it must be resonating like a drum in this chamber of stone.

"By the tomb?" a second man answered. "This place belongs to the dead, and they don't walk by day!"

Had she pulled all of her draperies within? She strained to see over the curve of her hip.

"Then why're ye hangin' back, eh, Izri?" This, in the accent of the north. "The chief says we're to check ev'ry farm, ev'ry hiding place. I don't know if ghosts can hurt ye, but Ramdane surely can!"

"This land has too many tombs," came the second voice again. "The dead aid their sorceress, or we would have found a trail."

A little earth sifted down as someone climbed up the mound. Anderle fought a vision in which his weight shifted the balance that held the stones, of great masses sliding to crush her and the child. At least, she thought grimly, they would have a worthy burial.

"By the Hunter's prong, it's a *goat!*" the first voice exclaimed.

"Then I thank him—" answered the northerner. "'Twill be a nice change from boiled barley."

Anderle tensed, unconsciously squeezing the child. But Mikantor's protest was covered by Ara's sudden bleat.

"Leave it alone!" one of the other men cried. "It might be an offering!"

Old Ones, hide us, and I will give you an offering in truth! the priestess prayed. *Set fear in their hearts until they flee!* Abruptly she sensed that she was not alone. The warriors could feel it as well.

"If you want your balls to wither and your crops to die you go right ahead, but I'm getting out of here now!" The sounds of crushed leaves and breaking branches told her when first one, then the second man went away.

"Very well, but I think ye spineless fools," the northern man replied. "Still, if ye had any backbone, I suppose we'd not have taken Azan." His muttering faded as he too retraced his steps through the wood.

For a long time Anderle lay trembling, but presently her heartbeat slowed and her tense muscles began to ease. Reason told her that the warriors had been too frightened to return, but just now that was not enough to persuade her to leave this earthen womb. It had never before occurred to her to envy the ancestors. But here they were sheltered by eternal stone, all passion spent, all danger past.

Or at least a part of them, she thought then. Another part lived in the blood and bone of their descendants, and yet another moved from life to life across the centuries, seeking to work out its destiny. And that one would outlast even these stones. . . .

From time to time a memory of other times would surface in the meditations of one of the people of Avalon. Even little Ellet had dreamed of using an antler pick to hack at the soil of the Tor to create the spiral path around it; the elder priests thought it likely that she had been one of the acolytes who came to Avalon from the Sea Kingdoms that lay now beneath the waves. But Anderle's visions were of the Sinking, of the last cataclysmic explosion when the mountain shattered and her city died in flame.

If I was indeed there, then I did not survive it, she realized suddenly. *Perhaps that is why foreseeing the destruction of Azan frightened me so. . . .* Mikantor stirred in her arms and she turned on her side to make more room. *And who were you in those days, my little one? Are you the child who was saved to inherit a new land?* At the moment, it was enough to have saved him from the burning.

It was said that Micail, who built the great henge, had come from a line of kings, though he had lived his life as a priest, not a ruler. It seemed to her then that the darkness had become a tapestry on which dim figures moved, fighting, dancing, shifting great stones. Still striving to understand, she slept as deeply as any of the ancestors.

When Anderle woke again, the band of light that filtered in through the opening to the tomb was barely brighter than the gloom inside. For a moment she could not think where she was, much less what had awakened her. Then she heard the bleat Ara made when they had not given her enough water or food. Whoever had come was someone whom the she-goat expected to take care of her. The priestess smiled in the darkness and gathered her forces to send a mental call.

"My lady!" came Ellet's soft voice from outside. "Where are you? Have you turned invisible?" Her voice wavered. There were stories that some adepts of Avalon had known how to do just that. "It's safe now—the evil ones have gone!"

Mikantor squeaked in protest as Anderle pushed him through the opening, and Ellet gasped. When she got her own head and shoulders through the gap, she saw the girl staring, fingers twitching in a warding sign.

"I'm no ghost—" The priestess suppressed a laugh. "But I am surely grateful to the spirits who sheltered me. When the Ai-Ushen came, they thought Ara was an offering. If you have brought any food, we should leave some in the tomb."

Ellet recovered enough to hold out a bulging sack. "You must be hungry, and poor Ara is more than ready to be milked again." She took a wooden bowl and a waterskin from the sack and let the goat drink, then settled herself at the black-spotted flank and laid Mikantor in her lap.

Anderle stretched carefully. The last light glowed in the west, and the new moon was already high. She sensed that Ellet had spoken truly, for a palpable peace lay on the land. She rummaged in the foodsack and drew out two barley cakes, setting one at the entrance to the tomb.

"But what happened to you?" she asked as she began to eat. "Did the wolves come to the farm too?"

"They did indeed, and we owe Chaoud and his people the blessing of Avalon! The wretches lined us up in the farmyard while they poked their spears into the thatching and the storage pits. Chaoud told them that I was his sister who had never been quite right since she had the fever, and I pulled my hair over my eyes and gibbered and drooled until they gave up any ideas they might have had about raping me." Ellet grinned.

"They carried off what food they could find," she went on, "but in these times folk have learned how to hide their supplies. There was enough left to feed them, and spare us some provisions as well. Surely another day or two will bring us to the Tor . . ." She looked at Anderle hopefully.

The priestess nodded. *And what will I do if the Ai-Ushen follow us?* she wondered then. The Lake People had no warriors. *Our magic is for healing and growth, not destruction. If only I could draw the marsh mists around us and hide us from the world!* Perhaps by the time they reached the Tor the gods would have given her some counsel.

But first they had to get there.

THREE

*A*nderle and Ellet came to the village of the Lake People on the fourth day after the fall of Azan. The sky flushed with pink as the sun lifted over the eastern hills, but mist still swathed the platforms on which the villagers had built their dwellings so that from the higher ground the buildings seemed to float above the water.

A few dogs began to bark in answer to Ara's bleat, and in moments people were appearing at the edge of the platforms. Presently Badger shouldered through the crowd, still rubbing sleep from his eyes, with his mother, Willow Woman, behind him. He was young to be headman of the village, named for the white streaks that had appeared at his temples when his father died.

"Holy One, you are here!" He hurried across the causeway, bending to make the sign of reverence at heart and brow. "We hear of the burning, and then no word. We feared . . ."

Anderle suppressed a grimace. She could well imagine how the news of the fall of Azan would have been received at Avalon. "What have you heard?"

"They say king and all his family dead." His gaze moved to the baby. "Irnana and her baby burned in fire."

"My cousin ran into the Children's House to try to save him," Anderle answered truthfully, "and the roof fell before she could escape." She shuddered, remembering.

"We hear Durrin was killed in fighting—" Badger sent her a quick glance. "Some say the Ancestors take you to live with them in the mounds."

The priestess nodded, wondering at the way people could sometimes sense the truth even when they did not understand it.

Ellet's laugh was a little too shrill. "We have had such a journey! But the Goddess watched over us—she sent Ara here"—she rubbed the goat's poll between the horns—"so that we could feed the child!"

Eyes rounded as the people realized that Anderle held a baby in her arms. "This is an orphan we rescued on our journey," she said clearly.

Clucking, Badger's mother pushed past her son. "Baby not the only one needs feeding—you two come with me. There is porridge hot on the fire." She lifted the corner of the blanket and Mikantor opened his dark eyes and favored her with a searching stare that made her laugh.

Willow Woman had been Anderle's nurse when she was a baby. Anderle's own grandmother came from the same family, and there was no one whom she would rather trust to watch over Mikantor. She was still thinking about that as she settled gratefully onto a down-filled leather cushion. A fire burned on a stone slab in the center of the long room. The clay plastering of the smoke-stained walls rippled slightly over the woven withies beneath. The scents of drying fish and woodsmoke were among her earliest memories. Avalon was her life, but this felt like home.

"Irnana's boy?" asked the older woman as Anderle unfolded the baby's wrappings and she saw the red hair. "He looks strong."

"Thanks to Caratra," answered Ellet. "Or he might well have died before we found the goat."

"That too was a miracle," Anderle said then. "It was all as I saw in my vision, mother, except that I was there. This child has a destiny. But until he is old enough to claim it, the world must think that he *did* die."

"Even the folk of Avalon?" The old woman's dark eyes gleamed.

"Especially them," Anderle said ruefully. "The Ai-Ushen, and the traitors who aided them, will come seeking Mikantor when they hear I have returned, and those who are sworn to serve the Truth find it hard to lie."

"Then he must be hidden. You know Redfern, Osprey's woman? She has new baby and much milk. She will take him if I say." Willow Woman reached out to stroke the bright hair. "We shave his head for now. Later we use nut dye. He is big already as a child of five moons. Anyone sees him, they will think him older, and ours."

Anderle sank back on the cushion, only now allowing herself to recognize that the anxiety she had carried had been a greater burden than the child. She sipped gratefully at the yarrow tea the old woman ladled into a cup carved from oak wood.

"Ellet, you go find Redfern, tell her to come—" When the girl had gone, Willow Woman turned to Anderle. "Now you tell me how it is with you."

For a moment Anderle could only stare. "I don't . . . know," she said slowly. "I have thought only about the next danger, the fear. Durrin died to save me. I want to mourn for him, but I feel nothing, not even gratitude to be alive."

"That will come." Willow Woman nodded. "Now you need rest."

Anderle nodded. Her backache had returned, and she wriggled on the cushion, trying to ease the strain. From outside she heard laughter, and turned as Ellet pushed past the hide that curtained the doorway, followed by a round-faced woman who must be Redfern. She clearly had some of the blood of the tribes. She might even be able to pass Mikantor off as her own child. But what inspired instant trust was Redfern's smile.

Anderle reached out and Willow Woman passed the warm bundle across. She cuddled the boy to her breast and felt her eyes fill as he nuzzled against it, searching lips making soft sucking sounds. He began to fuss as he found nothing there.

"After the past few days I will miss him as if he were my own child. But he needs to be fed." She looked up at Redfern. "Willow Woman tells me that you have the milk, and the love, to take another child. All children are sacred to the ones who care for them, but the gods have told me that this boy's life is important to all the people of this land. Do you understand this? Do you understand that because of it he has enemies? We will do all we can to protect you and him, but you could be in danger. Are you willing to run that risk and care for this child?"

"Give me the boy—" said Redfern simply, opening the doeskin cape she wore over her skirt. Beneath it, her full breasts were bare. As she took the baby into her arms the milk began to flow. An expert adjustment popped one dark nipple into the seeking mouth, and the woman sighed. Then she looked at Anderle once more.

"You speak true, Holy One. All children a gift of the gods. This I say to you. As I give this boy my milk he becomes my own flesh. As my own I protect him. No more can I do for any baby, no matter whose son."

"Yes . . ." breathed Anderle. "The Goddess speaks in me— She will watch over you, and I will come to see him when I can. Thank you!" She shifted on the cushion, felt moisture and looked down, wondering if she had spilled her tea. But the warm wetness was spreading between her thighs.

She looked at Willow Woman in confusion and tried to rise. "I am sorry, I think I've wet myself and spoiled your cushion—"

Willow Woman and Redfern exchanged glances, and the younger woman laughed. "I take this little one away now and feed him more. I think that soon you will have baby of your own to fill your arms."

For a long moment Anderle simply stared. Then she felt the muscles of her belly contracting and understood that her labor had begun. Durrin had promised that when the child came he would sing her past all pain. She wondered if she would be able to hear him from the Otherworld.

"The baby is coming?" Ellet squeaked. "Now? Lady, shall I send for Kiri to come over from Avalon?"

Unable to speak until the next contraction had passed, Anderle shook her head. "Willow Woman has helped dozens of babies into this world, and with Caratra's blessing I trust her to deliver mine. Send no word to Avalon. They must know only that I arrived here with a baby, and I will leave as I came, with a baby in my arms. And to that, all of you can truthfully swear!"

TIRILAN . . . THE NAME FELL from Anderle's lips like the chiming of a sistrum. Her sign was that of the Peacemaker. Belkacem had read the stars for her and Merivel scried her future in the sacred pool. *"She will be a singer, and much loved . . ."*

Anderle treasured the words. *Like her father,* she thought as she leaned over the cradle to tuck the blanket more closely around the sleeping infant. Like her father, the child had curling fair hair, and Anderle did not think it was only a mother's besotted love that saw in her child's sleeping twitches the beginnings of Durrin's heart-stopping smile.

Since Tirilan's birth, thoughts of Durrin had often been with her, moments of grief alternating with a bittersweet memory, an anguished joy.

As winter's rain flooded the marshes, life continued at the Tor almost as before. The mist that hung above the reeds seemed to separate them from the world, as the old lore said the People of Wisdom had known how to do. But occasionally someone would come from the Lake Village with information. Even in this season when men huddled close to home, rumors still swept the land. It was said that in the fire Uldan's son had been transformed like copper ore in the furnace and been taken up to live with the gods; it was said that the ancestors had taken him into the mounds; it was said that he was hidden in a dozen different places across the land, from which he would return to destroy his enemies when he became a man. The stories about her own journey were equally fantastic. Now they said that she had spent those four lost days in the Otherworld and given birth to her daughter there, or within a mound, which was very nearly the same thing so far as popular belief was concerned.

They may well think you a child of the Hidden Realm, thought Anderle, bending over the cradle once more. The cradle was very old, carved with the symbol of Manoah's winged sun that the Wise Ones had brought from the Drowned Lands. The sleeping child frowned a little in her sleep, then turned and settled once more. *You are not a child of the hollow hills,* her mother thought then, *but of the gods.* She looked up as Ellet pushed through the door.

"Lady!" At Anderle's frown the younger woman straightened and took a deep breath. "Lady, a boy from the Lake Village has come. He says that Galid of Amanhead is here with a dozen warriors. He demands a boat to bring them across to the Tor."

"Have they searched the houses?"

Ellet shook her head. "They are only interested in Avalon. Badger told the lad to say he can hold them for a little, but they will start killing if he delays too long."

"Send him back," she said swiftly. "Tell Badger to let them come."

ANDERLE CHOSE TO AWAIT the traitor beneath the winged sun on the pediment of the Temple of Light, with her senior clergy behind her, all of them robed in shining white, brows bound with the diadems of their grades. The robes were woven of heavy linen, bleached to the whiteness of a cloud on a sunny day and embroidered around the hems with sigils in gold. As the visitors approached, she realized that Galid was followed by men of his own clan. Belkacem stepped forward to bar their way with his staff. Carved and gilded to resemble a serpent, it was a thing of beauty, but no match for a spear.

"Who comes in arms to disturb the peace of Avalon?" The old man's voice still had power. "Lay aside your weapons, men of blood, or depart, for you will find no answers here."

Galid's grin broadened, but the men behind him were glancing about uneasily. "Do you think such tricks will scare me?" he began, then realized that his warriors had begun to edge away. "Still, I believe that we are more than a match for women and old men," he added swiftly. "We will put down our weapons if they make you afraid."

"They will be safe here—" Belkacem said pleasantly, indicating a bench set in the hillside. "I will appoint a worthy guardian." He gestured again, and Linora, who at seven was the youngest of the maidens they were training, came gravely forward and seated herself on the grass.

The warriors looked faintly scandalized as they unbuckled sword belts and laid their spears beside her upon the ground.

Anderle bit her lip to hide laughter. "If you come in peace, you are welcome." Linora's older sister offered them a golden cup that brimmed with ale. "Drink without fear," the priestess said sweetly, though she could see that it was amusement, not anxiety, that glinted in Galid's eyes. But it did not matter what the traitor thought if they could overawe his men.

Galid handed back the cup, his scarred features as carefully grave as those of the child. When Anderle looked at him, she saw that face overlaid by the soot-streaked image of the man who had laughed as Irnana burned, and struck Durrin down. For a moment she closed her eyes, knowing that she had to deal with the man he was *now.*

His frame was heavy with muscle, and the frustrated hunger in his pale eyes had become a wary confidence. The cruel droop of his dark mustache had not changed. He had dressed for this meeting like a king, though the Ai-Zir queen had refused to make him one. How badly did that eat at his soul? His kilt was of fine russet wool, the mantle that covered his sleeveless tunic of the same weave. Heavy golden bracelets circled his forearms, and cloak and belt were clasped with gold.

But if he had changed, so, she thought, had she. No longer ungainly with pregnancy, she stood straight as an image in the formal robes, her face a pure oval within the draped veils and the headdress that added a handspan to her height, bearing the triple moon of Avalon. Galid eyed her as if he would like to unveil the woman behind those stiff folds.

Imagine what you will, the priestess thought with bitter amusement. *I am not a woman now, but the Voice of the Goddess, and* She *will make you hear. . . .*

"Come—" With the graceful, gliding tread she had learned when she was no older than Linora, Anderle led the way to the hall.

"We are honored by your greeting," said Galid when they had been seated near the hearth. "But you need not have taken the trouble. Our errand is simple. Now that the country is becoming more peaceful, we have come for Uldan's child."

Anderle met his gaze without blinking, glad her veils hid the racing pulse at her throat. "And what would you do with the boy if he was here?"

"Queen Zamara has asked us to find her nephew," answered one of the warriors, "so that we may raise him as heir to the Ai-Zir."

He might even believe what he was saying, thought Anderle as she considered him. But she had not missed the cynical glint in Galid's eye. "Alas, this is only Avalon, not the Otherworld," she replied bitterly.

"Do not play with me!" Galid's tone sharpened. "Irnana passed the baby to you and I saw you carry him away. It is known that you brought an infant with you when you returned to the Tor."

"Both those things are true, but the one does not guarantee the other," Belkacem said sadly. "Irnana's child never reached Avalon. The infant of whom you have heard is the Lady's own child."

If they had not stood on the knife-edge of disaster, Anderle would have laughed at the confusion of frustration, uncertainty, and disbelief in Galid's eyes.

"You may understand why I did not understand that you were searching for us so that you might care for the boy," she said tartly. "But the way was hard, and we had no milk for him. My own babe was not born until we were nearly here or I would have fed him at my own breast. I am sorry . . ." she added with lowered gaze.

"I don't believe you!" Galid snapped.

Anderle looked up at him. "Do you not? Ellet, bring Tirilan to us here—"

They sat in stiff silence until Ellet returned with the baby, awake now and fussing softly, in her arms. At three months old her hair was a golden halo. Anderle had not known many infants, but surely it was not only a mother's partiality that saw beauty in the tiny features despite the dubious gaze with which the baby was regarding all these strange men.

"This is my daughter, the heir of Avalon," Anderle said calmly. "Would you like me to undo her clout so that you may assure yourselves that she is indeed a maid?"

One of the men flushed and the others had the grace to look embarrassed. It was clear to all that this delicate child could not be Uldan's strong redheaded son.

"That will not be necessary," Galid said stiffly. For a moment longer his gaze held Anderle's, an odd mixture of lust and respect in his eyes.

Tirilan's face reddened and Ellet thrust her into her mother's arms, where she began to rootle against the heavy fabric, and then to cry. Abruptly Anderle realized that there was no opening in the ceremonial robes through which she could nurse her, and in a moment her breasts were going to begin leaking in response to the baby's cries.

"You may search the isle," Belkacem offered earnestly, "but I swear by the Light that this is the only infant of either gender to be found among us here."

"Search if you will—" Anderle rose, settling the baby against her shoulder. "But for this child, at least, I have milk, and I had better feed her before she deafens us all!"

"If you swear to it, then I am sure it is true, but even truth can sometimes lie." Galid lifted his hand like a fighter saluting his foe. "I will not forget, Lady—" Their eyes met, and she heard the unspoken words *"And I will be watching you . . ."*

As a chilly winter unwillingly gave way to an equally wet spring, the people of the village reported an unusual number of strangers in the area. Galid was keeping his word, thought Anderle, and denied her heart's craving to go to the Lake Village to visit Mikantor, whom Redfern, following Village custom, called Woodpecker. Thus, it was not until just after the boy's first birthday, when the priesthood on the Tor had finished the ceremonies surrounding the summer solstice, that she crossed the lake to preside over the villagers' Midsummer Festival.

Anderle sat on the platform on which the headman's house was built, helping Willow Woman to plait wreaths for the evening's dancing from flowers and leafy branches the children had brought in from the marsh. Tirilan lay sleeping in a cradle by her side.

"If I did not trust our observations of the heavens, I would think we were celebrating the Turning of Spring." She threaded a few primroses among the yellow cresses already twined into the braid of bullrush with a sigh.

"It's so—" the older woman agreed. "Many trackways through the marsh are underwater still."

"This year the isles of the Summer Country are islands indeed." Beyond the platform sunlight glittered on the open waters of the Lake and the channels that wound through the reeds.

"The water meadows are still water. Not many places for the sheep and goats to graze, or gather seeds. Next winter I think we will live on dried fish and waterfowl and berries."

"Be thankful you have them," Anderle said grimly. "They tell me that it has been too cold to grow much on the old farms on top of the downs, and those that lie too low are so wet the cattle are getting hoof rot and the seeds drown in the fields."

She turned as a trill of laughter rippled up from below. One of the older girls was watching over the toddlers as they played on the ground that had been bared beneath the pilings as the waters receded. Mikantor was among them, walking already and tall and strong.

"The boy looks well, and he has grown. If anyone asks, we can say he is a year older than his milk-brother, Grebe."

"Redfern's milk is good," Willow Woman replied. They both laughed as he sat down suddenly in the mud, brows lifting in an expression of comical surprise. In the next moment he was pulling himself upright once more. The sun struck rusty glints from his dyed hair. "She loves Woodpecker as if he's her own."

"I know, but we cannot keep him here forever. Tiny children all look much the same, but as he grows older, even the hair dye will not be enough to make people think he comes from here. Already there are legends that Uldan's son was reborn from the fire."

"To take Woodpecker while he is young will be very hard on both him and Redfern," the older woman said slowly.

"I will wait as long as I can." Anderle sighed. "It may be safest to move him from one village to another."

"Maybe, but that is the future," Willow Woman replied. "We have to keep him safe now or he has no future. You still know mighty magic— protect the Lake Village and he will stay safe within."

Anderle stared at her, the new wreath into which she was plaiting purple loosestrife and flowering rush trembling in her hands. "Not just the village. When we make the circuit of the seven sacred islands," she said slowly, "then I can weave the spell."

THE ALLIANCE BETWEEN THE people who had once hunted the marshes and the sun-haired priests and priestesses who had come from across the sea had endured for a thousand years. Each race had its own Mysteries, and the two strains, mingling, had given birth to a tradition that drew on the powers of both the earth and the stars. From this had come the spiral path that linked the inner and outer realities of the Tor itself, and knowledge of the paths the earth energies followed as they flowed through the land.

The Tor was linked to several of the smaller hills that rose above the fens. A map of these islands formed a shape that they also saw in the stars. The priests knew it as the Chariot of Light, or Caratra's Wain, but the people of the marshes saw in that constellation the upper part of a bear. To honor that protecting power it had become the tradition to follow the path from isle to isle upon Midsummer Day.

The long low boats set forth at midnight. When the boats moved from marsh to river, she could feel the difference in their motion, but beyond that, it was as if they floated between the worlds. By the time the sound of voices roused her, the sky was growing lighter. Before them rose the tree-clad hump of the Watch Hill. Already the birds were chorusing their own salutation to the coming day. As the first sliver of gold edged the eastern hills, the boatmen flung their torches into the water and Anderle began the song—

> *How beautiful, how beautiful upon the horizon,*
> *The Lord of Day is coming, robed in light!*
> *Awaken, children of earth, as he arises.*
> *Light fills the soul as it fills the land.*
> *Awaken, oh my people, to light and to life.*

She bent, hands moving in the Sign of salutation. *Hail to thee, Manoah, Lord of Light.* She called on the god by his ancient name. *Touch the path we take today with power, that we may be protected from those who would wish us harm.* Slowly her arms lifted as she stretched to embrace the light that spilled down the hillsides and lit the waters as if the torches had set them aflame.

Her breath caught as she felt that same fire ignite within her. Only afterward did she learn that to the others she had seemed limned in light. She turned to the north.

"As light blesses the land I invoke the spirits of this hill to ward against all foes."

As she went back down the path, Anderle could feel the power she had raised spinning out behind her like a thread of light.

Men from the settlement below the hill waited to pole them on the return journey. This first leg was the longest, following the winding course of the river. To either side long grasses waved from a raised bog, interspersed with heather and a tangle of birch and alder. Dragonflies were already flitting above the water, and now and again a fish would leap to greet the day.

By the time they reached the low isle where once a great warrior had fought a spirit of darkness, the sun was halfway toward noon. They left an offering and made the short crossing to the hill of the wild powers. This place also was not meant for human habitation, though hunters came here sometimes to keep vigil and beg the favor of the powers who guarded the game. Some, it was said, came away with the favor of those powers, but others fled, maddened by sudden fears, and ran until they collapsed from exhaustion or the bog sucked them down.

Anderle sensed the spirit of the hill as a chaotic but not unfriendly energy. As she drew the sunfire past she felt it waken. *If enemies come, fill them with your terror,* she prayed. *Witless and wandering may they find their doom!* And it seemed to her that something on the island grinned in answer.

Now they wound their way southward through level lowlands. Herons stalked where the petals of the yellow flag curled on their proud stalks and the blue flowers of brooklime captured bits of sky. Just at the hour of noon they came to the Isle of Birds. Badger's village was just beyond it, built out into the marsh to leave the solid ground for growing crops and grazing sheep.

The only structure on the hillock was a shrine. Flocks of clamoring waterfowl sought the air around her. As she scattered the grain that was their offering, they settled once more, gabbling in satisfaction. Anderle gazed back at the way they had come, strengthening her hold on the thread of power. She stood, hands lifted to the sky.

> *Hail to thee, brightness of the nooning,*
> *Oh sun in thy splendor, ruler of the sky.*
> *Each leaf and each blade, each bird and each beast*

Lives by the love of the Lord of Light.
Blessed be the sun's holy fire. . . .

When she returned to the boats, Willow Woman was waiting with food and drink. Redfern had come too, with Mikantor slung on one hip, gazing around him with the same eager curiosity as the ducklings that followed their mothers in chuckling lines among the reeds. As Anderle embraced the other woman, she dropped a kiss upon the boy's brow.

"Rejoice in the Light, Son of a Hundred Kings. Can you see the shining web that stretches yonder? I am spinning it to protect *you.*" And though she knew her words could mean nothing to a child so young, it seemed to her that his eyes were tracking that invisible radiance across the waving reeds.

Leaving the village and the hill behind them, the boats turned westward toward the isle where the sacred oak tree grew. When age and the winds of winter brought an old tree down, an acorn that had been saved was carefully nurtured until it could stand alone against the storms. Here, the priestess poured out ale and tied a riband of fine linen around the trunk as the custom was, but she bound the line of light to the tree as well.

The sun was curving westward as they turned toward the Maiden's Isle. Eran came down to meet her, in a clean tunic for once, for on this day the forge was cold, and the only fire burning was the one in the sky. As he saw her, his eyes grew wide.

"Lady, walk in the Light. . . ." He bowed.

Anderle smiled, for he was the first, except for the child, who had seen that she was attempting something more than the usual ritual.

"Mastersmith, I ask your blessing on my work, and the blessing of the Lady of the Forge."

He bowed again and stepped aside to escort her into the smithy. The image of the goddess in the niche in the wall was shaped out of lead from the hills north of the Vale, with a cylindrical base to suggest a skirt and nubbins of breast on her torso. Years had blurred any features that might have been sketched beneath her headdress, but she stood like a priestess with upraised arms. This was one deity whom the People of Wisdom had not brought with them, but recognized as the upwelling spirit in the human heart and in the land. Eran had garlanded her niche with summer flowers. Anderle came to a halt, feeling the sun-thread as a warmth against her back, and reached out to gather and offer it to the power that image represented.

"Achi, Old One," she murmured. "Here is another fire for you to hold. Strengthen this barrier and guard this land. Guard the child who is our hope, and when he is grown, forge the weapon that will bring him victory!"

She waited, and heard a rushing like the sound of the wind in the trees or the fire hissing in the coals. But the fire was out and the air was still, and the sound was a voice that whispered to her soul.

"In the crucible he will be tried, shaped in the mold, forged until he is a weapon fit for my hand."

She must have staggered, for when she opened her eyes Eran was holding her arm and offering her water. She accepted it gratefully, but even to him she could not explain.

Only the Tor remained. Anderle could feel the tension as she climbed and circled the stones that crowned it, for the sun was beginning to sink toward the distant sea. But the power in the hill was stronger than she had ever felt it, as if eager to accept her binding. She stumbled down to the boats that waited to push off toward the Lake Village once more.

As they crossed the last open water toward the village, the sky was flaming with its own Midsummer fires. It had been a very long day and she felt weary to her bones, but the skein of light stretched taut behind her. The boat passed the village and drew up on the high ground beyond it. With the approach of night the birds had hidden themselves among the rushes, and the hilltop was very still. In the west, the sun set fire to the cloud banks above the distant sea. She slitted her eyes against that final blaze of glory as she chanted the evening hymn.

> *How beautiful, how beautiful upon the horizon,*
> *The Lord of Light is descending, seeking his rest.*
> *Sleep, oh children of earth, as earth is sleeping;*

Light lives within you, lives in the land.
Sleep and find healing until he comes again.

As the last fiery sliver disappeared, she grasped the thread of light and linked it to the pulse flowing down from the Watch Hill where they had begun, a loop of power to safely bind the seven islands of the Vale of Avalon.

FOUR

$\mathcal{W}$oodpecker! The Lady of Avalon is here!"

At his brother's words Woodpecker's eyes flew open and he surged upright, casting the blanket of woven rabbit skins aside. *The shiny lady. . . .* He always called her that in his mind, even though she was as small and dark of eyes and hair as any villager. She lived on the magic island to the south of the Lake Village. Maybe that was why light seemed to gather around her. Woodpecker belted his kilt, flung the rabbitskin blanket around his shoulders, for this early the spring air still held a chill, and followed his brother to the hearth.

"They got here last night," chattered Grebe as they gulped down the hot porridge that Redfern insisted on setting before them. "I heard the voices."

The shiny lady visited them once or twice a year. Somehow, things would always be arranged so that she saw him. Of course she saw all the village children, and sometimes there were sweets to go with her blessing, but Woodpecker always had the feeling that she was looking at him especially closely. It made him uneasy, as if he was different from the others. But he already knew that. There was something wrong with his hair. His mother kept it cut short, and every month she had to treat it with a medicine that left it dry and dull.

"Slow down," panted Grebe as Woodpecker slung on his carry-sack and led the way toward the headman's dwelling. "They won't be awake yet. They were all up late talking."

"How do you know?" mumbled Woodpecker.

"I woke up when Papa came in and I heard, of course. As usual, you slept through it all."

"We'll wait, then. I'll play you at spellikins," he added conciliatingly, hunkering down at the edge of the platform. He pulled out the bag his father had made for him from the skin of a vole, and tipped the bundle of slender sticks into his hand. It was a game of which his little brother, who was sure-handed though not strong, was very fond.

"Why do you care so much anyway?" asked Grebe as Woodpecker evened the ends and tossed them into the air.

"She's pretty," he answered as Grebe took first turn, flipping sticks aside with the carry-stick and collecting them in one hand. "Like somebody I saw in a dream." He did not mention that sometimes the dreams were nightmares of fire and terror from which the bright lady rescued him. "And she gives me presents."

"Oh ho!" said the younger boy, then swore as his hand twitched and a tangle of sticks began to roll apart. "Your turn—" he conceded, but Woodpecker was not listening.

The door to the headman's house had opened, and *she* was there, talking to someone behind her. This time, though, was different. Beside her stood a girl, a little thing with light hair who carried with her the same kind of glow. The Lady turned, saw Woodpecker standing there, and smiled.

"Is that you, Woodpecker? You have grown!" The Lady of Avalon spoke the dialect of the Lake Village well.

As Grebe gathered up the spellikins Woodpecker shuffled his feet, recognizing the usual response adults gave when they did not know what to say. In his case it was usually true. He was as tall as Redfern's oldest boy, who was twelve and went hunting with the men.

"This is my daughter, Tirilan," the Lady said then. "Will you be kind to her and show her the village? But don't let her fall into the Lake—Tiri cannot swim."

Woodpecker and Grebe exchanged glances. The girl was small, but she must be at least six. By that age every child of the Lake Village could swim like a frog.

"We'll take care of her," Grebe said brightly, and earned another smile.

"Come on, then," muttered Woodpecker, leading the way back toward his mother's house, though he had no idea what they were going to do.

"Why are you called Woodpecker?" Tiri asked, using the mode of speech of the tribes. At least she was not shy.

"'Cause I always get into things, I guess," he replied, wishing he had paid more attention to Willow Woman's lessons in the tribal tongue.

"I thought it was maybe because your hair sticks out around your head like a baby bird."

There was no malice in her tone, but he could feel himself flushing angrily. "You look all pale and thin, like something under log. I think I call you Worm!"

"Are you going to gobble me up?" she retorted. "I'd like to see you try!"

He blinked; she seemed to be growing brighter. "A glowworm, maybe, warns off things that want to eat her 'cause she taste bad!"

She frowned, as if trying to work out whether that was another insult or a compliment.

By the time they reached Redfern's door, more children had joined them. Beaver, who at nine was almost as big as Woodpecker and inclined to challenge him; Alder, a leggy girl with a long black braid who looked at Tiri as if she had come from another world; and Goosey and Gander, who were twins.

"Does your name have meaning?" asked Alder when they had made introductions.

"Our names have meanings in the old language of the Wise," responded the girl from Avalon with her first smile. "Mine means 'sweet singer.' My father was a bard."

Woodpecker blinked and looked away. Definitely shiny, he thought, like her mother. It must be nice to know where your talents and features came from. He loved his parents dearly, but he found it hard to see anything of himself in them at all.

"We can teach her to swing from the branch of the willow tree?" asked Beaver.

"If it breaks she'll fall in and she can't swim and anyway the water is still cold," Alder replied.

"We could go out in a boat," Goosey offered shyly. He turned to the girl. "Have you seen marshes? They real pretty in spring."

"But she can't swim," objected Grebe.

"She had to go in a boat to get here, didn't she?" growled Woodpecker, though he would have believed it if they had told him the Lady of Avalon could fly. "You can hold on to her if you're afraid she'll fall in."

"I would like to see the marshes," Tiri said clearly. "Do you paddle, or push your boats with a pole?"

Woodpecker looked at her with more respect. At least she knew *some-thing* about boats. "Not tall enough to use pole well," he admitted, "but I paddle fast. I win boys' race at Midsummer last year." Beaver, whom he had beaten in that race, glowered.

"We don't need to go *fast,* Woodpecker, just safe," said Alder repressively. "Come on!"

The folk of the Lake Village were too accustomed to the gaggle of chattering children to notice the golden head among them as they scrambled down the ladders and piled into the long low boats that the villagers carved from the trunks of trees. Woodpecker helped Tiri to get into the boat behind him with Grebe and Alder, while Beaver and the twins took the other craft.

"There was wooden trackways through marshes," said Alder as they eased away from the pilings. "But they are underwater for long time now. Boats better. You go anywhere!"

Tiri gripped the sides as they slipped past the new green reeds and sedges that were pushing up through the yellow tangle where last year's crop had been cut for thatching, but settled back when a long stroke of the paddle sent the craft into the open water beyond. They called it a lake, but it was nowhere very deep, a sheet of water covering the low-lying ground to the west of the Isle of Birds and the Tor. The water glimmered with a nacreous sheen beneath the pale sky.

"Where are you taking us?" Tiri asked.

"If lucky, see animals," he replied. "The birds come north—" He pointed to a flock of mixed waterfowl bobbing on the water. Beyond them a flicker of white emerged from behind some reeds. "Look, a swan!"

More careful strokes brought them around the northern edge of the Isle of Birds and into what gradually resolved into a sluggish stream that fed into the lake from the rising ground to the north where fen carr and raised bog supported a tangle of trees.

"Will we see bears?"

"Do you want to?" He looked at her in surprise. She might seem weak and pale, but he was beginning to suspect that she had more spirit than any of them. He usually had to work pretty hard to persuade the others when he had a really interesting plan.

"We have a legend that there was once a bear, or maybe a bear spirit, that lived in a cave on Avalon."

"I never hear of bear in the marshes," observed Alder. "I think too wet for them, especially now. On higher ground sometimes deer."

"Oh . . ." Tiri said dismissively. "Well, it is very pretty here."

Stung, Woodpecker frowned. "You want excitement?" he said slowly. "We go to Wild God's Isle!"

"It's forbidden!" Grebe exclaimed. "We *can't* go there!"

"You can go back in the other boat with Beaver if you're afraid," Woodpecker said over his shoulder, digging the paddle into the water and driving the boat forward. A squawking pintail duck flurried up from the reeds as they passed, and Tirilan laughed.

"It's too far—" said Alder.

"No farther than from here back to the Tor," he answered, though he supposed it would take longer to thread his way through the fen than to cross the open lake. He had only made this journey twice, since he'd been old enough to accompany the Midsummer warding, and winter floods could change the channels, but all the children of the Lake had a good sense of direction. He could feel the invisible link between the sacred islands. If he followed it he would reach his goal.

"What will we find on this forbidden isle?" Tiri sounded amused.

"Wild things," Alder said tartly.

"Spirits—" added Grebe. "Sometimes they drive people mad."

"My mother commands spirits," Tirilan said dismissively. "You can't scare me with that tale."

Woodpecker was sure that was true, but her mother was not here. Distracted, he let the boat graze a hidden stump and dug the paddle into the water to ease it away. The craft was solid enough, but could easily be overturned.

By the time they neared the ridge of higher ground from which the hill rose, it was nearly noon and the breakfast porridge seemed very far away. Still, the marshes held food for those who knew how to find it. They would have to keep their eyes open when they reached the isle.

The stream narrowed, curving around the base of what seemed to be a hill, though it was hard to make out its shape through the trees. If he remembered right, a little ways ahead it joined another stream and continued on toward the Watch Hill. This was it, then. Woodpecker stood, balancing carefully, and leaped to a protruding root. Grebe tossed him the rope tied to the boat's bow, and when the others had clambered out, they pulled the craft onto the muddy shore.

"Now we walk." He grinned at Tirilan's expression as she eyed the morass of mud and scum and decaying leaves. "Better you take off your shoes," he told her. He and the other children were already barefoot. Relenting, he held out a hand to steady her until they reached firmer ground.

"I AM HAPPY TO see how well the Village has survived the winter," said Anderle. It was a fine day, and after weeks of cloud and rain they were grateful to sit on benches set on the platform on which the headman's house was built and take in the sunshine.

Badger grinned. "Here we already know how to live with water. Otter's house got wet, but this summer we build his platform higher."

"We look already at the places where we plant and gather," added his mother. "We won't have so much seed for bread this year, but more water is good for fishing and birds. We won't starve."

Anderle nodded. "I will send some of our younger ones to help you. It will be good for them to learn just how much work getting food can be. Most of our food used to come from Azan. We are still getting some from farmers who are grateful for our help in the past, but of course there is nothing from the king."

"I hear that Galid of Amanhead rules now in Azan-Ylir—" Badger, who was sitting on the edge of the platform, leaned over to spit into the water below.

"He *says* it is as protector for the queen. But Zamara is still kept at Carn Ava, and I am told that these days his house guards are all Ai-Ushen wolves." She shivered, remembering.

"I think King Eltan glad to have some place to send them, so they don't make trouble at home. Eltan's cousin tries to kill him last summer, but Galid owes him everything, makes a dependable ally."

"Dependable?" Anderle laughed bitterly. "He betrayed his own king. Why should Eltan think that Galid will not do the same to him?"

"Maybe the wolf warriors are there to watch *him*," observed Redfern's husband, who was called Stalker.

"I think there's few chieftains who sleep easy these days." Badger picked up his own clay mug of tea. "If good men, they grieve because they can't save all their people, or they use all their wealth to help, and get weak. And they fear their people if they are bad."

"Fear and hunger make good excuse for hate," said Stalker. "Many old scores get paid off now."

"Then everyone ends afraid of everyone else," observed Willow Woman, "and when enemies come they don't stand together."

Anderle shivered again, although the spring sun was warm on her shoulders. They could ask the stars whether there would be a good harvest, but if the stars foretold disaster, they could not conjure food from grass. Against the forces that were changing their world the magic of Avalon seemed to have little power. If the prayers of a priest had no more effect on the floods than a chieftain's curse, why should the clans share what little they had with Avalon?

"What we cannot cure, we must learn to endure . . ." Kiri's watchword came to mind. Surely the future held more than this slow disintegration of all

order, or why had the visions driven her to Azan to rescue Mikantor? *When the Son of a Hundred Kings is grown, he will restore our world,* she told herself sternly. *Our task is to preserve the pieces until then.*

She shook herself and looked at the others. "Surely it is past time for the noon meal. Shall we call the children to share it? I had only a glimpse of Woodpecker this morning. I should like to see how he has grown."

"Grown?" grinned his foster father. "He grows like the marsh reed in the spring. Every day taller."

"Go call them," said Willow Woman, setting a hand on her son's shoulder to steady herself as she got to her feet. "I will give another stir to the stew."

The old woman had brought out wooden bowls filled with a steaming mix of roots and grains with some dried meat before Stalker came back again, and when he climbed up the ladder to the platform he was frowning.

"It is good you started eating. The children are not here. People say my boys and your daughter go off with Alder and Beaver and the twins, the ones they usually play with. Their boats are gone."

Anderle looked from him to Badger. "They went out in boats? Is that safe?"

"Our children learn boats when they learn to walk," the headman replied. "But it's strange they don't come back for food."

"Could they have gotten lost in the marshes?" Suddenly the patchwork of greenery and gleaming water seemed more confused than beautiful. Anderle had grown up among the marshes, but when she had to cross them she stuck to the wood-paved trackways.

"I would not think so——" Badger said slowly. "Always you can see the hills to north and south, and today the sun shows the way west. They know the way to come. Still . . . they might be stuck somewhere . . ."

"Nothing in the marsh to hurt them!" Willow Woman said quickly. "But maybe you men best go looking, eh? We wait——"

"And plan how to make them sorry for frightening us so!" added Anderle. Tirilan was a good-natured child, but she had a mind of her own. This would not be the first time she had eluded her watchers.

By the time Badger and Stalker returned, the sun was halfway between its nooning and the horizon. They had searched the area around the Lake Village, but boats left no tracks upon the water and of the children there was no sign.

"They must have gone farther, but which way?" Stalker asked in frustration.

"When they see it's getting dark they come back to us," offered Willow Woman.

"If they can. . . ." Anderle got to her feet, staring out across the landscape. Which direction would they have gone? A priestess of Avalon might not know how to navigate the reedbeds, but she could ride the currents of power. She closed her eyes, inner senses extending to the borders she herself had strengthened the previous summer, feeling for the ebb and flow of energy within the area they protected, and the particular signature of her child.

She turned to the men. "We will go out again, and I will go with you. There is something that way"—she pointed northward—"that calls me. When we are closer, I will know for sure."

THE BANK OF THE stream was choked with willows whose lower branches were still draped with drying clumps of reed left there by the winter floods. Woodpecker heard a muffled squawk, and turned to help Tiri pick fragments of a wagtail nest from her hair. Beaver and Grebe followed. After a vigorous discussion, Alder had agreed to stay at the boats with the twins.

"I thought you said that people came up here sometimes," Tiri complained.

"At Midsummer," he answered repressively. "But comes winter, shoreline always change. Still, should be—there, you see, by birches? Path goes up the hill."

A stand of white trunks glimmered beyond the buckthorn thicket. When they emerged they could see a wavering line of short green grass leading upward. At first Woodpecker wondered if it really was a path, but presently he noticed where branches had been intentionally trained so that they would not block the way. The hair rose on his neck. Humans were only guests in this place, and not very welcome. But he was not yet frightened enough to turn tail.

"Be careful," he said aloud. "Don't break branches, and . . . keep your voices down."

Grebe gave him a curious look. His brother had always been a canny one, using wit to make up for his lack of size, and he would know that although Woodpecker could move as softly as any boy trained to hunt the small, cautious game that was all a child's bow could bring down, he was not noted for caution.

As the path grew steeper, the others glanced at him more often. They felt it too, he thought uneasily, that feeling that they were being watched by Something that, if not an enemy, was certainly no friend to humankind.

"I wish we had brought an offering," said Grebe softly.

"I have a piece of bannock," whispered Tirilan.

I should have thought of that. Woodpecker bit his lip. That was the least of the things he should have thought of. When they got home, *if* they got home, Redfern would have his hide. But he sensed that to show fear now would attract the kind of attention they wanted to avoid. Finishing the climb carefully, but boldly, was their best choice now. *And then turning around and heading home,* and accepting whatever punishment his parents chose.

A soft piping from above brought all four to a halt, staring.

"A redshank!" stated Grebe, but it did not sound quite like the red-legged marsh bird he remembered. Suddenly it seemed very dark beneath the trees. The way had grown steeper and Woodpecker's legs were aching. He looked back to see how the others were doing. Grebe and Beaver were panting, but Tiri seemed to dance along. No doubt she was used to climbing, he thought resentfully, remembering the height of the Tor.

He jumped as the bird—it must be a bird—gave that odd piping call once more. It had sounded nearly at his elbow. He looked wildly around, but could see nothing but moving leaves. He had not heard the wind rising, only a vague whisper that seemed to come from all around him. Nor did there seem to be a direction to the movement of the leaves. It made his head swim.

He felt a small hand grip his elbow and turned. Tirilan had gone as still as a startled doe. "What is it?"

"Something is watching us . . ." she breathed in his ear.

He nodded, oddly comforted to know that she could feel it too. That sense of attention was all around them, but it seemed to him that it would only grow worse if they stayed here.

"There are no bears in the Vale," Beaver was muttering. "There are no bears."

No, thought Woodpecker, but there might be worse things. He wished he had paid more attention to the hunters' tales.

"Hush—" murmured Tiri. "There are spirits here. I can almost understand their words."

That doesn't take magic, Woodpecker thought, shivering. *They are telling us we don't belong here.* But the branches were swaying so he could hardly see the path.

"Then tell them we mean no harm."

"It's coming!" Beaver exclaimed suddenly, and gathered himself to run.

Woodpecker made a wild grab for his tunic. "Shut up and take my hand!" The need to take care of the others steadied him, and he started upward once more. Only Tiri seemed unafraid. He put Beaver between Tiri and Grebe and took her other hand.

As they inched their way upward he was aware of surprise at how natural that seemed. For a moment he remembered holding on to her as the world fell apart around them, but in that memory they were both grown-ups, so perhaps it was a dream. As they moved along he could hear her whispering words in some other language; he thought it was the old tongue the priests used on the Tor. Woodpecker tried to imitate her sounds and found them coming easily, which also seemed odd, since he had never heard them before.

The tumult around them was increasing. Branches lashed angrily, and sticks and stones seemed to give way intentionally beneath each step. *Stop it!* he thought. He ought to be able to stop it—he used to know how—but that was ridiculous, he told himself. That must have been in his dream.

Tirilan said another word. Woodpecker started to repeat the syllables and felt them change in his mouth. For a moment a *Word* hung in the air. In the next moment it was echoed by a rumble of thunder. The world went black and then bright again, and everything was suddenly still.

The children looked at one another, too surprised to speak, though Tirilan was eyeing Woodpecker with an odd, considering gaze.

"There's the path—" Woodpecker said finally. "Come."

Light filtered through the young leaves to dapple the earth before them, but though the woods were still mysterious, the tension that had threatened them was gone. A golden butterfly floated across their path. Grebe touched his shoulder and pointed and Woodpecker glimpsed the graceful shape of a deer. Now that he knew to look he could see more of them, moving, like the children, toward the top of the hill.

Golden light filled the air before them. As their eyes adjusted, they saw a small clearing carpeted with new grass and open to the blue sky. Deer were grazing there, the rich russet of their summer coats gleaming through the ragged remnants of winter's shaggy hair. He counted four hinds, two of them accompanied by dappled fawns. Beyond them, a little apart, another larger animal grazed.

As Woodpecker took a step forward, that other deer lifted its head. The boy stared as first the velvety half-grown antlers, then the massive neck and shoulders, rose into view. The hinds threw up their heads in alarm and vanished into the woods, followed by their offspring. But the stag's head turned, and for a long moment Woodpecker was transfixed by that dark, dispassionate gaze.

I know you . . . said that look, *but you are too young and weak to concern me. We shall meet again when you are grown. . . .*

With a snort the crowned head turned, and the stag paced disdainfully away. In moments the antlers had merged with the branches, the red-brown form with the shadows, until Woodpecker wondered if the deer had been there at all.

Where they had been, beams of sunlight moved and flickered as they passed through the trees, for the sun was already sinking toward the west.

Tirilan slipped beneath Woodpecker's outstretched arm and skipped across the grass, lifting her face to the light.

"The spirits are here!" she called. "Cannot you see them? Oh, come and join the dance!"

"What does she mean?" whispered Grebe. "Who is she dancing with?"

For Tiri certainly was dancing, her pale hair lifting, the skirts of her white tunic flaring like the wings of a swan as she dipped and twirled. She stretched out her arms, laughing, and for a moment Woodpecker thought he could see the radiant forms that danced with her. But he stood where he was. He had his vision and she had hers.

He never knew how long he stood watching that strange dance as the sun sank toward the distant sea. But a moment came when the sun's rays failed and Tirilan stood alone in the clearing, light fading from her eyes as it was beginning to fade from the sky.

Woodpecker went to her. "It's all right," he said softly. "But we must go. Powers of Day bless us, but I don't know about Powers of Night." As he took her hand he heard from below the voice of the Lady of Avalon, calling them.

ANDERLE SAT IN THE bow of the low barge with her daughter in her arms. Ahead, the pure peak of the Tor rose like the sure center of the world. It would be good to be home. But the more she thought about it, the more disturbed she was by the children's story of what had happened on the Wild God's Isle.

"Will we go back to the Lake Village soon?" Tirilan looked up at her.

"Do you wish it?"

Tiri nodded. "Woodpecker is fun."

Anderle suppressed an impulse to ask how she could consider clambering around in the wilderness all day and driving her mother half mad with worry amusing. She had yelled at them loudly enough the night before when she was not hugging her daughter until she squeaked in protest to assure herself that the girl was really unharmed. Stalker, who was clearly appalled at the danger into which his sons had led the daughter of the Lady of Avalon, had hauled both boys off for a switching and sent them supperless to bed.

"Are you still angry?" asked Tiri, who could read her mother very well. "He was very sorry. I think he was trying to show off for me."

Anderle wondered. The younger lad had yelled while he was being punished, but Woodpecker had made no sound at all.

"I was very glad when you came to get us," the girl added reassuringly. "How did you know where to look?"

The girl was priestess born, thought Anderle, and precocious. Perhaps she was old enough to understand.

"You know how each year I renew the wards around the seven sacred isles. I could feel a change in the energy connecting the islands, so I thought we should look there. The closer we got, the more I felt that something was wrong. That's why I was so upset with you last night—I was afraid."

"I understand," Tirilan said wisely. "I was afraid too. Something that did not like us was there. I was chanting all the prayers I could remember."

"Did you, my darling?" Anderle smiled. "I am glad that you remembered them. Which one were you saying when you heard that clap of thunder? The feeling changed." It had happened just as they were leaving the open water for the stream—thunder from a clear sky, and in the next moment an overwhelming sense that all would be well.

"Oh, that wasn't me," the child replied. "Woodpecker started to say the prayers with me, and when I got to the part about protection from wind and storm, he said a different word, and then we were safe, I could tell."

"What word?" Anderle whispered. "What did he say?"

"He said"—Tirilan shook her head—"I can hear it, but I can't say it. It isn't mine . . ." Anderle shivered as for a moment a much older soul looked out from the girl's eyes. "It was the Word of Thunder," Tirilan said then.

I must not let her see that I am surprised, Anderle thought numbly. *Woodpecker is a child of the Lake Village, but Mikantor is the Son of a Hundred Kings. Is it so strange that he should . . . remember?*

"What does Woodpecker think happened?"

"Oh, he doesn't know what he did." She grinned. "But whatever it was, I know that we've done it before. He's not like the other boys in the Village. I think you should bring him to Avalon."

"I wish we could—" Anderle's voice trembled. If the power was already emerging in him, he needed to be trained. It had been some time since she had caught the scent of Galid's spies. Perhaps she had finally convinced him that the child was lost. If she found other talented children to teach, she could hide Woodpecker among them.

"I would like that." She gave her daughter a hug. "We shall see."

FIVE

*A*s the first full moon after the Turning of Autumn drew near, the Lady of Avalon traveled to the great henge to honor the ancestors. The paths were already sodden with the approach of winter, the old bracken on the hillsides limp and brown. It was said that this feast had once marked the end of the harvest, but what harvest there was had ended a moon ago. The souls they had come to guide would have a wet journey home.

The great passage graves had been abandoned generations ago, but every seven years, the spirits of the dead still flowed down the river to make their pilgrimage to the Henge, and from there to the Otherworld. In every farmstead and village the oldest woman in the household would preside over the ceremonies for the dead of the family, midwifing their transition into the Otherworld as she assisted at the birthing of each new child of her line. And this year, as in most of the years that Anderle could remember, far too many families would have lost a member to whom they must now bid farewell. But the Sisterhood of the Ti-Sahharin, the seven priestesses who guided the spiritual life of the tribes, had another task. And for this they had called the Lady of Avalon, who served all the tribes but was bound to none of them, to aid.

They passed the crossroads and the line of mounds that Anderle remembered all too well from her flight from Azan-Ylir and came suddenly to the rim of the shallow valley that the Aman, swollen now to a small river instead of its usual gentle stream, had cut through the plain. To their left the storm-stripped branches of the oaks clawed at a cloudy sky. Across the river other travelers were passing the charred timbers that once had guarded the high king's home. As they drew closer, Anderle recognized the rain capes of tightly woven rushes that the Ai-Giru wore.

"Let us wait here," she told her men. "If they have trouble with the crossing, they may be glad of our assistance."

But the fens of the Ai-Giru country were even more extensive than those that surrounded Avalon, and the Lady's escort managed to ford the stream with a minimum of splashing and swearing. As the newcomers started up the bank, Anderle came alongside the tented wagon in which the priestess was riding.

"Linne—I hope you are well. I will not ask if you have had a pleasant journey," said Anderle as a thin hand lifted the leather flap and she glimpsed a pale face within.

"Let me see—by pleasant do you mean two lamed horses, and the coughing sickness that hit three of my men so hard they had to be left along the way?"

Anderle nodded. This was the beginning of the dark time, the season that belonged to the powers that dwelt below.

"And this year how have your people fared?"

"My country is like yours—mostly fenland, so we know how to deal with water, although if we truly had webbed feet like the frogs our tribe is named for we would be better off. But now we have to fight off raiders from the Great Land," Linne went on.

"I suppose that times are bad there as well."

"I don't know why they should think that things here are any better," she said bitterly. "But I questioned the one man we took alive. He told me their land lies so low that when the wind blows from the west it is easy for the sea to rush in. The great City of Circles loses ground every year. So the men without families take to their boats to see what they can find elsewhere."

"We should not be surprised." Anderle sighed. "Is it not the same here, as one tribe is forced from its lands and attacks another, and they attack their neighbors in turn. It's like an avalanche—one little stone falls, and before you know it half the mountain is moving."

Ahead the ground rose slightly. Now they could see the huddle of tents fashioned of raw wool or oiled leather and booths roofed with rough thatching that had been set up around the entrance to the Processional Way. This gathering was nothing to compare with the vast crowds that in former days had gathered here for the festival, but an impressive turnout all the same. Beyond them lay the pens where the hairy red cattle waited to be slaughtered for the feasting or traded to improve the stock of other tribes.

One of Anderle's men lifted a horn to his lips and blew three long blasts. People began to emerge from the tents, drawing their mantles over their heads against the fine drizzle that had begun to fall once more. She shivered, only now allowing herself to admit how welcome she would find a bowl of hot soup and the warmth of a fire.

"AT THE TURNING OF Autumn I gazed into the Mother's pool, but all I could see was the swirl of the water, everything dissolving, everything being swept away. . . ." Kaisa-Zan of the Ai-Utu looked up, firelight gleaming in the water that welled from her eyes. She was the youngest of the priestesses, a sturdy girl with a wealth of auburn hair.

"It takes no seeress to interpret that," observed Leka, who came of the Ai-Akhsi, the People of the Ram. "You are afraid of floods, so that is what you will see."

She dipped up another helping of stew, a mixture of mutton and beef and assorted roots and grains, as various as the women who were eating it. The flicker of the fire set their shadows to dancing with the images on the woven hangings that warmed the inner wall of the roundhouse. It was the only permanent building in the encampment, a sturdy structure with a roof of heavy thatch that came down nearly to the ground outside. Over the central hearth, a precious bronze cauldron of stew was simmering, and oat cakes toasted on flat stones at the edge of the fire.

"You can afford to smile," Kaisa-Zan answered bitterly. "You live in the Dales. But how would you like your hills to become islands? If that happens sheep are all you will be able to raise."

"Peace," counseled Linne. "We are here to take counsel for our people—it serves no purpose for us to tear at each other." She looked around the circle with a quelling glance, firelight lending a fugitive color to her silver hair. Nuya, who was the younger sister of Uldan and Zamara and high priestess of the Ai-Zir, sat as far away as possible from Saarin of the Ai-Ushen. They had not spoken to one another since they arrived. "Have we had any word from Olavi?" she asked.

"They say the roads to the north are already covered in snow," answered Saarin. "I almost did not come myself," she added with a glance at Nuya. "You have not made me feel very welcome here. But it is needful. Many of my tribe have died too."

"All of us have too many to call this year," said Leka, "but you can hardly blame the rest of us for resenting your king's way of trying to solve his problems. It is bad enough that Eltan has seized lands in the territory of another tribe. Those he does not kill, he enslaves, and they are grateful to glean the leavings from their own harvests."

"And his creature Galid is worse," added Kaisa-Zan. "His men scavenge like wild dogs, attacking farms and destroying what they cannot carry away. Does he think that if he destroys Azan, Zamara will approve him as king?"

"He is like a wild dog that attacks a sheepfold," said Leka, "rending and slaying for the pleasure of destruction."

"As does any beast divorced from its true nature," observed Shizuret, "whether dog or man."

It was true, thought Anderle, remembering the fallow fields and abandoned farmsteads she had seen as she rode here from Avalon. And over the years she had heard a steady series of tales from refugees. They need not wait for worsening weather to destroy them when they had worse men.

"I think that Galid's sickness is something deeper, an emptiness that no amount of food, or blood, can fill," she said then.

"At least when the wolf kills, it is in order to live," said Saarin. Nuya wrapped her shawl around her as if to protect herself from the other's contagion. And yet come the morrow they would all make the journey to the Henge, joining their powers for the sake of those they mourned. Anderle gazed around the room, seeking for the common quality that made them what they were.

She and Kaisa were the youngest, the others between them and Linne in age, for in the normal way of things a young woman would assist her predecessor for many years before death or retirement thrust her into the senior role. But of course these were not ordinary times. Leka was in her early thirties, strongly built with curly brown hair and a direct manner that was sometimes interpreted as harsh. It was said that the Ai-Akhsi had been warring with their southern neighbors, and she had received a few dark looks from Shizuret, the priestess of the Ai-Ilif, who was almost as old as Linne, and had had a husband and six children before a plague took them, along with the woman who had been intended to succeed the tribe's priestess before her. Perhaps the similarity was that air of self-sufficiency, as if having looked upon the Otherworld, they could not be defeated by any tragedy of this one.

"I can foresee disasters in plenty even if the Island of the Mighty remains above the sea," said Shizuret gloomily. "We are in for a hard time, my sisters, and we must set ourselves to endure."

"That will be difficult when our leaders put all their energy into fighting each other instead of addressing the ills that assail us," agreed Linne. "I am reminded of a litter of puppies someone tried to drown. The top of the bag had come open, and they were struggling to stay afloat. But every time one reached the surface, another would try to climb up and push his brother under again."

"Hard luck," said Leka.

"What happened to the puppies?" asked Kaisa-Zan.

"I pulled them out and found them homes . . ." Linne's smile faded. "But I cannot do the same for your chieftains." Her gaze lingered for a moment on Saarin and Nuya, then passed on.

"Our magic is for growing and healing," whispered Kaisa-Zan.

"And the chieftains doubt our ability to use it," agreed Nuya with a venomous look at Saarin. "The only power men understand now is the point of a spear."

Anderle closed her eyes, summoning up the image that had come to her more than once in dreams. She had seen Mikantor, grown to manhood, striding across a battlefield with a sword in his hand that shone like white fire. *Dare I tell them? They need that hope so badly, but it will be many years yet before what I have seen can come to pass.* She bit back the words with a sigh. So long as Galid lived, the world must continue to believe that Uldan's heir had died.

"And yet we *are* the Sacred Sisterhood." Linne straightened, the folds of her blue gown giving her gaunt figure a sudden majesty. "And if all we can do is to pull an occasional puppy from the flood we will do that."

Or from the fire . . . thought Anderle, remembering Mikantor, as she had seen him when she passed through the Lake Village on her way to this conclave. It must have been nearly time for Redfern to dye his hair again, for hints of red sparked through the dusty brown like a fire through ash. In the past year there had been no exploits as outrageous as the visit to the island of the Wild God, or not, at least, that involved her daughter, but he seemed to have twice the initiative and energy of any of his playmates. *I will have to do something about that boy.*

"We must work with the children," she said aloud, one thought leading to another. "This crisis will not be over soon. We must teach the children to trust each other, even the girls you are training, and we cannot do that if you keep them at home."

"What are you suggesting?" Saarin asked sharply.

"Send them for a few seasons to Avalon, both girls and boys. We will teach them healing and history, make them work together in the rituals. When they have learned and laughed and tested each other's minds, it will be harder to think of the folk of other tribes as those evil wretches from over the hill."

"As we do here . . ." Linne said dryly.

Anderle shrugged. "Send me the ones you think have talent. The ones with energy and inquiring minds. The ones who their parents think are troublemakers, but whose hearts are good. From each tribe, take two or three between the ages of seven and fourteen."

"With a load or two of supplies toward their upkeep?" snorted Shizuret, "or had you thought about how you were going to feed them? Children are always hungry at that age, and your marshes are not exactly the breadbasket of this isle."

"Neither is Azan, these days," murmured Nuya sadly.

"The men of the Lake Village will teach them hunting"—Anderle smiled—"but we will not turn down any supplies you can spare."

"Speaking of which, I believe that the oat cakes are almost done—" said Shizuret, "and to waste the good food would be a sin."

And that, thought Anderle, was a sentiment upon which all of them could agree.

TORCHLIGHT THREW THE EARTHEN banks that defined the Processional Way into high relief, leaving both the rolling plain and the river behind them in an even deeper darkness. Anderle held the edges of her cloak together with one hand, for the wind had come up with sunset, and the black wool flapped around her legs. At least it was also driving the clouds away.

The light brightened as Shizuret emerged from her tent to join the other priestesses who were forming up behind the Lady of Avalon, and her escort fell in around her. In the flickering light the black boar sewn to the back of her cloak seemed gathering itself to charge. A few more moments and Saarin and her wolf-warriors followed and took their places in the line, the priestess in the middle, her torchbearers to either side. Images of Wolf and Frog, Hare and Ram and Bull danced in the firelight, for all of the priestesses wore their tribal regalia here.

That was the last of them. Anderle held up her staff, crowned with the same triple moon that was stitched across her shoulders. A glance over her shoulder showed the real moon already well above the horizon, easing shyly in and out of the remaining clouds. As the staff lifted, the whisper of conversation ceased, until the only sounds were the crackle of the burning torches and the murmurous voice of the river.

"Sisters, the moon is risen. The season of Achimaiek is come. Is it the Hour of the Calling?" Anderle cried.

"The Hour of the Calling is come—" came the reply.

"Then let us seek the Gateway between the Worlds. . . ." She signaled, and the two lads with the bull-roarers began to swing their thongs. As they started forward, the eerie buzzing rose and fell, making the hair prickle on her neck with a chill that did not come from the cold.

The way led to the right and up a gentle slope before turning west toward the Henge. As the road leveled and they emerged onto the plain, Anderle saw the line of barrows extending to her left, and brought the procession to a halt to salute the ancestors who lay there. Before her, the avenue ran straight for a time, and the moon, escaping finally from the encircling clouds, revealed the plain with a cold light that made the torches pale. Here and there the smooth line of the horizon was broken by the tree-covered grave mounds of ancient kings.

As they resumed their march, Kaisa-Zan, who had a fine, clear voice, began to sing the verses that welcomed Achimaiek, whom the tribes worshipped as Grandmother, and whose season was the wintertime.

> *"High the eye of autumn's moon;*
> *Rain scours the hill, now winter chill*
> *Chides the flesh and flays the bone.*
> *With shortened days,*
> *The wild wind's moan*
> *Brings in the Crone."*

Anderle saw a point of light to the north where at Carn Ava the balefire had been lighted upon the Lady's hill. On this night the fires would be signaling from hill to hill from the farthest north to the southern sea, sending the living to huddle behind their doors, calling the dead to their long home. At the sight her heart beat more quickly. The dead whose spirits had clung to bone and ash were waking, hearkening to the song.

> *"She calls you home, no more to roam;*
> *She sets a light upon the height,*
> *Hails plain to hill, and softly calls,*
> *Past good or ill,*
> *Past praise or blame*
> *Your own true name."*

The priestess had a sudden awareness of the Henge before them, even though at this distance it seemed no more than a leafless thicket, barely visible in the light of the moon. Despite that clarity, shadows were everywhere, more sensed than seen. The ghosts of the ancient folk whose mounds dotted the plain were welcoming the more recent dead, whom Anderle could feel gathering behind them.

"Follow, shadows, that bright road
To its last end. The final bend
Shall bring you to the place where best
You may find peace,
Your Self, at rest,
There in the west."

The final note faded, and the bull-roarers began to swing once more, but this time that humming was supported by the voices of the priestesses, rising and falling in eerie harmonies. The tension thickened; the spirits in the barrows were listening. As the road curved once more to the left, Anderle could see the paired stones that marked the entrance to the causeway across the ditch. The shadows of the priestesses lengthened before them as the torchbearers fell back to follow in single file. Anderle paused again when they reached the upright that marked the Midsummer sunrise and unhooked the flask of beer from her belt to pour over the stone in offering. Then their line bent around it and they continued forward.

As they crossed the gap in the bank and ditch and passed between the three boundary stones, their shadows changed again, for the men who carried the torches were turning aside to form a circle of fire outside the Henge. As they moved, light and shadow began to weave a wavering pattern through the linked stones of the sarsen ring. The priestesses slowed their steps so that they entered it at the same time that the men completed their circle. But though only seven living women had entered the circle of stones, a far greater company had followed them.

Now the light steadied, raying between the linked standing stones and the circle of smaller bluestone pillars within them so that as the priestesses arranged themselves within the semicircle of great trilithons, they seemed to stand at the center of a great wheel. But only light entered the circle. If there was any sound from outside they could not hear it, and Anderle knew that the men outside would hear only the faintest murmur from within.

She closed her eyes and took a deep breath, directing awareness to tap into the current of power that coursed beneath the surface of the soil. Across the great island it flowed, from the southern coast through the Henge and Carn Ava and thence northward all the way to the Ai-Siwanet lands. A lesser current connected the Henge to the Tor. She stood at a crossroad, invisible to the ordinary eye, and as she brought the power back up her spine, activated a third channel that linked Above and Below.

"Sisters, are we gathered?" she called.

"We are gathered!" came the reply.

On this night they stood between life and death. The people of this isle had chosen their site well, and her other ancestors, fleeing the fall of the Sea Kingdoms, had done well to recognize the native wisdom, even those—or so said the legend—who had sought to appropriate the power of this place for their own ends. Anderle glanced toward the southern side of the Henge, where the sarsen stones that had formed the fallen segments of the ring lay scattered on the dead grass. At Avalon the story of how those stones had been knocked askew in a battle of magic between the priests of the Henge and of the Tor was taught to the senior adepts. It was said that after the conflict the survivors left the sarsens where they fell as a permanent warning to those who would misuse their power.

And now, thought the priestess, they no longer had the craft to erect the fallen uprights and replace their lintels even if they would. The secret of shaping sound to make such magic had been lost in the generations that had passed since the stones were raised. But they still knew how to use the unique qualities of the Henge. When you were standing inside the circle, sound had a peculiar quality, a vibration that was not quite an echo. Voices seemed particularly clear.

"Call upon those who now must make their passage!" she cried.

Leka of the Dales was the first to move to the center and lift her hands.

"Ultakhe son of Izora I call. You lost your life when the rocks of the sheep-fold gave way before the flooding stream as you were trying to save the last of the lambs."

"Blessed be your life and blessed your passing," chorused the priestesses.

Anderle felt the vibrations of their voices passing through her, took another deep breath, and as she let it out, opened her mind to the spirit who had been called. In the darkness behind her eyelids she could see the glimmering outlines of the Stones, and the misty shape of the man, gazing about him in wonder. What was he seeing?

"*Ultakhe, hear me—*" She sent out an inner call. "*Your flesh is ashes, your spirit body unbound. Now comes the final sundering. Will you leave a part here to watch over your family and hold your memories?*" She waited, and felt a strong assent. No doubt an echo of the man would haunt the scattered stones of that sheepfold. She hoped that his descendants would be able to rebuild it one day.

"*It is well. But now I call your higher soul, the Self that survives all changes.*" At those words the image of the man grew brighter, but it was shifting, the bone structure altering, the scars and lines of care fading away. A succession of faces flickered across that countenance, combining at last into an image that was beyond race, beyond age, beyond gender, and yet unlike any other soul. "*This is the face you had before you were born. Go into the west, Child of Light, to consider what you have learned in this lifetime, and to rest until the time is right for you to take a human body again.*" Anderle could feel the flow of power intensify in the direction of the Tor. She turned in that direction, the arms of her spirit body lifting, releasing that bright spirit into the west.

This was the task to which the Ti-Sahharin had called her, the wisdom brought from lost Atlantis, to ease the natural confusion of passing and speed the spirit beyond the circles of the world. There, it had been a deathbed ritual performed by a priest for an individual, but the Sacred Sisters of the Isle of the Mighty already gathered their dead when the harvest of the crops was done and called them to the Henge. Some early priest or priestess of Avalon had been inspired to guide the passing of the dead of all the tribes at once. The tribes called the goddess into whose keeping they consigned their dead Achimaiek, but it was Ni-Terat on whom Anderle called, the Dark Mother who cradled the seeds in the tomb of her womb through winter's cold until it was time for them to be reborn.

As she relaxed from that first effort, she heard Kaisa summoning the next spirit. "Hilmi son of Koucella. You raised three children to follow you, and died of the coughing sickness in your forty-fifth year."

"Blessed be your life and blessed your passing," the others replied, and Anderle took another breath and prepared to receive the Ai-Utu man. The first spirit was always the most difficult, but with each successive calling it felt more natural to inhabit this space between the worlds. One after another, the priestesses summoned the spirits of those who had died during the past seven years.

She recognized Saarin's voice, harsh with pain. "Krifa daughter of Bou-jema, you died bearing your second child."

This woman had been beautiful, and Anderle was aware of a moment of regret, quickly suppressed, for a life cut off too soon.

Shizuret lifted her hands. "Amruk son of Abrana, you were killed de-fending your farmstead from warriors from the Dales."

Even in her detached state Anderle could feel a chilling of the circle's energy. Yet she knew this would not be the only one dead by violence. They were always the hardest to send onward. The ones who died of old age or sickness were generally glad to be free of the pain. But the fighters still hungered for vengeance. The spirit parts they left behind were all too eager to continue the war. But Amruk's primary emotion was a great sadness, al-most as hard to bear. With an effort she encompassed his spirit, and was rewarded when his darkness at last gave way to a luminous joy. She sighed, releasing him. As the white moon passed the zenith and began to arc west-ward the litany went on.

Linne called, "Massine daughter of Izoran. You died at the age of seventy-seven, leaving behind six grandchildren and fifteen great-grandchildren."

This was a spirit matured and serene, already half transmuted to realiza-tion. As Massine moved on, the priestess warmed herself at her light.

"Blessed be your life and blessed your passing."

"Kalinna daughter of Auris, you died after being raped by men of the

Ai-Ushen." That was Nuya's voice, shaking with anger. Anderle wanted to tell her to stay calm—her grief would hold back the soul she was calling—but voice and vision were fixed upon an inner reality. Only the flow of power that linked above and below kept her upright, limbs locked, suspended between directions, between the worlds. Dimly she was aware of Linne's soft voice, soothing and supporting, and gradually the image of the violated woman became clear and she too passed onward.

The energies around her were beginning to shift. She could feel the moon low in the west; the air had the damp chill of the gray hour before dawn. Somewhere a bird chirped hopefully, then fell silent. But much more palpable was the emptiness of the spiritual sphere where once so many spirits had thronged. *"Hurry,"* her spirit cried. *"Soon it will be day!"*

There was a pause; then Saarin spoke. "Barkhet son of Eilin, you died of cold and starvation while your mother wept, when you were only five years old. . . ."

Anderle reached out to the small spirit, too intrigued by the strange place in which he found himself to move. *"Come, little one, where you will be warm and well fed and dry. You had no time to learn much this time around. May you be reborn in a better time. Come now, it is time to rest—"* As if he had been her own child, she took him in her arms and whirled him around, releasing him like a captive bird to seek the skies.

"Blessed be your life and blessed your passing," the priestesses sang, and in that moment light from without merged with the light within as the newborn sun shouldered up over the eastern rim of the world.

As the darkness retreated, Anderle saw that sweep of shadow as the mantle of a mighty figure, the Crone Herself, in all her sere beauty and terror, gathering the scattered spirits and shepherding them away. For a moment She looked back at Anderle, Her eyes luminous with love and sorrow.

"Do not weep for those who are gone. Can you regret that I have taken them into My keeping, knowing that in time they will be reborn?"

But Anderle could not forget the words with which the priestesses had mourned their dead. Whatever they had come into the world to be and do would not be completed now.

"Forgive my sorrow. I see only the time that is given me. You see eternity . . ."

she replied, remembering Irnana and Durrin. She had saved Mikantor, but who could tell if he would live to become a man?

As daylight filled the circle, the other powers that had flowed through it began to sink back into the land. With them went the energy that had sustained Anderle. The image of the Goddess disappeared in a blaze of light. There was a moment in which inner and outer realities whirled dizzily, and then she was falling in a slow subsidence as if she had no bones. She felt the damp grass beneath her, Linne's thin arms supporting her, and then she knew no more.

WOODPECKER SHIFTED UNCOMFORTABLY ON the wooden bench, wondering if folding his mantle into a cushion would make sitting through the lesson easier on his skinny rear. He had been excited when word came that he and his brother were to join a dozen other youngsters as students at Avalon, but today the sun was shining, and he found himself longing for the freedom of the fens. He was not the only one to chafe at sitting in the stone room on a warm summer's day.

"I am sorry if I am boring you," said Larel as Rouikhed stifled a yawn. He was a tall, big-nosed boy from the Dales who vied with Woodpecker for leadership in the children's games.

"Sorry, master. I did not sleep well last night," the boy replied.

"Nobody sleeps well—" complained Vole, another lad from the Lake Village. "He wake us up yelling!"

"Did you have a nightmare?" Larel frowned. "It is true that children often have bad dreams, but sometimes such dreams hold seeds of truth."

"I suppose." The boy hung his head. "I dreamed again about the flood that washed away my family's farm. Every time it comes, I'm trying to find another way to save them, but it never works, and when I wake it's like losing them all over again."

"I understand," Larel said softly. "I know it does no good to tell you that there was nothing you could have done but die with them. I believe that you were saved for a reason, and when you find your work, those memories will fade."

"I know—but—" The boy looked up suddenly. "This dream was different. I stood on the hill, watching, and saw the floods spreading until they covered everything. It wasn't only my own home—the whole world was being washed away. . . ."

A whisper ran through the children, and Woodpecker wondered who else had had that dream.

"What can we do?" Rouikhed wailed. "Is everything we know and love going to be destroyed?"

For a moment Woodpecker glimpsed an answering panic on Larel's face—did he too fear destruction, or only the prospect of dealing with a roomful of hysterical children? Then the young priest got himself under control.

"Do you think we are the first to face disaster?" he asked sternly. He pointed to an image, its colors now faint with age, that adorned the plastered wall. "Have you ever really looked at this picture? Do it now! What do you see?"

A dozen pairs of eyes obediently turned to the wall.

"I always thought it was a mountain," Tiri said finally. "With some kind of cloud on top."

"And more clouds around it—" added Vole.

"I suppose they do look like clouds." Larel sighed. "The image was clearer when I first heard the story, but the damp has blurred it. Listen now, for this is how the picture was explained to me. This peak"—he rose and traced the outline—"was called the Star Mountain, and it rose in the center of Ahtarrath, an island in a far southern sea. What you see above it is not cloud, but fire and ashes, and what you see around it are the engulfing waves of the sea."

"It doesn't look much like it," Tiri said absently.

"What do you mean?" The priest's voice sharpened.

Tiri looked up in sudden confusion, blinked, and flushed a becoming pink. "I don't know!" she exclaimed. "It just seemed . . . wrong to me."

"How could a mountain have fire?" Woodpecker asked quickly. "Did the forest burn?"

"The way the story goes, everything burned. In those lands fires live beneath the earth, and the mountain exploded from within. Those who could reach their boats escaped and sought refuge in other lands."

"Like this one!" Tirilan smiled once more. "My mother told me that story when I was a little girl."

"Exactly. They had lost everything, and had to make a new life in a new land. But they survived and brought their wisdom to Avalon, and blended their blood and their magic with that of the Seven Tribes."

"But we will never match their wonders," said Ganath wistfully. "We cannot even restore the glory of our own people. In the old days, they say, the kings of the Ai-Zir marshaled armies of men to move the great stones and everyone drank from beakers of worked gold."

"Nonetheless," Larel said firmly, "they are our ancestors. If we do all we can to preserve the truth we've been given, I do not believe that the gods will allow our traditions to be entirely lost." Larel finished on a ringing note, and Rouikhed managed a smile.

"But he doesn't say we all survive . . ." whispered Grebe.

"I know," murmured Woodpecker, but he was determined that whatever happened, he *would* live, and make sure that Tiri, and Grebe, and everyone he cared for lived too.

"Do you think one life is all?" the priest challenged then.

"What does it matter how many lives we've had if we can't remember who we were and what we did before?" complained Analina, who came from the Ai-Utu lands, and thought herself sophisticated because she had helped her father deal with the traders who came from Tartessos to buy tin in Belerion.

"My mother says that a trained priestess can help the soul remember who it really is when it journeys to the Otherworld," Tiri put in then. "That's what she went to the Henge to do last fall."

Ganath, who like Tiri was the child of a priestess, nodded. "My mother told me that when you are alive you only remember those other lives when you really need to know something you learned then." He was a usually cheerful boy with a fine clear voice.

"Sometimes I think I remember," Vole said slowly. "Different for you— you been here all your life and heard things, so how could you tell? But some things I learn here, it's more like remembering something I know before."

Woodpecker grimaced, remembering how he had echoed Tiri's words in the Old Speech on the island of the Wild God. Had he been a priest of Avalon and known those words before? And then there was that Word that had banished the evil powers. Anderle and the others had asked him endless questions, but he could not even remember what the Word had sounded like, much less what it meant.

But though he would not have admitted it to the other boys, if he had had another lifetime, he was pretty sure that in it he had known Tirilan. Though he had forgotten the Word that brought the thunder, he still remembered the solid warmth of her small hand.

SIX

*W*oodpecker feinted with his staff and felt the shock vibrate all the way up his arm as Larel blocked it. The staff was a priest's weapon, but the boy had learned to respect the bruises it could leave when wielded by skillful hands. He ducked, slid a little on ground still squishy from the last rain, and recovered with a swift twist that brought him in under the young priest's guard. Sheep kept the grass short in the field below the complex of buildings that he had come to think of as home. The youngsters in training took exercise here every day before the meal at noon.

In the three years since he had come to live at the Tor, the boy had learned many things. This was one of his favorites, though he wished that the staff had been a spear or a sword. Lady Anderle said that those who honed their spiritual skills required no physical weapons, but her magic had not saved Tirilan's father.

He sensed, rather than saw, the priest's staff whirling toward him and struck upward to deflect it, transferring the impact's energy to his own swing as he brought his weapon down and around to connect with Larel's side. At the last moment he tried to pull the blow, but the meaty "thwack" as it connected made him wince, although not nearly so badly as it did Larel, who reeled back with a stifled cry.

"Goddess! I think you've cracked a rib!" The priest grimaced as he felt along his side.

"I'm sorry, Larel—" Woodpecker tried to look ashamed, when in reality his heart was thumping in triumph. This was the best blow he had ever gotten in. "I didn't expect to hit you." *At least not so hard . . .*

"I suppose I should be proud of my teaching, if not of my skill," Larel said ruefully. "Ow . . ." he said again as he bent to pick up his staff. "I had better ask Kiri to bind this. It won't speed the healing, but it will remind me to be careful when I move."

Mist still drifted on the Lake, casting a ghostly veil across the trees, but as the sun rose, it was burning through the clouds. Woodpecker flushed as a brighter ray gleamed suddenly on Tiri's fair hair. How long had *she* been watching him?

"Shall I punish him for you?" she asked as Larel limped past.

"As if you could!" grunted Woodpecker, and the other boys laughed. She stepped forward to meet him eye to eye. In the past year she had been growing until she was almost as tall as he, graceful as a swan, and as strong. "What, are you going to put a spell on me?"

"Why, no . . ." she answered, wide-eyed. "That would be a misuse of my powers. But I know where you sleep—" A giggle spoiled her attempt at an ominous tone. "Spiders? Grass snakes? What shall it be?"

Woodpecker glared. *Boys* were supposed to do that sort of thing to make the girls squeal. But Tirilan feared nothing living.

"Do you know that when you stand like that you look exactly like a grouse ruffling up?" she said cheerfully.

He felt his skin heating, but could think of no reply. Turning his back he challenged Rouikhed to another bout with the staves. He could hear Tiri laughing with the other girls as they strode away.

THE NEXT TIME WOODPECKER saw Tiri she was weeding the little garden in the lee of the dining hall, where Ellet had been trying to get some of the wild herbs they used for healing to grow. When he realized who it was he hesitated, but she was already getting to her feet and holding out her hand. It had rained earlier in the day, and she had a smear of mud across her nose.

"Please, don't go—I'm sorry I teased you this morning, but you did look funny standing there and I was mad because you hurt Larel."

"Do you like him?" Woodpecker wondered why that thought should disturb him. He fixed his eyes on the row of chamomile daisies, avoiding her gaze. In the next row they had planted sunwort, and beyond it clumps of yarrow. Bees hummed happily as they moved from flower to flower.

"Of course—" she began, then laughed. "But I don't have a *passion* for him, if that's what you meant—"

It was, but he was not about to say so. "Of course not—" he echoed, careful to use the dialect of the Tor. "You're too young to be thinking about such things."

"I am as old as you are!" she replied.

"No, you're not. I am thirteen, and you are a year younger than me," he said stoutly, though he could not deny that in the past few months she had been changing. There were small but definite breasts beneath her undyed woolen gown.

"Really?" she said sweetly. "I heard my mother say that when I was born you were three months old, *and* you had bright red hair."

Reflexively he ran his hand over the hair he kept close cropped even though they had stopped putting medicine on it every month once he came to Avalon. When he let it grow it turned into a mop of auburn curls.

"There's nothing wrong with my hair!" A bee buzzed toward him and he waved it away.

"I know that—"She looked troubled. "It doesn't matter. It was something I heard my mother say to old Kiri one day."

Woodpecker blinked, then grabbed her arm as she started to turn away. "Tirilan! You can't come out with something like that and then just stop! What else did she say?"

Tiri looked at him and then at his hand on her arm until, flushing, he let go.

She frowned thoughtfully. "I didn't understand. She said they had to dye your hair because you looked so different from the other babies. Your enemies would have found you if you hadn't been disguised."

The medicine Redfern had used was a dye? For a few moments Woodpecker could only stare. "You must have misunderstood," he said at last. "My father isn't even the headman. How could I have enemies?"

"Perhaps I did," she said softly. "It doesn't make sense, does it? Although you don't look very much like Grebe . . ."

"Lots of people don't look like their families. You don't look like your mother at all."

"Yes, but— Oh, never mind. I shouldn't have spoken. Kiri always says that people who eavesdrop never hear anything good of themselves, or anyone else, I suppose." Her eyes glittered, and he realized that she was on the verge of tears.

"It's all right," he said gruffly. "It doesn't matter." But both of them knew that he lied.

ANDERLE HAD MADE A point of spending time with her daughter every day. Perhaps having lost her own mother so early had led her to idealize the relationship, but she was determined not to leave her child entirely to the care of those who might treat her with too much reverence because of her parentage, or for the same reason, resent her. And so, except when there was an evening ritual, the hour after the priests and priestesses had their communal meal she spent with Tirilan in the small chamber just off the dining hall that she had claimed as her own.

They sat now by the little fire, hands busy with needlework. Tirilan had inherited her mother's clever fingers, and when there were no ritual garments to be embroidered, someone always had a tunic in need of mending. Tonight, Tiri was fixing a three-cornered tear in a shapeless mass of gray wool. Anderle smiled a little, appreciating the picture the girl made with the firelight glinting on her fair hair. She was still a child, but she was growing fast, and every now and then one glimpsed the young woman, long boned and fine featured, that she would become.

"What are you working on?" she asked, gesturing with the bone needle with which she was setting a hem in a linen veil.

"Woodpecker's tunic—" Tiri shook it out and held it up for her mother to see. It had already been mended in several places, and was going to need work in several more. "I wish he was not so hard on his clothes, although if he would give them to me before they got torn so badly, they would last longer."

"You shouldn't have to work on the boys' tunics—" objected Anderle.

"I know. I only do it for Woodpecker. I thought I might as well get used to it. I expect I'll marry him someday."

"Has he been bothering you?" Anderle asked in sudden alarm. Of all the problems she had foreseen in preparing the boy to take his place in the world, this had not been one of them. And really, the child was at that awkward stage, all legs and elbows, when he was not likely to be attractive to anybody. "I would have thought him too young, but—"

"Woodpecker? Of course not. He still thinks of me as a nuisance." She looked down at the tunic with a secret smile. "When the time comes I'll have to tell *him*."

Anderle shook her head. "That won't be necessary. You may take him as your lover in the rites, but priestesses do not marry."

"What if I don't become a priestess?" challenged the girl.

"Nonsense!" her mother exclaimed. "You are priestess-born—it is in your blood. If you had no talent it would be another matter, but I have felt your energy rise in the rituals. You cannot deny that you feel the power. The potential is there. Your formal training will begin soon."

"Woodpecker has the potential too—will you make him a priest?"

Anderle stopped short, staring at her daughter. "Woodpecker . . . must follow another path." How quickly the time was passing. Soon, she supposed, she would have to find a way to tell him about that destiny.

"And I?" Tirilan had grown very still.

"You will be Lady of Avalon after me."

"Just like that?" asked the girl. "The council of priests will choose me because you have willed it? You may be Lady of Avalon, but who made you queen of the world? I don't see you having much luck in stopping the rain from falling or the tribes from fighting. I think the world has other plans, and so do I!"

"You have no idea what you are saying!" exclaimed Anderle, stung to an unaccustomed fury, not least because so much of what the girl had said was true. "You are a child who dreams of playing house. Have you seen how those women live who are so proud to be called wives? My cousin Irnana was the wife of the king of the Ai-Zir, and even she—" Anderle stopped abruptly, realizing she had almost let out the whole tale. One day Tirilan would have to know, but not now, when her head was full of foolish fantasies about the boy. "It does not matter—" With an effort she restored her voice to calm. "You are still a child and so is he. The time for choices is far away."

THE COMMUNITY AT AVALON had done their best to provide a well-rounded training for the children with whom they had been entrusted. In addition to their own genealogies, they were taught the stories and great deeds of every tribe. They learned to take pride in the achievements of those who had raised the barrows and stone circles, and to sense and tap the power that those monuments channeled through the land. They learned the names and stories of the gods and spirits worshipped in each region, how to calculate the turnings of the seasons by the movements of sun and stars, and the rituals for each festival, though with the weather so disordered the ceremonies no longer seemed to match their dates as well as they had in the past. The students were taught herb lore and divination and meditation, and lest all this mind work leave them feeble, they learned to spar with the staff, to paddle a boat, and to swim.

After that disturbing conversation with her daughter, for a time Anderle kept a closer eye on the students than she had done before. But whatever Tirilan might dream, there did not seem to be anything but friendship between her and Woodpecker, and the priestess began to think it had all been no more than a childish fancy after all. Still, she was beginning to worry about the boy. He, who had always been eager to speak up in the teaching sessions, now replied in monosyllables if he answered at all. He had been a leader in the games, but now played without enthusiasm. He had taken to long walks and sullen silences.

"It is only youth," said Belkacem. "Boys have these phases, and this one will pass." But Larel, who remembered his own youth more clearly, was not so sure. "Something is bothering the child," he told her one day toward the end of summer. "Even his friends have noticed it. But I cannot get him to talk to me."

Whether it is youth or some deeper cause, he is growing, thought Anderle as she watched him sitting in the circle listening to Belkacem lecture on the history of Avalon. *If he is to challenge Galid and rule the Ai-Zir, there are things he will need to learn.* Despite his sulks, Woodpecker had gotten bigger over the summer. He was taller than Tirilan once more. His hair had darkened from its baby brightness, but as he sat with his head bent, arms around his knees, the sun kindled fiery glints in his auburn curls.

"You all know that our community here comes from the fusion of two peoples," said Belkacem, "the ancient tribes of this land and the adepts that came here from the lost lands across the sea. It is said that one of them was not only a priest, but the prince of an island called Ahtarrath, the heir of a hundred kings. Micail was the leader of the adepts whose singing lifted into place the great stones of the Henge, and the husband of the first Lady of Avalon."

If there were a man of that stature among us, I might reconsider my position on marriage, Anderle thought wryly. Durrin had been a wonderful singer and a charming man, but she wondered sometimes if her love for him would have lasted once she had grown into her own power. *The truth is, I need a man whose strength will match mine.* But as leader of their community, she must be supreme, and although the Lady might lie with a tribal king in ritual, that role was generally taken by the high priestess of his tribe. To take a man of the tribes as a permanent partner in the rituals would upset the balance of power. There was always a Morgan to serve as Lady of Avalon, but a soul worthy to assume the title of the Merlin appeared among them rarely.

And so, she concluded with a sigh, *I seem fated to lie in an empty bed.* To be sure, for the most part she did not regret it. There had not been a man who could stir her blood since Durrin died. It was only on days like this, when the sun had broken through the clouds and every leaf and blade of grass seemed to shimmer with life, that she remembered that she was a woman, and still young, and alone.

Belkacem seemed to be droning to a conclusion at last. Anderle left the birch trees in whose dappled shade she had been standing and started down the hill to speak with the boy.

"Lady!" the old priest called, and the children who had been gathered around him made the gesture of reverence and stood aside. "Were you here when I was questioning them? They are doing well, very well indeed. So well I think we might give them some role in the Harvest ceremony."

"Yes, yes, we should do that—" Anderle answered, her eyes on Wood-pecker, who had said something to Grebe that made the other boy frown and was now striding up the lower slope of the Tor. By the time she was able to detach herself, he had disappeared into the tangle of oak and haw-thorn that girdled the base of the hill.

ANDERLE CAME TO A halt by the westernmost of standing stones that crowned the Tor and paused to catch her breath. She had intentionally kept to a moderate pace, for to greet Woodpecker windblown and sweaty would be equally undignified. But the boy was barely halfway up the hill. He walked with bent head, pausing now and again to examine a stone or detour around a flower. Sometimes he followed the wandering path the first priests had carved into the hill, but then he would gather his forces and charge straight on once more.

Her lips quirked as she looked down the grassy slope. She had rolled all the way from the summit once when she was a child. Kiri had smacked her bottom until it hurt as much as the rest of the bumps she had acquired on the way down, but it had been worth the pain. She still remembered the dizzy excitement when all direction disappeared in a whirl of sensation, as if she were about to spin bodily into the Otherworld. That was what she had hoped to do. It was said that from the Tor one could pass into that other realm that lay upon this one like an invisible veil.

Now, of course, she knew how to shift her awareness between dimen-sions as she had done at the Henge when she midwifed the souls. But it would be a fine thing to walk in her own flesh in that realm where there was neither sun nor moon, but only a perpetual luminous twilight, and to meet its ageless queen.

Her shadow lengthened as the sun sank toward the bank of cloud that usually hung above the sea. Its light gleamed on Woodpecker's burnished head as the boy made his way over the rim of the hill.

"Well met—" she said softly. He started, eyes widening, and began a bow whose depth lessened as his vision adjusted and he realized that it was Anderle. "I know who you were expecting. I am not She, but I *am* the Lady of Avalon, and you are in my care. Woodpecker, we have all seen that you are troubled. What is it, my child? We are alone here—you can speak freely to me."

"'Woodpecker,' you call me!" he blurted. "Who gave me that name, and when? *Who am I?*"

He knows! thought Anderle, mind racing in speculation. Had someone told him of the prophecy that the son of Uldan would return to save his people?

"Has someone said that you have another name?" she asked, playing for time to let her speeded heartbeat slow, and like an echo heard, *"I know the name you had before you were born,"* a phrase from the Mysteries. And was not the purpose of one's life the manifestation of that primal identity?

"No one had to tell me," he said quickly, but his flush told her that *something* that started him down this path. "I don't know if I have another name, but I have only to look in the reflecting pool to see that I am no child of the Village. They should have called me 'Cuckoo,'" he added bitterly. "Where did you find the chick you put into Redfern's nest?"

Anderle sighed. At least she could stop wondering how to tell the boy about his heritage. She should tell him to sit, but she was not sure he could bend without falling down.

"I suppose that we should have told you before, but you must understand—you are still a child. We did not think you would understand."

Try me—said his answering glare, and for a moment someone much older looked out of his deep-set eyes.

"You do have another name," the priestess said then. "It is Mikantor."

He blinked, trying to process that information. "That is not a name from the Tribes," he said at last.

"Your mother was my cousin Irnana. Like me, she came of the sacred line of Avalon that goes back to the People of Wisdom who came here from across the sea."

"Then why pretend I was a child of the Lake?" he exclaimed. "Why—" He stopped short, staring. "The lady Irnana was married to the king of the Ai-Zir," he said slowly. "I have heard that tale. He died when Galid opened the gates to the Ai-Ushen, and his lady burned with their child. . . ."

"So it is said," Anderle agreed. "But I got you away. Galid knows that you lived, but not what became of you afterward."

"Then it is because of him that my parents died."

What, she wondered, had the boy heard? "It is, indeed. So we must keep you hidden as long as we can." That would not be long, she thought, seeing already beneath the soft contours of childhood a hint of the stronger features he would have as a man. Though they had been refined by mixing with the blood of Avalon, he was still going to have the look of old Uldan. "It's as well that you know now. There are things you will need to learn if you are to defeat him. Your cousin Cimara has no brothers. As her closest kin, you have the best right to lead the Ai-Zir."

"What if that's not what I want to do?" he said mutinously. "It seems to me that you have all made very free with my destiny."

"You are the Son of a Hundred Kings!" she cried, temper snapping at last. "Azan is only the beginning. In times to come a Defender will be needed to lead all the tribes. The gods tormented me with visions until I went to Azan-Ylir to save you. It is they who have given you a hero's destiny. All I have done since then has been to make sure you live long enough to claim it!"

She saw him recoil and took a deep breath, fighting for calm. He could not know how she had suffered on that journey. It must be hard enough for him to assimilate the facts—it was far too soon to expect him to show gratitude.

"You are overwhelmed," she said, "and you have reason. I will leave you here to think about it. You are excused from lessons for the rest of the day."

———

WOODPECKER OPENED HIS EYES to a misty twilight. He was leaning against something hard. A dozen paces away he saw an upright stone about half his height that seemed to glow from within. Others stood to either side. It was the stone circle on top of the Tor.

He remembered climbing the hill and speaking with Lady Anderle, and then she had left and he had sat down because his legs would not support him anymore. Images from that encounter surfaced, dim and confused as memories from a dream. Once more he heard the Lady of Avalon calling him the "Son of a Hundred Kings . . ." Certainly *that* memory had come from a dream. Perhaps he was dreaming still. The top of the Tor was always a little uncanny, but this did not look quite like the world he knew.

He got to his feet. The Vale of Avalon lay before him, a marvelously variegated tapestry of marsh and meadow and woodland that, like the stones, seemed lit from within. He could see the seven sacred islands clearly, though from here they seemed no more than radiant green hills in a landscape whose proportion of land to water was far greater than he remembered.

How long had he slept? He could not see the sun, but perhaps it had just gone down, for the sky had that soft radiance that held the memory of light. But as he turned, his skin chilled, for the light to the east and to the west was the same. Where was he? *When* was he? He had heard tales of folk who wandered into the Hidden Land and when they returned found everyone they loved long dead and themselves no more than a distant memory.

He should have known better than to fall asleep in the circle. He should— He turned again and sighed with relief, for the shiny lady was standing there. He stifled a laugh, realizing how long it had been since he had thought of Anderle by that name. And then the Lady smiled, and he realized that although she too was small and dark-haired and beautiful, she did not look like the Lady of Avalon at all.

"Be welcome to my country, child of the ancient line—" Her voice held the ripple of water and the lilt of birdsong.

Without intending it he found that he had fallen to his knees. He could see now that instead of priestess-blue she was wearing a garment of pale doeskin, and her waving hair was crowned with summer flowers.

"Will you give me your name?" Once more she smiled.

He blinked, aware that like eating the food of the Otherworld, giving out that information might mean more than it appeared. But just now he did not care. "The Lady of Avalon called me Mikantor."

"And what do you call yourself?"

"I do not know."

"Then I will call you Osinarmen, for that was your true name when I knew you long ago."

He realized that he was gaping and shut his mouth. If he could say nothing sensible, at least he could avoid sounding like a fool.

"You were older then, grieving because you thought that your only child was dead and your line would fail." She shook her head. "You children of earth have such strange fears. In my realm we never die, but you who do may still return again. Do you not remember?"

"I am not Osinarmen—" he stammered.

"His blood flows in your veins. You carry his soul."

And the Word that brought the thunder . . . he thought with an inner tremor.

"Anderle doesn't want me to be a priest," he replied, although another part of his mind was telling him that this whole conversation belonged to some feverish dream. "She wants me to be a warrior-king."

"And what do *you* want to do?"

"In this life?" he challenged. This was getting easier, so long as he didn't think of it as real. He could even allow himself to answer her question. "Keep my people safe, . . ." he said, remembering some of the stories he had heard. "And I suppose it's my duty to get back at Galid for what he did to my . . . parents."

"That seems an appropriate ambition for a warrior-king."

From her tone, he could not tell whether she approved. "Do I have a choice?"

"There is always a choice," she said gently. "To act as your nature impels you or to refuse the challenge. To stay here with me, or to go back down the hill to embrace your destiny. Be warned, the path I see before you may take you to places you cannot imagine, but if you are true to yourself, you will achieve your goal."

Now, she *did* sound like Lady Anderle. And with that realization, a longing awoke in him for the honest warmth of a hearth fire and the sight of familiar faces. If she had offered him food, he might have been tempted, even knowing the dangers, but she stood silent, watching him with that same tender smile.

He shrugged. Compared with all the other revelations, to realize that he was a year younger than he had thought was a minor adjustment. Hard as it was to accept that he was the son of King Uldan of the Ai-Zir, to think of himself as the priest Micail who had sung the stones of the great henge into position was stranger still.

"I will go back," he answered finally. "I don't believe half of what you have said to me, but I won't desert the people I love."

"Then you have my blessing," she said gently, moving toward him. She scarcely had to bend to kiss his forehead. "And my farewell."

And then she was gone. Gone too was the strange light that had surrounded them. Woodpecker who was Mikantor stood alone atop the Tor. It was getting dark, but her kiss still burned upon his brow.

SEVEN

*L*ook! A sea eagle!"

Woodpecker turned as Tiri touched his arm. Through the fringe of budding willows they could see the bird circling, black and white feathers flickering as they caught the sun. They hunkered down among the twisting trunks, more to stay hidden from any watching eyes on the Tor than from the osprey, whose attention was on the patch of lake gleaming in the watery spring sunlight. As they watched, that keen gaze fixed on a ripple, and then the spread wings tilted and the long glide became a lightning stoop that struck the water in a flurry of spray. A few mighty wing-strokes launched the osprey upward once more, clutching a wriggling stickleback in her talons, and she beat across the marsh toward the Oak Tree Isle.

"We'll miss *our* breakfast if we don't go back soon!" muttered the boy. His belly was beginning to remind him how long ago last night's dinner had been. "I don't understand why your mother won't let us have any free time together. We've been slogging away at all those extra lessons she added last summer, and we are doing well."

"I still think you should tell her about the queen of the Hidden Realm," said Tirilan. As she turned her head, a little wind stirred the branches and let a dappling of sunlight through to play on her amber hair. After his encounter with the Otherworldly Lady, Woodpecker's standards for "shiny" had been considerably raised, but he saw some of that light in Anderle when she put on her robes to conduct a ritual, and sometimes he sensed the same glimmer around Tirilan.

"She rules every other part of my life," he said mutinously, stabbing a piece of broken branch into the muddy ground. "She told the priests she had a vision that I should get special training. I've heard them congratulating her on my improvement. If I tell her what the queen said, she'll try to turn me into a priest or make me learn the genealogies of the Sea Kings as well as those of the Ai-Zir. Don't you tell—"

"I've sworn a solemn oath to keep your secret, Mikantor . . ." she reproved.

"Don't call me that."

"It is your name—"

"A dangerous name, until I am old enough to defend it," he replied.

"I know, but if you never think about it, you'll never grow into it. That other name she said—that was another life, another man. You have to find your own path. My mother is determined to make me a priestess, but I think your task is more important, and I will help you any way I can."

He dropped the stick and met her steady, searching gaze. Nothing that had been said to him by Lady Anderle, or even by the queen of the Hidden Realm, had shaken him like this simple declaration.

"If you believe in me . . . that much, I swear to do my best to be . . . a king." Suddenly self-conscious, he looked away. "But I can't do anything if I starve," he added brightly. "Let's get back before the porridge is all gone!"

ANDERLE TOOK A DEEP breath as Badger dug the long pole into the lake bed and propelled the narrow dugout across the water. It was one of those days that in recent years had come even in summer, when the morning mist clung to the reeds until past noon, veiling the distinctions between air and water and solid ground until crossing the Lake felt like a visionary journey through the Otherworld. She had forgotten how much she enjoyed the stately rhythm of this progress. Behind her, old Kiri, who did not enjoy being on the water, gripped the boat's sides. It would be pleasant to spend a whole afternoon simply sliding across the smooth water, but she only had the opportunity when she was on her way somewhere, usually worrying about whatever she would have to do when she got there.

Badger's face gave her no reassurance that this trip would be any different. He had come to the Tor that morning with the news that Willow Woman was sick with some illness they had never seen before. Kiri had argued that *she* was the community's most experienced healer, and there was no need for the Lady of Avalon to leave her duties on the isle. But Anderle, remembering the many times Willow Woman had helped her, knew that she must go, especially if this sickness proved to be beyond Kiri's skill.

"How long has your mother been ill?"

"Three days now," came Badger's reply. "When the moon was new, a man comes up from the coast with cloth to trade, says people sick down there ever since traders came from the Middle Sea. He was fine when he comes, a little fevered when he goes away. Willow Woman told him stay till he's better—likely he's dead in the marshes somewhere by now. Guess he didn't go soon enough—a few days after, my mother starts feeling tired, has a fever, can't swallow food."

"Has anyone else fallen ill?" Kiri asked.

"Beaver, Sallow's son—he was always hanging around the stranger, asking questions. He throws up a lot, and now his neck swells like a bull."

It was a contagion, then, thought Anderle with a sinking of the heart, not some nameless illness that attacked the old. The raised platforms that supported the houses of the Village were looming up out of the mist. Soon they would know. The dugout rocked and she held on to the side as Badger brought it alongside the ladder and made it fast.

The look on Badger's face as they gathered around the sick woman's bed told the priestess that Willow Woman must have gotten worse even in the time he had been gone. The sound of her breathing was loud in the quiet room.

"She fades in and out—" said Badger's wife. "Says it's hard to move."

The headman nodded. "Mother—here's the Lady of Avalon. Won't you say hello?"

Willow Woman had always been active, out in all weather and brown as a nut with exposure to wind and sun. Now she was deathly pale. Anderle knelt beside the bed and grasped the thin hand, her apprehension increasing as she felt the pulse in the woman's wrist racing like the heart of a frightened bird.

"The blessing of the Goddess be with you, my dear one," she said softly.

Willow Woman's eyelids fluttered open and her lips twitched in what might have been a smile. "Night Lady . . . takes me . . . soon. . . ." she got out between labored breaths. "Watch over . . . the . . . boy. . . ."

"Kiri, she is in pain! Is there something you can do?"

The older priestess gripped Anderle's shoulders and moved her aside. "Let me see to her now. Go out and purify yourself. There are evil spirits here."

"You have seen this before?" Anderle got to her feet, blinking back tears.

"I have." Kiri's face was grim. She had always been a big woman. Now, as she interposed herself between the high priestess and the dying woman, she seemed to have the enduring solidity of one of the great standing stones. "The throat swells and becomes like leather until the sufferer cannot breathe. Unless she has great strength to resist, she will not survive, and she will not be the only one."

WOODPECKER STOOD WITH THE other students in the Hall of the Sun, trying to ignore the apprehension that coiled in his gut. This plague that had struck the Lake Village was like some terror in a nightmare, the faceless, voiceless kind that could be resisted neither by strength nor by magic. Willow Woman had died from it, and his old playmate Beaver, and then Redfern, whom Woodpecker had thought of as his mother until a year ago. Even old Kiri's legendary strength had failed. She had sickened and died, and Vole, who had been her student in healing, had succumbed as well.

He tried to comfort himself with the knowledge that Tirilan was still healthy, and Lady Anderle must be all right, for she had ordered them to meet her here, and she would not have done so if she were sickening. But the early summer sunshine that filtered in through the openings between the lower part of the roof and the upper canopy that let out the smoke from the central hearth had little power to dispel the fear that chilled his soul.

Had someone else died? Since Vole fell ill, the students had been kept isolated from the rest of the community. *Waiting to see if anyone else was going to get sick,* the boy thought dismally. Each morning, food had been left for them at the dormitory doors. *Perhaps the danger is over, and she will assign us roles in some great ceremony to mourn those who are gone.*

But he knew this was not how such news would have been given. And Anderle's face, when she appeared in the doorway, was gaunt and grim. Woodpecker saw with shock the first threads of silver glinting in her dark hair.

"I am happy to see you all in good health," she said as she took her seat in the carved chair, and as Woodpecker and the others made the formal obeisance, they knew the sentiment was no empty formality. "This disease seems to strike first at the young and the old. Belkacem has died, and Damarr is stricken." Without giving them a chance to respond to the loss of a teacher who, if not beloved, had seemed as eternal as the distant hills, she went on.

"But we have lost only one of you children, and we mean to keep it that way. Avalon is no longer a safe haven. To continue to expose you to this danger would be to betray the trust of those who sent you here. I am sending you all back to your tribes."

"On foot?" asked Rouikhed.

"Alone?" echoed Analina. "What if the plague is at Belerion too?"

"So far the illness seems confined to the south coast." Lady Anderle answered the last question first. "I have gone out upon the spirit roads and spoken with the Ti-Sahharin. You will follow the old trackway through the marshes to the east until you come to the hill of the Winding One's spring. Some of you, at least, know how to follow the flow of power that goes that way, even if you lose the path. Your tribes will send men to meet you there and take you home."

Woodpecker reached out to grip Grebe's shoulder as the others began to ask questions. The Lake Village was the only home they had ever known.

"Tirilan, you will go to Nuya at Carn Ava," the high priestess said then. "Woodpecker and Grebe, you will be taken westward to dwell with the shepherds on the high moors."

Woodpecker let go of his foster brother and took a step toward Tirilan. Why couldn't Anderle have sent them off together? But a look at the Lady's face told him that it would be useless to protest. He did not think he had ever seen anyone who looked so desperately tired. She probably had not even been trying to separate him from her daughter, only to find safe nests for all the chicks she had gathered here.

Will I ever see you again? his gaze asked Tirilan.

I will not forget you— hers replied.

SUMMER PASSED INTO FALL, and the plague ran its course. A messenger was sent to take Grebe back to the Lake Village, but Woodpecker was given a new name and ordered to spend the winter with Lady Leka in the Dales instead of returning to Avalon. As spring approached he saw swans flying eastward and wished he was seeing them on the marshes once more, descending in such numbers their white backs covered the pools. But when the priest Larel came to the Ai-Akhsi lands, it was to escort him to stay for a time with the family of Analina, in a coastal village in Belerion.

"I don't understand," the boy said as they made their way southward. "The Lady talked so much about all the training I must have, but the plague is over, and still I am being herded from one place to another like a one-horned goat that nobody wants in his herd. Is Tirilan back at Avalon?"

Has she changed? He bit back the question. *Have I?* He knew that he was growing when his tunic sleeves got too short and tight across the shoulders, and he, who had always been graceful, found himself stumbling over feet suddenly too large and legs too long. He supposed that was to be expected now that he was fifteen. A glimpse of his face in a woodland pool showed him serious brown eyes and a beak of a nose beneath a shock of dark red hair.

They were crossing a long valley between two lines of rolling downs. On the slope to the south someone had cut the stylized figure of a horse into the chalk. Every year the people of the Vale scoured the encroaching grass from its outlines as part of a great festival. As they followed the shaded land across the valley, the image of the horse appeared and disappeared through the trees.

Larel laughed. "The Lady said that you would ask. Tiri came home again at Midwinter, and we all wish that you could be there as well. I am to tell you that there are two reasons for keeping you away. The first is that a leader needs to understand the lives of his people. By living in different regions you will learn things that cannot be taught on Avalon."

Woodpecker sighed. It was true that the windswept rocky moors of the northern Ai-Utu were a world away from the close marshes that protected the Tor. For the first few moons he had been dreadfully homesick, but in time he had learned to love the great sweep of open sky and the way the green turf clung to the bones of the land.

"And the second reason?" he asked then.

"It would appear that your secret has not been kept as well as we believed. One of the other students, no doubt quite innocently, must have said something about the bronze-haired boy who was so good at games, and set your enemies to wondering. Galid has been making inquiries. He fears that if you live to manhood, one day you will come after him."

And if I live, I will. He will be right to fear. . . . "Are you moving me now because they know I was in the Dales?" he said aloud.

"That is what we have heard," the priest replied.

"What story will you tell to explain my presence this time?" On the moors, he had been an orphaned cousin needing a home. By the time he was moved to the Dales, he had learned enough about sheep to be taken on as a herdboy. But he did not think there would be many sheep by the sea.

"Analina's father needs another clerk. The port where the tin traders put in is a busy place, where people from all over the island come to trade. Your northern accent will not seem too strange. You will be known as Kanto there."

Woodpecker sighed. This would be the third name they had given him, and none of them was his own. Until they let him settle down somewhere, he would never learn who *Mikantor* might be.

"It's not my accent, but my counting that will sink me," he said when the silence had gone on too long. "If you want sheep counted, I'm your man, but I don't know about anything more complicated than that."

"When we camp for the night we shall practice." The priest grinned. "I have brought slates along for that very purpose. You were quick at your sums, as I recall. We'll have you calculating higher numbers in no time at all."

Woodpecker groaned. He had been very glad to leave the sheep behind, but suddenly he missed them.

ANALINA'S FAMILY LIVED IN a village that bordered the curve of a bay that faced south. When Woodpecker looked through the open door of the store shed, he could see across the thatched roofs of the houses to the water, blue today, with a ruffling of whitecaps fluffed up by a light breeze, to the pointed island that guarded the bay. After the windy silences of the moors and the Dales, to share the busy life of a community again had been a shock. The clustered houses reminded Woodpecker of the Lake Village. Whether raised in argument or laughter, you could always hear human voices in Belerion. Although at first he had started at every sound, people, however noisy, were much more interesting than sheep. The sea breeze made the blood race in his veins. He fancied that beneath the briny scent of the ocean he could smell more exotic odors from lands whose names he was just beginning to learn.

Or perhaps it was the things in Master Anaterve's store shed that he was smelling, he thought as he picked up his lump of chalk and his slate and turned back to the pile of fleeces he was tallying. Logs of a wood called cedar lay across the rafters, and bags of aromatic herbs hung from the walls, brought by the winged ships that everyone said would be returning as soon as the season of storms was past. Until now, it had never occurred to him to wonder where the traders who brought oxcarts full of goods to the great festivals got their wares.

Master Anaterve was a dealer who collected anything he thought might sell, but especially the bun-shaped ingots of tin he got from the miners who scraped the ore from the "tin streams" on the moors and smelted it in rude furnaces. In the world of the great, bronze was more valuable than gold, and since the gods in their wisdom had chosen to place the sources of copper and tin in such widely divergent regions, to create bronze required trade.

But the relative value of the ingots in relation to a hundred other commodities was a constantly shifting calculation. How much was a fleece worth, or a golden earring, or an ingot of tin, when the basic unit of value was a cow? Within a few days Woodpecker had realized why the merchant required the services of a servant who could count a pile of ingots more than once and get the same total each time.

And after half a year with the merchant he thought he understood why the Lady of Avalon had sent him here. A sheepherder worried about taking care of his family. A king had to care for a whole tribe, and the key to getting all those things a family could not make for itself was trade. To acquire those things, and to make the weapons to defend his people, a king must have bronze. If the Great Land needed tin from Belerion, no less did the Isle of the Mighty need the copper with which it must be combined, and the supply of accessible ore in the mines from which the Ai-Ushen had derived their wealth was coming to an end.

He cast an indulgent glance at Master Anaterve, who was examining the latest load of tin to come down from the hills. The merchant was a good man, who drove a hard bargain but an honest one, and believed that men would always act rationally if they understood where their best interest lay. But two years with the tribes had shown Woodpecker another side of humanity. When times became too dire, he thought unhappily, men gorged like starving wolves. That was not really greed, but the desperation of those who grabbed what they could because there was no predicting what they might need.

Just as I can't predict my future, he thought with a return of the depression that had kept him from forming close ties in any of the places he had stayed. In his mind he knew that he had been moved around because Galid was actively seeking him again, but in his heart he suspected that Lady Anderle had some magic that told her when he got too comfortable. *The day I admit, even to myself, how much I like it here, I expect Larel to come striding down the road.* But he couldn't help hoping that they would let him stay long enough to see the trading ships come in.

"Fair weather . . ." said the merchant, coming out to stand at his side and shading his eyes with one hand. "The ships from Tartessos will be arriving soon, with their white sails like the wings of swans."

Had he picked up the older man's eagerness, Woodpecker wondered as Anaterve took up the list he had been working on, or was it something in the air? The ships came at the time when the swans winged eastward across the clearing skies, and he had been hearing them off and on all day. His nose wrinkled as the scent of smoke mingled with the briny scent of the sea.

"Is someone burning brush?" he began, and then, "Look—smoke is rising from the island. There must be a fire . . ."

He broke off as Anaterve turned, a smile lighting his face like a new dawn. "A beacon fire!" the merchant exclaimed. "As soon as the weather clears we post a watcher there. It is a ship, lad!" He pounded the boy's shoulders gleefully. "The Tartessos wing birds coming at last! Run and tell my wife to start cooking. The word will spread like lightning, you'll see, and everyone and his cousin will be coming in to see what they have brought this year."

But a messenger was hardly needed, thought Woodpecker as he hurried down the hill to the house. He was not the only one to have seen that column of smoke, and the hubbub of excitement was echoing through the town.

MASTER ANATERVE HAD SPOKEN truly. By the time the two ships had anchored in the lee of the island, the meadow outside the town was sprouting tents above the trampled flowers. Beyond them, rough pens had been thrown up to hold the sheep and cattle that would feed all these people. The foreigners would be buying animals and grain as well to replace their stores. Anaterve's store shed acted as a clearinghouse for much of this barter, and Woodpecker was kept busy tracking credit amassed and expended. The primary reason for the Tartessans to make so long a voyage was the ingots of tin that had been collecting in the merchants' sheds, but luxury items like river pearls and jet and the pelts of wolves and bears would not take up much room, and a few captives and criminals sold as slaves would serve as extra labor on the voyage home.

It was not until the day before the Tartessan vessels had announced for their departure that things grew calm enough for Woodpecker to take an afternoon off to wander down to the harbor. Beneath awnings of striped wool they had laid out trays with ornaments in bronze and gold. One neck-lace had gold beads interspersed with others of a shiny blue that they told him was called *faience*. It would have suited Tirilan. With what Anaterve owed him he might have bought one bead, he thought, and laughed, and moved on. Another booth held a display of bronze daggers from the Middle Sea whose ivory hilts were wound with wires of gold. Weapons fit for a king, if any of their kings still had the wealth to buy. All those he knew of had spent it already to keep their people fed. There were lengths of wool and linen woven in patterns no one here knew, and pottery vessels bur-nished to gleaming smoothness inside as well as out.

Not from here . . . all those bright objects seemed to say. *We come from another world where the sun shines warm on a blue sea.* That sun had browned the skin of the men who sold them, dark-haired, wiry men in white linen kilts and striped cloaks who chattered in a strange swift language and wore gold in their ears. Arganthonios was the name, or perhaps the title, of their king. Anderle wanted him to learn about the world—what if he went with these men to see the lands where the geese went when they flew southward in the fall? But even as the thought came to him, he knew he would never go so far, not when he still woke from dreams of the Vale of Avalon with his face wet with tears.

As the day waned, a rougher element was coming into the village, drov-ers who had brought the animals that were now mostly consumed or sold. They had credit markers in their pouches, and a healthy appetite for ale and that strange blood-colored drink called wine that was made from some fruit that grew in the southern lands. Woodpecker had tasted it in Master Anaterve's house and not liked it much. Some of the men were drunk al-ready, swearing or singing and offering convivial swigs from their wooden beakers of beer to passersby.

Woodpecker took a moment to gaze across the water at the ships, their high carved prows gilded by the setting sun. The trading had gone well and Analina's mother was cooking something special to celebrate. But it was time he was getting home.

As he turned, a heavy body lurched against him, throwing him against a wall.

"Why'd ya shove me?"

"I'm sorry—" the boy began, recoiling from the blast of beery breath as the man reeled toward him. "I didn't mean—"

"Drink wi' me!" the fellow said then. He was a stocky man in a stained tunic whose face was mostly obscured by a brown beard. There was something familiar about him; Woodpecker thought he might be one of the men who had escorted the trader who came down from Azan with a load of hides. The man had hung around Master Anaterve's shed, asking stupid questions, until his master and the trader had finally come to terms.

"Thank you, but I'm late for my dinner, and—"

"Don' wanna fight? Gotta be my frien'." The man went on as if he had not heard. "Come on—have a drink wi' me!" A hard hand closed on Woodpecker's shoulder.

If he made a fuss, he would sound like a little boy. He supposed he could spare the time for a sip of beer, and clearly the fellow would not give up until he gave in. Shaking his head, he let the man propel him around the corner toward the drink stall.

But at the end of the alley there was no drink stall, only three more men with cudgels, and suddenly the one who had hold of him did not seem drunk at all. Woodpecker started to struggle, trying to remember the wrestling moves he had learned at the Tor. A lucky kick hooked one man's leg and brought him down. Woodpecker twisted, wrenching his shoulder free, and dove for the emptied space. He glimpsed the other man's cudgel whirling toward him; then a blinding pain exploded in his head and he knew no more.

CONSCIOUSNESS RETURNED WITH A wave of nausea and a throbbing ache as if a bronze smith was beating out a spearpoint on his skull. The earth seemed to be moving up and down, and there were two moons in the sky. *Did I get drunk?* He could not remember it, but he dimly recalled that was often the case. He took a careful breath, and the nausea eased a little, but the surface beneath him was still heaving, and the fresh air smelled strongly of the sea.

It *was* the sea. He could hear it, and feel the stretched hide covering of the boat beneath him, the kind that fishermen used to fish the bay. He tried to push himself up so that he could see, and it was then that he discovered that his hands and feet were bound.

"Hey, Izri, the calf has decided to join us again!" Someone gave a rough laugh.

Woodpecker twisted around and saw the man who had accosted him, as disreputable as ever, but no longer inebriated, if he had ever been drunk at all.

"Who are you?" he managed. "Why have you taken me?"

"Who we are don't matter. 'Tis what we are, and that's Galid's men," said one of the others. "An' ye've led us a fine chase. Thought we had ye at the shepherd's, but someone heard we was sniffing and got ye away. But to put ye with a trader, now, that's like hidin' a bull calf at a fair. People always comin' by—one of 'em's bound to tell Galid 'bout the smart lad with the red hair." The third man, who was rowing, gave a grunt of agreement.

The shock of that name left Woodpecker's mind for a moment far too clear. He pulled at his bonds, but whoever had tied them knew his trade.

"What are you going to do with me?" His voice still had a tendency to squeak under stress and he tried to keep it low.

"Galid hears you're in Belerion an' sends us. He wants to see you—"

"So's he can finish what he started fifteen years ago," said the one called Izri, and they all laughed.

"Queen Zamara's got no male kin left—you're the last of that line. When you're dead, she's got no choice but to make Galid king."

Woodpecker swallowed. They were angling eastward across the bay. On their right the island bulked black against the stars. Ahead a gleam of light showed where the Tartessan ships lay at anchor, preparing for tomorrow's journey.

"I hope he rewards you well," he said bitterly. "Of course the Lady of Avalon would pay better—" he added then. "Lots of gold at the Tor, from ancient times." Of course most of it was attached to ritual robes and gear, but although he had sometimes wondered whether Anderle even *liked* him, he was unhappily certain that to get him back she would strip Avalon bare. "And when she learns who gave me to Galid, she'll hunt you down," he added into the silence. "When she begins to sing to the spirits, I don't think his luck will cover you."

Was he imagining that the man at the oars was rowing more slowly? "I promise you I'm more valuable alive." He waited, poised between hope and dread.

"'Tis true, he's a likely lad—" Izri said thoughtfully. "Pity to waste him, especially if Galid's a niggard with the reward."

"What d'you mean? He'll have our heads if we let the lad go."

"Sell him—" the first man replied. "There's the Tartessan ship over there, all set to haul anchor and go. We give them the boy; they give us gold. He's gone from the island, so there's Galid's purpose served—"

"He'll slit our throats—" repeated the other man.

"Not if we tell him the lad threw himself overboard tryin' to escape and got drowned."

"Hunh! Well, let's find out what they say—"

Woodpecker felt the boat dip as the left-hand oar bit deeply and the craft began to turn. Soon—too soon?—they bumped up against the big ship's side. *Wait,* thought the boy. Suddenly this didn't seem such a good idea after all. He might have found a way to escape his captors between Belerion and Azan-Ylir, but unless he wanted to swim home, from the sea there was no escape at all. But the man who had hit him was already climbing up the rope ladder. Then the others dragged him over the side and dropped him like a netted fish at the captain's feet.

"Is so—" came the foreign voice. "Is a well-grown boy. Ugly, like all you folk, but seems strong. I give you, hmm, three good daggers for him, and a jar of wine."

Such an easy transaction? Was his fate decided so soon? Woodpecker's head throbbed as they hauled him to his feet. For a moment only his captor's hands kept him upright.

"Thank you for my life—"

"You think that was mercy?" came the equally low-voiced reply. "May be you'll come to wish you'd died, before you're done. But make of your life what you can. . . ."

And then they were gone. Someone cut the rope that bound his feet and pushed him along the walkway to the end of the ship. From the smell, he guessed this must be where they were keeping the wretches they had bought already.

"What they call you, boy?" said the man—one of the sailors, he supposed.

For a moment he could only stare. In the past two years he had had so many names.

"Woodpecker," he said finally. He would have to wait a long time to claim the name of Mikantor now.

BY TORCHLIGHT THE WATERS of the sacred pool looked as red as the stain they left upon the stones. Anderle sat on her carved chair, a silver bowl that had been filled with that water on the little table before her. Her long hair fell down to either side of her face, blocking distraction and focusing her vision. The ornaments of the high priestess trembled on her brow.

The regalia and the ceremony were traditional, intended to impress the priests and priestesses who formed the circle around her so that they could raise the energy to speed her on her way, but tonight Anderle knew that she needed those symbols just as much as they did. She felt old and empty, drained of power. Woodpecker, no, *Mikantor* was gone.

Did it matter? Did anything matter now? She had raged when word came that the boy had disappeared from Belerion. By the time Larel got there, Galid was proclaiming that the last heir to the royal line of the Ai-Zir was drowned, and where he had ruled as a robber, he claimed now the name of king.

And she could not tell whether the ritual for which they had gathered was the wise response to the need to plot a new course, or a desperate denial that the hope for which she had suffered and sacrificed so much had finally failed. But whatever her reasons, she must attempt it now. She gave a short nod, and the others began to sing, a minor, wavering chant whose words had been ancient when the priests from the Drowned Lands first came to these shores.

"Sink down, sink down, release the mind, go deep—
Beyond the door of dreaming and of sleep,
Take now the path beside the holy tree,
Behold the sacred waters and be free."

The priestess took a deep breath and then another, letting the air out slowly, counting, in and out and in and out again, relieved to find a lifetime's discipline overcoming the madness of a single moon. Thank the gods for the ancient methods. Already she could feel her heartbeat slowing, awareness narrowing to the familiar focus of trance. She could remember what had happened, remember even her anguish, but now she observed it with a detached curiosity. Passive, she waited for Larel's word.

"Lady, we seek to know the fate of the boy Mikantor. Open your eyes and look into the water. Tell us what you see—"

For a moment all Anderle saw was the gleam of torchlight on water. Then she was falling into the fire. She gasped, believing that she was back in Azan-Ylir, but this time she too was caught in the flames. Yet she could not pull away, and now she saw that this place was much larger, as if a whole village had been built of stones like the Henge. It was not a village; it was a fortification with mighty walls. But they had not been able to keep out the army that surrounded it, and now it was burning too.

"Where is Mikantor?" she cried, and what she had thought were stones resolved into a pile of glowing coals in a forge. Within that pulsing glow lay a sword of light. A shadow bulked beyond it; she saw the burly shape of the smith as he lifted it in his tongs and laid it on the granite anvil. Sparks flew as he struck again and again.

"Before the metal can be shaped it must be heated," the answer came, *"forged and honed before it can serve a king. In fire the old world shall be destroyed and a new one born."*

The smith lifted the sword, and white fire ran down the blade. He held it out to a hero, crowned with flame. Then there was only Light. Anderle felt herself being swept away. When she could focus again, she was lying back in her chair and her cheeks were wet with tears.

EIGHT

*V*elantos was in the smithy, working on a dagger with a narrow triangular blade, when the new slave came to call him to the king. His arm muscles quivered as he whispered a prayer to the Lady of the Forge and tipped the crucible to let the molten bronze pour smoothly into the mold, but there was no tremor in his hand.

The smithy was set in the Lower Citadel that had been added to the north wall of the palace at Tiryns when they rebuilt after the great earthquake in his great-grandfather's day. His workshop was walled on three sides, with doors that opened so that the flames could be fanned by the wind. When it did not blow, the heat could be stifling, but Velantos was accustomed to the sweat that rolled down his broad chest and spattered sizzling into the fire.

"Lord, the king your father want you—"

The smith sent him a quick look from beneath bushy brows, suspecting irony, but Woodpecker was new, a lanky adolescent with a jutting nose and hair a little darker than bronze, brought down to the Middle Sea from some impossibly distant northern land. No doubt they had told him that Velantos was the son of the King of Tiryns, but not that his mother had been a weaving woman, little better than a slave herself, who had caught King Phorkaon's eye as she served in the hall.

"A moment—" He turned back to the mold, watching carefully as the flicker of flame above the new casting died away.

"Great lord, he want you *now* . . ." The slave's voice wavered, and Velantos realized that despite his height, he was only a lad, still learning the language of his new home.

"Be easy; if there is delay, I am the one he will blame—" Carefully, the smith set the crucible aside, then lifted the stone mold and set it on the broad rim of the raised hearth. As he straightened, his gaze fell on the niche that held the image of Potnia Athana in her aspect as Lady of Craft, upright in her one-shouldered garment and pointed hat. Broad-shouldered Epaitios brooded from the other wall. Velantos nodded with a respect that had become so ingrained it was instinctive.

"He say quick," Woodpecker replied, coloring up to his bronze hair. "A messenger come."

And why should that make any difference to me? Velantos stretched muscled arms until the bones in his back clicked. A breath of air drifted through the open door, carrying the scent of baking bread to mingle with the smoke. Though the brightness told him the day was hot, the air seemed refreshing after the heat of the forge. But the lad looked truly anxious, and Velantos had not the heart to worry him further by delay.

The dagger would cool no more quickly for being watched. Consigning the work to the goddess, he stepped to the corner of the shed and dipped water from the big terra-cotta pithos, pouring it over his head and torso and using a length of rough linen to scrub the worst of the sweat and soot from his body. Another dipperful sluiced back the dark, curling hair that was escaping from the leather thong that tied it back when he was at the forge. His linen kilt hung from a peg. He wrapped it over the loincloth in which he worked and clasped the broad belt around his slim hips. A decade of smithwork had filled out a naturally burly build. Velantos had never taken any prizes at the footraces, but at the Festival Games he was a regular winner in the wrestling, and when the discus was thrown.

With visible relief, Woodpecker turned to lead the way.

"Have you seen this messenger?" Velantos increased his pace to match the boy's long-legged stride.

"He come from Mykenae, from the Overking."

Well, that was not unusual. The kings of Tiryns ruled from a small hill on the fertile plain just above the harbor. The site offered good access to trade and raid, both of which had been a constant in its history. Though Tiryns was older, Mykenae loomed from the knees of the mountains to the north, a stronghold that had never been taken by an enemy.

But Tisamenos, who ruled there now, was young in both age and power, eager to prove himself worthy of heroic ancestors. He was, in fact, the same age as Velantos. Did King Phorkaon think that youth would speak better to youth? Was that why his father wanted him?

They crossed the open space in the center of the Lower Citadel and climbed the roadway through the corridor to the great gateway that guarded the citadel's eastern side. They stepped into the shade beneath the high roof of the passage. The two sets of doors at its end, banded with bronze, were open, and something within him that had been tensed in apprehension began to relax. Whatever news had come with the messenger, there was no imminent danger, or the palace would have been buzzing with armed men, and the great door barred. Up and around they climbed, through court and corridor, until they passed the painted columns of the propylon and emerged into the open air of the outer court.

The citadel of Tiryns crowned the small hill. Velantos paused a moment to savor the breeze from the bay that sparkled below. Beyond the walls spread the tile-roofed houses of the city, and then the fertile plain, divided into plots of tilled earth or orchards of olive trees and fenced fields green with vines. To east and west, the sheltering circle of the mountains ran down to the sea. It was a good, rich land, and one that many folk had desired. On the summit of the great headland a watch post guarded a beacon, ready to give warning of attack from the sea, as once it had waited to signal the end of the war in Troia.

At the thought, Velantos felt a flicker of unease once more. Without warriors, what use was warning? The strength of Akhaea was not what it had been before the Overking led the flower of its warriors to Troia. That conflict had left not loot but legends as its most enduring legacy. So many of the heroes who survived the victory had failed to survive their return. Certainly the House of Atreos was diminished. In Mykenae, the grandson of Agamemnon still ruled, but Velantos wondered if even the gods could purify the family from the stain of that bloody kin-strife, wife against husband, mother murdered by son. Surely their blood still polluted the ground.

"Lord, you must *come!*" Woodpecker's touch on his elbow brought Velantos to himself again. He realized that he had been staring unseeing at the shimmer of the sea beyond the wall.

Light and shade succeeded one another as he led the way between the columns of the smaller entry and across the central court toward the megaron, pausing to honor the sacrificial altar as he passed. He blinked as he came into the shadow of the prodomos, taking a moment to allow his eyes to adjust. When he could see the blue rosettes in the frieze that ran along the walls, he passed through the easternmost of the three doorways that led to the megaron.

One of the four red-painted pillars that supported the ceiling blocked his view of the king, but he could see the messenger, standing between the throne and the great circle of the hearth. A reflexive glance told him that the queen's seat by the pillar was empty. No doubt she was in her own rooms beyond the hall. Did the easing in tension come from this additional evidence that there was no emergency, or simple relief at not having to meet her flat glare? Perhaps he wronged her—it was well known that Naxomene's vision was poor, and perhaps she did not see him at all. That was, after all, the way a Royal Woman was expected to view her husband's chance-got child.

But the Lady of Tiryns was a priestess of E-ra as well as queen, and the wife of the Cloud Gatherer had a history of hostility to the fruits of her husband's love affairs. Her hatred had hounded Erakles and driven his children from the land, so that it was a princess of the House of Persaios whose marriage had made the line of Pelops the city's lords. But E-ra was still Lady of the Palace. Only in the forge did Velantos' own bright-eyed Lady hold sway.

Potnia, be with me, he said silently. *Grant me the wit to understand and the will to meet whatever test faces me here today.* Composing his features, he crossed the stone threshold and entered the room.

Tall and gaunted now with age, King Phorkaon looked up, greeting him with his usual tentative smile, as if wondering how he could have begotten such a broad-shouldered, burly son. When he was small, Velantos had thought that perhaps the king was right to question. He had always had a fellow feeling for the persecuted Erakles. King Phorkaon was descended from a bastard brother of Atreos, but Erakles was heir to the Perseids, and his descendants were Tiryns' rightful kings. In his more exalted moments, Velantos had dreamed that his mother's lover had been Erakles himself, returned to the kingdom he had loved and lost. One day he would stand forth and proclaim that he was a child of the great hero, come back to claim his own. But at other times, when his half brothers had been tormenting him, Velantos would feel gloomily certain that some slave or guest must have begotten him, and not the king at all

He crossed the patterned tiles and moved around the right side of the hearth to stand before the throne. The messenger must be of some importance, for Phorkaon had put on the cap of kingship, and the fringed wrap that left one bony shoulder bare, and his sword.

"You have called, my lord, and I am here. What is your need?"

"The Overking has had strange news. War is brewing to the west of us and in the north. Some say it is only a few ragtag bands of barbarians that are raiding, but others whisper that the Children of Erakles have come at last to reclaim their land."

Velantos blinked, hearing that name, but his wildest fantasies had never included a barbarian horde.

"It may be no more than rumor," the king went on, "but we should take precautions. Go as my voice to the Overking. You know our strengths. Confer with him on how we may defend this land."

Our strengths . . . and our weaknesses . . . thought Velantos. He was the one who supervised the workmen when they repaired the walls, and the one to whom the warriors came to repair a piece of harness or edge a new spear.

"Alone?" he asked.

"If Aiaison comes back from Argos before you return I will send him after you. He will need to talk to Tisamenos' commanders. But for the essentials, yes, you are the one who knows."

Velantos bowed, as much in gratitude for that recognition as to cover his unexpected pleasure in receiving it. The arms of the octopus painted on the tile at his feet seemed to flex, seen through unshed tears. However accidental his birth, he was valued. Only now did he realize that he had never been quite sure of that before.

"I am at your service, but if we are to go now, there is a thing I must finish at the forge."

"Nay, nay. The enemy, if there *is* an enemy, is not at our gates. Finish your work and gather your retinue. I will entertain our guest as he deserves and the god requires."

A retinue? Velantos lifted one eyebrow. Apparently the king wished his standing to be clear. "My manservant is ill," he replied. "May I take the boy?" He nodded toward Woodpecker.

"Why not? I purchased him for the queen, because I thought his novelty might amuse her, but she does not care for him. If you like him, he's yours."

Velantos cast a quick glance at his new possession and was surprised to see a look of relief in the slave's dark eyes. Had the woman been so unkind to him?

"Come then," he said to the boy. "If you are going to serve me, you may as well begin by learning to assist me in the forge."

As they passed through the propylon, Velantos caught the flicker of a gown in the door that led to the women's quarters, and he turned. It was a purely physical reaction, for his mind was full of calculations, but the motion brought him back to himself and he smiled to see Tanit waiting for him there. In a simple belted robe, with a band of bronze flowers that he had crafted for her holding her dark hair, he found her more beautiful than any court lady in her bodice and tiered skirt sewn with gold.

"Good morning, little one—" he began, his frown easing into a smile. "I'd hoped we could be together tonight, but the king—"

"Never mind that," she interrupted him. "The queen wishes to speak with you."

For a moment the conflict between the quickening in his flesh and the chill invoked by the queen's name held him speechless.

Tanit's mouth twitched at the corner, just where he would kiss her when she was slow to warm to him, but she maintained the dignity suitable to the servant of a queen. "She will not eat you, you know—"

Of that, Velantos had never been quite sure. But he was a man now, not a child. Stiffening his features, he followed the girl into the queen's megaron. Its plan was the same as that of the king, except that it was smaller, and the hearth was rectangular instead of round. Like her husband's, Queen Naxomene's throne was on the eastern side of the room. Over her gown she had put on the robe of the high priestess, and the golden headdress with its pendant lilies bound her brow.

Clearly, whatever she wanted him for, it was not personal. Whether this was more or less disturbing Velantos could not decide. He made the obeisance due a priestess and stood waiting, trying to read meaning from the sculpted planes of her face, smooth as one of the golden masks that covered the faces of the dead.

"What did the messenger from Tisamenos have to say?"

For a moment, Velantos thought of replying that if the king had not thought fit to tell her, it was not for him to say. But it was well known that it was the queen who was the strong one in their partnership, and if she did not know already, surely she would soon. There must be another reason why she was questioning Velantos now. He looked up, disturbed because the dangling ornaments kept him from seeing her eyes.

"There's some tale of raiders, but such vermin have always prowled our borders. There is no reason to suppose—"

"The goddess is uneasy," the queen interrupted him. "The Children of Erakles trouble the land."

"Does she still hate him?" Almost instantly, Velantos regretted the question.

The golden lilies trembled as a shudder passed through the queen's frame, and Velantos felt a chill without understanding why.

When she spoke again, her voice had changed. "Erakles is now a god but his children are men. This enemy is very old, but the war will be new, a kind of fighting that you have never known."

Tanit took a quick step forward, then stopped, biting her lip. Abruptly Velantos understood what had happened. He had seen Naxomene carry the goddess before, at the festivals, but there had never been any reason for him to be near. His skin prickled as it did sometimes on days when the wind was high, though the air here was warm and still.

"Yes, Lady," he answered her as both goddess and queen. "What would you have me do?"

"A new war will need new weapons."

New weapons? How could he make new weapons when he did not know what the danger was? "I will do what I can," he whispered.

"You will—I will make sure of it. That is what I do." There was something terrifying in her smile. "Knowledge will be given to you. Epaitios is my son. He will show you what to do." She sank back against the throne.

"Go; go quickly," whispered Tanit as Velantos stood staring. He had never been more glad to obey a woman's command.

"YES, *THAT* ONE—PUT it into the chest—fold it carefully, now!"

Woodpecker glared at Estaros, the thin and grizzled upper servant who was supervising the packing, and picked up the robe. The man had been yammering at him since morning, as if he should somehow know not only what Prince Velantos would need for his journey but where to find it. Barely a day had passed since he had been transferred to the prince's service. He was beginning to wonder if his early relief had been a mistake. Would Velantos beat him if he wrinkled a garment? He looked strong enough to do it himself, not like the boy's second master, or was it the third, who liked to watch as his slaves were whipped by his musclebound bodyguard.

He shook out the folds of linen, as if by instinct knowing how they should fall, straight across the shoulders so that the garment formed a square and then folded inward so that the design on the back would lie flat. But of course it would be familiar. He had often assisted Larel when he wore such robes in ritual. He banished that memory, then turned the robe and stilled, staring at the emblem embroidered there. It was the head of a bull with curving horns and a sun disk upon its brow.

Why should he be surprised? These people valued cattle—he had seen the stylized horns set up outside their shrines. It meant nothing that he should find such an image on a princeling's robes. But for a moment what he had seen was the bull's head emblem of the Ai-Zir.

He thanked the gods that such moments came rarely. Everything here— trees and flowers, the very shape of the hills, and the scent of the air—was so different from his homeland that he could go for days at a time without remembering. And then some chance sight or scent, like the smoke of Ve-lantos' smithy, would overwhelm him, and for a moment he would be lost.

"You! Mooncalf! What are you staring at?" The servant's voice seemed to come from some great distance. When the man slapped him, his cheek barely felt the sting. "Do you think—"

"Estaros!"

The deep voice that overrode the man's next words brought the boy around, flushed with mingled embarrassment and apprehension. Velantos filled the doorway, heavy brows meeting as he frowned. His forehead and cheekbones had the strong lines of cast bronze above the short black beard. Estaros flinched, and Woodpecker braced himself for a blow. This morning Velantos wore the long linen tunic appropriate to his rank, but when Wood-pecker saw the prince stripped and sweating over the forge, he had been amazed at the strength those muscles implied.

"How should the lad know what to do when he never saw my belong-ings before? We do not leave for two days. Give him time."

Woodpecker flushed again, hearing beneath the rough timbre a warmth that he found oddly comforting. He brought his fist to his forehead in salu-tation, then, with nimble fingers, finished folding the robe.

BEYOND THE CURVE OF the road Anderle glimpsed a glitter of blue water and the pointed top of the isle that guarded the bay. It was time for the festival that welcomed summer in Belerion, and the clouds had lifted at last. Creamy primroses were blossoming beneath the oak trees, and the hedges were starred with hawthorn blooms. But the cheerful sparkle of the blue waters before her seemed a mockery. In that sea all her hopes had drowned. Ellet tried to console her with the memory of the prophecy that had come from her own lips after they heard that Mikantor was lost, but the words the others had taken down were no more than a disjointed rambling, and she herself had no memory of what she had seen. A great clanhold of stone? What could that have to do with them here? And as for the Sword, if the hero who was to wield it was dead, what use could it be?

But even to her priestesses, she could not admit how completely her faith had failed. And so when the king of the Ai-Utu sent to tell her that Kaisa-Zan had died and a priestess was needed for the rites, she had agreed to come herself. If the queen had been young, she and her consort would have performed the ritual that welcomed summer in, but she was failing. Kaisa should have been able to take her place until it was her daughter's turn to rule. The sudden fever that had carried the priestess off was no more than the latest disaster. King Sakanor did not need to know that Anderle had begun to doubt that even the magic of Avalon would stop the storms or drain the sodden fields. She would go through with the ritual, and trust that the gods had hope even though she had none.

That night they were guests in the house of the family that guarded the stone circle called the Maidens. Near the house was a mound where a thorn tree grew. Beneath it a long chamber had been carved. In the old days it had been a place of initiation, sunk into the earth where the power flowed from the stone circle north and eastward across the isle. That night she took a lamp and made her way down the slope past the stone where a carven warrior warded the opening, and settled to open her awareness to the spirits of the land.

The stones of Belerion had been old when the priests from the Drowned Lands raised the trilithons of the great henge. The earth energies that they channeled flowed strongly, and would continue to flow no matter how much rain might fall. Anderle sat up straighter and let her breathing deepen, sensing the loves and lives of the people whose spirits had become part of this land. *Ancestors*, she prayed, *watch over your descendants. Give us the wit to change what we can, and the strength to endure what we cannot change.* And in that confined space it seemed to her that the pressure of the air grew greater, as if a crowd of invisible companions had joined her there. And though no clear message had come to her, when at length she left the chamber to seek her bed, she found that her spirit had been eased.

The next day was the eve of the festival. She spent it in seclusion, and when the day drew to an end, Ellet and the local women bathed her and set a hawthorn crown above her veil and led her down the road to the circle of stones. From ahead she could hear drumming, and knew that the king awaited her there. Compared with the great henge these stones were modest—no more than waist to chest high. But they were far older, and on this night Anderle could feel the energy that sparked from one to the next. *Perhaps,* she thought as she entered the circle and felt that power shock through her, *the gods have not abandoned us. Holy Caratra, bless the work we do.*

The part of her mind that was still her own noted that King Sakanor's beard was growing gray. But her body was swaying to the beat of the drum. She sensed the glow of power begin to gather around him as it must be limning her. Laughing, she led the maidens weaving in and out among the stones of the circle, and when men and women came together at last, the king was no longer a middle-aged man with arms a little thinned and belly broadened by the years, but the virile protector, and she, no longer small and dark, but the glowing lady of the land. Man and maid surrounded them, singing, as they lay down together, and Anderle felt the power she had sensed in the underground chamber surging upward, to be intensified and channeled in a river of light to bless the land.

It was not until the next morning that she was able to talk to the king, when the Powers that had worked through them had departed and they were no more than man and woman once more.

"Lady Anderle, I thank you. Kaisa-Zan was a fine woman and a strong priestess. She was taken from us too soon. The girl she was training is still young. We would be grateful if you would take her with you when you return to Avalon and finish her teaching there."

"I will take her," said Anderle, "for the land must be served, even though each time I see her I will remember what happened to the boy I sent to you."

King Sakanor sighed. "That Galid could send his wretches to carry off a lad from the midst of my country was a great shame to us all, and yet I am not entirely satisfied by his story. We lose a fishing boat from time to time, and the sea eventually sends those that drown in the bay to shore. But your boy's body was never found, and I assure you, my lady, the fisher folk searched long and well."

"I believe Galid capable of any lie," the priestess said sourly. "But if the sea did not take him, where is the boy?"

"The ships from Tartessos left on the morning tide. And I've heard that Galid's creature Izri was seen with a shiny new southern dagger at his belt the next day. The traders buy slaves, my lady, though I forbid it. It's possible that Galid's men sold him to them instead."

Anderle realized she had seized the king's arm and let go, seeing the prints of her fingers white on his arm. She became aware how heavily her heart was thumping when he reached out to steady her in turn.

"This is truth?" she breathed.

"As much truth as I know," he replied. "It is always hard to lose a youngster, but why should you care so much about this boy?"

"Mikantor was King Uldan's son, my own cousin's child—let that be enough reason for his fate to matter to me."

"Uldan's boy!" The king's eyes widened. "The child of the prophecy?"

"You have heard it?"

"The whole land has heard it," he replied. "This is heavy news indeed, for whether he has been taken to Tartessos or the Land of the Dead he is equally lost to us."

"Maybe . . ." Anderle said slowly, "but if the gods are good, from Tartessos, he might someday return."

In the end Velantos' new servant spent more time organizing his master's belongings than he did learning smithcraft. For that, as the boy diffidently told him, there would be time, whereas the king wanted them on their way to Mykenae *now*. Velantos was surprised to find himself responding with amusement to the boy's insistence. His other servants, more used to growls than smiles, decided to treat the newcomer as an ally rather than a competitor for his favor. That surprised the smith as well. Accustomed to doubting his own status at Tiryns, had he been so thoughtless a master? Velantos was still mulling over the question as they turned off the main road across the plain and started the climb to the Overking's citadel.

As they ascended the last slope and rounded the bend, he was recalled to himself by Woodpecker's whistle of surprise. The boy was staring at the fortress that seemed to have grown from the summit of the hill before them, an eminence that would have been called a mountain in most lands. Here, it was only an outcrop, dwarfed by the sheer peaks that rose behind it. Walls of massive honey-colored stones wrapped it round, tier upon tier, crowned by the royal halls, their russet crenelations glowing in the afternoon sun.

"Impressive, aren't they?"

"Tiryns is mighty," breathed the boy, "but Mykenae greater still. Giants moved those stones?"

"That is what they say." Velantos smiled. "It was built by the Cyclopes for King Persaios, when Tiryns was no longer enough for him. Of course that was before Odikeos put out Polyfemos' eye on his way home from Troia. Even for a son of the Cloud Gatherer I do not think the Cyclopes would be so helpful now. Have they no such mighty stoneworks in your own land?"

"Not for the living," the boy said, frowning. "I . . . remember a thing like a great stone table, where a flood washed the grave mound that covers it away. There's great stones in the Henge where priestesses do sacred rites, sung into place by masters of magic who come to my land from across the sea. But that was many lives of men ago. My people live in houses roofed with thatch and surrounded by wooden walls—easy to burn."

He stopped, the emotion leaving his face as a sculptor smooths the clay of an image. Velantos did not press him. For all his uncertainty about his status, the smith had never doubted his physical security. Not until now.

Dust rose from the plain in swirling clouds, through which the shapes of the maneuvering chariots appeared and disappeared like images in a dream. The walls of Mykenae, three times the height of a tall man, topped a hillside that already loomed above the sloping plain. From here you could see all the way to the hills that sheltered Argos, which was no doubt why Persaios had chosen it for the site of his citadel.

The area where the chariots were training was closer, just beyond the road that carried the trade through the mountains from Korinthos down to Tiryns by the sea. From his place near the king, Velantos squinted to see their movements, memory imaging the braces and hinges, buckles and bits and all the other hardware that passed through his workshop. When the warriors boasted over their wine in the hall, it had always amused him to reflect that no amount of courage could save a man from being dumped in the dust if he lost a wheel.

"Look at them go!" King Tisamenos leaned over the wall. "We had so much rain this winter, the pastures are still green, and the horses are fat and feisty. They can run rings around any enemy!" He straightened, laughing, a tall young man with wildly curling black hair.

"How can you tell?" Velantos softened the comment with a laugh. "Dust clouds are all I can see—" Folk sometimes wondered how he could stand the heat and smoke of the smithy, but the dust of a battlefield was thicker. And he could strip to his loincloth to do his work while the chariot fighters sweltered in leather coats sewn with plates of bronze.

"Ah, but there are patterns in that dust," observed the Master of Chariots, "that the experienced eye can see . . ."

That puts me in my place, the smith thought wryly. The night before they had sat late in council, and the warrior had clearly wondered what Velantos was doing there, much less why the king paid him any attention. It had ended with a bland assurance that Mykenae could not be taken. Tisamenos promised to call for men and supplies to withstand a siege, but it was clear that he did not expect to need them. *To each man his craft,* Velantos thought then. *I can tell when to put the bronze in the fire by looking at the color of the coals, where you would only know not to put in your hand.*

"If they send chariots, your men will surely prevail. But they won't. That's what I've been trying to tell you," muttered the man from Korinthos as if he didn't care whether anyone heard him. Thersander was his name. Certainly the king did not seem to have been listening so far.

"Tell *me*—" said Velantos, taking his arm. "And since neither of us seems to be wanted here, perhaps we could go somewhere cooler to talk."

They made their way along the wall, almost as wide in places as it was tall. The chariots might fail, but when Tisamenos said that Mykenae could not be taken, Velantos believed him. No human force could dislodge those mighty stones. Just past the grave circle from which the spirits of the mighty dead continued to watch over their descendants, a stair led down to the granary.

The guards at the Lion Gate saluted as Velantos passed and Thersander lifted an eyebrow.

"My apologies, Prince—I had understood you were a bronze smith serving the court at Tiryns."

"Can I not be both?" Velantos decided not to go into the details of his parentage. "In my land, the crafting of bronze is one of the royal Mysteries, and the kings are required to know something of its lore. It is tradition for at least one son in each generation to become a master, and I was the one whom Potnia Athana called."

"And you are a master of the craft?" the other man asked as they climbed the road, taking the left-hand way that led to the workshops and other buildings on the other side of the palace, where guests were lodged whose standing did not require they be given beds in the xenonas near the megaron.

"They call me so," Velantos said curtly. It still felt like hubris, to claim mastery when he knew he had so much to learn. "And what is your skill, man of Korinthos, beyond the bringing of news that no one wants to hear?"

That made the messenger laugh. "My father trades in wine and often sends me abroad. I am only a middling hand with a spear, but I have seen a great deal. My kings thought that I might be able to explain what is hap-

pening in words that King Tisamenos would understand. They do not expect you to help us, but even if we fall to these barbarians, our people will
not be entirely without leadership if the heir of Agamemnon survives."

That made Velantos stare. The Danaans had not been able to agree on
the price of olive oil, much less obedience to an Overking, since Agamemnon led the hosts to Troia.

"Are they really barbarians?" he asked as they passed into the shade of
the colonnade that surrounded the courtyard. "I had heard they call themselves the Eraklidae—the Children of Erakles, and speak some northern
dialect of our tongue."

Thersander shrugged. "Who knows?" He eased down on one of the
benches with a sigh. "By all accounts, Erakles was a bull who sired as many
sons as Diwaz Himself. It was only his legitimate children by Deianeira who
took refuge in Athina. Erakles may be a god now, but he made a lot of enemies while he was a man."

Velantos twitched, hearing an echo of Queen Naxomene's words.

"I suppose his get took after him. Tiryns was not the only city where his
offspring were not welcome. So they went north—some of them, anyway—to
the lands where men are as lawless as they are," Thersander went on.

"Even if they were all as potent as Erakles himself, they could not have
bred the hordes you're speaking of." Velantos took the other end of the
bench and signaled to a passing servant for wine.

"Tell *them*! Don't you see? This man Aletes who is attacking Korinthos
says he's a grandson of Thestalos son of Erakles. Other cities have been attacked by Shardana from some island to the west of here, or men of the
north beyond Olympos. It doesn't matter who they really are—they have
convinced themselves that they are something more than greedy barbarians
out for loot—these freebooters have a *story*! They are the Children of Erakles, and they have returned!"

"Like our grandfathers, when they went to Troia . . ." Velantos said
slowly. "They swore they went to avenge the honor of Menelaos and recover Helena."

Thersander nodded. "But they looted and burned the city all the
same."

But they were Danaans, thought Velantos. *If our warriors could take Troia, so far from home, how much stronger we will be when we are defending our own land!* "They haven't burned Korinthos—" he said aloud.

"Not yet. I got out just before they laid siege to the citadel. The city below could not be defended, and most of the people have fled. But the akropolis has a good spring, and a lot of stored grain. King Doridas thinks that disease and boredom will make Aletes give up before hunger forces us to give in. King Hyanthidas is less hopeful, but then he was always less bold than his brother." He sighed. "The thing that your king does not seem to understand is that when they came marching up to the city, we sent out our chariots to destroy them, and they defeated us."

"They came marching. . . . They were on foot, then." Velantos frowned. "Every army has some foot soldiers to skirmish in rough country and clean up after the chariots, but how could they get close enough to do massed chariots any harm?"

"They've learned a new way of fighting," Thersander said solemnly. "Even if we survive, we will never make war in the same way again."

"What do you mean? No warrior on foot can stand against a chariot . . ."

"Separately, that's so. The runners that go out with our chariots are there as backup, to finish off enemy wounded or help get our wounded to safety. Caught in the open, they can be run down. But Aletes' men fight in units. Their round shields are big enough to fend off arrows, and one of their heavy javelins can bring down a horse. Then they charge in and hamstring the others with one slash of the sword."

"I don't understand—" His brothers carried long swords when they rode in their chariots, but they were meant for thrusting, and rarely used. A disciplined body of chariotry mowed down their foes with arrows, and only the occasional skirmisher got close enough to require fending off with the long spear.

Thersander got to his feet as if he had reached some decision. "I'll show you. I think that *you* may be able to understand—" The Korinthian man made his way down the colonnade and disappeared. When he returned, he was carrying a long bundle.

"This is what they use—" Laying it on the bench he turned back the leather wrappings to reveal a sword. But it was like no sword that Velantos had ever seen. As long as a rapier, the blade swelled gently from the tip before curving in again, and the edges on both sides were wickedly honed. The smith reached out a tentative hand, let one finger drift along the smooth surface. The hilt was of bone, held by a netting of gold wire.

"The work is good . . ." he said slowly.

Thersander nodded. "Can you make one of these?"

Velantos grasped the hilt and got to his feet, testing the weight of it, the way it balanced in his hand. In a rapier he would have called it point-heavy, but the blade swung easily, as the head of a serpent swings in search of prey. *It hungers for the blood of men . . .* he thought, but surely that was a good sign in a blade.

"With this as my model, I think so. In time."

Thersander responded with an abrupt bark of laughter. "All I can do is give you the sword. Only the gods can give you time."

NINE

*F*or a while, it seemed that the gods had heard Velantos' prayer. The bare, bright days of the southern summer faded into fall, the ripe olives gave up their oil, and the winepresses ran red with new wine. The winter wheat was sown, and soon the rains, more abundant this year than ever, brought up the first sprouts in the fields and living green covered the hills. Despite the rumors of war, men looked forward to a good year.

As the grain grew in the fields, the pile of weapons grew in Velantos' forge. Copying his sample, the smith had carved a blade of wood to make the first mold. But not well enough, for though the blade looked like the model, the balance was awkward. It took Velantos several weeks of trial and error to create a weapon that felt right in the hand. By then it was becoming clear that it would take a very long time to make enough swords for all of Tiryns' warriors, and supplies of bronze were running low.

Word came that Korinthos had fallen, but the enemy seemed to have settled down to enjoy their conquest. With Mykenae standing in the way of any further push, few in Tiryns were losing much sleep over the danger. Of all Velantos' brothers, only Aiaison seemed to pay much attention to his warnings. Sometimes Velantos thought the war leader was only humoring him, but Aiaison did take the first leaf-shaped sword that came close to meeting Velantos' specifications, and began drilling his men in close-order fighting with sword and the new round shield.

So it went as storms lashed the citadel day after dismal day. In the summer, the land was filled with light, but when winter's clouds closed in they felt cut off from the world. It mattered less in the smithy, but not even the heat of the hearth could cheer the smith when he cracked the clay from his latest effort and found that several flecks of charcoal had gotten into the mold.

He glared balefully at the bronze, then gripped the flawed blade and broke it across his knee. In the past months Woodpecker, hovering now in the doorway, had learned a great deal about smithcraft, including when to get out of his master's way. But this time the rage that the boy clearly expected did not come. It was too dark, too cold, too impossible a task. The metal clanged as Velantos tossed the pieces on the scrap pile and sank down on a bench, his head in his hands.

Lady, why can I not master this craft? I don't labor for wealth or glory but to serve my people! If you want me to succeed, why won't you show me what I need to know?

A cold breath of wind filtered in around the stout timbers of the door, waking the coals to sudden life and chasing shadows across the familiar shapes of the smithy. The painted lips of the clay image seemed to curve in an enigmatic smile. Velantos' gaze moved from hearth to bellows, passed unseeing across the smooth granite of the anvil and the small broom they used to brush away the particles struck off by the graduated hammers of stone and bronze. Fire tongs, sharpening stones, bronze swages, the heavy clay vessel of water, each in its place, and every one of them useless, it seemed to him now.

After a few moments, Woodpecker picked up the pitcher that had been keeping warm next to the hearth, poured some wine into a kylix and brought it to him. Velantos stared into the dark surface, cradling the shallow bowl, but saw only his own distorted reflection. He sighed, lifted it by the arching handles, and let the wine slide down his throat. The heat had intensified the flavor so that he could not tell if the wine had been watered. Scent and taste were for a moment overwhelming. He drank deeply. It hardly mattered if he got as drunk as a northern barbarian. He would get no more work done today.

"Did you think I would beat you because the sword failed?" he asked the boy after a while. "The fault was not yours—"

"Some masters would," Woodpecker replied. The boy's mastery of the Akhaean tongue was improving. "The first man bought me, treated his slaves worse than his hounds, and a dog that barked at the wrong time he kicked across hall. When he died and his heirs sold the slaves, I was glad."

"How many masters have you had?" Velantos straightened with a frown, a little surprised to realize that he had not thought to ask that question before.

"Not sure . . ." the boy said after a pause. "There are times I don't want to remember. Not now though—" he added quickly. "This is the best place I've been."

"The best? With a surly bear of a master who half the time forgets to feed you, in a city that may be soon attacked by some mysterious enemy?"

Woodpecker shook his head. "I eat when you do, sir, and you work harder than me!"

Velantos noted that the boy had not mentioned the enemy. Well, he would rather not think about them either. Perhaps that was why he drove himself so hard. Enough work would leave him too tired to worry, or even dream. These days he feared dreams, for too many times he had dreamed true.

Clearly the slave's past was a painful subject, and Velantos forbore to ask him any more questions, but that night he slept lightly, and when he heard a sob from the pallet at the foot of his bed where Woodpecker was sleeping, he found himself wide awake. For a moment he lay where he was, unwilling to embarrass the boy by letting him know he had heard, but as the whimper became a cry he rolled out of bed.

With a sigh Velantos bent over the sleeping form. He told himself that half the palace would be wakened if this turned into a full-blown nightmare, and more to the point, that he himself would get no sleep if it went on—a more acceptable reason than the realization that for some reason he was hurt by Woodpecker's pain. He gripped the boy's shoulder and shook him gently.

"Woodpecker—wake up, lad. You're here, you're safe. Wake up and look at me!"

The muscles beneath his hand tensed, and the boy surged upright with a cry. "Fire!" The word came out half muffled by Velantos' hand. "Burning . . . can't breathe!" The boy shuddered, seeming to relax, and as Velantos began to let go, uncoiled with a blow that left him gasping. But muscles trained at the forge gripped the boy's long limbs tightly until at last the trembling ceased.

"It's all right . . . you are safe with me," he murmured, knowing even as he spoke that he lied.

Life was uncertain. A thousand disasters could overwhelm them even if the Children of Erakles never arrived. And so, he reminded himself, it was for all men everywhere. But in this time and this place, this moment in which he felt the boy's taut muscles gradually easing beneath his hands, he could protect this—he did not quite know how to define him, for he had surely ceased to think of Woodpecker as a slave some time ago—this fellow human who lay in his arms.

Woodpecker was no longer a child, so why this surge of protective feeling? He sensed only that the Fates had somehow spun their threads together. Whatever the reason, the auburn-haired slave had entered the small circle of those for whom Velantos allowed himself to care.

ON THE HEADLAND ABOVE the harbor, orange flames blazed against the cool evening sky. Klytemnaestra had set the beacon there during the years when the flower of the Danaans, led by her husband Agamemnon the High King, bled at Troia. By the queen's command, men built the beacons that would declare from peak to peak that the black-hulled ships had at last set sail for home. The Akhaeans had praised her devotion, not knowing that hate fueled those fires.

In the years since that bloody homecoming, the more distant beacons had been abandoned, but as pirates became more active in the Aegean, the posts along the coast had been rebuilt. These days, the men who tended them watched not with hope but in fear.

And now the beacons burned once more. Velantos stood upon the wall that curved outward from the western face of the rock of Tiryns, noting with a detached aesthetic appreciation the vivid contrast of the fire against the deepening blue. Smoke alternately veiled and revealed the first stars. The plain below swarmed with activity as people carrying bundles and pulling creaking wagons bore their possessions toward the citadel. Velantos tried to tell himself those supplies might not be needed. The beacon had signaled only that warships had been seen. It was always possible that a few pirates were hovering offshore, hoping that a fat trader might put out from the harbor. In a day or three the alarm might pass and the worst of their labors would be the confusion of setting all to rights once more.

But the cold lump in Velantos' gut said otherwise. The green hills and warming weather proclaimed that the season when men might safely put to sea had arrived. The king had hoped they would come south from Korinthos and blunt their teeth first on Mykenae. But there had always been the chance that Aletes would send one of his cousins to tackle Tiryns, and crush Mykenae between Tiryns and Korinthos once they had both in their hands.

"My lord Velantos—" Woodpecker was standing on the stair. "My lord, they need you at the gate. A wagon lost a wheel—I already told them to take your tools down."

The smith nodded. Thus, it began.

THE MAIDENS OF TIRYNS danced before the king, a sinuous line that twined and straightened as it wove around the great hearth. In the megaron the feasting tables had been cleared away and the commanders of the chariot squadrons lounged on their benches, watching the dance. Faces smoothed by concentration, the girls curved forward, only to arch their backs once more, turning toward each other and then away, supple bodies obeying the sweet call of the flute and the patter of the drum. For this moment, it did not matter that the striped and patched tents of the enemy horde sprawled along the curve of the bay. There was only the next step, the next dip and turn, the discipline of the dance.

Perhaps, thought Velantos, it was so for men in battle as well, when existence contracted to a confusion of snarling faces in which all that mattered was the unthinking rhythm of attack and defense trained into muscle and sinew. At times it was like that for him in the smithy, when he would straighten, suddenly aware of the ache in his arm as he hefted a finished blade, and realize that sunlight from the westward window was slanting across the packed earth floor.

The coals in the great hearth pulsed as if to keep time, deepening the red of the painted pillars, sending the maidens' shadows leaping in their own dance across the tiled floor. The king watched with face smoothed to attention, but his gaze had gone inward. Since the enemy's arrival, events had progressed with the deliberate order of a ritual. There was no question of surprise or strategy—the city could not run away. Tomorrow the chariotry of Tiryns would drive out to do battle, and Velantos would find out if Thersander of Korinthos had spoken the truth about the new swords and their power. In a way, he thought grimly, the slaves who survived the destruction of the citadel had the least to fear, though from what Woodpecker had told him, he doubted their new masters would offer them so civilized a captivity. He hoped the boy would find better fortune. He himself did not expect to survive.

He looked up to see that the dance was ending, the maidens' circle unwinding as they moved toward the door. Tanit was last in the line. She met his eye with a smile and his own spirit surged suddenly in response. What was he about, to respond to their performance with such gloom? The walls of Tiryns were mighty, her people stouthearted, and her warriors strong. Even the gods could not deny fate, but until the folk of Tiryns had done all that men might to defend the citadel, it would be the act of a coward to give in.

THE HEAVENS BLAZED WITH the clear blue of spring, skimmed by the swallows that had gathered to harvest the insects disturbed by all these feet and hooves. *There's no disaster that does not benefit someone,* Velantos told himself with determined cheer. His fingers tightened on his brother's helm, testing the strength of the rows of boar's tusks and the hardened leather and lacing and wool cap beneath, wondering how they would stand up to one of the new swords. Somehow it was not much consolation to realize that no matter who ruled Tiryns the swallows would continue to scour the skies.

"My lord, it is time—"

The voice of Aiaison's charioteer recalled him to earth, where King Phorkaon's forces were forming up into three ranks, spread across the plain. The ponies stamped and shook their heads, plumes tossing as their drivers reined them down. Warriors set their spears in the rests and slung their small shields, loosened the arrows in the quivers that hung from the chariot rails, and began to string their layered bows, diffusing their tension with laughter.

Velantos handed up the helm. How beautiful his brother was, with the sunlight gleaming on the polished curves of the bronze neck guard and shoulder plates of his armor, sparking from the bands of metal riveted to the leather corselet and the bronze greaves. His dark hair was bound up in a warrior's knot. Melandros, his driver, shared his splendor, his armor less elaborate, but equally well kept. Even the turn of his head echoed that of the prince, but then they had been lovers since boyhood. It was some consolation to know that in battle the two would fight with one mind.

As the elder prince settled the helmet, his white teeth flashed in his beard.

"May the gods ride with you," Velantos said gruffly. Of King Phorkaon's five legitimate sons, Aiaison, the eldest, had been the kindest to him when he was small. The smith's gaze checked greaves and arm guards one last time. They were of his own crafting, and he had blessed them every time his hammer hit the bronze.

"The gods, and your good blade—" Aiaison slapped the hilt of the sword that hung at his side. "I am only sorry that we have no more of them."

Velantos shook his head. "We did not have the metal to make so many, and it made sense to give them to the runners, who are accustomed to fight with swords. My hope is that you will kill all your enemies with your arrows before they have time to test the strength of that shining armor you wear!"

Now was not the time to complain that most of the proud chariot warriors who faced the mass of foot soldiers spreading across the plain had refused to exchange their father's tapered thrusting swords for the new blades. And why should they believe Velantos, a man who swung a hammer, not a sword, and who had only the word of a chance-met merchant's son regarding what one of those new swords could do?

"I hope that you have kept one of those blades for yourself!" With one of his unexpected leaps of intuition Aiaison responded to the words his brother did not say.

"The last blade I cast is still in the mold, but you will not fail!" Velantos replied heartily. "Our grandsires brought proud Troia to ruin. Surely their blood runs true."

"Now we are the ones defending our citadel," Aiaison replied gravely, "and they are the Ellenes, however barbarous, who seek to conquer." For a moment the shadow of Erakles fell between them.

Velantos took a deep breath, smelling horse and leather and dust and the male musk of fighting men. A horse's flank and the hard muscle in the arm of a warrior shone with the same beauty, moving with the grace of a thing whose form was mated to its function, like one of the new swords. The paired curves as an archer flexed his bow and released it again were like the movements of the dancers he had watched the night before, and for a moment he understood them all as part of a single unity. Then the rough chanting of the enemy surged above the stamp of hooves and mutter of conversation around him. They were banging out the rhythm on their round shields with the flats of their swords.

Aiaison brought up one armored arm in salute, but his gaze, and his attention, were already turning toward the enemy. The runner who would go with them hopped onto the chariot, shield bumping his back, gripping the curved rail with one hand. Velantos saluted in turn, knowing his brother would not see him. In their hearts they were already gone.

Athana protect you, brother, he prayed, *and Arei strengthen your arm!*

There came a sharp call from the commander's horn, and the earth trembled as the chariots began to move. Velantos threaded his way among them toward the citadel. He had played his part in this battle. To wait with the slaves and the women was all he could do now.

———

MOST OF THE FOLK of the citadel were gathered on the wall already. But not the king. Tangible heart of his kingdom, Phorkaon would be on his throne by the great hearth in the megaron with the queen beside him, waiting to learn the fate of his city and his sons. Velantos wondered if he had left it to sleep in his bed the night before. He could understand. Coming up the stair to the western bastion he had felt a momentary impulse to continue on to the smithy. But that refuge was for a time when all hope was gone. If his brothers could fight this battle, he could bear witness.

He pushed through the crowd on the bastion that curved out from the citadel and used his rank to gain admission to the tower, where the men of the king's personal guard had gone. From here he could see the curve of the bay and the black ships drawn up on the shore, the jumble of tents and the enemy horde, gathered in irregular groups that might represent clans. The chariot squadrons were maintaining their spacing, those to the left and right gradually increasing their pace to encircle the foe.

At this season, the land to the west of Tiryns was divided into pasture-land and newly planted fields, the one already indistinguishable from the other as the armies advanced. Although the ground was not so dry as it would be later, dust was beginning to rise. By nightfall red blood would soak that ground.

Velantos tensed as the chariots neared arrow range. For all their valor and skill, the chariotry of Tiryns had never been blooded. There had been a brief conflict with Argos when his father was a young man, but until they began to train for this invasion, the only combat the current crop of warriors had seen was the yearly war games when the fields lay fallow in the summertime.

The first volley of arrows streamed like smoke across the lessening gap between the armies, but the enemy had met this kind of attack before. In the midst of each cluster of warriors the round shields swung up, overlapping to cover those below. Some got through; but the momentary gaps were covered as the shields joined once more.

Faint from below he heard the horns blat as the charioteers shook the reins on their ponies' backs and urged them into a flat run. Surely no man on foot could withstand the avalanche of horseflesh that was bearing down upon them now. A quiver in their ranks—they were breaking—no, groups were withdrawing in staggered sequence all along the line to let the first chariots through, then closing in around them. Another horn call, and still shooting, the second line of chariots wheeled away with the sweet unity of a flock of birds. But the first rank were trapped, held at bay like bulls surrounded by wolves.

"Diwaz Thunderer be with them!" whispered Velantos, knowing that Aiaison had been in the forefront of that first charge.

Now the groups of enemy who were not engaged flowed around them and moved forward, opening their loose line again as the chariots charged once more. These maneuvers had made them a little more vulnerable to the showering arrows, and the second line of chariots had learned from the fate of the first, but some, unaware of the danger or unable to control their horses, drove forward and were engulfed in turn.

The scene before him was disintegrating into a chaotic mass of plunging horses and struggling men, but Velantos had imagined the possibilities too often not to have a very vivid image of what must be happening down there. The mobile archer was safe enough so long as he was moving, but once his chariot was stopped he must try to fend off attackers with his spear. In combat, Thersander had said, the leaf-shaped slashing sword would defeat the older style of blade.

"Athana shield them," he murmured again and again, and never knew that his clenched fist had driven his nails into his palm until he saw the marks there later on.

Close to three hundred fifty chariots had sped forward in that first charge across the plain. Velantos could see less than half of them still moving now. A few were fleeing. It occurred to Velantos that they had better be prepared to close the gates if the enemy sought to follow up on their victory by attacking the citadel.

But surely they were not defeated yet—the surviving chariots could keep moving, picking off the foot soldiers from a distance . . . until they ran out of arrows. . . .

How many of the men of Tiryns would make it home? Velantos' heart keened at the certainty that Aiaison could not have survived that turmoil. *How many of his brothers still lived?* a deeper part of his awareness dared to ask. Was it possible that he would be the sole son left to King Phorkaon by the end of the afternoon? There was a time when he would have welcomed that knowledge. It made him gibber in panic now.

Another chariot wheeled away from the battle and headed homeward, and then more. They were fleeing, and though even tired horses could gallop faster than men burdened by shield and armor, the enemy would be on their heels.

"Xanthos!" He gripped the guard captain by the arm. "Take half your men and get those people off the wall. Give the others to me—we must be ready to close the gate and hold it when the last of our men have come in!"

"Tap . . . tap . . . tap . . ." WITH exquisite care Velantos drew the sword blade between the bronze anvils, hardening and shaping the curving edge. This last blade had come whole from the mold, the best one he had yet made. The hilt lay ready on his worktable, waiting to be riveted on. It made sense that his skill should improve with practice. With another decade or two of work he might even become a master. A pity, he thought bitterly, that he was not likely to have those years.

Night had come to Tiryns, but there was little sleep for anyone in the citadel. It was clear to everyone that in the morning the final assault would come. At first, when the Eraklidae surrounded the fortress, Tiryns had expected a siege, a prospect that the people of the citadel, their granary full of winter wheat, could face hopefully. Sickness in a camp often made a siege as deadly to the enemy as to the defenders. And the longer they held out, the more time there would be for the men of Mykenae to come to their rescue.

But Kresfontes and Temenos, the brothers who were leading that army, wanted the grain for themselves, and had no mind to sit waiting while the people of the city consumed it. The walls of the citadel were mighty, but determined men with ladders could get over them. The walls of Tiryns were strong, but her king no longer had enough men to guard every foot of them. If the sons of Aristomakhos threw all their strength against the citadel, it would fall.

At least Prince Aiaison had received due honors, even if for the rest of them the citadel would have to serve as a pyre. Velantos wondered if it had taken courage for the queen to lead the women of the city out to search the battlefield, or whether she was too numbed by grief to care. He was still haunted by the image of that doleful torch-lit procession of black-clad women with ashes in their loosened hair. They had gone out to seek their sons and husbands when darkness put an end to the battle, and the Eraklidae, fearing to see the Kindly Ones turn to Furies, had not dared to hinder them.

Aiaison and Melandros had been found, as all expected, together, limbs mingling in death as they had so often done in love. Melandros must have died first, speared in the back, for he was hardly marked except for that great wound. Aiaison had straddled his body, defending it until they hewed him down. The queen had identified him by the fragments of embroidery that edged the tunic he had worn under his armor. If she could no longer recognize the child of her womb, still she knew the work of her own hands.

When for a moment Velantos ceased his tapping, he could hear drumming and the sound of drunken laughter. Closer still, a woman's moan of pleasure told him how others were passing the time. That was better than the quiet weeping he had heard as he came down into the lower citadel. In such moments, he thought, people showed what they really cared for. He might have tried to find Tanit, but the queen and her women were keeping their own vigil. It was perhaps inevitable that he should take refuge in his craft. If this blade was the last piece he would make, he was determined it should be a worthy memorial.

And he had made a private vow that it would drink deep of enemy blood before it fell from his hand.

He knocked loose the blocks that held the anvils and took up the sword, reaching at the same time for the sharpening stone. This, at least, could be done sitting down. With even strokes he drew the stone the length of the blade. Presently he became aware that Woodpecker was humming in time to the scrape of stone on bronze. It was a strange, wandering melody in a minor key, unlike any music he had ever heard in his own land.

"What are you singing?"

Startled, the boy looked up. "An old song from my country—" he stammered. "Don't quite know why it comes to me now."

"What are the words?"

Woodpecker shook his head in frustration. "It is hard to put the words in your tongue. I can't say it in poetry."

Velantos waited patiently, for the boy to gather his wits, for the bronze he was polishing to shine. From the passage outside came a burst of drunken laughter. The voices faded as the men went on.

"'Tis the wild geese . . ." Woodpecker said at last. "That fly in autumn. They come in great crowds, crying, crying. Fill the lake. Sky echoes with noise. Then one day they know it's time. First some, then all, lift into air, wing higher, higher. The lake is dark, lonely. Only a few feathers float on water. All gone. . . ."

"By the gods, your people must be cheerful souls!" Velantos mocked gently. But he was thinking that he had never heard Woodpecker say so much about his home.

The boy shook his head. "I don't know why I think of it," he repeated.

But to Velantos it seemed quite clear. His eyes smarted with a sudden vision of his city turned to a waste of tumbled stones where owls nested and sheep huddled for shelter from the wind. When the spring that warmed his own land now reached the north, the wild geese would return. Even now one heard them overhead, winging toward their distant summer home. But what would the folk of Tiryns leave behind to tell the men of some future year that once they had lived here?

Sighing, he took up his hammer once more and began to rivet the hilt of the new sword to the blade.

TEN

*V*elantos turned as Woodpecker came up the stairs to the watch post above the outer court, a sweating earthenware jug of water in each hand. As the boy reached the platform, the wind changed and he bent over, coughing. The town below the walls had been burning since early morning, and acrid black smoke rose in a shifting column to stain the sky. Velantos set down his bow, lifted the cloth he had tied over his nose and mouth, and took one of the jugs. The cool water slid down his throat like a blessing.

They had wondered whether the wells in the lower citadel would last them through a siege. That was no longer a concern. The assault had begun early that morning, and it was now becoming clear to friend and foe alike that Tiryns no longer had enough warriors to man her walls. The Eraklidae had begun with attempts on the main gate and the passage that led from the western bastion, though both were well fortified. Now they were beginning to send groups to assault selected points elsewhere. It was only a matter of time.

"You think they meant to burn the town?" asked Woodpecker, shielding his nose with his hand. Velantos glimpsed a new knot of men trotting up the ramp, handed the jug back to Woodpecker, and grabbed his bow. He had not his brother's precision, but his work in the forge gave him a range they would not expect, and packed as they were, any arrow he loosed was bound to hit someone.

"I doubt it," Velantos replied as the enemy recoiled and swung up their shields. "It's been abandoned since they arrived, so they've had time to collect any valuables left behind. The fires they built to light their fire-arrows must have gotten out of hand. The smoke must be making it hard for the men who are trying to get up our walls. One advantage of being a defender," he added with bitter humor. "It takes less energy."

"My lord—" One of Aiaison's slaves appeared in the stairwell. "They are running low on arrows above the gate."

Velantos turned, trying to assess the activity on the other walls. "Go to the western bastion and see if they have any to spare. That wall will give the scum a hard time no matter what we do." It still seemed strange for men to come to him for orders, but he was not only the king's son, but one of the only unwounded men of fighting age. "Wait—" he added as the man turned away. "If they break through, I want you both to take refuge in the Lady's shrine. That may stop them from killing you out of hand, and when they know you are slaves you will be spared." The goddess who had watched over him since the first day he picked up a hammer seemed very distant now, but perhaps her image still had power.

"I loved Prince Aiaison—" the slave said reproachfully. "And I am still a man. You cannot prevent me from doing what I may to avenge him."

Velantos closed his eyes against the pain of that reminder. The stones of the great courtyard were still black from the pyre on which Aiaison and his brothers had burned. *May the ancestors receive him kindly,* he thought grimly. *May they welcome us all.*

"And I will stay with you!" Woodpecker gave him an impudent grin when the other man had gone.

Velantos glared. How could he expect to command warriors when he could not make one young slave obey? But a dead body was neither slave nor free, and all of them were dead men now. His anger gave way to a wave of sadness. Before this began he should have freed the boy and sent him to follow the wild geese to his northern home.

Another contingent crowded through the opening in the wall and up the corridor toward the gate, overlapping shields like the scales of some great serpent. He straightened with an oath as he realized they were bringing up a battering ram. The main gate of Tiryns was as mighty as the one at Mykenae, but the weakness of any gate was its timbers. Theirs had come from the mighty oaks that grew in the mountains, but wood could not endure like stone.

A rending crash from below brought him to his feet, staring, Woodpecker leaped to the parapet.

"The gate! The wood is in pieces. They'll use axes now."

Velantos nodded. "In a moment they will be through."

He was surprised to hear his voice so calm. He could hear a muffled clamor as the attackers pushed through the roofed corridor beyond the Gate. The defenders had broken holes in its ceiling through which they were shooting, but on the roof they had no cover and the enemy had archers too.

The life he had known was shattering. It was odd how little he felt, now that the time had come. He began to understand why his brothers had yearned for battle. Everything had suddenly become very simple. He nocked another arrow and sent it toward the men who were still crowding up the ramp. He would shoot until he had no arrows left. Then he would draw the leaf-shaped blade whose form he had learned from his foes, and strike—not until there were no more enemies, but until they cut him down.

More crashes told him that the enemy had broken through the double doors at the end of the roofed corridor.

"Woodpecker"—he cleared his throat—"you have done more than enough. It is time to seek what refuge you may."

The boy shook his head. "I told you already. I stay with you."

Unexpectedly Velantos grinned. "You have put muscle on those skinny arms, helping me at the forge, but even your strong arm will do no good once they get this far. There are too many, lad. Go to the smithy. Your hair and skin will tell them that you are no man of this land. Tell them you understand forgework and they will spare you."

Reflexively he touched the hammer he had thrust through his belt that morning when he said farewell to the smithy. It was not a warrior's weapon, but if—no, *when* it came to close enough quarters for him to use it, no one else would be left to care.

"Lord, I want no other master. I know them, or men like them. Better to die with you."

Were those tears that glimmered in the boy's dark eyes? It must be the smoke, he told himself. His own eyes were smarting too.

"Must I make it an order? Or bind you and have you carried below?" Velantos glared. "I will do that if you do not obey! You have served me well, but this is not your fight. We are not your people. Go!" For a moment he thought the boy would continue to argue, but Woodpecker gulped, bent suddenly to seize and kiss his master's hand, and clattered down the stairs.

Velantos let out his breath on a long sigh. Everything that he had said was true. He told himself that at least he had saved one of those he cared for, but his post seemed suddenly very lonely. No matter, he thought grimly as the sounds of slaughter grew louder. He would have plenty of company soon.

The sound of combat echoed from the lower levels but a great quiet seemed to surround him. "Goddess, I've had little time to speak to you and nothing to offer," he whispered, "and now all the time is gone. I thank you for the help you've given me. Farewell . . ." He closed his eyes, seeing in memory the image below which Woodpecker was no doubt sheltering now. And in that moment he felt a stir in his awareness and a voice in the silence of his soul.

"Do not lose hope. We have work for you still . . ."

Before he could wonder what he had heard, or if indeed there had been anything at all, the first rush reached the court below. He set another arrow to the bow, feeling his muscles creak as he drew the string back to his ear. He could hear the thud of axes once more as the enemy reached the barricade they had thrown up across the passage to the Great Propylon. But the monumental entry, with its red pillars and painted processional scenes, had been intended to impress with its beauty, not its strength. It would not hold them long. As more and more men poured through, he continued to shoot into the crowd, dodging as javelins arched upward, bounced off the parapet, and rattled across the floor.

A shriek from the southern side of the citadel brought him around, staring. Velantos had known the attack on the western bastion to be a feint—it was the strongest of their defenses. But he had thought the southern face of the akropolis too sheer to tempt an assault. The oversight hardly mattered, for even if he had suspected its vulnerability they had no men to defend it. He could see the first foes to get over threading through the passageways between the buildings now.

He tried to remember whom he had put in charge of defending the propylon.

"Andaros—beware behind you!" he yelled as they burst into the open space before the entry to the courtyard. He nocked an arrow and shot, saw a man near the leader fling his arms wide and fall with the black feathers sticking from his chest, reached for another and scraped his fingers on stone. All his arrows were gone.

With an oath he flung down the useless bow and reached for his sword, leaped from the platform to the roof, and from that to another and ran across to the Archive Room, praying that the ladder by which in other times the women had climbed up to watch the moonrise would still be there. As he reached the ground, he saw the defenders edging back from the inner door of the propylon into the outer court, swinging around to face the new threat behind them. No need to guess what the enemy intended—the citadels were all built to the same plan. One had only to go upward to reach the central courtyard and the megaron beyond it. And there they would find the king.

Velantos drew his sword as the first foes reached them, bracing his feet as the shock drove the man in front against him. He gaped as a spearpoint burst through the man's back, swung up his blade as the slain man slumped, and chopped down as his killer struggled to withdraw the spear. The sword caught in the man's collarbone and he nearly lost it as the enemy in turn began to fall, wrenched it free with a gasp, and swung against the next contorted face beneath a bronze helmet, aware at the same time of a dim wonder that it should feel so much like hitting the goat carcass on which he had tested the blade. And why not, he told himself as the man reeled back from his blow. They were meat, man and goat alike, compacted of bone and muscle and red blood that fountained when the sword bit through. He whirled and struck again, understanding at last the meaning of the battle dance the priests of the Kouretes taught the boys when they were initiated as men.

"Retreat to the entry! We'll hold them there—" he gasped, dodging a spear and sprinting between the pillars of the smaller gatehouse beyond with the others behind him. They had not barricaded it, for the best defense in this narrow space was a hedge of spears. Orange sunlight poured through from the central court on the other side. He ran out into the court. A quick glance showed him the warriors of the king's guard forming up on the far side before the entrance to the megaron.

"Be ready—" he called. He turned at a sound more sensed than heard, and reeled aside as a javelin sliced across his upper arm. There was a man on the roof of the smaller propylon. In the next moment another appeared behind him, then more. The ladder! He should have brought it with him. But that did not matter now. He dashed back to the shadow of the propylon.

"Andaros, they're behind us! Everyone, to the megaron!"

Men tumbled out of the shadows of the smaller propylon as more and more foes reached its roof. They were the ones who could throw down missiles now. But they were too eager to come to grips. They brought up the ladder from the other side and began to scramble down. It became a chaotic running fight between the retreating defenders and the foes who were streaming after them.

Panting, they attempted to form up in front of the king's guard. With a shout the Eraklidae charged. The first men clutched at the spears that spitted them, tearing them from the defenders' hands. Then it was work for swords. Accustomed to using either hand in the forge, Velantos hewed with the blade in his right hand and swung the hammer with his left. At such close quarters, the one was as effective as the other. The sword bit deep into flesh, but the hammer shattered bone. In such a scramble no one could go unscathed, but Velantos never felt the blades that stung him. No decisions remained, no care, not even for his own life, only the need to strike and strike again until he could strike no more.

He blinked as he found himself forced into the shadow of the porch, only then realizing that he had been retreating across the court. Four of the king's guard stood with him, all that remained to guard the three doors that led within. A swing of the hammer missed and smashed into the alabaster rosette on the wall, blue-painted chips flew into his opponent's eyes, and the man reeled backward. Velantos edged back through the middle door and cast a quick look behind him, glimpsed the king on his throne with the queen standing beside him, tried to turn back as foes filled the doorway, and went sprawling as they crashed through, sword and hammer sliding across the floor.

He expected that moment to be his last, but a curt order halted the rush that followed him into the room. Velantos started to lever himself upright and stopped as a spearpoint swung down to prick his throat, the instinct to flinch battling the desire to lean into the blade and show his father that he too could die like a prince of Tiryns. In the distance he could hear the clamor of battle, and from somewhere closer, a woman's scream, but in the megaron, all was still.

Heart hammering, Velantos tore his gaze from the spearpoint and looked around him. A dozen warriors stood between him and the throne, big men in red kilts with scars on their bare chests, carrying spears and swords. Through their legs he could see the king and the queen.

There was no point in trying to prove his courage to his father, he thought numbly, seeing the old man slumped as if he had fallen asleep in the great chair. The king was dead already, had been dead, perhaps, since word came that the Gate was down. Had he taken poison, or had his heart mercifully given way? The queen stood like an image beside him, the same faintly disapproving expression as always on her lips and brows. For a moment their eyes met, and he saw in her gaze a flicker of something that might have been pity, though he found that hard to believe.

There was a stir at the doorway and men stood aside to let in another group of warriors, better armed, and unwounded as the men of the king's guard had been until a little while ago. Behind them came an older man in a red cloak with grizzled hair tied up in a warrior's knot, the scars on his face deepened by the lines of passion and power.

"Queen Naxomene . . . I am Kresfontes, son of Aristomakhos, and my brother and I claim this citadel."

The queen nodded. "I see that it is so," she said harshly. "I will not bid you welcome."

He shrugged. "Your husband has escaped us, but it is you who carry the sovereignty."

"Do you think to claim it by taking me to your bed?" She laughed. "It is long since the Lady of Love shared her gifts with me. My sons are all dead, and my daughters all married into other lands."

"Then you shall act as nursemaid to the children I get on other women."

"How kind! Shall I give you a gift in return? You have taken Tiryns, but in times such as these the women of my line receive the gift of prophecy, and though you have asked no question, I will be your oracle. The line of Pelops is ended, and with it the Age of Heroes. From this time forward, the Plain of Argos will be ruled by the Children of Erakles, but it is our stories that your sons will tell. And though you may have captured this citadel, you will not hold it for long."

Now Kresfontes was the one who laughed, although through the ringing in his ears Velantos seemed to catch a note of strain. "Do you think Tisamenos will thunder down from Mykenae to avenge you? Once we have finished here, his citadel will be the next to fall."

"You may conquer men, but can you stand against the gods?" asked the queen.

"We are the heirs of Erakles," Kresfontes said proudly, "and we come to claim our own. Will the gods not support our right?"

"Erakles was denied this city by the will of E-ra, and she opposes his blood still," the queen replied. "Posedaon Enesidaone will shake down these walls rather than leave them in your hands." Some of the warriors made a sign against evil and she smiled. "That is not a curse; it is a prophecy."

"I give this for your prophecy—" Kresfontes made a rude gesture, and his warriors laughed. "You are no longer a queen. You are my slave, and you shall grind the grain to bake my bread. Bind her—"

Velantos realized that all the warriors were staring at their leader and the queen. He raised himself on one elbow. The hilt of the leaf-shaped sword lay just behind his hand. If he could reach it—what could he do? Leap between Naxomene and the men who were starting toward her, to delay for a few more moments the death of her pride? *I can die like a smith,* a deeper knowledge replied, *with my last work in my hand . . .*

As the first warrior reached for the queen's arm, Velantos grabbed for the sword, but before either could reach their goal another blade flashed. A twitch of her wrist brought the dagger the queen had held reversed against her inner arm out and up and into her heart. Bright blood blossomed on the fine stuff of her gown as she curled around the blade, sank to her knees, and then to her side on the tiled floor.

"It is my blood that curses you. . . ." she gasped, and then a last shudder took her and she lay still.

Velantos surged to his feet, the sword whipping out to take the nearest warrior in the side. Beyond him he saw Kresfontes and lunged toward him. But the enemy were already recovering. Swift as hounds they turned on him. His left leg gave way as a spear slammed into the calf. Swords that would have pierced him clanged above his head. As he hit the floor, a heavy sandal stamped down on his arm and the sword was torn away.

At least, he thought with a last flicker of triumph, *the boy will live. . . .* He saw blades gleam above him and turned to welcome them.

THE SOUNDS FROM THE upper levels had changed. Woodpecker lifted his head, listening. The full-throated shouts and the clangor of arms had given way to footsteps and voices. Except for the screaming when some woman was seized, it might have been the noise of a crowd on a festival day. But the clamor was all from above.

Here, nothing moved but the dust motes that swirled in the shaft of sunlight that came in through the high window. But Woodpecker knew that the safety of the smithy was an illusion. When the palace had been secured, the enemy would begin to search the rest of the citadel, and they would find him, and he would be a slave once more. He tried to tell himself that nothing had changed, that he had been a slave since— His mind shied away from the image of a grinning bearded face. The harsh reek of smoke merged with memories of mist that clouded a rocky shore.

To Velantos, he had been a companion.

And he had abandoned him.

Velantos rejected me! He answered that inner accusation. Woodpecker thought he had found a home in Tiryns. To be told he had no right to die in its defense hurt. Was that why he had obeyed Velantos? Or was he afraid? He clasped his long arms around his knees and rocked back and forth. Fear was an old companion. There had always been an undercurrent of anxiety even when he was a child, in the days when he had thought himself free.

For three years he had been at the mercy of his masters. He had learned every gesture of submission, every way by which a slave might placate wrath or evade a blow. For three years all he had remembered was that he must survive. That was what Velantos had told him to do. He grimaced as he realized he was still obeying a master. In the smithy, everything, from the tools on their shelves to the scarred leather apron hanging from its peg on the wall, resonated with the smith's identity. Velantos was still here, grumbling, teaching, and all too rarely, loosing that deep-throated roar of laughter that seemed to roll up from his toes—Woodpecker had not left him on the watchtower after all.

No . . . He shivered. *He's dead. When he sent me away, it was because he meant to die.* His gaze sought the clay figure of the goddess that always reminded him of the image above the forge on the Island of Maidens at home. *Why couldn't You save him? He loved You!*

There was a shift in the light as if a bird had flown by the window, though he saw nothing pass. A phrase repeated itself in his awareness—*"The god gives the power, but we are the tools . . ."* He could not, would not, remember who had said that to him. Perhaps it was the goddess herself, Potnia Athana, who in his own land had another name.

Velantos had expected to die, but Woodpecker knew from his own experience that sometimes those who were supposed to die lived. What if the smith had not found death in battle? What would they do to him? Without intending it, the boy unfolded from his fetal crouch, legs tingling as he forced numbed muscles to move.

They will kill him without honor, he thought grimly, *enslave him to some wretched work that will grind him into the dust.* Woodpecker knew all about the kind of labor that suffocated the spirit and deadened the senses. But such treatment would only goad Velantos to a rebellion that would end in a death more wretched still.

Now that he was standing, cowering until he was hauled off to a new captivity was no longer an option. He looked up at the goddess once more.

"You want me to do something, don't You?" he said aloud.

Frowning, he took down the leather apron. It would go twice around him, but it might identify him as a skilled craftsman long enough to keep him from being skewered the moment he appeared. And he should take something to demonstrate Velantos' skill—not a weapon— His gaze fell on an earring in the shape of a pendant lily that Tanit had brought to the smith for repair. He tried not to think about what her fate would be now. He had heard stories from captive women in households where he had served. First rape, then, if they were pretty, service as a whore to the warriors until they were sold. To know that had happened to a girl he had loved must be as great a torment as defeat itself. Woodpecker understood why Velantos would prefer to die.

But perhaps the prince was not dead.

He twitched at the sound of voices in the street outside. They were coming already. A swift step took him to the back entrance that led to the sheds where they stored the charcoal and from there to an alley. After a year of doing errands for Velantos he knew all the back ways and shortcuts, and the ladder, if it was still there, that would get him into the Upper Citadel.

"TAKE HIM OUTSIDE AND kill him—there's too much blood already on this floor . . ."

The voice seemed to come from a great distance away. The sword whose point was already cutting into Velantos' breast twisted, and he forced himself not to flinch from the pain. Rope rasped his left wrist as they bound it; he grunted in agony as they grabbed his right. But he had only to endure a few more moments and he would be done.

"Bind him, but do not kill!" A new voice cut across the moans of the dying and the jeers of his captors. Velantos' head jerked round, his eyes widening as he saw Woodpecker, the leather apron flapping around him, standing beside the hearth. "He's a master smith, valuable. See, that's his hammer on the floor. You want him alive."

"And who may you be, to give orders here?"

Velantos' relief that Kresfontes' voice held amusement warred with his own wrath that the boy had disobeyed.

"I help him; I learned from him! I have some skill too. But look—" Gold gleamed in Woodpecker's hand. "He made this earring—it's beautiful, yes?"

"Our women are already weighted down by the golden gauds that we have won," said one of the warriors. "We have all of yours already, and the gold of Mykenae when it falls. We don't need a smith to make more."

"You still need swords!" came the swift rejoinder. "He saw your kind of sword last year and learned. That one—" Woodpecker pointed to the leaf-shaped blade that had come to rest against the curb of the hearth. "He made it. Look at it. Keep him and he'll make more."

With a detached amusement Velantos noted how the sight of the weapon had changed the expressions of the men who guarded him. Woodpecker had made a good try, but if they thought he would work for them they were mistaken, and he would die after all, in some worse way. The gash where the spear had brought him down was still bleeding and his leg was beginning to grow cold. If they waited much longer, it would not matter anyway, for blood loss would finish him.

Someone had picked up the sword and set it in Kresfontes' hand.

"A year?" The enemy leader extended the blade, swept it in a circle and brought it down once more. There were a few nicks in the edge, and it would need to be sharpened before it was a really effective weapon again, but Velantos was distantly pleased that it had held up so well. *And killed so many . . .* His lips curved a little as his eyes closed.

"Very well—" The words came from somewhere far away. "Bind up that leg and take him away. You spoke for him, boy—you take care of him. If he lives, we'll see what he can do."

Velantos gasped as a rough bandaging woke the wound in his leg to screaming agony. But the fingers that untied the rope from his damaged wrist were precise and sure.

"Soon, I'll get you water," came Woodpecker's whisper. The voice was a line that held him to consciousness through the waves of pain, the long-fingered hands cool as they smoothed the matted hair from his brow. "Don't die, Velantos. You've given me my soul again. Don't leave me alone. . . ."

"As bird and beast find mates and couple, so it is with men, for none can prosper alone. . . ." Anderle lifted her hands in blessing, and Cimara blushed rosily, casting a swift look at the young man who stood at her side. "May the gods grant that your lives will be long and happy, and your offspring prosper in the land!"

The queen of Azan was old for a first wedding, but her mother had not allowed her to take a husband for fear of Galid's wrath. Queen Zamara had died just after Midwinter, though it seemed to Anderle that her spirit had succumbed many years before. It had taken some months of secret negotiations to find a suitable bridegroom to sire the next generation of Azani sovereigns. Agraw was from the eastern edge of Azan, where they had not suffered so much from Galid's depredations. He was a second son, and no doubt his mother had been pleased to settle him so well.

Agraw was not a bad-looking boy. Beneath the wedding crown his brown hair was thick and curly, and the shoulders draped by the leather cape looked strong. Cimara's worn features had a youthful radiance beneath a felt cap banded with amber beads to which a rectangle of tubular jet beads had been added on each side. Lappets hung down her back, and her brown hair had been intricately braided behind. Necklet and bracelets were of gold, and her shoulder cape was held to her gown by long pins of bronze. Even Galid had not dared to steal the regalia of the queen.

The party assembled to witness their vows was small, but Anderle had persuaded enough representatives of Azan's noble families to come to the sacred grove to validate the ceremony. And they were almost done. The couple had exchanged bread and salt, and on the stone altar the fire that had witnessed their handfasting still burned. Once they had made their offerings to the gods, they could be put to bed, and if the gods were good, Cimara would conceive.

And what will we do if she bears a son? Anderle wondered then. *Must I try to hide him as I did Mikantor?* Her heart twisted with the old pain. King Sakantor's words had eased her sorrow but brought little hope. It had been nearly three years since Mikantor had been captured. Even if the boy still lived, he was lost to them.

"Come, and we will offer our gifts to the gods in exchange for their blessings." She gestured, and two of the men picked up the chest that held the offerings. Hand in hand, Cimara and Agraw led the way along the path from the grove to the place where the river had spread wide to form a marshy bog. Planks had been laid across the mud to allow the pair to get closer to the water. As they neared, a pair of mallards flew up, quacking. The dessicated head and hide of a bull dangled from a pole among the reeds, left from the last ritual conducted by the old queen. Today they ought to have offered another, but that would have left evidence that Galid would question. Instead, Cimara was offering her remaining treasures—a bronze bowl with its side beaten in; a gold pin, bent; and then a good bronze blade that Agraw broke over one knee.

Metal flashed pale in the sunlight as the items were tossed into the bog. Anderle closed her eyes and reached out with her other senses, and it seemed to her that she could feel a change in the pressure of the air. The spirits were listening.

To make offerings to the waters was a new thing. Her mother had begun it, in one of the first years when the rains threatened to engulf the land. The sacred stones still got a little milk and bread, but the sight of dark waters closing over something so valuable was clear evidence that a sacrifice had been received. She hoped the gods were pleased. It had been disturbing to feel the land so uneasy as she crossed Azan.

Cimara and her new husband offered the last gold pin and turned. She was smiling with relief and pleasure, he serious, as if only now understanding that although he would not rule, his was the power that made the queen fertile to bless the land. The witnesses set up a cheer as they reached the grass. Startled by the noise, it took Anderle a moment to realize that she was hearing another sound. She bent and felt a vibration in the earth, and recognized it as the rattle of chariot wheels.

Some of the kings in other lands had chariots, but only one man would be driving so furiously here.

The others had heard and were turning. Anderle hurried toward the bride and groom. "Galid is coming! Agraw, take off the crown and cloak and hide yourself among the other men!"

Cimara's face had gone white. She stood her ground as Anderle bundled the groom's gear into the box that had held the offerings, but as the chariots surged over the rise, she reached out to take the priestess's hand.

Galid's charioteer reined in the ponies, a pair of chestnuts whose coats glowed the same color as his cloak, pinned with a great brooch far finer than anything Cimara had been able to give to the bog. Behind him came five other chariots, each bearing several men. Their bronze spearpoints gleamed in the sun.

"What a fine pair of birds—" he observed with a nasty smile. "And what fine feathers. But why the celebration? Have I somehow forgotten a holiday?"

"Does it require a holiday to make an offering to the spirits of the land?" Anderle replied.

"It does at least require a reason," he said slowly, scanning the faces of the others. Flushed or pale, they avoided his gaze as if they had been guilty of some crime. "Has there been some disaster of which I was not informed?"

You are the disaster, Galid, thought Anderle, but she bit back the words as he went on.

"If you wished to make a sacrifice, why was I not invited? I see no beast, no fire, no blood on the ground. Surely you would not insult the gods with a paltry offering."

"Bring us a bull, if you can find one among your herds that is not someone else's rightful property, and we will be happy to offer it," she said evenly. "You have left these people little to celebrate with, or for."

"Is that so? But I was told that you were planning a very special cere-mony." His lips smiled, but there was venom in his gaze. "A queen's wed-ding," he whispered. "And not witnessed by the protector of this land?"

"You are not my protector," Cimara said coldly, though Anderle could feel the trembling of her hand. "Not my war-king, nor my husband. You have no authority over me or over this land!"

"Only this!" he hissed, jerking a spear from its holder and swinging it toward her breast. "Here's a plow for your furrow, if you're so hot to breed!"

"Even you, Galid the Greedy, know better than to kill a queen," Anderle cut in.

"I don't have to kill her, only her heirs . . ." The spear lifted, and swung toward the others, who now stood surrounded by his men. "If she's wedded, I'll swear she's not been bedded, nor will be." He nodded to his charioteer, and a touch on the reins brought the cart closer to the witnesses. "Seven men stand here, shaking in their sandals like so many girls. And not a one has the stones to step out and face me, much less sire a ruler. Still, to make sure, I suppose I had better kill them all."

He grinned, letting the spear drift back and forth along the line. Some of the men had knives, and one, a sword, but against those numbers none had dared to draw. As the spearpoint moved, first one, then another, edged away from Agraw, who stood with his eyes tight shut like a man trying to deny a bad dream.

"Is that the one?" Galid asked softly. He dropped the spear suddenly to prick old Orlai's breast. "Is that trembling lamb the bridegroom, or shall I kill you instead?"

"It was him . . ." Orlai's answer could barely be heard. One of the other men glared, but none of them had reckoned on paying such a price for witnessing a wedding. Agraw opened his eyes then, looking at Galid with a dazed expression, as if he had not understood. Perhaps that was a mercy, thought Anderle.

She took a deep breath, gathering her power. "Galid!" she cried, but his arm was already swinging. "Ni-Terat curses—" Her words were lost in Agraw's scream as the spear drove in. For a moment the young man flailed, but Galid's aim had been true. As he sagged, the spear jerked free. Blood spread across the front of his tunic as the victim sagged to his knees, and then to the ground.

"The food you eat, the ground you walk on . . ." spat Anderle, "Ni-Terat curses them all. Neither long life nor luck nor child nor wife shall you have, cursed by all the gods—"

"Bitch, be silent!" Galid swung the bloody spear around and Cimara clutched at Anderle's arm. "Don't you yet understand? The gods have abandoned us! Do you think I could have killed him if the gods cared what men do? But just in case I'm wrong, pitch the body of that fool into the river and let them have their sacrifice!"

"Your doom may be delayed," whispered Anderle, "but one day it will come for you—" Even in her own ears her words sounded hollow. As the current took Agraw's body, she put her arm around the weeping queen of Azan, who this night would sleep alone.

ELEVEN

*J*n the heat of the afternoon, cicadas strummed from the hillside above the road like lyres that had lost their tone. Woodpecker pulled the length of brown wool that was one of his few remaining possessions across his nose and mouth to screen out the dust. By night it was his blanket, by day a drape to shield his fair skin from the sun. They had been marching for six days, from Tiryns north on the graded and graveled road to Mykenae, and then turning off before they reached the akropolis and going on toward Nemea. That had been the moment when the boy hoped for rescue, but his captors made a night march, and King Tisamenos had stayed behind his mighty walls, hoping the Eraklidae would think them impregnable. And now the high valley that sheltered Nemea was also behind them. The way ahead curved downward along a slanting ridge. Beyond the stark curves of the hills he could see the green of cultivated lands and the blue glimmer of the sea.

Korinthos, where Aletes now is king, he thought grimly, trying not to wonder what would happen when they got there. First—he glanced anxiously at the wagon where Velantos had been unceremoniously dumped atop piled sacks of grain—they had to reach the city alive. He could understand why Kresfontes, on learning who Velantos was, had not wanted to keep him in Tiryns where he might lead the surviving populace in an uprising. But the prince should not have been moved so soon. Woodpecker had protested, but slaves, as he understood only too well, had no choices. And Kresfontes and Temenos had decided to let the gods choose whether to preserve King Phorkaon's last son or relieve the Eraklidae of a problem.

The officer whom the kings had put in charge of this collection of loot rode in a chair-litter, out of the dust at the head of the column, shaded by oiled cloth stretched over hoops. A dozen warriors tramped after it, though the boy could not imagine from what dangers the man thought he needed protection. All the scary people were guarding *him*.

Perhaps if Woodpecker could find a stick he could use it to prop his bit of wool over his eyes so he could have shade without sweltering. *I am a slave,* he told himself. *What I cannot change I must endure.* With Velantos he had almost forgotten that, for a while.

He thought he heard a grunt from within the wagon and stepped closer to see. Velantos lay curled around one of the sacks, his head pillowed on another, apparently asleep. But he knew that the prince feigned sleep even when pain did not exhaust him, as if by closing his eyes, he could shut the new reality away.

It did not work for me, thought the boy, *and the gods know I tried.* On the voyage from Belerion to Tartessos he had been too seasick to care where he was. By the time they arrived, he could count his ribs. He did not know why they had not simply tossed him into the sea.

He leaned over the wagon. Velantos had grown thinner even in the past week. Above the black beard the strong shape of cheekbone and jaw stood clear. Even wasted, the powerful lines of the smith's body were still apparent, but the tension that had enabled him to manifest that power was missing, or rather disrupted, as limb locked against limb to resist the pain. Velantos' features tensed as the wagon hit a deeper rut, throwing him against the side, and Woodpecker heard a moan the older man could not deny.

"My lord! I know you're not sleeping—this jolting would wake the dead," he babbled. "Would you like water? And maybe I can fix something to keep off the sun."

"Not dead . . ." Velantos echoed. Woodpecker wasn't sure whether that had been a confirmation or a complaint. "Water would be . . . good."

Woodpecker wondered if they had given him the skin of water to test his devotion or his self-control. But after three years in this dry land he could go without if he had to. He pulled the stopper and held it to Velantos' lips, steadying the man's head with his other hand.

As they descended, they began to pass scattered farmsteads. Men and women were working in the vineyards, hoeing weeds into the soil and trimming shoots to concentrate growth in the hard green grapes that were beginning to swell on the vines. They looked up as the soldiers came into view, then returned to their labor, satisfied that this was the enemy they already knew, unlikely to ravage fields where food could grow.

"I suppose the worst has already happened to them," Woodpecker said aloud. "Farmers are like that, even when the world is falling apart. I remember—" He faltered, and then, seeing interest replace the pain in Velantos' eyes, forced himself to go on. "In my country, after the floods came, or the human wolves, they would go back to the fields."

"Earth must be served," said the older man. His gaze grew inward. "I tell myself that it doesn't matter who rules. The kingdoms of men rise and fall, but the peasants remain. So long as the crops still grow, life will go on. The blood of the slain fertilizes the fields."

But if the sun doesn't shine, the crops can't grow, thought Woodpecker, remembering some of the bad years at home. *Men and beasts alike prey on each other.* For the first time, it occurred to him to wonder if the disasters that beset the Island of the Mighty had troubled other northern lands. Could such disturbances have pitted one people against another until the pressure set the Children of Erakles in motion? If the whole world was sick, he shouldn't envy these farmers. They too were doomed. They just didn't know it yet.

"Is something wrong?"

As Velantos spoke, Woodpecker realized that he had been silent for too long. But his reflections would be a poor medicine for a wounded man. He shook his head with a bright smile. "Thinking about farmers. This land is so different from my home—"

In other circumstances he might have enjoyed this opportunity to see the interior of Akhaea. His earlier journeys had mostly been made by sea. At the summer's beginning the grass had already ripened to gold. Though patches of brush dotted the hillsides and taller trees clustered in the ravines, the shape of the land was still clear. The dark green pillars of holy cypress were scattered across them like the columns of a temple for the gods of the wild.

"They say that long ago there were more trees here," muttered Velantos. "We cut them for houses and firewood and charcoal for smelting copper ore. There were lions too, but none has been seen in Akhaea since the one that Erakles killed."

"If I could I would summon a lion to chase his children home again—" said Woodpecker, and was rewarded by the twitch of a smile.

The hill they had been descending began to level off. At its base clustered a few oak trees and some bushes with leathery pointed leaves and pink flowers, surrounding a stone basin that collected the trickle of water from a spring in the side of the hill. An order from ahead turned the line toward the trees.

When they came to a halt, Woodpecker assisted his master to sit up and found two sticks over which he stretched his bit of cloth to provide some shade. It was hot. When he went to refill his waterskin, he plucked a spray of the pink flowers. They had five petals with squared-off tips and a faint sweet smell.

"It's so dry here, I'm always surprised to find flowers." He held them out to the older man. "These are pretty. What are they called?"

"Bitter Laurel—highly poisonous." Velantos' wry smile became a bark of laughter as Woodpecker snatched the flowers away. "But only if you eat them. A grown man would only become sick, but a little can kill a child."

Woodpecker relaxed, but he did not return the flowers.

"You need not fear I'll try to poison myself," Velantos added bitterly. "I have no wish to add a bad belly to the pain I bear. Though I do not know why you should take the trouble to keep me alive, or for that matter, what gives you the right to do so."

Woodpecker gave him a sidelong glance, trying to decide whether this was a convalescent's petulance or a justified anger. He wondered suddenly if he had fretted so much about Velantos in the days since the fall of Tiryns to avoid asking himself the same question.

"My reasons are selfish, of course—" he said flatly. "Taking care of you gives me a purpose . . . again. When I was growing up, I was told I was born for great things. But I think now that those who said so were fighting their own despair. If the gods had a plan, they should have given me more protection! If I can't serve myself, at least I can serve you." He stopped short, breathing rather quickly. It had been a long time since he had allowed himself to feel that particular pain. He cast a quick glance at Velantos, who was looking thoughtful.

"Then I suppose I should try to deserve your devotion, though it seems rather thankless when I am a slave too."

"Maybe that is why," Woodpecker replied shortly. "I serve you because that's what *I* choose. And what I choose now is to take a look at that leg of yours—" he added, and Velantos, interpreting the look on his face correctly, stretched out his leg with a grimace and a sigh.

The Eraklidae had rousted them awake early, allowing no time for Woodpecker to dress the wound. His lips tightened as he unwound the bandage. The spearpoint had gone deep, and though the wound had bled profusely, who could say what filth still hid within? The skin around the gash was an angry red, hot and hard to the touch. Velantos flinched when he bathed it and applied powdered sage to poultice it anew. For whatever good that might do, the boy thought grimly. It should be opened up so that the medicine could reach it. Velantos needed a healer, not a barbarian who could only try to apply what little he remembered of the ways old Kiri had treated his scrapes at Avalon.

He could feel Velantos trembling, though the man made no sound. He wrapped a new bandage around the leg and took the old one to the spring to wash. When he came back, the prince's eyes were closed. Woodpecker looked more closely and saw that he had stopped sweating. That was not a good sign.

VELANTOS WRITHED IN WAVES of heat. He could see the rim of the crucible around him; he was the raw ore, the essential metal liquifying as the dross rose to the surface. He groaned as a harsh touch scraped his skin, scooping it away. He hoped the smith knew what he was doing; If the fire was allowed to grow too hot, even copper would burn. Perhaps that would be best—the pyre would consume his pain.

"Velantos—open your mouth. Drink this!" The order came from some other world, but his body must have responded; he tasted cool bitterness, and suddenly the heat gave way to racking chills. His sensitized skin screamed at the touch of a woolen blanket, and then he was back in the crucible, and the cycle began once more.

Each time it happened the sensations were more intense, more divorced from any human reality. The crucible became the body of a woman formed of flame, slender and supple, with glowing eyes. He gave himself to Her more fully than ever he had with any mortal lover, pouring out his essence in Her embrace.

"Now you are fire . . ." said the goddess, *"by giving all, you become everything."*

"But can do nothing—" came a voice like thunder. *"If he would serve You, he must be shaped and hardened, hammered and honed."*

"Then I give him to You!"

I don't want . . . the spark that was Velantos protested, but already the grip of the goddess was tightening; he felt himself changing in her arms. Still glowing, he was lifted and laid upon an anvil. He convulsed at the first blow, and again and again as each particle of his body was realigned.

He screamed as he was plunged into water. He felt the new shape solidifying to contain him, to constrain him, and opened his eyes to meet Woodpecker's frightened gaze. He closed them again, striving to recapture the vision, weeping with the pain of that loss, and slowly became aware that his whole body was wet, that he lay in a cold pool.

"Lift him out now," said a deep voice, "before he takes a chill."

He could neither help nor resist as many hands maneuvered his body. He felt as if he had no bones. They put him on something yielding, covered him with something soft.

"Velantos, can you hear me?" came Woodpecker's voice, and then, "Have we saved him? Did the fever burn his mind away?"

"Give him time, lad," the deep voice replied. "He has been to the gate of Hades. To return will take a little while."

Velantos took a deep breath, a little surprised to feel his body responding to his will, and opened his eyes once more. Woodpecker knelt beside·him. In the flicker of lamplight he could see that behind the boy stood an older man in the white robe of a priest of Apollon Paion. The priest bent closer, meeting his gaze, and seemed to read something there that satisfied him.

"I think he will sleep now. If the god is merciful, when he has rested he will be able to speak to you. Watch beside him, and call me when he wakes."

As if that had been an order, Velantos felt himself sliding down into a darkness that was neither hot nor cold, but infinitely comforting.

ANDERLE WOKE FROM DREAMS of fire. That was not unusual, but for the first time it was not a nightmare of the burning of Azan-Ylir. In fact, she had an unaccustomed sense of well-being, as if from some pleasant exercise. For a few moments she lay blinking, trying to remember what it had been. At least it had kept her warm. She had not only kicked off all her covers, but somehow her sleeping shift had come off as well.

What had she been doing? There had been fire, no, she had *been* the fire, and there had been one man whom she embraced and another with whom she argued—no, he was a god, with a smith's hammer in his hand. And then somehow they had become one man, dark of hair and beard and very strong. The tingle of arousal as she thought of him made her flush again. But now she felt in the air the chill that heralds the dawn. She pulled the covers back up to her chin.

The man was not anyone Anderle had ever seen, but she would surely know him again. Was she so desperate for a man's touch that she was inventing dream lovers? Somehow she did not think that she would go to the priests for an interpretation, but perhaps she might find some illumination in the forge fire on the Maiden's Isle.

Lady, if this dream holds some message, show me what it means! she prayed, and as she slid back into sleep it seemed to her that she heard the Goddess laugh.

At the shrine of Paion the Healer, you could always hear the sound of water. The springs of Lerna gushed forth from the rock like the nine heads of the hydra that gave the place its name, fed by snowmelt from the mountains behind the town. Woodpecker liked to sit here in the morning when sunlight shafted through the branches of the pines. Their scent and the sound of the water reminded him of home. As he sat on the bench beside the bathing pool, it was possible to forget how much of the city was now a charred and depopulated ruin. But the Eraklidae had spared the holy places, or perhaps the god had taken care of his own. In any case, he was grateful that Kresfontes' officer, fearing the loss of a valuable slave, had allowed him to take Velantos to the shrine.

He turned at the sound of a footstep, and saw one of the younger priests standing there. The priest's nod of greeting held neither deference nor superiority. Woodpecker supposed that everyone—conquered and conqueror, slave and free—were equally suppliants here.

"Your master is awake and calling for you."

Woodpecker gave him a sharp look. Had there been a hint of relief in the man's tone? "Is he in a bad temper?" he asked aloud.

"Convalescence can be very difficult, especially for a strong and active man."

Woodpecker interpreted that to mean "yes." He was not surprised. When the icy bath broke Velantos' fever, they had hoped for a speedy recovery, but it had been nearly a week now, and although the flesh was no longer decaying, the hole in the smith's calf remained raw, and did not heal.

"He no longer wants to die," the priest went on, "but he does not want to live. We have discussed the case. We believe that it will improve his mood if he leaves his bed, perhaps to sit in the sun. But for healing, he must be willing to ask the help of the god."

Woodpecker could translate that too. They had already tried to get their patient up and moving, and now they were hoping the slave boy could succeed where they had failed.

Velantos was lying on his side with his bad leg propped up on pillows, face turned to the wall. An uneaten bowl of porridge sat on a low table nearby.

"It is a fine morning, master," Woodpecker said brightly. "Far too nice a day to stay cooped up inside. The grounds here are very peaceful. Let me help you into a tunic and we can see how well this crutch they've made you lets you get around." He saw the man's shoulder twitch, so he knew Velantos was awake, and went on. "You may have scared off the priests, but I am not going to go away or stop talking until you sit up and answer me. I saw a hawk circling above the trees. It caught a mouse. Isn't Paion fond of mice? I would think—"

The bed groaned as Velantos heaved upright. "Will you be still? A man can't sleep through your stupid prattling!"

"You are not supposed to be asleep. It's morning. Here, take the crutches and haul yourself out of that bed. You'll want to relieve yourself, and then—"

Woodpecker dodged back as Velantos snatched the nearer crutch by its long end and jabbed, bringing up the other to guard as he had learned when practicing staff work at Avalon. The smith swore as the movement jarred his leg and swung again. Wood cracked against wood and the boy laughed.

"Come here, you barbarian swine! I should have beaten you before. Come here and get the thrashing you deserve!"

"First you'll have to get up," taunted the boy. He wove back and forth, feeling his own heartbeat speed as he avoided the man's blows. Weakened Velantos might be, but fury could give a man a hero's strength. The boy was pretty sure that in his right mind, the prince would not harm him, but that suffused face and those blazing eyes did not look very sane.

"Ungrateful! Stupid little turd!" Velantos raged. "I'll sell you to the Eraklidae for a whore. If they'll take you, ugly as you are!"

He's angry. . . thought Woodpecker. *Angry men will say anything.* But that, surprisingly, had hurt.

"I've coddled you. See how you like—"

"Catch me!" the boy cried, threw the other crutch at his master, and darted through the door.

I'VE GROWN WEAK AS a pup, thought Velantos, levering the crutches forward, swaying as they caught against his loose robe, and taking another step. *No wonder the boy laughed at me.*

He remembered shouting. He supposed he ought to apologize. He shifted his weight to the crutches and swung his good leg ahead, wincing as the movement jarred the other. It ached fiercely, but then it did that most of the time.

Hop and swing, hop and swing, he made his way into the herb garden. Woodpecker was sitting on a bench, eating dried figs. He looked up at the scrape of the crutches and flinched. Velantos closed his eyes against a pain that had nothing to do with his leg. *What did I say to him?* His mind felt curiously empty, with the stillness that comes after the storm.

"Sit down before you fall down," said Woodpecker when the silence had gone on for too long.

Velantos nodded, maneuvered himself to the other bench, and eased onto it. He took a deep breath. The air was heavy with the scent of laurel and sage, thyme and tarragon and other plants whose volatile oils were released by the heat of the sun. It was a relief to stretch out his leg, but sweat poured from his brow and his heart was pounding like a drum. "I've been told that I . . . say things . . . when the rage takes me," he said stiffly. "Whatever I said to you, I hope you will forgive."

"You threatened to sell me—"

"I can't sell you. I'm a slave too—"

"I thought of that," said Woodpecker, "but I didn't want to depress you."

For a moment Velantos could only stare. Then, surprising himself as much as he did the boy, he began to laugh. That first bark of sound rasped his throat. He could not remember how long it had been since he had allowed the sheer painful paradox of life to overcome him. Perhaps he had forgotten how. Then the next convulsion took him, a racking sob of laughter, repeated again and again. Woodpecker thumped his back, pressing a clay cup of water into his hand. He drank, choked, drank again, and then fell blessedly still.

"I'm sorry I tried to hit you—"

Woodpecker shrugged. "You couldn't hit a tethered lamb right now. But I understand why the priests didn't want to disturb you. Get well, and maybe I'll be afraid of you again."

Velantos jerked his head in denial. Had he lost the boy's trust forever? But Woodpecker's hand still gripped his shoulder. He leaned into that strength, confused by a pain for which he had no words, and forced himself to focus on what Woodpecker was saying now.

"You can't go on this way, you know. The priests need your bed for other patients, and King Aletes has sent more than once to ask whether the master smith his cousin gave him has decided to live or to die. The priests have done all they know how. They want you to sleep in the temple and ask the help of the god."

IN THE LAST LIGHT of afternoon the procession of sick and wounded made its way up from the sea where they had been purified. Velantos had ridden down in the wagon, but he had sworn he would make the journey back on his own. Willpower had gotten him the length of a running track before his leg, raw flesh still stinging from the sea, had buckled beneath him, so he was in the wagon again.

At least now he could sit upright, bracing himself against the wagon's sway with arms that constant use of the crutches had strengthened. But he had a long way to go to rebuild his powerful frame. Now was not the time to ask himself what he was trying to heal his body *for.*

Woodpecker walked beside the wagon. His sunburned face bore its usual half smile, as if he was secretly amused. For a year Velantos had taken the boy for granted, too busy with his own concerns to wonder who Woodpecker had been before fortune betrayed him. He had an excuse for that—he had been concerned with the fate of a kingdom, but he was no longer his own master, much less the boy's. Now that he dared not wonder about his own future, all he had left was Woodpecker. At least when the boy looked at him now, that hurtful hint of apprehension no longer flickered in his eyes.

Velantos shifted position on the bench, skin itching with salt. There was sand in his robes. They all smelled of Posedaon's briny blessing—the Dorian warrior who had lost a leg and the Korinthian harness-maker whose skills were too valuable to lose. They said that the Earthshaker owned all the shorelands, while the sun-washed bare heights belonged to Helios. Korinthos had honored the other gods between the two in the town that had clustered at the foot of the akropolis on an eminence that looked over the coastal plain. Most of the buildings had burned. The Dorian warriors now camped in tents on the field where they had destroyed the Korinthian chariotry while King Aletes kept their former rulers captive in the citadel.

The road curved around the western side of the town. Velantos could see the dark-fringed pines that shaded the shrine, and the sunset-gilded gleam of the buildings beyond. By the time the wagon came to a halt before the sanctuary, he was sufficiently recovered to take his place in the file of suppliants who moved one by one to the altar to offer a honey cake to the flames. Within the wall the shrine was roofless, four pillars supporting a canopy that protected the image of the god. Gold foil had been attached to simulate hair and ornaments, but the body of the god was hewn of oak wood, dark with age. From the pillars hung images of body parts placed there by grateful patients whom the god had healed. *Heal me, Lord, and I will craft a leg of bronze to be my testimonial,* thought Velantos. He gazed at the impassive features, but he could read no promise there.

Then it was time for another sluicing. Velantos was grateful to wash off the salt, but at least the sea had been warm. Still shivering, he let them belt the white sleeping robe around him and followed the young priest to the sanctuary.

By the time they had all been settled on the pallets on which they would sleep, it was full dark. Resigned to a sleepless night, Velantos lay listening to the snores and whistles of his companions, but he had not counted on the effects of exertion and sea air. He was still trying to figure out which sufferer sounded as if each breath was about to be his last when suddenly he found himself in another place entirely and knew that he was in the country of the god. It was, he realized immediately, a land made of light, light that filled each rock with meaning and shone with sourceless radiance from the blue bowl of the sky. And he was not alone. The light had taken the shape of a man, white-robed, glowing from within as bronze glowed in the mold.

"Velantos son of Phorkaon, what do you ask of Me?"

He trembled, knowing that even as he had offered his gift he had not believed that anyone would receive it. He had gone through the ceremony to please Woodpecker and the priests. But the Presence beside him was more real than anything in the waking world. This was not a deity with whom one could make deals. He had submitted himself to Paion's judgment when he made his offering.

"Healing . . ." was the obvious answer, but Velantos knew even as he spoke that it was not true. "The destruction of my people's enemies—" he said then.

"As the people of this place have been driven from their homes, the children of the Children of Erakles will be driven from this city in turn," said the god. "But that day is a thousand years in your future. So I ask you again. What do you want?"

In this light, thought Velantos, everything was visible, even his own heart. He could not go back to his old life—all that he had loved was gone. Even freedom had little meaning now.

"Purpose . . ." he said aloud. "Repair my body well enough to serve my will, and give me a worthy deed to do before I die." That had the ring of truth. He could hear its echo resounding through unimaginable distances, and knew that the Fates themselves bore witness to his words.

His eyes were becoming accustomed. On Paion's face he glimpsed an enigmatic smile and eyes that gazed with implacable calm through his seeming to his soul.

"Your Lady chose well," the god said then. "A purpose you have, already destined. Unknowing, you have set your feet upon that path. Where you are going you will find Me once more, though day be turned to darkness and warmth to cold. Where the human wolves howl, My wolves shall hunt them, and My silver bow shall slay your enemies."

"And what must I do in return?'

The serene smile blazed. "What you most desire. You shall forge a Sword from the Stars for the hand of a king. . . ."

"Where? And how?" Velantos cried, but the shining figure only reached down and touched his leg. Pain blazed through him, so intensely he could not even scream. When he could think again, he saw that the scene was shifting, golden light whirling away in mists of silver into which the figure of the god disappeared.

When Velantos became aware once more, a cock was crowing, and the cool gray light of dawn filled the room. He lay without moving, savoring a feeling of being at ease in his body that he had not known since he was a child. The light strengthened and the white-clad priests entered the room, moving from one patient to the next.

"I have no need to ask how *you* fare," said the old priest, bending over Velantos. "The god's glory still gleams in your eyes." He lifted the light woolen blanket and with a delicate touch unwound the bandaging. "Look"—he called to the others—"Paion has touched him indeed."

At that, Velantos heaved himself onto his elbows to see. There was still a depression in the calf of his leg where the dead meat had sloughed away, but the raw flesh was now covered by smooth pink skin.

WOODPECKER DIRECTED THE MEN to set the heavy chest down on the stony ground and motioned them away again, watching Velantos warily. The smith stood beside the empty hearth in the workshop King Aletes had given him, waiting with the same serene smile he had worn since his night at Paion's shrine. The workspace was little more than a shed built on to the side of the megaron. The narrow space atop the akropolis left little room for a palace. But it would have to serve.

"They are all here—" The boy indicated the box. "All your things from the smithy at Tiryns. Kresfontes sent them with us. He said no use to have a smith without the tools of his trade. . . ." His voice faltered.

What had Velantos dreamed? He must have told the priests, for they seemed pleased. And the king must have been informed that his captive's wound had healed, for two days later men had come to fetch the two slaves to the citadel. Woodpecker had been told nothing at all.

He frowned resentfully. *Why won't you talk to me? Why do you gaze around you with that exalted smile?* He wanted the old Velantos back again, temper and all.

"That was thoughtful," said the smith. "Perhaps we should open it. My muscles are like clay." He laughed softly. "I will have to get my strength back before I can work again."

That sounded like an order, and Woodpecker bent to wrestle with hasp and pin. Sunlight gleamed warm from the metal within. "Here's a small hammer for you to begin on—" He held out the tool.

As Velantos took it his posture changed, the lines of his face firming, the hammer becoming an extension of his hand. Woodpecker sighed in relief. This was more like the man he knew.

"A good choice," the smith said softly. "My first teacher gave it to me when I was so young this was the heaviest tool I could hold. This is a hammer for fine work, not for weapons. But that is just as well. Before I make anything for the king, I have promised a votive offering to the god."

TWELVE

The third winter after Mikantor had disappeared brought cold such as the community at Avalon had never known. The water in the marshes froze and the Lead Hills were covered with snow. The houses where the priests and priestesses slept had never been intended for such harsh weather. As the cold increased in the black months that followed Mid-winter, Anderle gathered everyone in the pillared hall where they took their meals, built of solid stone with a central hearth. Hangings stretched between poles gave them a little privacy, but the air in the chamber was heavy with the scents and sounds of crowded humanity.

To Anderle, huddled in her heaviest woolen tunic, two shawls and a cloak, the pressure of so many other souls and bodies was almost unendurable. She knew how to shield her spirit at the great festivals, but this was Avalon, and these the people to whom she had spent her life learning to open heart and soul. Now, what she was picking up from them was physical discomfort and an undercurrent of fear.

Fear, she decided as she took the earthenware beaker of hot mint tea that Ellet handed her, was as debilitating as the cold, sapping heart and will. She cradled the beaker between her hands, luxuriating as its warmth penetrated cold fingers, and felt the tightness in her chest relax as she breathed in the fragrant steam. She wondered how were they faring in the Lake Village. They could insulate their walls with bundled reeds, but the stilts that kept the platforms that were the bases of their houses above the floods also lifted them into the wind. At least, in this weather, no one was traveling, and the only illnesses they had to fear were the ordinary coughs and fevers that came with the cold. Perhaps she should send to see if they needed more feverfew or white willow. With the Lake frozen there was no need to call for a boat. One could walk across it, with care.

No—she thought suddenly—she would go herself. In this cold even Galid must keep close to home, and for the moment the gray skies seemed to hold no snow. After their confrontation the previous year, she had hardly left Avalon, and then only when she was well guarded. After murdering Agraw, the warlord had held Cimara prisoner for a time before exiling her to a small farm. His threats to Anderle had been scarcely less dire, and there had been moments when she wondered if he would let her return to Avalon. But whether it was fear of the Goddess or some buried superstition of his own that constrained him, he had not raped or murdered either the priestess or the queen.

She glanced around her. Larel was telling a story about snow spirits to the children. Swathed in sheepskins, he looked like a snow monster himself as he acted out the tale. Ellet had joined Tiri and the younger priestesses near the fire, the only place where it was warm enough to spin. The whirling weight of the spindle drew out the thread, inducing its own trance as the spinner found the rhythm that would allow her to wind it onto the shaft, add more wool, and let the spindle spin downward once more. Conversation was only a surface distraction from that perpetual motion, in which an afternoon could easily be lost. The others had likewise found occupation for their hands or minds, or rolled up in their blankets to sleep some more.

She swallowed the last of her tea and moved quietly to the door, muting her energy so that no one would notice or question her. She spooned more herbs into bags, working quickly as the chill of the still-room numbed her hands, then shrugged on her own sheepskin cape, fleece side in. Lambskin mittens protected her hands. At the door she turned back and selected one of the walking sticks whose ends Larel had sharpened to give a grip on ice or snow.

Anderle nearly turned back as she came out into the cold air, but there was peace in that silent chill, and the air held no scent at all. She strode out strongly, willing her heart to pump, her muscles to kindle heat within. By the time she reached the center of the Lake, she was almost warm. She paused, breathing carefully, allowing herself for the first time to open her awareness to this strange white landscape that had replaced the world she knew.

The sky was covered by high clouds, through which a pale light diffused to illuminate the white world below. The Lake's expanse was a mottled mixture where storms had broken the ice and driven the slabs against each other in tumbled windrows, white shading into blue and gray. Here and there the surface shone where the wind had scoured away the covering of snow. Beyond, ice gleamed from reed and shrub and tree, and farther still, the white hills were studded with the black arrows of the trees. Only the Tor, kept treeless now for centuries, rose like an ancient pyramid in pristine white, crowned by the ring of stones.

She had huddled, trembling, beneath the howling fury of the winter's storms, but on this day what she felt was a profound peace. This was not the immobility of death but a focused stillness, as if the world had contracted all its forces into this cold kernel to await the moment when the time was right for those pent-up energies to break free.

The priestess took a careful breath, filling her lungs gradually to mute the shock of the icy air, then let it slowly out again. In and out she breathed, in the pattern to which she had been trained since childhood. Beneath the ice she could sense the gelid depth of water; above, the shimmer of ice crystals suspended in the air. To either side she extended her awareness, then behind and before, until she stood poised at the intersection of three axes of power. She took one step, maintaining that balance of forces, and then another. From here she could go anywhere, do anything. She stood poised at the still point of possibility.

This was not the unthinking liberty of a child, but a freedom created and upheld by a lifetime of discipline. *I have found the Center . . .* Anderle realized in wonder. *What can I, should I, must I do?*

From somewhere deeper within came the answer. *Change. . . .*

Ever since her childhood it seemed to her that the world had been not so much changing as running down, becoming colder, wetter, less organized, and the more people clung to the old ways, the more they seemed to lose. Even Galid's violence was a symptom of that decay of order, the spasmodic convulsions of a dying beast that does not understand its doom.

Or perhaps the warlord understood what was happening only too well. He felt free to flout their ancient customs because he believed that the floods that devastated the land were washing away the foundations of all law. With an inner chill that owed nothing to the cold she remembered the look on his face when he speared Agraw. He had *enjoyed* that. For such as he, even rape would have affirmed life too strongly. She doubted that even making him king of Azan would give him ease. The only feelings intense enough to reach Galid now were pain and fear.

"Goddess!" her spirit cried. *"If there is no hope, why have You sent me so many dreams and visions? If You have abandoned us, why am I still compelled to fight for Avalon?"*

Change . . . The word resonated in her awareness once more.

Balanced between earth and air and water, Anderle sensed within herself the one element that was lacking, the living warmth of fire, and recognized the moment when love and will could set the world in motion once more.

"Lady of Light . . . Fire of Life . . ." she said aloud, and the fire within began to pulse and grow. "I call You! Consume me, transform me! I offer myself as a channel for Your power. Change me, and change the world!"

For a moment she stood, the surging heat within contained by the cold outside. Then she whirled, arms opening, releasing the power within her to flare out before and behind her, to either side, above and below. Light exploded around her. When she could see again, she stood in a world of rainbows and crystal. The clouds had opened, and sunlight flashed and flickered from ice and snow. She laughed for sheer delight in the sudden beauty of it, and again as her cheek was kissed by a breath of air in which a hint of moist warmth had replaced the cold.

She struck her stick into the ice for support as it quivered beneath her, and looking down saw a crack angling toward the farther shore.

Goddess! Don't let me escape freezing only to drown! Still grinning, she hurried back toward the Tor. When she reached it, she looked behind her and saw the six intersecting cracks radiating from the place where she had stood.

In their center a gleam of open water mirrored back the light of the sun. But what she could see was only a visible expression of the energies she could feel vibrating in every direction. The transformation she had invoked was beginning, though she might never know what changed or how.

It was a few days later, when the snow was still melting, that Badger sent her a bouquet of small white lilies drooping on slender stems that they had found blooming at the edge of the hills. "Snowdrops," the hunters called them. Anderle had never seen them before. She found a vase to hold them and set them on the altar in the Hall of the Sun, beside the eternal fire.

WHEN WINTER CAME TO Korinthos, the mountains grew white with snow, heavier, men said, than any they had known in recent years. No doubt the men who were rebuilding the town appreciated the view, but Velantos and Woodpecker very quickly learned to hate the icy winds that swirled around the citadel. Even at the end of winter, when the lambing season had begun below, they wrapped themselves in wool. The walls of the fortress were not impressive, but they hardly needed to be, with such sheer slopes below. The megaron, too, was small in comparison with those of Tiryns and Mykenae, but it held enough benches for communal meals. When the body heat of Aletes' household was added to that of the central fire, it was almost warm enough to take off a layer or two.

Woodpecker reached for another beef rib and began to gnaw the bone. Soon after dinner began, he had stripped off not only the moth-eaten sheepskin he wore over his shoulders but the shapeless woolen garment beneath it. He had found the dry cold of the mountains affected him less than the damp chill of the marshes at home. It was Velantos, who had spent all his life in the milder climate of the Argolid, who warmed his hands in his armpits and muttered and swore. The serenity the smith brought from his temple-sleep had gotten him through the crafting of an image of his healed leg in bronze. Since then, their work had been a succession of repairs to utensils and jewelry and weapons, with nothing that was challenging and little that was interesting at all.

The city's former owners had not taken their cattle with them, so despite all the discomforts, there was plenty of meat, even for the slaves. Velantos had filled out again, and Woodpecker had put on more inches. He was taller than his master now, taller than most of Aletes' men, though some of the royal guard were from some northern land where they grew long of limb and light of hair.

King Aletes himself was a rather small man who wore the tall cap of kingship so habitually it was rumored he slept with it on. His queen, who was Doridas' daughter, sat on a stool beside him. He had put aside his northern wife and married the Korinthian princess in order to legitimize his rule. Woodpecker pitied the girl, who was even younger than he was, but at least she did not have to watch her father and uncle paraded on display at this informal meal. Aletes' first marriage had produced a daughter called Leta, a sallow, brown-haired adolescent with her father's big nose who sat at her youthful stepmother's side. Woodpecker wondered how they got along. From all he had heard, most of Aletes' life had been spent in a series of army camps. Perhaps the girl was so glad to live in a house she did not care who ruled it.

He tossed the beef bone to one of the hounds that Aletes kept in the hall and carefully wiped his mustache. It was still a little wispy, and the beard was no more than a fringe. It was coming in a much brighter red than the rest of his hair. The elaborate plucking and shaving by which the nobles tended their facial hair was not for him, but at least a smith could make his own razor, and he and Velantos kept each other trimmed.

As he passed Velantos the wine jug, the twanging lyre ceased and the megaron grew still. Aletes had risen, swaying a little. He did not water his wine.

"Cold enough for you?" The king laughed. Woodpecker shivered refexively. There had been a scattering of snow on the ground that morning and tonight would likely bring more. Their bench was at the very edge of the room, near the door. An icy draft stirred his hair.

"You southern men know nothing about cold! In Thessalia snow covered the fields, but even that's nothing to what they have in the north. In my youth I was a great traveler—" Wine sloshed from the golden cup as he gestured. Woodpecker took a drink from his own mug and sat back, wondering which of the stories they were about to hear again.

"I crossed the great mountains that hold up the sky, so tall they bear snow all year around, looking for the copper mines in the region beyond. And then I went even farther, into a land of mighty trees. I was a guest that winter of the king of the Tuathadhoni at Bhagodheunon. That was snow! Heaped up in drifts all the way to the thatching! It lasted until the Turning of Spring!

"He made me his guest-friend. Gave me gifts when the weather warmed at last, and sped me on my way. And when the time came for the Children of Erakles to return, I sent word to him, and he gifted me with good fighting men—" He gave a nod to the benches where his bodyguard were lingering over their wine. "Now the time has come to repay his generosity. A new messenger has come with agreements from the king.

"My daughter Leta shall cross the great mountains to marry the son of King Maglocunos, and with her shall go bridewealth from the treasure of Korinthos—gold and bronze, a chariot and horses from Thessalia, and a master smith of the Middle Sea!"

Woodpecker felt Velantos stiffen and cast him a quck look—clearly this was a surprise to him as well.

"The trade of the north will come to Korinthos," the king proclaimed, "and the trade from the rich lands to the south that our allies now rule. Ships shall come to the isthmus from east and west. We sit at the crossroads of the world, and we will make Korinthos wealthy beyond our dreams!"

The warriors surged to their feet with a mighty shout, cups raised high, and then, still chattering, began to stream out of the megaron. The little queen and the princess rose as well. Woodpecker wondered if *Leta* had been informed of the honor in store for her before this announcement was made. Her face showed no reaction, but she had clearly learned to hide her thoughts at an early age. He sympathized.

Velantos rose and picked up the striped blanket that served him as a cloak during the day. "You go—get a fire going in the brazier. I am going to talk to the king."

"Be careful." Frowning, Woodpecker watched the older man limp across the tiled floor and bow before the throne. Then he shrugged himself into his own wraps and went through the prodomos to the court beyond. As he turned down the staircase to the small chamber that he shared with Velantos, he caught sight of a woman—no, two females, one carrying a lantern, passing through the lower gate.

Where could they be going in this weather and at this hour? Silently he followed. The tiny flicker of light was bobbing down the path that led to the shrine of the Lady of the Doves. He had visited it once himself to make a thank offering after one of the serving maids had initiated him into the Lady's Mysteries. That had been on a sunny summer morning. It would be freezing down there now, with no shelter but the perimeter wall and the few cypresses that clung to the side of the hill. They would be lucky if the wine stayed liquid long enough to pour a libation.

The statue was a weather-worn stone whose contours barely suggested breasts and the cleft between curving thighs. But each year they gave her a new spear and shield. Up here on the akropolis even the Lady who presided over love had weapons, but perhaps that was just as well. In the marriage to which Leta was going, she might need to be armed.

"MY LORD, I BEG the favor of a few words with you," Velantos said in a low voice, and wondered why Aletes looked so apprehensive. *Perhaps he feels guilty about disposing of my future so blithely,* he thought with a bitter satisfaction. *Even though I wear rags, he remembers I was not born a slave.*

"Do you think I should have consulted you about the journey to the barbarians?" snapped the king. He edged to one side so that Velantos, who had been standing with his back to the hearth, had to turn. He supposed that with the bulky blanket broadening his shoulders and his face in shadow he might have appeared somewhat menacing.

"You are the king. You do what you will," rumbled the smith. "But I would ask . . ." he added carefully, "if you are unhappy with my work."

"Unhappy?" The king looked genuinely surprised. One of the guards started toward them and Aletes motioned him away again. "No, not at all.

Really, your talents are wasted here. What we need now, any man who can bang on a blade can do."

"You think they will appreciate me more in the northern wilds?" Velantos said dubiously.

"Not so wild as you might think." Aletes grinned, stroking his grizzled beard. "Great lords there, you will see. Think a lot of themselves. Before they seek our trade, they'll have to be impressed by our skills."

The smith strove to keep his expression bland, but his heartbeat had quickened with something that was not fear.

"They will not be impressed by the skills of a slave," he said flatly.

The king flushed and frowned. "You will go where I say if I have to send you in chains." The king moved back to his throne. He motioned, and Velantos knelt before him, hearing his knee joints crack as he got down.

"You can constrain my body," the smith agreed, "but not my craft. You can kill me, but I work for the Lady of the Forge, not you."

Aletes blinked, striving to assimilate the idea that he did not own his captive's will. "What do you want?"

"Set me and my forge boy free."

"Do you value him?" A spark of cunning flickered in the king's gaze. "Perhaps I shall keep him here as a hostage for your cooperation."

He thinks that fear will chain me, thought Velantos, and realized with surprising pain that it was almost true. But then, Korinthos could not have been conquered by a stupid man. The smith could play for his own life, but dared he risk the boy? Life, or that which made life worth living? Which would Woodpecker choose?

"I need him," he said quietly, hoping that his voice did not betray in how many ways that statement was true. "Send us together, outfitted like men of worth, and I will do marvels."

"Is he your *eromenos*?" the king asked curiously. Velantos was grateful that he did not use a cruder word. If Aletes thought he understood their relationship, it was more than Velantos did himself. But it didn't matter what the king believed, so long as he agreed.

Velantos managed a shrug. "Separate us and you might as well set us to herding goats on the hills, for all the use we will be."

"You won't go running back to Tiryns?"

Velantos felt his face grow bleak. "Tiryns—my city—is dead. Mykenae is fallen. There is nothing for me there, nothing for me in any of the lands of the Middle Sea."

Aletes sat back, rubbing his bare upper lip. "I didn't get where I am by refusing to take a chance—" he said finally. "I suppose we will have to find you some proper clothes . . ." The king sighed.

WOODPECKER JERKED AWAKE AS the door slammed. "Are you drunk?" he asked as Velantos stumbled against the bed frame. "Are you hurt? What did he *say* to you?"

The rawhide straps groaned as the smith sat on the edge of the bed and began to unwrap his woolen leggings.

"We're goin' on a journey—" Velantos gave an uncharacteristic snort of laughter. Woodpecker's nose twitched at the scent of wine. "Cap, cape, an' sword. Goin' to the end of the world, but we're gonna be *free . . .*" He swung his legs onto the bed, gave a hiccup, and fell over onto his side.

"Velantos!" Woodpecker exclaimed, but the only answer was a snore. He had seen men drink to drown sorrow, but why dull one's wits for joy? If there had been any wine in the room, he would have taken a swig himself to dull the frustration he was feeling now. The headache Velantos was likely to have in the morning would not improve his temper, but at least he would be conscious. He would have to give up the whole story then.

Woodpecker pulled the covers up and curved his body against the other man's to make a cocoon of warmth against the chill. His mind raced with speculation. *North . . .* he thought, with a curious lurch of the heart. In Tiryns the northern horizon had been walled by mountains. It had been easy to pretend the world ended there. But the citadel of Korinthos faced northward, and now they would be traveling into the heart of the Great Land.

But that was still a long way from home. . . .

———

WOODPECKER HAD HEARD OF mighty mountains in the country of the Ai-Ushen, but except for the very highest, men said that their coverings of snow melted when summer came. The mountains the travelers from Korinthos were facing now were surely the pillars of the sky. Tier upon tier they rose, snow and bare rock frowning above darkly wooded slopes and patches of meadow.

He drew in a harsh breath, feeling the chill air sear his lungs. The mountain dwellers they had hired to guide them through the passes laughed when they saw the lowlanders panting and said they had been spoiled by too much fat air. They might be right, thought Woodpecker as the path leveled and he paused to catch his breath. Certainly he had never known air so clear. A peak like a god's hat looked close enough to touch, though he knew it was many leagues away. Only the eagles traveled freely here.

This is Diwaz Pitar's land, he told himself, or at least it did not belong to Posedaon. They had been in Istria, waiting for the passes to clear, when they had felt the earth shake. He had still been recovering from the journey north along the coast, and for a moment thought he was at sea again. It was many days later when a battered ship brought news of the earthquake that had leveled what remained of the citadels of Tiryns and Mykenae. Queen Naxomene had been a true oracle. Korinthos had not fared much better, but even before they left, King Aletes had been planning to build a great house on the ruins of the old town below. The Dorians did not need the citadel. *They* were the enemy it had been built to repel.

He heard stone crunch behind him as the line of porters caught up, and started into motion again. They had abandoned the wagons several days ago. No wheeled vehicle could manage these paths. The princess was the only one riding, in a covered chair carried by the sturdiest slaves her father had been able to find, and when the way grew too steep, even she had had to get out and climb.

At least the trail was well marked. At regular intervals they would find a cairn of stones piled up in offering to the mountain spirits, or perhaps to honor men who had perished here. There was one just ahead—he bent to pick up a shard of granite to add to the pile. With all its dangers, this was a major trade route. The wealth of the northern lands—furs and amber and copper from the mountain mines—flowed over these passes, and in return came amphorae of wine and rolls of fine cloth and weapons and ornaments of worked bronze and gold.

"Move, boy—" grunted Velantos, and Woodpecker shook his head and continued to climb.

THAT NIGHT THEY CAMPED at the edge of a mountain meadow, in a three-sided shelter of rudely piled stone they roofed with a length of oiled wool. Velantos, who by the end of the day was limping badly, eased down by the fire with a skin of wine, too tired to do more than glare when Woodpecker asked if he wanted to climb up the slope a little to watch the sun go down.

Still grinning at that answer, the boy found a spot beneath an overhang of rock that gave a little protection from the wind and settled himself on a flat stone. Below him a fold of the mountains wound northward, its depths lost in shadow while the western sides of the peaks flamed with rose and gold. Earlier, he had seen some kind of brown goatlike creature bouncing from crag to crag, but now the mountains were still, the hush so deep it echoed in the ear like a sound. *Peace . . .* he thought, caught in the timeless moment, in which he was one with the pine tree that clung to the rock and the starry white flowers that nodded where a little soil had collected among the stones.

He jumped at the sound of voices and turned to see Leta clambering up the slope, followed by a panting maid. He rose politely, wondering why she had dragged the poor woman after her. Since her betrothal the princess had been strictly guarded, but her virginity was hardly in danger here, where no one in his right mind would take off his clothes. They were all wearing northern breeches and leg wrappings, as well as long-sleeved tunics, sheepskin vests, and cloaks of tightly woven wool.

"My lady—" He gestured toward the flat rock. "Will you be seated on your throne?" She had a pretty laugh, which was why he had said it. He grinned and remained standing, leaning against the cliff. "And enjoy this beautiful evening—" He gestured toward the distant peaks, where banners as deeply pink as the flowers that grew in another pocket of soil just below him flew now in a golden sky.

"It is beautiful," she echoed softly. "I will not forget this. To have seen it almost makes up—" She bit back her next words.

For being sent to the back of beyond to marry a stranger? He knew better than to say that aloud. The warm light gave her skin some unaccustomed color. She might be almost pretty if she were happy. He hoped her barbarian prince would be kind to her.

"Were you born a slave?" Leta said suddenly.

I was a king's son, so they say— thought Woodpecker. But if all the slaves who said they had been nobles before they were snapped up by pirates and sold were telling the truth, there would have been no one left to inherit the land. Anyhow, he supposed she would have thought his own homeland even more barbarous than the place to which they were going. *I must not think of that . . .* He fixed his gaze on the mountains once more.

"I don't mean to insult you—" she went on. "I used to think that nothing could be worse, but I have no choices either, only a more comfortable captivity."

Woodpecker cast a quick glance at the maidservant, who was doing her best to pretend deafness. But if she was her mistress's confidante, she would have heard all this before.

"We always have choices," he said slowly. Before they left, the king had formally given him his freedom, but their guards still treated him as a slave. "I choose not to think about what I was before, only about what I am going to be."

She nodded without speaking. The light was fading, the shadowed slopes deepening to purple as the sky turned to rose. The peaks on the other side of the valley were etched in black against that glowing sky. Warmth as well as light was ebbing with the end of day.

He was about to suggest they go back to the fire when a flicker of movement brought him around. The princess screamed as a lithe shape soared from the cliff, but Woodpecker was already in motion. His leap landed him on something with muscles like writhing snakes encased in thick fur. A feline screech assaulted his ears as he clutched with arms and legs, grabbing for a stranglehold. A clawed foot whipped past, searing his thigh. He yelled and tightened his grip convulsively, feeling the impact of each stone as they rolled down the hill.

He heard shouting, a javelin rattled past. A stone scraped his shoulder; another loomed up before them and they crashed to a halt. He could feel the muscles beneath him contracting; he yelled and wrenched and heard the crack of bone. The beast convulsed and then went limp. He collapsed atop it and lay panting as every part of his body began to complain.

"Woodpecker!" Someone had brought a torch. The light flickered over Velantos' agonized face, the princess behind him, the tall figures of the guard.

"I'm all right . . ." He struggled to sit up, blinking.

"Is it a lion?" asked Leta, leaning over him to see. Woodpecker turned and looked. Stretched out, the cat's body reached his shoulder; it was longer if you counted the tail, covered in grayish dun fur mottled with black spots. In death the creature was still snarling. There were black tufts on the flattened ears.

"A lynx," said their guide. "He hunt the chamois on the cliffs. It's good there's no cut. The skin will make a fine cape to witness your glory."

"My glory?" Thinking back, Woodpecker wasn't at all sure the cat hadn't broken its head on the rock before he broke its neck, but the men who had been sent as Leta's escort were grinning. One of them brought up his arm in a salute Woodpecker had never received before.

"Come on, hero," said Velantos, getting a muscular arm under his shoulders and heaving him upright. "We'd better see to your wounds."

THIRTEEN

*K*ing Aletes had boasted of the forests beyond the great mountains, but not until the travelers left them behind and crossed the plain that rolled away from their feet did Velantos begin to understand. On the other side of Danu's river the countryside belonged to the trees. Except where humans had hacked them down for field and meadow they flourished, a mixed forest of oak and beech and ash, of chestnut and elm, and the occasional glimmer of white where graceful birches grew. He did not believe the hills of his homeland could ever have been so thickly wooded. Such growth needed deep soil and abundant rain.

At first he had enjoyed the luxuriance, but soon he began to find the thick growth claustrophobic, or perhaps it was the atmosphere at Bhagod-heunon, where the king's smith and the king's son saw him and Woodpecker as rivals. He had done his best to keep his promise to King Aletes, but he felt a sneaking gratitude for the accusations, however unwarranted, that, after no more than two moons at the Dun had set him and Woodpecker on the road once more.

He heard the boy swear and saw that the pony had stopped short in the path. That was not unusual—the wretched animal had shied at the prospect of crossing streams, stopped short to snatch at every tempting hummock of grass, and spooked each time the wind stirred the trees.

"What is it this time?" asked Velantos wearily. They had been on the road since before dawn, if you could dignify the trail they were following by that name.

"I think the girth is rubbing his side," came the reply.

"Would it help to loosen it?" Velantos stumped back to see. Neither he nor Woodpecker had much experience with horses, a fact of which the pony, a sturdy chestnut-colored animal with a white blaze down his nose, seemed determined to take advantage.

"Only if you want your tools all over the road," grumbled the younger man. "I suppose we must be grateful to the king's smith for packing them, but they do unbalance the load."

"Yes, we should thank Katuerix—" Velantos said repressively. "Wherever we end up we will need to make a living. Those tools are more valuable than gold."

"I'm sorry!" Woodpecker burst out, stopping short in the road. "But it's not my fault! Princess Leta was kind to me because I reminded her of home. I never touched her, never even spoke to her alone! That would have been crazy. What did I ever do to make King Maglocunos doubt my sanity?"

"I know, I know." Velantos pulled a bit of leather from his pack and set about devising a pad. In truth, he suspected the princess had been attracted by Woodpecker's broadening shoulders and sweet smile. Now that he was growing into his height, he promised to become an impressive man.

"It is not your fault, lad. He doesn't know you as I do, and he seems to be one of those who believes in striking first and working out the rights of the matter later on."

"And I've no kin to demand compensation if he had succeeded in killing me," Woodpecker added bitterly.

Velantos finished adjusting the pad and tugged at the rein. They had left the Dun in a hurry, when Katuerix came with a warning that the king was sending men to kill the boy at dawn. *Go north*, the smith had told them. *"You'll be out of Maglocunos' territory when you reach the coastal plain. Go to the City of Circles. Rumor is they have had some bad floods, but they should be all the more willing to welcome another good smith there."*

"Are you sure he was telling you the truth?" asked the young man. "Maybe this was a clever way to get rid of his competition."

"I suppose so. I never could convince him I had no ambition to take his place with the king. But I thought he wanted my help experimenting with those bits of bog iron he found."

"I thought the war band *liked* me!" Woodpecker echoed, suddenly sounding very young.

"The men who came with us from Korinthos like you," Velantos corrected. "The others, the ones who've never traveled past the river, much less the great mountains, are suspicious of anything they don't understand. Be grateful the dog-king isn't hunting us with his hounds. His reasons have nothing to do with his feelings. If he decided to remove you, it is because he thought it the most practical way to deal with a threat. If he is not chasing us, it is because we have solved his problem another way."

"I suppose you would know . . . I may be the son of a king, but I did not grow up in a royal hall."

"A king's son?" Velantos looked at him in astonishment, then wondered why he had not recognized the breeding implied by the boy's manners. "You have never spoken of your history, and I am ashamed to say that I never thought to ask you."

"Why should you?" Woodpecker looked back with his swift grin. "I was doing my best to forget it myself. He ruled no great city like yours, and he died when I was only a few months old. I grew up in hiding, not that it matters now. Slaves have no history."

Velantos nodded. "I was beginning to learn that. But in the past year I have also learned that there is a world beyond my forge." He broke off as a grouse flew up in a clatter of wings and the pony reared. By the time they got the beast calmed, it was almost noon.

They were passing through a grove of mixed oak and ash; bracken grew thickly on the forest floor. Ahead of them sunlight glowed golden through the green leaves. In the next moment they had come out into a clearing where the ferns gave way to grass and summer flowers. In its center grew a group of three silver birches, fair as maidens bending in the dance.

"Potnia!" he breathed, making a gesture of reverence, for surely they were worthy of the goddesses. Clearly he was not the only one to think so. An image braided of straw and ornamented with strips of cloth had been bound to the trunk of the middle tree, its ribbons fluttering in the slight breeze.

"Should we be here?" breathed Woodpecker, his eyes going wide.

Velantos nodded. "We need to eat and let the pony graze. If we are respectful, I don't think that the Lady will mind. Help me unload the beast. While we are resting, maybe we can devise a better harness as well."

Katuerix had brought them hard loaves and a mixture of dried meat and fruit for the journey. Velantos laid a little of each at the foot of the tree and poured out some water.

"Potnia Theron, I salute you. Receive this gift, which is all I have, and ward our journey, and if we come safe to a place where I can earn my living, I will make you a better offering." If their pony kept misbehaving, she might get a horse. He stepped back, wondering if this was like one of the sanctuaries they had at home where the god spoke through the whispering leaves, but the air was still.

When he returned, Woodpecker was still looking anxious, but he had started eating with the appetite of the young and healthy as soon as the offering was set down.

"Have you ever thought of going home?" Velantos asked when he had taken the edge off his own hunger.

"No!" Woodpecker replied—too quickly? "It has been too long. They will all have forgotten me!"

Velantos looked at him from beneath bushy brows. The lad sounded very sure . . . and yet ever since Woodpecker had admitted his lineage the smith had been thinking about what Apollon Paion had said to him. *Where* was he destined to forge the Sword from the Stars? And for the hand of what king?

He had no answers, but when they continued on after their meal he began to suspect that some god had heard his prayer, for the pony settled down and they made good time. They slept that night within the protection of a copse of holly, and the following one in the barn of a farmer who traded them a good meal for mending a cauldron and sharpening his sword.

In this way they moved northward, crossing a range of low mountains and then faring downward through the forest. They passed from one steading to the next, sleeping in sheds or under the stars while the moon waxed from a sliver to nearly full. The country changed as the land sank toward the sea, the trees becoming more sparse, then giving way to bog and heathland except where cuttings and dikes protected rich fields.

WOODPECKER STOPPED SHORT, NOSTRILS flaring, as the changing wind lifted his hair. *Fire* . . . He had always feared it, but only when Anderle told him how she had rescued him from the burning house had he understood why. The scent faded with the wind, then returned, stronger. With time he had grown accustomed to the smoke from the forge, but this was no charcoal burner's fire. The reek of burning thatch was unmistakable now . . . the smell of a burning home.

He turned and saw that Velantos, who was leading the pony, had smelled it as well. "A house is burning—" He pointed across the heath, where purple heather covered the rough ground between stands of yew and pine. Now they could see a black plume of smoke beyond the trees. It was leagues away—whatever was happening would be over by the time they reached it. Even with a trail to follow, getting across this country took time.

These days Velantos had a few nightmares about fires as well, and in the past few days they had seen the charred timbers of more than one steading. Despite its apparent state of peace, this was a troubled land. They both kept their swords loose in the sheath and their spears within easy reach as they continued on their way.

Presently the heath began to give way to mingled marsh and pasture and winding channels that bordered isles of trees. It reminded Woodpecker strongly of the Vale of Avalon, and he found himself amusing Velantos with tales of his childhood there. That was not all he was remembering. Spending so much time outdoors had awakened skills he had learned hunting in the marches. And as the sun sank toward the west, he began to have the uncomfortable feeling that they were not alone.

He stopped the pony and leaned over to fiddle with the harness, scanning the heath from beneath the animal's belly. A clump of buckthorn trembled—was it the wind?

"What is it?" Velantos called.

"The fastening here seems to be loose," Woodpecker said loudly. "Could you take a look?" As the older man bent beside him he murmured, "I think we're being stalked. Can you reach your bow?"

The smith's eyes widened. "You may be right—have to unpack a bit to see . . ." Fortunately they had put the weapons where they would be accessible. Carefully he eased the bow from its place, holding it between his body and the horse to bend and string. He slung the quiver casually over his shoulder.

Woodpecker loosened the ties that held his spear and looked around him. The path wound among scattered clumps of thorn and alder, any one of which could conceal an enemy. Beyond them he glimpsed reeds. He couldn't see anything that offered good cover near the road. If he had been alone, he would have taken to the water, but that would mean abandoning the pony, and it was probably the gear the beast carried that the wolf's-heads wanted anyway. The pony's head lifted, nostrils flaring. *He smells them . . .*

As he straightened, Woodpecker caught another scent, the smell of baking bread. "They're out there, but I think there's a farmstead nearby. Move as fast as you can and be ready."

Velantos lifted an eyebrow at the decisive tone, but nodded and strode ahead, holding his bow casually under one arm. Woodpecker jerked on the pony's rein and hurried after him. They passed a tangle of trees and saw ahead a well-built house on its own isle, with a new fence of logs around it and bridges and wooden walkways to connect it to pastures and fields. In the next moment an arrow flicked past his ear and stuck trembling in the box that held the smith's tools.

"Run!" he yelled, jerking at the ties that held the spear, but Velantos ducked back to the pony's other side, fitting an arrow to his drawn bow. *Right,* thought the younger man. *He won't leave the gear.* But it was true that the horse was the closest thing to cover they had. The chestnut pony, sensing its danger, tossed its head and jerked diagonally across the road. Woodpecker followed, hoping the beast's movements were confusing the enemy as well, and grinned as more arrows skittered harmlessly across the path.

"Ho, the house!" Velantos' deep voice rang out. "Aid! Aid!"

Whether or not the farm had heard him, the call brought the bandits leaping from their hiding places. Another arrow parted Woodpecker's hair; then it became a race, with the snorting pony in the lead. As the animal, thank the gods, headed toward the gate at the end of the path, he found himself facing a tattered fellow with a spear.

He swung up the shaft to block a thrust as his training with the staff at Avalon came back to him, shifted to horizontal to jab, gulping as he felt the point go in. Not far enough—instinctively he had pulled the blow. The man yelled, but he was still fighting. He heard the dull ring of bronze and knew that Velantos had drawn his sword, but could not turn to see. Woodpecker whirled the spear around to block another blow, the steel shod butt striking with the strength of desperation. The man reeled back and Woodpecker thrust at the first one again, but only managed a slash. Then a third man knocked the spear from his hands and they were all around him.

He got his own sword free and began to swing, with so many targets, connecting more by chance than by design. He felt the sharp sting as a blade scored his arm. What a *stupid* way to die! Then arrows were falling all around him. The man who had cut him fell back, screaming, an arrow sprouting from his chest like some strange flower. A blur of shouting figures came across the road, led by a monstrous figure shrouded in dark fur.

"Run for the house, fools!"

As Woodpecker forced his limbs to motion, he saw his rescuer advance upon their enemies, a sharp bronze war ax whirling in each hand.

VELANTOS STRETCHED OUT HIS arm, biting his lip as the farm wife poured hot water over it and began to swab the wound. He told himself he should be grateful to have suffered nothing worse. He ought to endure at least as stoically as Woodpecker, who had made not a peep as the woman sewed up the long gash across his thigh.

The house was not so great as Bhagodheunon, but built on much the same plan, with a long central hearth in the middle section, where most of the household slept in beds built against the wall, and private quarters at one end for the master's family. At the other end was a space that in the winter might shelter the family's most valuable cows. The fire had been built up, and the merry blaze blessed the room with a warm golden light that reminded him oddly of sunset on the walls of Tiryns. In both cases, it gave a deceptive sense of safety.

He forced his attention back to their rescuer, not the master of the farm, as he had at first supposed, but his uncle, a warrior from the City of Circles who went by the name of Bodovos the Bear.

"The city was never the same since the great storm that struck us twenty-five winters past," said Bodovos. "But I think now the trouble began before, when the princes who should repair the gates and dikes spent the gold on their fine houses. Or maybe it would have happened anyway. When the gods line up in the heavens and then send a storm against you, there is not much that men may do."

He upended the elmwood cup from which he was drinking and held it out for more beer. A blond boy called Aelfrix was acting as cupbearer. He was the heir to the steading, if he could hold it. That was looking less likely, as whatever the weather did not destroy, the masterless men who now roamed the heath tried to take away.

"We heard there was work for smiths in the city," rumbled Velantos.

"Oh, aye, for fixing," said the older man. "Not so much call for things made new."

"And for warriors?" asked Woodpecker.

Bodovos fixed him with a sardonic smile. "You have not had your fill of fighting?"

"Was I fighting?" the young man said bitterly. "Seems to me I was about as effective as a maid with a milk ladle out there."

Velantos suppressed his own smile. After killing the lynx and winning the race, Woodpecker had been thinking himself a hero. It was better to learn sooner than later that he was not invulnerable, so long as the lesson did not prove fatal. Growing up in the shadow of his brothers, the smith had never had any illusions about his own skills.

"'Twas not so bad," the warrior said kindly. "You got in a few good knocks with the spear."

"Good knocks—and that was all. I had some training with the staff long ago, but I don't know what to do with the point."

"You understand that, do you?" Bodovos' gaze was suddenly intent. "Then you might make a warrior. Is that what you want to be?"

Woodpecker flushed. "If I am going to carry a sword, I should learn how to use it. I was hoping to find someone to teach me, that's all."

Bodovos began to laugh. "Perhaps you have. For my sins, I've the task of commanding the City Guard. A recruit who doesn't think the sun shines out of his arse would be a welcome change."

"You'll be leaving us, then?" The woman finished tucking in the bandage on Velantos' arm and rose.

"Buda, you know I must, and if you're wise you and the boy will come with me. Today's exercise should make that much clear. I can't stay with you, and without your own war band you will not survive."

The woman cast an anguished glance toward her son, who had brightened at the mention of the city.

"You can come back when times are more secure and Aelfrix is a man. The land will still be here—" Bodovos spoke heartily, but Velantos was not so sure. From what he had seen of this country, if they did not maintain the ditches constantly, the fields might very well be marshes by the time they returned. From the despair in Buda's eyes, he thought she knew it too. Face set, she turned and made her way to the door at the end of the room.

"We will go with you—" said Woodpecker with a quick look to make sure Velantos approved. The smith nodded. He could not help the woman, and despite Bodovos' gloomy words, the City of Circles sounded like a civilized place where he might almost think himself at home.

WOODPECKER DREAMED THAT HE was fighting. That was not unusual, since coming to the City of Circles he had trained with Bodovos almost every day. But this was not the exercise ground with its raked gravel and seats cut into the grassy bank around it from which observers could watch the play. He was on a hillside of sheep-cropped turf, where scents of gorse and heather mingled with a briny breeze from the nearby sea. The warriors who fought beside him were the boys with whom he had studied at Avalon, grown now to manhood.

Instead of staves they wielded spears, but even less effectively than he had used his in that fight outside Aelfrix's farm the spring before. Clumsy, they fell back before the band of wolf's-heads who were attacking them, and one by one they were brought down. At each death he redoubled his own efforts, but however many he killed, there were always more.

"Help me!" he cried, swinging his spear in a swift circle that repelled his foes, and like an echo, heard another voice that he knew to be Anderle's.

"Help *us*—" she called. "You are the only one who can! Mikantor, come home!"

He turned, seeking her, but the woman he saw bore first Redfern's features and then, for a moment, the bright eyes and red hair of the mother whose face he could remember only in dreams.

"I have no home!" he replied. "You abandoned me!"

At that, his enemies closed in. Someone grabbed his arm and he struck out, heard a yelp. Then cold flooded over him, cold *water*! As sensation shocked through him, consciousness shifted with a jerk and he opened his eyes.

Aelfrix was standing at the foot of his bed, rubbing his arm. Beside him Velantos held an empty bucket, his grim frown easing as he saw the sanity return to Woodpecker's eyes.

"Had a bad dream, did you?" asked the smith. *Another one. . .* Shivering, Woodpecker nodded. Velantos turned to the boy. "Did he hurt you?"

"Not much—" Aelfrix said valiantly. Since they arrived in the City of Circles, he had followed Woodpecker like a puppy.

"Next time, try the water first," the smith said sardonically. "Much safer."

"For you . . ." muttered Woodpecker. "Throw me a dry blanket, someone, before I catch an ague standing here."

"You'll warm up fast enough on the training field," Velantos said cheerfully, "or had you forgotten you were scheduled for an early session of spear drill with the guard?"

"Aren't *you* due for some more work with the axes?" Woodpecker tucked in the tail of his breechclout and reached for his tunic. Aelfrix was already trying to untangle the sopping bedclothes. Bodovos had judged that the same muscles that swung a hammer so efficiently would swing a war ax as well, and amused himself by tutoring the smith in his own favorite form. Velantos said it was like the war dance of his own country.

"Tomorrow," said Velantos, handing him his wide belt with the round bronze clasp embossed with the concentric circles that were the emblem of the town. "Today it's a conference with Lord Loutronix about a new mechanism for working the sea gate."

The city was built on the more or less circular series of embankments that gave it its name, based on islands dyked and raised by mud dredged out of the channels in between. Like the bank-and-ditch system of a clanhold, they provided successive rings of protection for the central island that housed the homes of the nobility and the temples and the palace of the Tuistos and the Mannos, twin monarchs of the city, and the Sowela, their sister and queen. The channels were linked by staggered openings, but the outermost ring was closed by a massive arrangement of chains and timbers, which could be raised or lowered to keep out enemy vessels or mute the fury of their greatest enemy, the sea.

"Good luck—" he replied. Lord Loutronix was notoriously resistant to any change. But in truth, there were times when Woodpecker wondered if any human ingenuity could stand against the anger of the gods. Not that he would ever have said as much to Velantos. The smith had found powerful patrons here, and, except for his complaining about the cold, he seemed happier than he had been since Woodpecker had known him.

He picked up his cloak, for even at the end of summer, mornings were cold, and started for the stairs. "I'm sorry I hit you," he said to Aelfrix, tousling the boy's fair hair.

"What about breakfast?" asked Velantos. "It won't help your spear work if you faint from hunger on the field."

"No time—" Woodpecker said cheerfully. "Besides, men have to get used to fighting on short rations in war!" He frowned as his gaze passed across the water on the floor, but the details of the dream were already fading. Shaking it off, he clattered down the stairs.

———

"Move forward together," barked Bodovos. "Cuno, get that shield up! You can't cover each other if you're wandering all over the field."

Woodpecker felt his movement mirrored by the man beside him, the slide of muscle beneath the other's skin as familiar as his own. In close-order drill everything became very simple. Their movements were as ordered as a dance. Of course the row of posts on which they were advancing were not going to do anything to upset that rhythm. The real test of their discipline would be the first time they faced a living enemy.

"Shield *up*! Sword *out*! Thrust left, thrust right, that's the way. Keep together and none of the misbegotten scum can get past your guard!" Bodovos' voice was already cracked by years of parade-ground bellowing. He never seemed to tire. He had promised to lead them against the lawless men who roamed the coast as soon as summer had dried the roads. Then they would find out how well they had learned the drill.

Beyond the heads of his companions he glimpsed the bright robes of the nobles who had come to watch them. Woodpecker did not mind putting on a show for them—they were paying for the food he ate and the armor he wore. He found himself straightening, head cocked at a more martial angle, and grinned.

The posts seemed to rear up suddenly before them. He thrust, felt the vibration of impact all the way up his arm as the blade bit wood, jerked it free, and strode past, two steps forward and then the turn in unison with his fellows, ready to face the foe once more.

"That's enough!" Bodovos' call carried above the smattering of applause from the banks where the observers were sitting. From the next field he could hear drumming where the acrobatic dancers who served the temple were practicing.

"Stand down. Red and Blue Files, that will be all for this morning. Greens and Yellows, take your javelins to the butts and see if you can hit them this time." There were a few good-natured protests and grumbles, but the men knew that their commander was not only tough, but fair.

"Woodpecker, 'tis your day for sword work, yes?" When the younger man nodded, Bodovos grinned. "Just as well—you'll give a good performance for our audience. The Tuistos himself has come to watch us today."

Woodpecker suppressed a twitch of nerves as he took his place in the ring. He knew he had improved. The bruise from the last time Bodovos had landed a solid touch to his ribs with the wooden blade had almost disappeared. It did not matter what a king thought of him. As the commander had told him far too often, in a fight, the only person whose opinion mattered was the one coming at you weapon in hand.

"We'll start with the standard drill, I think. You know the moves, but they don't know that—we can go a little faster and it will look good—"

Woodpecker gulped, but nodded agreement. Knowing the sequence didn't always help when Bodovos stepped up the pace, and the older man could swing that wooden blade very fast indeed. He settled into position, slightly angled with his left foot forward, shield up, sword ready.

Bodovos picked up his own gear and moved to face him, weaving in place, though whether that was to loosen his muscles or confuse his opponent Woodpecker did not know. He took a deep breath and let it out slowly in the way he had learned at Avalon, focusing, centering, letting his own tight muscles ease.

"Very good," murmured his teacher, moving in. "Sword high, now low, shield high, to the side, again . . ." The snick of the wooden blades and the hollow thud on the shield created a counterpoint to the dancers' drumbeat; he let himself relax into the rhythm, as if his motions were also part of the dance.

The commander stepped back, inviting Woodpecker to initiate his own attack, the same sequence of moves, but this time the younger man increased the pace, a decision he began to regret as his opponent grinned. Bodovos' response was another degree faster. Woodpecker narrowed his focus and attacked, then found himself abruptly on the defensive as the commander began to push him backward. One step and then another, now it was all he could do to keep that darting blade at bay.

His concentration wavered as his heel struck something behind him. He got his shield up as the next blow came in, but his balance was going. Bodovos' sword was a brown blur that he could barely see, much less counter. His own blade flew from his hand as the sword hit; a blow to the ribs knocked the breath from his body and he was falling, vision a whirl of stars.

When he could focus again, he realized that he was lying on his back on the grass and Bodovos was holding out his hand. He worked his left arm loose from the shield strap—the right was now throbbing fiercely, and he knew he wasn't going to be using it much today—gripped the man's callused hand and came to his feet.

"Sorry—" he said, looking around, and realizing his opponent had driven him to the edge of the field.

"Just so." Bodovos nodded. "It is as important to be aware of where you are going as to see what your enemy is doing. You won't be fighting your battles on a newly cropped and raked field. But I'll admit it was a low trick. The thing is, I wanted a dramatic finish, and you were doing well enough I couldn't be sure of taking you any other way."

Astonishment overwhelmed Woodpecker's pain as he realized that the light in the commander's eyes was pride.

"I'm getting better?"

"You are indeed—your early training laid a good foundation. Come on now, and I'll introduce you to the king."

FOURTEEN

*I*n the City of Circles, the harvest was celebrated at the Turning of Autumn. It was the city's most important festival. For weeks the people had been crafting sheaves of emmer and rye from straw and wood, for every grain that the fields had borne was needed for food. The early storm that had washed away part of the outermmost ring of the city had flattened much of the harvest. The shadows cast by the arrangement of rods used to calculate the seasons still marked solstice and equinox, but the movements of the heavens and the turnings of the year no longer seemed to correspond.

Velantos squinted upward, hoping to glimpse a patch of blue, but clouds still covered the sky. Last year's festival, the first year that they had been here, had been the same—more blessed by rain than by sun. Still, as an act of faith if not of affirmation, the people hung out their banners and festooned their balconies with green branches and fruits carved from wood when their orchards were bare.

And who was he to say they were wrong, thought Velantos as he stuck out his elbows to make room for Buda and Aelfrix to stand next to him. If he had learned anything during the three years since the Children of Erakles destroyed his home, it was that people needed hope, whether or not that hope was justified. The street was filling with people whom he had begun to recognize as friends as well as neighbors. That still seemed odd to him. When his own city died, he had been certain that he would never belong anywhere again.

"I can hear them," exclaimed Aelfrix. From somewhere beyond the

houses came the clash of brass cymbals and the regular vibration of the deep
drums. The boy bounced on his toes as he strained to see. He had grown
during the past year until he was as tall as Velantos, leggy as a young colt.
No doubt by the time he reached manhood he would be as big as Woodpecker, who seemed to have reached his full height, half a head taller than
Velantos himself.

"Of course you can hear them," Buda replied. "They must be right over
there—" She pointed at a gap between the buildings on the other side of
the street, where one could just glimpse the sheen of gray water. "But they
will have to go all the way around the fourth and third circles before they
cross the bridge to start around ours."

And a depressing circuit it would be, Velantos thought then. Last winter's
storms had taken the seaward houses of the Fifth Ring, and the docks
where the large ships moored. Now they anchored in a makeshift shelter
between the city and the mainland. Velantos had repaired an anchor chain
for one of the captains, a man called Stavros who traded with the cities of
the Middle Sea. It was pleasant to talk and share a cup of wine with someone who knew the warm lands of the south, but Velantos had learned not
to do it too often. For one cup could easily become several bottles, and a
sore head only added to his pain.

In more than one place the water had broken completely through, and
they had had to build makeshift bridges before the festival. The openings of
the circles were offset, so that a boat could reach the moorings below the
palace only by making a series of turns. Oared ships did so under their own
power, but those that depended on sails moored outside or were warped by
a system of lines and pulleys from one circle to the next. The circles were
linked by arched bridges, but many of the houses at the edges of each ring
kept small rowboats tied up behind their back doors.

A lad came down the street bearing a tray of the tiny sausages fried in a
twist of pastry that were a local delicacy, the tray suspended from a strap
around his neck. Velantos got enough for Aelfrix and his mother. The house
he shared with Woodpecker stood on one of the twisting lanes that ran
between the Processional Way and the shore. Those with the wealth to live

on the road were watching from their balconies, but the smith's breadth of shoulder and black glower had won a place for him and his household at the edge of the paved road.

He thought that the palace and circles of the city had about the same population as the citadel of Tiryns and the town that had sprawled below. Many of the traditions here reminded him of home. There too, families had gathered for the spring festival while more formal observances took place in the citadel. Their first year here, the servants they had inherited with the house had insisted that they must participate in the festival. Somehow, Buda and Aelfrix and even Bodovos had become part of their family.

A stir of anticipation rustled through the crowd as the sound of the procession grew louder. Now he could hear the tramp of hobnailed sandals. Two of those sandals belonged to Woodpecker, newly promoted to lead the Red File. Velantos found himself smiling.

"They're coming!" Aelfrix's voice squeaked in excitement. Above the heads of the people the carven images of the Powers that protected the city bobbed on their poles as if they were marching too. The crowd retreated in a wave of motion as the standard-bearers appeared, followed by the men with the drums.

First marched the Blue File, wearing mantles the color of the sea on a sunny day, edged with a spiral wave pattern. They were followed by the guild of fishermen, wearing their nets like ceremonial garments, and carrying the image of the Kraken, part god, part monster, who ruled the waters. If his powers were not quite the same as those of Posedaon, they were surely no less, here in this place that men had wrested from the sea. The leading merchants followed them, bearing models of the ships they sent to lands north and south in search of trade. This holiday signaled the end of the season for safe sailing, though these days they saw few vessels from the Middle Sea at any time. Next marched the Green File, whose mantles were embroidered with a stylized pattern of sheaves. They carried the veiled image of the goddess who gave fertility to the fields, and were followed by farmers and cooks and all whose trade had to do with feeding the city.

There was a pause, during which some of the neighborhood's children scampered into the road to strut in imitation of the soldiers. Then they heard more drums and cymbals, suddenly much louder, and the children scurried back to their families.

"There he is!" exclaimed Buda as the Red File came into view. "And doesn't he look fine!"

Woodpecker was leading his men, marching just behind the fellow who carried the image of a god whose pointed cap bore the horns of a bull. Woodpecker had laughed oddly when he told them of his promotion, and only later did Velantos remember that the younger man had once mentioned that his father's people were called the Tribe of the Bull.

From the bronze that banded his helm to the buckles on his sandals he was polished and shining, marching with an easy stride, as if his corselet of heavy leather sewn with plates of bronze weighed no more than Egyptian linen, and his wooden shield, painted red with the image of a bull, no more than a serving tray. Velantos had made the sword that hung at his side, almost the only bronze work he had done here, for with trade so disrupted, scrap bronze had become as valuable as gold. Woodpecker's crimson mantle bore a frieze of animals.

As the file tramped past, the reason for the delay became apparent. Farmers from the lands that supported the city had brought their finest livestock, among them, the beasts destined for sacrifice, and one of the bulls was balking. The people laughed as the herders struggled to get the creature going again, but Velantos frowned. If this animal was intended as an offering, its recalcitrance was not a good sign.

When the animals were finally past, Velantos sighed in relief. After them the Yellow File was coming, their standard a goddess who reminded him of Potnia Athana, their emblem the bird they called the oystercatcher here. She was the patroness of the artists and artisans of the city, those who worked in wood and stone, in thread and clay and glass. The smiths walked here also, hammers in hand. Velantos nodded respectully as they passed. Few in the city were his equals in skill, but he had not protested when they insisted that he should serve his period of testing before being admitted to their ranks. Perhaps next year, he would wear out a pair of sandals in this procession as well.

The palace musicians marched toward them, those who played flutes and horns walking, while the harps and lyres were borne in a wagon from which they could hear the occasional twang over the cheers of the crowd. The people hushed as behind them, the banner of the royal house appeared— two swans flanking the sun on a field of blue. Two trumpeters paused to blare a commanding note on the curving bronze lur horns. A chariot followed, drawn by two white horses. The box was carved and painted with spirals and chevrons, with gilding on the rails and the spokes of the wheels. In the box stood the two kings. They wore fringed kilts and white mantles sewn with gold, a wise choice, as it was said that the rich fabric covered a pair of rather flabby torsos. On their heads were pointed helmets of gilded leather with curving horns whose ends were tipped with tiny golden birds. And each king bore an archaic double-bladed ax, the Tuistos in his left hand and the Mannos in his right. Velantos leaned forward, wishing he could get a closer look. In the lands around the Middle Sea, kings bore such axes in the most sacred rituals—it was a design that had been ancient when Tiryns was new.

There was another space, and then more flute players, followed by girls shaking sistrums that filled the air with a shimmering sound. The priests and priestesses walked behind them, each arrayed in the vestments of their grades and gods. The temple dancers came with them, stripped to clouts and brief skirts of twined wool cords, interpersing cartwheels and backflips with the sinuous movements of the dance.

Velantos glimpsed a blaze of gold and turned. Everyone was shifting to stare down the street, as flowers turn toward the sun. A light wagon was coming, drawn by a chestnut mare. Sides, spokes and all were covered with gold. In the wagon rode the queen, robed in a saffron mantle so thickly sewn with golden oranments that she seemed an image cast in gold, steady and strong. From what he had heard, her image reflected reality. There was no need for the wagon to bear an image of the sun. She *was* the sun for her people, her rayed headdress scattering light each time the orb in the heavens peeked through a gap in the clouds.

"Sowela! Sowela!" the people cried, casting their remaining flowers into the road before her. "Bring us warmth and life again!"

Her face was painted so that one could not tell her age, for the sun had no age, unlike the ever-changing moon. In the south, men thought a god, bright and merciless, ruled the solar orb. But Velantos could understand why folk might seek light from a goddess here. He lifted his hands in adoration as she passed. It was going to be a long winter. *Bring us life,* he prayed as he felt the first drops of rain . . .

WOODPECKER TOSSED ON HIS straw mattress, twitching too badly from exhaustion to sleep. The guard had been ordered out to help the people of the Fifth Circle, and muscles he had thought hardened by Bodovos' training were throbbing with pain. At least he was finally warm and dry. Rain pounded dully on the thatching over his head, driven by a wind from the west that moaned around the eaves. Winter had been cold and relatively calm, but as the wheel of the year rolled toward the Turning of Spring the elements seemed determined to hold off summer's coming with a defense more violent than anything the city had ever known. For three days storms had battered the coastline, with the promise of worse to come.

Tonight he would have welcomed one of his dreams. He no longer fought the visions, frustrating himself and frightening his friends. To walk the green fields of the Island of the Mighty—the native land that his conscious self had tried so hard to deny—would have been a relief after such a day. However soggy, the island was at least solid ground. He hoped that Velantos believed that the nightmares had ceased. At least it had been some time since they had used a bucket of water to awaken him.

He told them he did not remember what he had been dreaming, but it was not true. More and more often, the memories were bleeding into his waking awareness, so that sometimes it was the City of Circles that seemed unreal. And he carried his knowledge of the City with him when he walked on Avalon. Still, if he looked hollow eyed with strain, he was not the only one whose face bore witness to his anxieties. Tonight, he could probably have shouted without disturbing Velantos, who lay snoring on the other side of the bed. The smith had spent all his waking hours with the builders.

By the time he fell into bed, he was far too tired to worry about the younger man.

When Velantos returned today, he had worn a look Woodpecker had not seen since Tiryns fell. All their efforts were failing. Those who lived on the outermost circle had been told to seek refuge in the inner rings. Finding room for them would not be a problem—many of the City's people had already fled to the mainland, preferring to battle human foes than pit themselves against the Powers of the Sea.

And yet, would one of his dreams have been any improvement? His visions had shown him Belerion sacked by seaborne raiders, and the farm where he had herded sheep crushed by a rockslide. He saw Galid's men tormenting a captive while their leader laughed. There had been other scenes in places he recognized as belonging to other tribes. By now he probably had a better idea of what was happening on the Island of the Mighty than anyone but the Lady of Avalon. The state of affairs was not much better than things in the City—he suspected that things were not much better anywhere. But in this liminal state between sleep and waking, he could admit to himself that the island was *home.*

He wondered if he could summon a vision of the holy isle. Surely he would find peace there. He took one breath and let it out slowly, and then another, closing his eyes. He would imagine he was looking at the Tor by moonlight. He smiled a little, seeing the pure line of the slope, the faint gleam on the standing stones that crowned the hill. But the image was not quite what he had expected—within the circle he glimpsed a warmer glow. As the light grew stronger, he realized that someone had lit a fire on the altar stone. At least, at Avalon tonight there was no rain.

As he drifted toward that light, he felt a vibration in the air. The priests and priestesses of Avalon stood within the circle of stones. They filled the night with a full-throated shifting shimmer of sound. This was no full moon ritual, but one of the great magics, forbidden to uninitiated eyes. The elder priests had been quite explicit about what could happen to any child who dared to spy. He willed himself to turn away, and realized with a thrill of fear that he was still moving toward the hill.

A stand of Singers . . . they had called it, when seven notes were sounded to weave a tapestry of harmonies. Like a leaf caught in the current he floated toward the sound. A single trained voice lifted above the others.

"I call the one who will bring us hope!" Anderle scattered incense upon the fire that burned on the altar stone and a sweet smoke swirled upward. "I call the one who will comfort the bereft and rebuild what is broken, he who shall defend the weak and command the strong!"

At each word, Woodpecker remembered the visions of disaster that he had seen, and felt once more his frustration at being unable to do anything to change them. With every tone the buzz along his nerves intensified, if he had nerves here. He struggled to escape, but this was no current; it was a vortex that was drawing him inexorably in.

"I summon the hero who will save our people! I call the Defender!"

The smoke of the incense was spreading in a luminous cloud above the altar, curling around him. He had always been an invisible witness before.

"Holy Goddess, show us the one who will save us! Hear and appear! Hear and appear! Hear and appear!"

Anderle's eyes widened and he realized that she could see him. The sound wavered as one of the priestesses fainted, then steadied as the others gathered their forces and sang on.

"Mikantor—" the priestess whispered, reaching out to him. "They said you had died, but I knew the gods would not be so cruel! Come back to us! Come home!" Her fingers passed through his arm.

He trembled, torn between the desire to save the people whose suffering he had seen and the memories of all his failures.

"I am no hero—" He shook his head, not knowing whether she could hear. "I cannot help you!"

"You are the Son of a Hundred Kings!" she exclaimed. "For this you were born! For this you have been saved!"

He was still shaking his head. Could he persuade her that this was his ghost, returned from the Otherworld? Meeting Anderle's fixed and glittering gaze, he suddenly doubted that even death could release him from her demands. For a little while, between his twelfth and fourteenth years, he had believed that he was destined to be a king. Instead he had become a slave. His body had been freed, but invisible shackles bound him still.

I am not . . . I cannot . . . I am not worthy. . . .

"Goddess!" Anderle flung up her hands. "Show us Thy will!"

At the words, the fire on the altar blazed. Glowing within the smoke he saw the shape of a woman with laughing eyes and fiery hair. Then it thinned and sharpened, until what hovered before them was a sword. From the wonder in the eyes of the priests, it was like none that they knew. But he had seen it, or one that was similar, in Velantos' hand. And yet not entirely like, for this blade was a brand of silver fire.

"Will a Sword from the Stars convince you?" came her voice, sweet and low. "The priestess summons the Defender, and the Defender will bring the smith to My forge!"

Velantos! thought Woodpecker. Had this path been laid for both of them by the gods?

The Sword flamed wildly and he was whirled backward, outward, in an explosion of light and sound, until he found himself sitting upright in his bed, heart pounding as if he had run a league, sweating as if he stood next to a fire. Rain drummed on the roof—no, there was a sharper sound to that pounding. Someone was beating on the door.

From below he heard voices. Aelfrix or Buda, who slept by the hearth, must have answered. He could not make out words, but the sharp tone was enough to launch him from the bed. He was already shrugging into his tunic when Aelfrix flung open his door.

"Woodpecker!" cried the boy. "Waves have washed across the Fifth Ring, and the Fourth is in danger. They want every man who can lift a sandbag to build up the barriers and carry people to safety."

He finished tying his sandal and jerked his head toward Velantos, who had not stirred. "Wake him if you can—he'll be needed. I'm on my way to the guardhouse. May Ni-Terat preserve us all!"

It was only when the door had closed behind him that he realized he had invoked the protection of a goddess of Avalon.

VELANTOS ROSE FROM EXHAUSTED sleep like a man fighting his way up through deep water. That was not so far from the truth, from the sound of the rain. He rubbed his eyes and recognized the fragile flicker of an oil lamp instead of the gray dawn-light he had expected. Aelfrix was standing with the lamp in his hand, mouth opened to call him again. Woodpecker's side of the bed was empty, the covers tumbled on the floor. He took a deep breath and tried to focus on what the boy was telling him.

Waves . . . the storm . . . He found it only too easy to interpret Aelfrix's stammering attempt to repeat what he had heard. Swearing, he heaved himself out of the bed. Every muscle still ached from yesterday's labors, but the storm would not wait for him to heal. By the time he had dressed and wolfed down the bannock Buda pressed into his hand, it was raining even harder, the wind howling like the Kindly Ones in pursuit of a sinful soul.

The streets were clogged with sodden refugees bent under bundles or pulling wagons crammed with whatever they had managed to save. Velantos pushed past them, suppressing an urge to apologize. His head told him that he had done all he could; his heart cried that he should have done more. *This is not my city!* he told himself, but guilt rose in a tide as dark and as devastating as the sea.

As he neared the bridge from the Third Ring to the Fourth, he saw collapsed houses, and then a section where the ground had washed out all the way to the road. Someone ran toward him, shouting that the western bridge was gone. Velantos groaned. His first home had perished in fire; this one seemed to be dissolving around him.

He forced his way back through the crowd toward the southern bridge. Surely it would still be whole. He could see better now—the sky was growing pale. Beyond the rooftops the masts of the ships that had taken refuge in the lee of the city tossed in the swell. He hoped that Captain Stavros was weathering the storm.

The southern bridge was blocked by a broken wagon. By the time Velantos had helped to drag it free, it was full day. When he reached the Fourth

Ring, he found men knocking down houses to brace makeshift dikes with their timbers. The rain had eased up, but the sea was still rising as a strong offshore wind pushed the water higher. There had been some talk of an evil alignment of sun and moon that lent strength to the waves.

Even as Velantos labored, a conviction was growing that the City of Circles had been abandoned by her gods. The work had left him no energy to curse them, but he vowed silently that while he had the strength to defend his new home, she would not be deserted by men. He had failed before; he would not give up again. Some distant awareness told him that this was not entirely logical. No man could fight fate. But he was too locked into the work before him—the next wall, the next piece of wood, the next dissolving bank—to care. His right arm grew weary from swinging the granite hammer and he switched to his left. It required neither precision nor skill to break down walls. With the sun invisible behind the clouds, the day seemed endless. They said that in Hades the wicked were doomed to repeat the same endless tasks. Perhaps he *had* died in Tiryns, and was only now receiving his punishment.

And yet a moment came when he realized that the light was fading. The storm had driven them back to the bridge and someone was shouting that they must abandon the Ring. Shivering, Velantos thrust his hammer through his belt. Water lapped at his feet, but for a moment the wind had stilled. Beneath his feet the ground was trembling. As the road crumbled, he ran.

The Third Ring was in chaos, even the pretense of organization maintained by those who had fought to save the outer circles gone. Velantos saw the Tuistos trying to move down the street with his guards, his elegant tunic muddy and a bruise on his brow. He was giving no orders. The smith doubted that anyone could have heard him, or would have obeyed them if he had tried.

As he neared the bridge that led toward the center of the Third Ring, the brazen note of the lur horn cut through the moan of the wind and the clamor of the crowd. He glimpsed white robes and the glint of gold. The Sowela was coming across the causeway from the palace. Rumor said she was the real power in the family, but what in the name of the goddess did she think she could do here?

Her attendants shared his opinion. One of the priests had knelt in the road, begging her to return to the palace. It was built of stone, proof against the sea.

"And what of all those whose homes are not built of stone?" she said clearly. She wore no face paint now, and she looked her age. He recognized the expression he had seen when his brother faced the foe. "My place is here." She picked her way toward the broken bridgehead. Beyond it there now lay a clear strip of tossing water that stretched all the way to the open sea. The priests fell back as she climbed to the edge of the shattered stonework, lifted her hands, and addressed the waves.

"Master of the Deeps, I, the Sowela of the City of Circles, stand here before you." Her voice seemed suddenly louder, and he realized that the wind had eased, as if the gods of sea and storm were waiting to hear. "You have taken so much already, let your hunger be appeased. Spare my city! We will give you many fine bulls and stallions, and if no other sacrifice will content you, I stand ready to make the offering . . ."

A cry of horror went up from those who had been close enough to hear. One of the priests started toward her, but something in her stance held him still. Velantos' stomach clenched as he realized it was not Aiaison whom she resembled now, but Naxomene. He had been amused by the pretensions of this northern royalty, but now he found himself bending in the full formal obeisance he would have offered his own queen.

For a moment it seemed that her prayer had been heard. Then someone screamed. Velantos looked up. A surge greater than any they had seen yet was rolling in from the sea. Water crashed against the remains of the outer Rings, demolishing what was left of them in an explosion of spray. But the original wave, focused and forced inward, rolled straight toward the queen.

Shouting, he tried to reach her, slid on a patch of mud, and went down. As the wave hit he saw the Sowela plucked from her perch; then the spray whirled around her and she was gone. In the next moment the same mighty force had seized him. He had a moment of wonder that his death should come by water instead of fire; then he was slammed hard against some unyielding surface and fell.

———

VELANTOS SURFACED IN A whirl of pain, an agonizing pressure in his chest that came and went until he arched, coughing furiously, and nearly passed out again.

"Stay with me, damn you! I won't lose you now!"

He looked up, saw an agonized face above him—the boy—no, the man, bright spirit shining within. Woodpecker held his face between his two hands, forcing the older man to meet his gaze, and Velantos felt his heart lurch at what he saw in those eyes.

"You *will* live!"

"You keep . . . saving . . . me. . . ." Velantos breathed.

"You have saved *me*, more often than you know," muttered Woodpecker. "Can you walk? Never mind," he added, as Velantos winced. "I can carry you."

He nearly fainted once more as Woodpecker hoisted him up and got his right arm across his shoulder.

"Where—" He grated as they lurched along. The wind seemed to have died down. In the street, people were picking through the sodden tangle of debris and belongings that the storm had left behind.

"Stavros' ship is waiting. Bodovos arranged our passage."

Velantos tried to stop. "The city—the queen—can't desert—again!"

"The queen is lost, and the gods know what has happened to the kings," Woodpecker said flatly. "Her sacrifice seems to have stopped the storm, but the city is broken. Bodovos' oath holds him here. He released me from mine in exchange for my promise to save his sister and her son. Men are looting already. Stavros wants to weigh anchor before someone else realizes the ship is a way out of here."

Velantos groaned as Woodpecker stumbled over a loose board and continued on more slowly. "Leave me, and go . . . while you can." He felt the younger man shaking his head.

"Your tools are already loaded, and you are going with us if I have to knock you out again!"

"Where?" Velantos coughed.

"To the Island of the Mighty . . ." The younger man's voice wavered oddly. "There is nowhere else to go."

WOODPECKER WOKE TO THE sound of water and the briny scent of the sea. What dim recollection he could muster told him that this was to be expected. But it seemed odd that he should be wrapped in something soft and warm with the rank smell of cured leather, hearing voices that he ought to know above the slap of the waves against a wooden hull. His memories of the last week were a chaotic mix of heaving seas and battling winds that had tossed the ship like a toy. There was a foul taste in his mouth, his throat was raw, and the muscles of his belly sore.

I'm in a boat, he thought, breathing carefully. *The sea nearly killed me on the way to Tartessos too.* And yet the surface below him was no longer moving. He seemed to be lying at an angle, and his stomach, though cramped with emptiness, was at peace. Above him a piece of tightly woven cloth stretched over hoops provided shelter. A new realization came to him. *The boat has come to shore.*

The last few days were a series of distorted images, including some that must have been dreams. He hoped they were dreams. He had been in a city that was being drowned by the waves, but his most vivid images were of an island greater still, crowned with temples and palaces and a great mountain that exploded in a column of ash and flame. There was someone he had lost—the grief of that parting brought tears to his eyes, but now it was all slipping away and he could not even remember her name.

He tried to sit up and found himself weak as a babe, but his grunt had been heard. Aelfrix ducked back under the shelter and knelt beside him, grinning triumphantly.

"You're awake! Velantos said that reaching solid ground would help you. He'll be so pleased!"

"He's all right?"

"His ribs still pain him, but he's getting around," said the boy. "When we first lifted anchor, what with him raving with fever and you puking your guts out, we wondered if either one of you would survive."

Aelfrix helped him to sit up and gave him some water, and he began to feel some strength coming back to him.

"Where are we?"

"Somewhere on your great island. Stavros says it's a place where many ships put in to trade. If you feel up to it, come and see."

He nodded, and managed, though his head swam and he had to sit down several times, to crawl from his bed to the ship's side. They were beached on a muddy shore where a broad river had cut a channel toward the sea. Tall grasses waved in the sea breeze, and beyond them the land was a mixture of marsh and meadow rising to some low hills. He looked at the blue sky beyond and realized that it was beautiful. There were huts on the shore, and from one of them smoke was rising, but at present no other ships were drawn up on the sand. At Aelfrix's shout, Stavros and some of his crew came down the strand, with Velantos hobbling after them.

They lifted him over the side of the ship and set him down. He took a step, breathing deeply of the sweet air.

"Woodpecker, thank the gods—" Velantos reached out to grip his hand.

He shook his head, a wellspring of inner joy that had been frozen for five years beginning to melt at last.

"No—you must call me Mikantor now, for I have come home, and I will never deny my name again."

FIFTEEN

*T*irilan, daughter of Anderle, why have you come here?"

She took a deep breath, feeling the wind that came through the open doorway stir her fair hair, still damp from the bath with which the ritual had begun. Mist lay heavy on the marshes around them, but the Turning of Spring had come, and the sun was shining on Avalon.

"I seek to know in order that I may serve . . ." It was the expected answer, and Larel and Ellet, who were presiding over the ceremony, smiled.

Tirilan stood in the Hall of the Sun before the assembled priests and priestesses of Avalon. Light shafted through the upper windows to illuminate their veiled or hooded heads and the frescoes that told the story of the People of Wisdom who had come here from across the sea. She had already demonstrated her mastery of the skills required of a priestess and been purified. At any time during that process she could have withdrawn. But there was no retreat once these vows had been sworn.

And what if I had answered that I am here because my mother willed it, and since Mikantor is lost to me, the calling of a priestess will suit as well as any? Tirilan wondered then, but she did not say so. Those who regretted the loss of the laughing child she had been five years ago ascribed the change in her to maturity, not knowing of the grief she had not been allowed to show. At first, that had been because Anderle refused to believe Mikantor dead, and later because to mourn him openly might make people wonder why they cared so much about one Lake Village child. Although if he was dead, why did it matter if everyone knew how the Lady of Avalon had saved Uldan's son from the fire? Confirmation of his suspicions could hardly make Galid hate her mother more. She glanced at Anderle, who presided from a great chair below the altar on which burned the eternal flame.

The priestesses praised Tirilan's gravity, and whispered that she would make a fine High Priestess when they thought she could not hear. *I would have made a better wife for Mikantor,* she thought rebelliously. She closed her eyes, trying to summon up his features. But by now he would look different anyway. If he lived . . . She had always thought she would know if he died, but if he was still alive, why had he sent no word?

"Know that the vows you take here bind you to a holy calling," the priest said then. "If you do not fulfill them in this life, you will be called to do so in another. This is not an obligation from which we can release you. Indeed, some of us fulfill that obligation by serving the gods in this life, and some have pledged themselves to serve from life to life until all others walk in the Light as well."

In the Light, and in the Divine Darkness, Tirilan added silently, remembering what she had been told in the women's Mysteries.

"When you were initiated into womanhood, you were taught that your body is the Temple of the Goddess," Ellet said then, "and that it was your right to choose when and with whom to share it. But now we lay upon you a greater commitment, for when the will of a trained priestess is focused in the act of love it can raise a mighty power. Can you swear that you will give yourself only in the sacred times and seasons at the festivals, or as required for the good of the people and the land?"

To lie with Mikantor would have been a holy ritual . . . thought Tirilan, but her lips moved in the required answer. Chastity was not a problem—she had no desire to lie with anyone, and if it was required of her, she could hope the Goddess would use her body and she would not remember.

"Do you swear that you will not speak of the Mysteries to those who are unsworn?" asked Larel, and again Tirilan agreed. She hardly ever even *saw* anyone who was not an initiate, living here on Avalon. She looked at the faces of those who stood in the circle, old and young. They had loved and taught her. She would try not to disappoint them.

"Do you swear that you will always seek to serve the Divine Spirit whom we see in the goddesses and gods? For all the gods are one God, and all the goddesses one Goddess, and there is one Initiator. Will you look for that Spirit in the soul of each woman and each man? Will you offer whatever help you may to those who come to you?"

That was the vow that had been most discussed among the students. It was, if you thought about it, a terrifying commitment. And yet this was the promise that troubled Tirilan least of all. *Perhaps I* have *been a priestess in some other time,* she thought then, for she found it hard to understand why anyone sworn to serve the Goddess would not seek to share Her love.

"Do you swear to obey all lawful commands given in the Lady's name?"

Tirilan suppressed a shiver, knowing her mother was watching her from beneath that veil, for surely any "lawful command" she might be given would come from the Lady of Avalon. *I have no choice now, having agreed to all the rest,* she thought numbly, and swore.

And now Anderle was rising from her throne, coming forward to take the place of the hierophant between the priest and priestess.

"Daughter of the Goddess, you have proven your fitness to stand as priestess before us, and you have taken your vows, but know that consecration comes not from us, but from the gods. If the Goddess does not accept you, then no human power can do so. Go forth, then, to face your ordeal, and return to us as a priestess of Avalon."

Tirilan made her obeisance. *It is a dance. We bend and sway and play our parts, and so I will play mine . . .* Sometimes people were lost during their testing. Perhaps she would die, and it wouldn't matter after all, except, of course, that she had just promised to fulfill the initiate's oath in another life if she failed in this one. But the next time around, she would not be mourning Mikantor.

THE TOR LOOKED AS it always did, a pointed hill covered with green turf, its long slope notched where the spiral path had been carved out generations before. To climb it did not seem much of a challenge, thought Tirilan as she gazed upward. She had been scampering up and down that hill since she could walk. She had hoped for a day of sunshine like yesterday, but what she had was swirling clouds, as if the mists off the marshes had decided to complete their conquest of the Vale by overwhelming the Tor. *Just so the waves rose up to cover the kingdoms of the sea,* she thought then. No doubt the image was a memory of the frescoes in the Hall of the Sun. She closed the gate behind her and started up the path.

Once, when she was about ten, she had vowed to count the steps on the spiral path, and been insulted when the priestesses laughed at her. Later she had heard that it had been tried many times before. It made sense that the number should vary with different lengths of stride, but it was said that even for the same person, pacing carefully, the distance would never be twice the same.

"In the name of the Goddess I shall ascend the holy mountain," she began the ancient prayer. *"In the name of the Lady of Wisdom, in the name of the Lady of Darkness. In the name of the Lady of Sovereignty I shall walk, and in the name of the Lady of Ravens. . ."* The names of those who ruled light and love, mind and emotion, and the solid, supporting strength of earth itself, all these she called, and if a male initiate climbing this hill had called upon the same powers in the name of the God, it was only the images, not the essence, that would have changed. Or one might pick and choose, or call both together. Another watchword of the Temple came to her—"The symbol is nothing, the reality all . . ."

Now I understand, Tirilan thought in amusement. *The purpose of this climb is to make me review everything they tried so hard to stuff into my skull!*

The prayer brought her to the first turning of the path, and she paused and bent to dig her fingers into the soil. The scent of moist earth and green grass rose around her, more heady than incense. *This!* she thought. *This, not some priestly abstraction, is what I serve. While we are in bodies, this is where it begins. The priests forget that sometimes, with their meditations and austerities. Earth is holy. Our bodies are holy. We must learn to live in that harmony.*

For a moment, then, kneeling on the green turf, she glimpsed a truth that, if it had been part of her training, she had never recognized. If she must be a priestess, she would not stay safe at Avalon. Anderle had plenty of people to say the prayers and perform the ceremonies. Tirilan would go where the need was, to teach and heal if she could and where she could not, to bear witness and offer comfort. The decision released a surge of warmth—or perhaps the sun was coming out. She looked up and saw the clouds thicker than ever, but they held a golden glow, and it was warmer, as if the sun was trying to break through. That was a good omen, she thought, as she started walking once more.

Exercise had lifted her mood as well as warming her body. As she continued to climb, she found herself humming the prayer. She had brought down the power; it was only sensible to follow its path upward, even if she must first forgive her mother in order to receive the blessing of the Lady of the Moon. Why, she wondered, were they so often at odds? She had heard that mothers and daughters were often so, and she supposed it must be harder when her mother was responsible for her as a priestess as well.

But the result is that she tries to rule me body and soul, she thought resentfully. She made the next turn, and a playful wind stirred her hair and stroked across the long grass. She sensed that she had entered into the presence of the Lady of Craft and Song, and surely this was where she would find the words to make her mother understand her need.

She laughed, her spirits unexpectedly lifting. *Anderle had to let me take this journey alone. No one else can live my life. No one else can give it meaning, not my mother, and not—*the thought came to her suddenly—*even if he had lived, not Mikantor.*

Tirilan strode out more strongly as the path curved around to the right and across the long axis of the Tor. Wind swirled the mists around her, carrying the scent of flowers. Was that perfume borne up from some protected meadow in the marshes? Certainly there was no such garden on the Tor. She felt soft turf beneath her feet and looked down. Could she have strayed from the path? In this mist, anything was possible, but she had gone neither up nor down. More slowly, she continued, striving to see.

And then, between one breath and another, the mists were gone.

She stood in a world of green—turf whose color was so intense it seemed to glow from within, verdant hedges, a rowan tree whose leaves burned with green fire, and beneath it a woman dressed in a floating garment of the color of sunlight through new leaves, crowned with white flowers. For a moment Tirilan thought it was her mother, for this Lady had the same dark hair and eyes. But Anderle had never allowed her hair to flow so freely, had never considered her with such a luminous gaze. This was the Lady Mikantor had seen.

"And yet I will call you daughter," said the Lady, as if Tirilan had spoken aloud, "for you are all like children to me. Be welcome, Eilantha, to my realm."

"Why do you call me by that name?"

"It was your name, when first we met upon this hill." The Lady smiled. "You do not remember, but I remember each face you have worn when you found your way between the worlds. I offer you now the choice that I have offered before—stay with me, and you need fear no loss again."

Tirilan blinked as she realized that faces were appearing and disappearing among the leaves. Beyond the trees deer were grazing in the meadow. She smiled, remembering how she had danced with them on the Wild God's Isle. She had sensed the life in the earth before, but here that spirit could be *seen*. The hedge encircled a grassy dell, and there a cloth was laid, covered with all manner of good things. And somewhere a lyre was being played, and fair-faced people beckoned to her to join them as they danced. The Mikantor she remembered was no more than a clumsy boy. Any man of this realm was far more beautiful.

The Lady had known how to tempt her, she thought then. But though this might be the soul of the land, it was not the gritty reality she had just sworn to serve.

"I cannot—" she stammered, and the Lady sighed.

"Each time I hope that one day you will decide to stay here, but that oath of yours always draws you back again."

Well, that answered the question about whether she had been a priestess before, thought Tirilan. She made the reverence she would have offered to the Lady of Avalon.

"Do you have some wisdom to offer me?"

Tirilan trembled as the Lady laughed. That merriment was not unkind, but it pierced the heart and set the blood pulsing in her veins. She could not tell whether she wanted to scream or to sing, but suddenly she knew that the measured existence that had been hers was enough no longer.

"Heart fire or hearth fire—you will seek both, my child. You will burn with passion, though now you believe yourself so cold. Your mother would make of you a priestess, and so you shall be, though not in the way that she foresees. You have vowed yourself to the earth, and you shall be a priestess to this land. You have vowed yourself to the people, and you shall hallow the Lord who will lead them."

Tirilan took a deep breath. Those words carried their own intoxication, but she sensed that here she must be very careful to avoid illusion, or self-delusion . . .

"What do you mean?"

"Behold, and remember . . . and one day you will understand. . . ."

The Lady gestured, and the air between them began to shimmer. Within that radiant sphere images stirred and shifted—a woman who was also a deer, a woman who stood bathed in moonlight upon a snowy hill, a woman standing before the great henge, holding a sheathed sword. There were other images beyond them, but she could not see them. Her vision was focused on the three. And as she gazed, words vibrated in her awareness—

"Without Me . . . no life shall come to birth,
Without Me . . . no night shall see the morn,
Without Me . . . no lord shall save the land,
Without Me . . . no hope shall be reborn."

———

MIKANTOR TIPPED BACK the beaker and took another long swallow of thin ale. The shape of the houses, the language, even the wind off the marshes teased at his memory. But he could not fault their hospitality. When the party from the ship trudged up the road, the farm family had welcomed them and made space in the storage sheds for those who would not fit under the round roof.

Traveling with Velantos, he had grown accustomed to new places, but here it was he and the smith who were the foreigners. Buda had begun helping the women, and Aelfrix, with his usual sunny good nature, had already started to make friends with the children. Aelfrix, he suspected, was the kind of youth who would land on his feet anywhere. Velantos, on the other hand, glowered from his place by the hearth. Even a winter in the north had not faded a skin clearly bronzed by a warmer sun, and scrapes and bruises only emphasized the strength of the swelling muscles of his chest and arms. With several cracked ribs, he had found the climb from the shore quite taxing, and even if the farm folk had dared to approach him he could not say much, for the farmer was the only one who had any of the traders' tongue.

He'll have to learn, Mikantor thought with anxious amusement, *just as I did when I came to his land.*

Mikantor himself, on the other hand, seemed to fascinate them. The farm wife was hovering before him now, a pitcher in her hand. Her words made sense to him, though the dialect was strange, but he was not quite sure what language would come out if he tried to answer. He held out his beaker with a smile. He had managed to remember enough to tell them his lineage, in hopes of gaining help for his band of refugees, salt stained and exhausted by three days of tossing on the sea, but not much more.

Do they think I have come to help them? Do I? he thought then, remembering his vision of the Tor. He was beginning to have the uncomfortable suspicion that it was the gods who had arranged this unexpected homecoming. And in that case, had the gods also arranged for him to be enslaved? If gods would do that to a boy, he did not think much of them.

Anderle would probably have said that the gods worked neither for men's pleasure nor for their own, but for the greater good of all. *She wants me to be a king . . .* he thought grimly. *And if I remember the vision correctly, there's a goddess who wants me to be a hero.* He didn't feel much like either one, although the good meat of the sheep that the people here had killed to feed them was already making him stronger. Velantos had promised to repair the farmer's plowshare, which seemed a fair exchange for their hospitality.

The sound of a new arrival brought Mikantor upright. He had his hand on the post where he'd hung his sword when a young man with light brown hair pushed aside the cowhide that curtained the door. Those snub-nosed features looked familiar. He was clothed in the pale tunic of a local priest with a healer's green belt of woven cord. He stopped, gray eyes moving from one stranger to another, widening as they fixed on Mikantor.

"Woodpecker? Is it really you? I heard you'd been carried off, but there can't be two men with a scar on the shin where I nicked you when my stave splintered one day. But the message from the farm gave another name—" he said with an odd, considering look, half hope and half suspicion.

"Mikantor"—he cleared his throat and felt the speech of Avalon coming back to him—"son of Uldan. It actually is my true name. The other was a disguise. You are Ganath, aren't you? You have grown."

"So have you, my friend," said Ganath, looking him up and down. "And you are Uldan's son, eh? Much becomes clear."

"Then that is more than I can say," Mikantor replied. "Sit down and tell me how the folk here get on. I saw the mark of fire on one of the sheds, but the farm seems prosperous. I can't speak the local dialect well enough to ask more."

"Oh, we've had enough trouble from raiders," said Ganath, accepting a beaker from the farm wife with a smile.

"How do you deal with them?" asked Mikantor, remembering the campaigns into the countryside on which Bodovos had led the guard. "Can't you get help from the king?"

"King Iftiken tries, but by the time word can reach him, the raiders are gone, and then when he is on the coast, Galid's bandits attack the interior."

"Galid!" Mikantor exclaimed, at the sound of the name aware of a sick roiling that he thought he'd outgrown. Why was he worrying about Anderle, he wondered then. Galid wanted to kill him; Anderle only wanted his soul.

"When enemy ships are sighted, the people drive their beasts to hidden pastures in the marshes and hide. They watched you for a day before sending the boy to lead you here, and they sent for me, though I don't know what they expected me to do. I'm a healer, not a warrior, but they know I studied at Avalon."

"And a pretty pathetic lot we must have looked," Mikantor said ruefully.

"Nice to know it was useful. Since we made contact, they have treated us like long-lost family."

"They would, of course," said Ganath thoughtfully, "because of the prophecy."

Mikantor stared. "What prophecy is that?" he said at last.

"The lost prince . . . The child who was reborn from the flames and will return to heal all our ills and protect us from all our foes. Uldan's lost son," Ganath replied with an odd smile. "I thought that *you* would know."

"Anderle said something once . . . but I did not understand," Mikantor said numbly, fighting an impulse to make a dash for the shore and beg Captain Stavros to put to sea.

"I have to get to Avalon," he said instead. "I'm glad you're here. I doubt these folk have traveled more than a score of leagues in their lives, and I need information on the roads."

"It is not quite that bad—they do go to the festivals at the king's steading north of here, which reminds me that I must send a message to Lady Linne. As for the road, be easy. I'm coming with you to Avalon."

NEXT TO THE HOUSE of the High Priestess there was a small garden where Anderle liked to sit on sunny days. This did not interfere much with her other duties, as the weather rarely made it a temptation, but it was sheltered from the wind, and today a few blossoms of sun's-blood were opening, translucent red spots on the leaves glowing as five-petaled golden flowers opened to the light. It was unusual enough to see something bloom in advance of its season that she took it as an omen. Perhaps she would pick a stem and tie it over the door for a blessing, though few unfriendly spirits could penetrate the wards of Avalon.

She eased down upon the stone bench and took a deep breath, savoring the peace. The peace . . . and a relief she would have admitted to no other soul. Her daughter had taken her vows and returned from her ordeal. Tirilan was a priestess now, bound to the path Anderle had dreamed for her child . . .

The garden was also a good place for meditation. At their meeting the previous autumn, the Ti-Sahharin had agreed to go aside every day at noon and seek communication on the spirit roads. And if no one had any tidings, in these times, a period when Anderle could sit and relax was always welcome, especially if her people believed she was working.

She settled herself more comfortably, back straight, hands open upon her knees, and closed her eyes. Perhaps, she thought, she would nap, lulled by the singing of the bees. Students always thought they were the first to discover that one could sleep sitting up while appearing to meditate, but Anderle had learned that trick long ago. If she needed rest that badly, she did not think the Goddess would mind. But first she ought to see if any of the other priestesses had news.

The priestess took a deep breath and let it out slowly, drew breath once more, savoring the scents of life and growth as the garden basked in the sun. This was one of the first skills she had learned, more than thirty years ago, and it still took an effort of will to let the clamoring memories go. In . . . and out . . . the old disciplines took hold. Awareness of the bees, the garden, and Avalon itself faded, not forgotten, but no longer at the forefront of her attention. She waited, opening her soul.

Despite her preparations, the contact, when it came, nearly jolted her out of trance. Or perhaps it was the exultation, so intense she barely recognized the source as Linne. *I am not accustomed to receiving good news!* she thought, sending a mental plea to the other woman to calm down.

"Ganath sent a message . . ." came Linne's thought. *"You remember, he's one of the lads who studied with you on Avalon. I had placed him on the coast near the river Stour where the traders from the Great Land come."*

When the raiders let them, thought Anderle.

"A ship came from the City of Circles. They say the City is drowning, but this ship escaped. Ganath's old friend Woodpecker was on it! Would you believe he has turned up alive after all these years? But now he calls himself Mikantor!"

Once more the contact wavered as blood drained from Anderle's head and surged back again. She trembled, caught between shock and joy.

"Where is he?" she sent a mental cry.

"Ganath got supplies for them. They're on their way to Avalon!"

"Fine news! The best of news, my sister. You have my endless thanks!"

"Then I must go. You will have things to do, and so do I."

As the contact broke, Anderle sank back into her body, uncertain whether to laugh or to cry. This was the confirmation of their vision on the Tor. *This* was the reward for all her labors. He was alive!

She stood, stretching limbs stiffened by sitting too long, and took a small dance step of delight. She saw a figure in priestess blue in the doorway and smiled radiantly as it moved into the light and the sun glistened on her daughter's bright hair.

"Tirilan! Listen—" *Now* she could share her joy—

"Mother, why didn't you *tell* me!" Tirilan's accusation cut across her words.

"How could—I only just learned—what do you mean?"

"Ellet says you saw Mikantor in your ritual!" Tirilan exclaimed. "Why didn't you tell me he's alive?"

Anderle's joy congealed as she saw her daughter's face, contorted in the image of the goddess of wrath. But *why?*

"Tirilan!" She put all her authority into the snapped command. The girl gasped, stopped in midword, and fell blessedly still. "What do you mean?"

"Ellet told me," Tirilan replied. "Now that I'm safely pledged, as a fellow initiate, she thought I should know about your little ritual on the Tor."

"Yes, of course," Anderle began, "but—"

"You saw Mikantor," repeated the girl. "Didn't you think what that would mean to me?"

"It was a vision . . ." stammered Anderle, wondering how her daughter had managed to put her on the defensive. "We hoped, but we didn't *know. . . .*"

"*Hope!* That's just what it would have been! Do you think I would have shackled myself to Avalon if I had known the man I love still walked the world?"

So *that* was it. "You still fancy yourself in love with him? You were children. You have changed. *He* will have changed. What makes you think that whatever was between you will not have altered as well?"

"That's not the point," Tirilan countered bitterly. "By tricking me into taking vows, you have denied me the right to find out if I still love him. You denied me the right to *choose* . . ."

Anderle felt her own wrath kindling. How dare her daughter accuse her, when she had given her the greatest gift in her power?

"Until Mikantor returns, how can I know?"

"You won't have to wait long, then," Anderle said coldly. "He will be here before another moon grows old. Weep now if you must, but when he arrives, be ready to greet him with a smile. If Ellet has told you what we saw, you know that the gods have granted him no easy destiny."

SIXTEEN

*M*aidenhills consisted of several roundhouses clustered below a spur of the downs where a lumpy line of barrows crowned a hill. A crowd of people waited to greet them. Mikantor sighed. He had hoped that they might pass unnoticed, one more anonymous band of refugees wandering across the land, but Ganath seemed determined to turn his homecoming into a parade. In all this winter- and war-battered countryside, there were bound to be some who would report his presence to Galid and his wolves. He could only hope to outrun the rumors, which seemed to be growing with every league.

Mikantor braced himself against the naked need he read in their eyes. There were seven men and three women, a gaggle of children peeking from behind their skirts, and one individual grown genderless with age. But the buildings were in better repair than many he had seen; in fact two of them seemed to be new. An eye educated by his recent travels noted the size of the livestock pens—empty at this season, when the beasts had been driven up to graze on the hills. Beyond the houses long fields were veiled with the hopeful green of emmer wheat, and gardens sprouted poles to support the first spiraling stems of beans.

When he looked back at the people, another figure had joined them, a tall young man in a tunic like Ganath's whom he surely ought to recognize.

"Ah, *there* he is!" Ganath was grinning broadly. "Do you remember? He always was a long lad, though we never thought he would turn into a young tree . . ."

"Beni—Beniharen . . ." the name surfaced. Mikantor's gaze traveled up and up as the newcomer hurried toward them. *My old companions have all grown,* thought Mikantor, *but that's excessive . . .*

"So you're back," said Beniharen. "It's about time. They said you'd been killed, but I never believed it."

"Why not? There were surely enough times when I thought I was going to die—or wished I had!"

"You have luck," Beniharen said simply. "Noticed it when we were at Avalon and you always seemed to end up with the last piece of bannock. And you usually have a plan."

Mikantor flushed. *But perhaps it's just as well. I think we're going to need both luck and a plan very badly soon.*

"This is your village?" he said aloud.

"This is where Lady Shizuret put me when we were all scattered after the plague. We haven't done too badly. I thought people might be safer if we lived closer together. There's more to tempt a robber band, but they have to be larger and better armed to take us on. It has worked so far." He shrugged, the unspoken *"And if a real war band attacks, we are doomed anyway"* hanging between them.

"You might build a fence of brush and bramble," Mikantor said aloud. "It would not stop a determined attack, but it would slow them." He had seen such defenses in the countryside beyond the North Sea. "Even a poor archer can hit a man pinned by thorns."

Beniharen nodded. "A plan—didn't I say it? We'll try that when summer comes. Now let me introduce you," he went on. A wave brought forward the two couples and the extra men, and finally the elder, who proved to be an old woman, the grandmother of one of the wives.

Mikantor took her hand carefully. He did not think he had ever met anyone so old. "A blessing on you, good mother. I hope you are well."

The woman fixed him with an eye still bright and gave a snort of laughter. "At my age, young man, to be up and moving is enough to hope for. When it is damp, my joints pain me, and in these times wet days are all we seem to have. These hands will no longer serve for spinning—" She held out fingers gnarled into claws. "But I am still lively enough to stir the pot and bore my granddaughter with tales of how much better things were when I was her age." She gave the younger woman a gap-toothed grin. "Still, sixty-seven winters should earn one some respect."

Mikantor nodded, remembering that Kiri had been that age when she died of the plague. They had thought her old, but she had seemed much younger than this woman appeared. He had never before appreciated the advantages of living at Avalon. Their food had been simple, but they did not have to grow or gather it themselves. Ganath and Beniharen, too, were bigger and stronger than other men their age. Perhaps there was a virtue in the very air of Avalon.

But why couldn't everyone live so long and so well? Even when the seasons were harsh, if properly managed, the land could feed the people. At least it could if they worked together.

The granddaughter was next, a sturdy young woman with an infant held against her breast who refused to meet his eyes. Her granddam had been bolder, but perhaps the old had less to lose. Still, he did not understand why she should be afraid.

"Will you give a blessing to my babe?" she whispered.

Mikantor blinked. "Sister, you and yours have all my goodwill, but I am no priest to give blessings!"

"You are something more—" Now she did look up, and he flinched before the hope in her eyes. "You are the child of the prophecy who will lead us against the evil ones!"

I am only a man . . . I am only a man . . . cried a gibbering voice within, but from somewhere deeper came the answer, *Only a man can help them, and if you do not stand forth, who will?* The worst that could happen was that he might fail. *At least,* he thought, *if I die helping my people, there will be a reason!*

"If you believe that," he found himself saying, "then I will try." He touched the baby's hand, and jumped as the tiny fingers gripped his own. "If you are as strong in manhood as you are in infancy, you will make a mighty warrior!" he said to the child. "Whatever blessings I have to give are yours with my goodwill!"

The young mother turned away to join the other women, who were already welcoming Buda. Velantos and Aelfrix, who was leading the pack pony, stood with Ganath, looking around them with interest.

"Well said!" Beniharen laughed. "Now come and talk to the men about that thorn fence."

"It's a simple idea," he said when they were all gathered around the fire in the largest of the roundhouses. "You make a framework of willow withies and thread bramble through them, or you can use branches from hawthorn or the like. Make it high enough so that anyone trying to get over will make a good target, and have some wicker hurdles handy to hide behind when you shoot. You do have bows, yes?"

The men nodded, but they did not look confident. Mikantor tried to remember what Bodovos had dinned into the heads of the guards.

"Well, then, practice! Every day, with different targets and distances, until you can hit something the size of a man every time. If your bows are not strong, we will try to find someone who can teach you to make better. Spears are good, but it's best if you never have to come within arm's length of your enemy."

"Flint will punch as good a hole as bronze," growled one of the men, "and there's more of it."

"The ancient ones who lie in the barrows up there used flint," said another.

"Then ask their blessing," agreed Mikantor, "and their curse upon your foes." That got some grins, and he gratefully accepted a beaker of beer while the discussion shifted to the health of the cattle and the state of the fields.

"There are other hamlets that might do the same," Ganath said thoughtfully, taking a seat beside him. "If someone were to show them how."

"I can't be everywhere—" Mikantor began, with the same sense of being carried along by unknown forces that he had at sea.

"Of course not, and besides, I expect you'll be training fighters. But we could bring people to Avalon, teach them all at once, and send them back again."

"While I train fighters . . ." Mikantor sighed. "You, or Someone, seems to have my future all planned out for me."

"Don't pretend you haven't thought about this." Ganath lifted one eyebrow.

"In my nightmares," muttered Mikantor. "You have to understand— I've seen the sack of a great city, and I've fought marauders as bad as any of Galid's men or these other bandit chieftains you say his example has spawned. Do you really think that if we take up arms against him, it will be one joyous romp to victory? The people here are not living well, but they are living. There are seven grown men in this hamlet. Leave three to work the land and send the other four to fight and how many will return home? Men die in battle, Ganath. I've gotten used to the idea of fighting myself, but leading other men to death still scares me."

"Mikantor . . . men *die*. No care of yours can prevent that. Will you not allow them the same choice that you have made, to die *for* something, instead of without meaning?"

Mikantor stared. It was so exactly what he had been telling himself not long ago. "Who taught you to strike so shrewdly?" he said finally. "You never used to be like this when we studied together at Avalon."

"You never used to stride like a warrior," Ganath replied. "We grew up, Woodpecker. If the gods are good, we will live to grow old."

Mikantor glanced across the fire at Velantos, who was sitting with the men, attempting to communicate with his fragmentary grasp of the language of the tribes. *I grew up thanks to you,* he thought soberly. As if he had spoken, Velantos looked up and smiled. *We will survive*— Mikantor tried to send the thought. *Somehow I will figure out a way.*

MIST SWIRLED LOW UPON the downs, alternately veiling and revealing the broad sweep of the Vale. It might have been as impressive as the view of the Argolid from Mykenae, thought Velantos, if they could have actually *seen* it. Mikantor had assured him that his homeland included mountains as noble as any in Akhaea, but ever since the ancient track they were following had climbed to the ridgeline of the hills, the view had consisted of a green slope disappearing into cloud.

The smith hunched more deeply into the sheepskin garment he had gotten from one of the farmers in exchange for an arrowhead of bronze. He had expected the damp wind that stroked across the grass to blow the mists away, but instead they swirled more thickly. His own people had tales of magic mists sent by the gods to spirit their chosen ones out of danger. He could wish for one of those mists now, if it would only take him somewhere *warm*.

What I need, Velantos thought morosely, *is a forge. Build the fire hot enough, and it won't matter what the weather is outside.* A forge, and his image of the Lady to watch over it, and metal to work. Then, wherever his *moira* led him, he would be at home. In his own country he could name the spirits of hill and tree. No doubt there were powers in this land, but they did not speak to him.

He watched Mikantor striding along at the head of their column with a new appreciation for the cheerfulness with which the boy had endured his exile. He tried to convince himself that his own fate did not matter—there was no life for him in his own land—whereas by coming home, Mikantor had come into his own. It was odd how since arriving here the boy had grown, perhaps not in actual height, but in *presence*. As he committed himself more fully to his people, with each day he was becoming the leader they desired.

All this time I thought Woodpecker was sent by the gods to aid me, thought the smith. *And now it would appear that I was sent to bring* Mikantor, *trained and ready, to the place where the gods want him to be.*

He looked up as the others halted. Mikantor was saying something about turning downhill to seek shelter at one of the farmsteads in the valley. The tall lad, Beniharen, did not think they could get there before dark. Velantos shivered again. Ganath pointed ahead and Velantos caught the word for an ancient tomb.

"To sleep near the dead is to sleep *with* them," muttered Buda in her own tongue.

"When I was an infant, Lady Anderle hid me in a barrow to escape Galid's men." Mikantor grinned. "They did me no harm!"

"These Old Ones, they friendly?" Velantos asked.

"If we show honor—" said Beniharen, speaking slowly. "This is where our people leave offerings to the thunder god. The People of the Hills come here sometimes—the first people in the land, who were here before the tribes. They are kin to the Lake Folk that fostered Mikantor."

"We'll camp," said Mikantor. Velantos wondered how much his decision had been motivated by a desire to escape the people who gazed at him with such hunger. The smith had felt like that during the last days of Tiryns, when he was Phorkaon's only surviving son. To have people look at him as if he could perform some miracle had cured him of any desire he might have had to be a king.

The stopping place was half a league further on, just past a slope where the grass had been carved away to reveal the white chalk beneath. Mikantor said it was the head of the figure of a gigantic horse carved into the hillside, but it was getting too dark to see much of it now.

While Aelfrix tied the pony where it could graze, Buda and Beniharen started a meal. Velantos walked off through the trees. He felt the ache of the day's march in his legs, but a restlessness he could not define drove him away from the company of other men. Between the tree trunks he glimpsed the solid gray of two great stones and stopped, eyes widening as memory overlaid them with an image of the pillars that flanked the great gate of Tiryns.

He moved forward more slowly. So far he had seen only wooden structures in this land, and thought them the best that these people could build. But the sarsen uprights he saw as he emerged from beneath the trees were the equal of any of the Cyclopean stones at Tiryns. And these, he sensed as he drew near, were older. A line of flat stones almost twice the height of a man fronted a long mound edged by smaller stones, with a ditch on either side. Near the entrance some of the earth had worn away to reveal the mighty uprights and capstones of a passage into darkness. In this land men did not build to defend the living, but to honor the dead.

He followed the path all the way around the length of the mound and came to the entrance. On a flat stone someone had laid the carcass of a grouse and a bunch of creamy primroses. Both were fresh. Velantos straightened, looking around him with the uneasy sensation that unseen eyes were watching. He felt in his belt pouch for something he might leave as an offering, and drew out a bronze brace that had come loose from a chest during the crossing. The box had proved to be beyond repair, but the bronze was a piece of his own forging and he had saved it. The metal clinked faintly as he laid it on the stone, and like an echo he heard a distant rumble.

Thunder . . . Velantos thought unhappily. The covers of oiled wool they had stretched between the trees suddenly seemed a much less desirable shelter. Shivering once more he turned away, tripped, and went down. As he tried to catch himself, he bruised his hand on something hard and smooth. He sat back on his heels, stifling an oath as the wrist that had been sprained when he was taken captive gave a warning twinge. The rock on which he had landed was still beneath his other hand. It was some close-grained stone, about half the length of his forearm, rounded at one end and widening and flattening to a blunt blade at the other, in fact, the same shape as the mound. No natural stone was shaped so evenly—it was a tool, he realized, something like the stone wedges builders used to split wood. It would hammer bronze as well, he thought, hefting it. It felt curiously right in his hand.

He slid it into his pouch and got to his feet, his heart lightened, even though the wind blew more strongly now, whispering spells to the trees. He could smell supper cooking—a stew of grains and greens and the meat of a hare that Aelfrix had brought down with his sling. It would be hot and filling, and Velantos had ceased to hope for anything more flavorful in this damp northern land.

When they had eaten, they banked the fire and unrolled their bedding beneath the shelters. All of them were tired from the day's march, and soon Velantos could hear the varied breathing as the others fell asleep. Only he remained wakeful, listening as the wind rose, whipping at the branches and flapping the cloth, hearing the thunder ever more loudly. He waited with mingled apprehension and resignation for the first hissing drops of rain.

Aelfrix, who was sleeping nearest the edge of one of the covers, must have gotten spattered, for he stirred, complaining. Then lightning flared, throwing a relief of black branches against the cloth. Velantos waited, counting, until thunder hammered the heavens, opening them to release a torrent of rain. Wind set all the cloth billowing; ropes parted; first one, then another cover flapped like a torn sail. Suddenly everyone was flailing free of their bedding, seeking shelter beneath the trees. Wind gusted again, driving the rain sideways. In moments they were all soaked through.

Velantos hunkered down in the lee of a beech tree, flinching as lightning flared again. The thunder followed more swiftly now.

"We can't stay here," came Mikantor's voice through the chaos. "Let us ask the ancestors for shelter!"

"You mean to take refuge in the mound?" Ganath's voice shook.

"No! Ghosts eat our souls!" Buda cried.

"Better to stay here," came Beniharen's deep voice. "The storm's moving fast and will pass soon."

Another flare of lightning glared on tossing branches; thunder cracked as the divine smith struck once more. Again came the lightning, and a great oak at the edge of the grove burst suddenly into flame. Sound rolled around them. As it passed he heard Mikantor ordering them all into the mound.

"I will go first—" The younger man half carried Buda. Aelfrix scrambled to follow. Ganath and Beniharen were pale shapes behind them. Still draped in the cloak in which he had rolled up to sleep, Velantos got to his feet and stumbled after them. The stone in his pouch thumped against his thigh. Had he inadvertently stolen an offering?

"Old Ones, we ask your mercy—" Mikantor's voice echoed against stone. "Protect my people, and if you are angered, let your wrath fall on me—"

Over the howl of the wind Velantos heard the murmur of supplication as the others followed. Another stroke of light showed him the opening to the tomb in stark relief, and Beniharen's tall form bending to enter the passageway.

The ancestors might be angry, but the wrath of the god of thunder was a certainty. For a moment Velantos hesitated at the threshold; then he slid between two of the great stones and clambered up the mound to stand above the entrance to the tomb. Hair streaming, sodden cloak flapping from his shoulders, he extracted the stone ax from his pouch and held it high.

"Diwaz Keraunos," he cried, "by whatever name they call you here, if I have done wrong, let me be the one to suffer. Spare these people who have done no harm!"

Lightning always struck at the highest. He would be—

Thought was extinguished as sound and light exploded around him. Every hair on his body stood up as the power passed over wet skin and cloth and into the earth below. And then he was falling. Still blind and deafened, he felt the hands of his friends pulling him down, still tingling and twitching, to lie on cold dry stone.

"VELANTOS—IT'S MORNING—CAN YOU HEAR me? Wake up, *please!*"

That was Woodpecker's voice. Velantos grunted, feeling each muscle complain as awareness returned. He had been ill, he remembered, so he must be in Apollon's temple, but why had the priests left him on the hard ground?

"Cold . . ." he mumbled. The air smelled of wood smoke and the fresh scent of earth after a rain.

"And so you should be," scolded the boy. "But Buda has the fire going and water heating for tea. Can you sit up now?"

Velantos felt a strong arm lifting him and opened his eyes. A pale golden light was shafting down a passage formed by mighty stones. The boy was holding him, no, the man, *Mikantor* . . . With the name came memory.

"Diwaz Keraunos save us . . ." he whispered. He felt weak and sick, but he was alive.

"*Somebody* certainly did," Mikantor replied, "and it's more than you deserve. What did you think you were doing, prancing about up there?"

"I thought . . . there might be need for . . . a sacrifice. . . ." With an effort Velantos got his feet under him and Mikantor helped him to stand. "Where is the stone?"

"The one you were clutching? It was all we could do to pry it out of your fingers. It's there, on the ground—"

"Give it to me . . . please." Velantos straightened, peering down the passageway. "Help me to take it inside," he said as Mikantor put the stone into his hand. "It belongs there."

"I . . . see," said the young man as he helped along. "I cannot pretend I don't understand, having made a similar offer myself. I am glad my ancestors were kinder than your god."

My god . . . Velantos had always given his worship to the Lady of Craft, with a nod to Epaitios. But here in the north, the powers of Diwaz and Epaitios were combined into a single mighty being whom the smith could no longer ignore.

The passage ended in three small chambers, like a hammer on a long haft. With a quick glance at their tumbled contents, Velantos bent to lay the stone ax down.

"Lie here in peace—" he murmured, "with my thanks for your blessing."

He let Mikantor turn him back down the passage. He was walking almost normally by the time they emerged into the light of the new day.

"How are you feeling?" asked Mikantor, using the Akhaean tongue. Three days had passed since the thunderstorm at the ancient tomb, but Velantos still worried him.

"Very well—" Velantos answered absently, smiling a little as two swans emerged from among the reeds that bordered the river and floated off like feathered clouds. The travelers had descended from the track along the hills and were following the Aman toward the springs of Sulis, for Mikantor had decided to approach Avalon from the north, avoiding Galid's land. The smith seemed to have recovered physically, but there was a brightness about him that reminded Mikantor of the way he had looked after his night in the temple of Apollon. He supposed that was only to be expected when one was touched by a god.

"Why are you smiling?" Velantos asked.

"I was just thinking that I am not the only one about whom the people will be telling stories now."

The smith's heavy brows came down in a familiar frown. "I told everyone not to speak of what happened at the tomb!"

Mikantor's grin broadened. "And we both know how much good that does when men are looking for heroes. When Ganath and I went into Carn Ava last night, Lady Nuya and the queen had heard how you were blessed by the Thunder Lord, and scolded me for not bringing you along. It was one of the People of the Hills who told them. It is said they have the gift of passing unseen."

"When I looked at the mound, I did feel as if someone was watching me," Velantos replied. "Perhaps I should have gone with you. A priestess might be able to tell me why I am still alive."

"Ask Lady Anderle," said Mikantor. "She always has answers." Velantos raised an eyebrow at a bitterness Mikantor could not quite keep from his tone. "What was it like?" he added to distract the older man. When they got to Avalon, Velantos could form his own opinion of Anderle. And for three days Mikantor had been wondering. This was the first time Velantos had seemed focused enough for him to ask.

"Like a piece of bronze must feel when the hammer comes down. . . ." the smith said slowly. "I have been changed—shaped—but for what purpose I do not know."

"I know *that* feeling well!" Mikantor exclaimed with a short laugh. "Well, I am grateful that you and I are treading the same path. And speaking of paths, . . .I had better find out what our guide is finding so interesting over there."

The ground was rising. The track wound among hillsides thickly wooded with beech and holly, while the river rushed more swiftly below. The boy whom they had brought from Carn Ava was staring at the muddy earth where a narrow path branched off from the road. He was a nephew of Lady Nuya's and ought to be trustworthy, but said little, as if overawed by his company.

"What is it?" He squatted down beside the boy.

"Many men have passed this way." The lad pointed to the overlay of footprints. "They came down the path and turned onto the track we are following, not too long ago. Big, strong men, carrying burdens, but nothing too heavy—see how the marks are pressed in, but far apart, as if the man has a long, fast stride."

"You have a good eye," said Mikantor.

"I learned to track raiders. I think these men carry weapons."

"I think so too . . ." *And I think they knew we were coming, and will be waiting for us up the road,* thought Mikantor. It would be little use to turn back, for if the travelers did not appear, their foes would track *them* and fall upon them from behind.

"Keep watch while I talk to the others," he said aloud, though he had no idea what they could do. He and Velantos were the only warriors, and he suspected the smith was still weak from his ordeal. Someone must have seen him with Ganath in Carn Ava and reported to Galid, unless this was some chance group of brigands. No one they had met earlier knew what route they were taking, and he did not think the elder folk would bear tales to Galid. So they could not know how many were in his party, or who they were.

"Everyone, listen—" he called. "We have to decide what to do."

MIKANTOR SHIFTED THE PAD beneath the box on his shoulder and bent once more as the warriors appeared at the top of the hill.

"Diwaz Keraunos, be with us now," whispered Velantos, who walked ahead of him.

He ought to be praying to Ereias, patron of travelers and thieves, thought Mikantor. Certainly, for this deception to work, some god was going to have to grant them a miracle. Velantos tugged uneasily at the veil that Buda had artfully folded around his head. Galid would not know that no such style of headgear had ever been seen in the lands of the Middle Sea. So long as Velantos looked foreign, it did not matter if he looked like a fool. Mikantor, his hair darkened with soot and skin covered with an artistic application of grime, was wearing a mismatched collection of garments borrowed from the other members of their company and bearing part of the pony's load.

If they brought this off, he thought with mingled exasperation and amusement, it would be because of Buda's costuming skills. And if their enemies saw through the mummery and attacked, bound within the bundle of sticks Mikantor carried was his sword.

Velantos lifted his hand and his followers came to a ragged halt, except for the pony, who kept going for several more steps, dragging Aelfrix along. The covers had been taken off the box of tools the beast bore, so that carving and brasswork shone in the sun. Mikantor's lips twitched as the smith straightened, thrusting out his chest in a pose that one of Phorkaon's stewards had adopted when he was about to deliver some especially pompous proclamation.

"Halt and give way, for a master smith of Tiryns," said Velantos in the tongue of Akhaea and then, "Stop, swordmen—what you want?" intentionally misprounouncing the language of the tribes.

"Outlander, what you got?" mocked one of the newcomers. From the others came a burst of laughter.

Peering beneath the shadow of his bundles, Mikantor counted nearly a dozen sturdy, dour men with shields slung over their backs, armed with swords and spears. Too many to fight. He was glad he had sent Ganath and Beniharen to hide in the forest, for they would surely have been recognized. Two could be hidden, but not all. They had begged him to go with them, but he could not leave Velantos to face enemies alone.

Hands went to swords as Velantos pulled his hammer from his belt and hefted it, the bronze head gleaming in the sunlight. "Bronze—" called the smith. "I make. You need?"

When they had played hide-and-seek at Avalon, they had learned to spin a sphere of protection that would deflect a seeking eye. Mikantor hoped his friends remembered how. Tirilan had been the best at it. She could stand in the middle of the playing field and remain unseen. He forced back the image of Tiri manifesting in a blaze of sunlight as she took down her shielding. Soon he would see her—the thought set his heart to pounding with a tension that owed nothing to his present danger. He would see her, but first he had to live through today.

The warriors spread out to block the road, grinning at the spectacle of this black-bearded hammer-waving man with his ridiculous headdress.

Mikantor squatted in the dust, one knee bent so he could spring up again if need be. *I am not a threat . . .* he projected the thought, *no one to fear. . . no one to think about at all.* During his slavery he had gotten quite good at being no one. His gut clenched at the effort it took to do it now, in his own land.

A man pushed through, shorter than some, but strongly built, with coils of gold wire binding the many braids of his grizzled hair. Over a shirt of heavy hide he wore a russet cloak, pinned with gold. Mikantor looked at those braids and felt a chill, remembering Anderle's story of the destruction of Azan-Ylir.

"What I need I take, and I stop whom I please. I am the law in this land."

I could grab my sword and reach him in six strides, thought Mikantor, trembling. After that, the warriors would cut him down, but if this was Galid, it might be worth the price. Or it would be, if Galid's tyranny were the only thing that troubled this land. Slowly, he mastered himself once more.

Velantos spread his hands in confusion. "No speak, no speak. You want bronze?" Mikantor's lips twitched, for although the smith spoke little, by this time he understood the speech of the tribes pretty well.

Galid gestured impatiently to one of his men, who stepped forward.

"Do you have trade talk?" he asked in a dialect close to the speech of the City of Circles.

"Aye, aye!" Velantos grinned broadly. "That is why I have come. I seek to buy copper and tin. I am told you have rich mines in the west—" He waved in the direction of the Ai-Ushen lands.

"Once," came the reply, "but no longer."

"Truly? Well, maybe then I will go south, where there is tin."

Galid muttered something to the interpreter. "My master asks who are those with you?" He nodded toward Buda, who had grimed her own face and hunched awkwardly to obscure her buxom figure, and Aelfrix, who hung his head.

"My servants—" said Velantos, as if surprised he should need to ask. "The woman cooks, the boy tends the pony."

"And the big one?"

"Ah, he is my Erakles—" Velantos grinned sourly. "He lifts the heavy things and works the bellows for the forge. Strong he is, but not too bright—" Mikantor felt Galid's gaze upon him and became even more still.

"See what he has in those chests."

"My master says to open the boxes," echoed the interpreter.

Velantos nodded. "Erakles," he said in Akhaean, "put down thy bundles and unload the pony. And *be careful,* in the name of all the gods."

Mikantor knew how to interpret that warning. He shrugged off his burdens and staggered to his feet. If Velantos could play the fool, then so could he. He let his arms hang loosely as he stumped over to the pony and began to fumble at the lashings. His muscles creaked as he manhandled the oak box, clanking faintly, to the ground. Velantos knelt on his left to undo the hasp, and picked out one of the spearpoints that lay on top, stepping between Galid and Mikantor.

"This is my work—do you wish to buy?" The warm metal glinted as he held it high.

"How many of these does he have?" Galid murmured to the other man.

"Six, lord—"

"Take them. Say it is to buy their passage through my land."

Velantos stiffened as the interpreter passed this on. "But this is robbery! I am a smith, blessed by the gods. They will not like that you treat me so!"

"Then let the gods reward you!" replied the interpreter.

As the man began to pick up the spearpoints, Velantos' hand came down on Mikantor's shoulder, squeezing hard. He stayed where he was, but his blood was boiling—surely steam must be coming from his ears.

"Be still . . . I can make more . . ." Velantos mingled the words with Akhaean fulminations chronicling the robbers' probable ancestry and certain fate while the warriors laughed.

Mikantor kept his head down, whispering his own curses as he listened to Galid and his bullies tramp away.

"Ssh . . . hush, be easy now," murmured the smith. "They are gone. Get up now and reload the pony, but carefully, for they may have left a scout to spy. We will continue on our way and make no trouble, and by evening it may be safe for your friends to join us once more . . ."

He spoke in a smooth singsong, thought Mikantor, like a man soothing a fractious mare. "And like a good slave I will obey . . ." he muttered bitterly.

"But no longer mine," said Velantos. "Now you serve this land."

Mikantor looked up and felt the tightness in his chest begin to ease as he met the older man's grim smile. "That's so . . ." he breathed. "But I promise you this. Next time I meet that man I will have a sword in my hand!"

SEVENTEEN

*M*ikantor had risen as soon as it was light enough to load the pony and roused the others, protesting and grunting, to pull on whatever clothing they had not slept in and get on the road. He himself took the lead rope to haul the beast along.

"At least you might have let us eat some breakfast," muttered Ganath, who was marching beside him. "Why the hurry? If the Tor has not moved in all the time you've been gone, it is not going to vanish today."

Like the land of the queen of the Hidden Folk? Mikantor shrugged. He himself did not understand his urgency. It had been almost seven years since he left the Tor. It felt like forever. It felt as if it had been a single day. *Will I wake again to find this all a dream and myself fourteen years old once more?* Even if he could have spent them at Avalon, he did not want to go through those years again.

"If we get there early enough, perhaps *they* will give us breakfast, and a far better one that we would have on the trail," he said consolingly. "It cannot be more than two leagues away."

They had spent the night on the last of the high ground to the east of the Vale of Avalon. The track they were following now wound through a mixture of pasture and woodland. As the sun rose, the sky before them warmed gradually from a misty gray to pale gold, deepening to pink with a nacreous shimmer like the inside of a shell.

The pony shied as something flapped among the trees. Two white swans lifted suddenly into the air, their first flurry becoming a smooth stroke that bore them skyward. In the next moment the travelers came out from beneath the branches and saw the Tor. Mikantor stopped short, gazing at the perfect cone that rose above the mists, silhouetted against the rosy sky.

After what seemed a long time he became aware that Velantos was standing beside him.

"Is that your home?"

"It was once . . ." Mikantor answered him, and did not know whether he was referring to his boyhood or to that other lifetime about which the queen of the Hidden Realm had told him.

"It is very beautiful," the older man said quietly.

Mikantor nodded. "It holds my heart, though I do not think I am destined to dwell there for very long."

Velantos gripped his arm with sudden strength, speaking swiftly in Akhaean, as he still did when moved. "Then do not go there! The gods gave Akhilleos his choice of fates, to die young and gloriously, or old and content. Have they given such a choice to you? We can leave this land and make our way south once more—"

Mikantor shook his head and covered the other man's hand with his own. "Be easy—the gods have given me no warning. But Avalon is for priests, and in this life, at least, my fate is to be a warrior. I do not know whether my time will be short or long, but it is in the country of the Ai-Zir and the lands beyond that I must fight my battles, and if I win them, it is there that I will make my home."

"That is the choice of a king," said Velantos.

"Or a Defender. This land is not like your own—here it is the queens who reign and the kings who guard them, so what Galid is doing is doubly a sin. But Avalon stands above all the tribes. Lady Anderle is the head of the Sisterhood of High Priestesses, an adept of great powers. Without her support I cannot even begin."

"She sounds like that witch Medea about whom we have so many tales." Velantos' lips twisted in what might have been a smile.

"Nothing so sinister! But she is a strong woman, to be sure."

"I look forward to meeting her . . ."

Mikantor laughed. Caught up in his own concerns, it had not before occurred to him to wonder what the smith would make of the Lady of Avalon, or she of him.

"The sooner we get there, the sooner you will," he said, starting down the hill.

The steepest side of the Tor faced eastward, rising from a tangle of wood and meadow. The path that led to it followed a ridge of slightly higher ground that stretched from the hills to the isle. Where the marsh had overtaken it, a trackway of split logs filled in, but most of it was on solid ground.

Now he could see the standing stones that crowned the summit. Below the smooth slope a band of trees separated it from a meadow where sheep grazed. On their left the marsh drew in. Swans floated on the open water beyond the fringe of reeds, perhaps the two they had seen before. The travelers fell silent. Even the birds had ceased their chattering. The sheep moved slowly across green grass jeweled with golden flowers.

Where the ground rose, the path divided. One fork would take them around the isle to the Hall of the Sun and the other buildings. The other led to the Tor. A bench stood at the turning. Mikantor glanced past it, then looked again. Someone was sitting there—one of the priestesses—why had he not noticed that blue robe before?

Had Anderle seen their coming by her arts and come out to meet them? As the woman rose, her veil slipped back, and he saw the sunlight blaze golden on her hair. Mikantor felt his heart stop and then begin a swift beat that shook his chest.

The woman came forward, her feet leaving dark prints on the dew-pearled grass. She was human, then, but why had he doubted? He knew those bright eyes and that curling hair.

She held out her hand. "You who have wandered, here is your goal. You who have been exiled, this is your home. Be welcome to Avalon . . ."

He knew that smile. But the child he remembered had gone. This was a woman, breast and hip neatly defined by the woven cord that cinctured her blue gown. Why had it not occurred to him to wonder how the years might have changed *Tirilan*?

"The blessing of the Goddess be on you, Lady, and on this isle—" said Ganath when it became apparent that Mikantor was incapable of producing words.

She drew nearer, her gaze passing from one to another, eyes widening a little as she looked Mikantor up and down. What must she think of him, with the dust of half the island ground into his skin and clothes?

She took each one by the hand as Ganath introduced them, coming last to Mikantor. For a moment she simply looked at him, then set her hands to either side of his face and drew his head down to kiss him on the brow.

"Son of a Hundred Kings," she whispered, releasing him, "I dreamed your coming. Be welcome to Avalon."

His eyes were stinging. The spot where she had kissed him burned like fire. Mikantor found that his knees would no longer support him. He knelt, and moved by an instinct he could not explain, kissed the ground.

"Lady, I salute you—" Words came to him at last. "I salute the Goddess whose image you are. I salute the holy earth of Avalon. . . ."

HE HAS GROWN . . . THOUGHT Anderle as the travelers made their way toward the Hall of the Sun where the Lady of Avalon and her priests were awaiting them. Her lips twitched as she remembered how many times she had thought that before. This time, though, it was easy to think of him by his true name. *He has grown into it—he really is Mikantor now.*

But was he the Son of a Hundred Kings, the destined Defender who would restore law and life to the land? The people seemed to think so. Word of his coming had run with the speed of sunlight across the land.

She had to admit that he looked the part—taller than his father, who in his youth had been a big man, with shoulders in proportion. The bare legs below his tunic were hard muscled as well, as they ought to be, after all the walking he had done. In the shadow his hair seemed dark, but it caught little fiery glints when he passed into the sunlight, and there was a coppery sparkle along his shaven jaw. Stronger suns than this one had turned his skin a ruddy bronze. From the priestesses behind her came a sigh of appreciation—yes, this was a man that women would favor. At the thought, she turned to see how her daughter was reacting to the return of the young man about whom she had made such a fuss not so long ago.

Tirilan's face was serene. *I do not believe that look of innocence, my girl,* Anderle thought dryly, wondering if her daughter had already managed to see Mikantor somehow.

If so, *he* did not seem to have been much affected. His gaze passed along the line of priestesses without pausing and returned to Anderle. Leaving his companions, he mounted the three steps to the portico and made the obeisance proper to her rank and grade with faultless grace, and if she found herself missing the enthusiasm with which he had hugged her as a child, she could hardly fault his self-control.

"My duty and love to the Lady of Avalon—" The pleasant deep voice was another surprise.

"Mikantor son of Irnana, Avalon welcomes you." It did no harm to remind him that here, his rank derived from the lineage of Avalon. Anderle held out her arms and offered first one cheek, then the other, in formal embrace. "You have long been lost to us. It is with joy that we welcome you home."

Mikantor ducked his head in acknowledgment, and oh, that *was* a heart-stopping smile, which a chipped tooth only made the more appealing. When he straightened, there was a light in his eye that lifted her spirits. With proper guidance, he might well have it in him to become a king.

"My dear, it is a good thing word of your coming came before you. We would hardly have recognized you," she said then.

"*You* have not changed," he replied, with another of those smiles, "nor has Avalon. But the holy isle is eternal."

Anderle shook her head, looking up at him. "Do not try to flatter me, my lad." And yet, on learning he had arrived she had put on her best robe and taken special care with the fall of her veil, and she did not think she was the only one. *We all have our vanity,* she thought ruefully, knowing he would probably not notice. "And who are these whom you have brought with you? The messages said you had a following, but not who they were."

"Ganath and Beniharen, you know—" He cocked his head at the two young men, who made the proper obeisance in their turn, "though there may be rather more of Beni than you remember. And these are Buda and her son Aelfrix from the City of Circles—" He motioned to the woman and boy to come forward. "They took us in when we arrived on the north coast of the Great Land. Her brother Bodovos trained me in the use of arms."

And thank the gods for that, thought Anderle. She had been wondering how a man who had never had a chance to use weapons could become a war leader. She looked forward to hearing the tale of his wanderings.

"And this is Velantos . . ." Some change in the timbre of Mikantor's voice focused her attention as the powerfully built black-bearded man who had stood behind the others came forward. Bent brows kept her from seeing his eyes, but he seemed to be somewhere in his late thirties, nearly her own age.

Stronger suns than theirs had browned his skin indeed. Everything about him, from the way he held himself to the gold rings in his ears, proclaimed that he came from a place of which she knew nothing. But whatever he was, she thought as he bent in a bow that, if not what she was used to, was clearly meant for someone of high degree, he was no barbarian. Rising, he intoned a resonant phrase in some foreign tongue.

"He does not speak our language?"

"Not much, great queen, but I learn—" His voice was very deep.

"We shall be glad to teach you." She smiled. With approval she noted the hard swell of muscle beneath the tunic. He must be a warrior of some note. With those arms and shoulders, anything he hit was not going to move again.

"Velantos and I have rescued each other from a thousand scrapes," Mikantor went on. "He has become my brother and my friend. But when I was first given to him as his slave, he was a prince of the great city of Tiryns, and a master smith of Akhaea."

A smith! The words took her breath. At that moment Velantos looked up and met her searching gaze. Without warning her other senses opened and she saw both body and the soul light that pulsed around him like the heat off a hearth. She knew this man! She had seen him—her cheeks heated as she remembered the dream in which she had embraced him in the fire of the forge.

And from the shock in his brown eyes, it seemed that he remembered it too . . .

Anderle's heart beat, slow and heavy as a ritual drum. *Goddess,* her soul cried, *what have you forged?*

"A master smith—" she managed to say aloud, for whatever his arrival might mean for them, it was not something to discuss before all the world. "Then you are doubly welcome. Our own smith has lately passed on and the smithy stands empty. Use it as you will."

Mikantor was asking about breakfast. Anderle hardly heard. She smiled and nodded as the party was introduced to the rest of the priests and priestesses and herded toward the dining hall, her inner sight still blinded by the vision of a flaming sword.

VELANTOS STOOD IN THE smithy on the Maiden's Isle, unable to believe that his journey had at last come to an end. The smithy was built to a familiar pattern, with three walls and a fourth that could be blocked by screens. In a niche set into the wall he saw a leaden image of the goddess of the forge, her crudely depicted garments reminding him of those worn for ritual by the ladies of his own land. He lifted the lid of the chest that had accompanied him for so many miles and released from her wrappings the clay image that lay atop his tools. He had been right—there was just room for his own image of the goddess beside the northern one.

As he stepped back, he heard a rustle of cloth from the doorway. He turned to see the Lady of Avalon standing there, sunlight shining through her veiling so that she seemed surrounded by a haze of light.

"Is permitted?" he pointed at the images.

"Oh yes—" Smiling, she put back the veil and came in. "Now we shall have two Maidens to guard the isle."

He bowed to cover the uneasy awareness she had produced in him since their first meeting the day before. She reminded him of Naxomene, but he had understood the source of the queen's magic. He knew nothing of Anderle's. *Medea. . .* he thought again. *She* had been useful too . . . and dangerous. He did not think Anderle would harm Mikantor—she was the boy's Dark Mother and would protect him, at least so long as he did her will.

I am the one who must be wary, he thought then. *She* wants *something of me.* Growing up in a royal hall he had learned to be careful with powerful people who wanted things.

"I see you have your own tools," she said pleasantly as he began to lay them on the workbench. "Is there anything else you will need?" Her voice made him think of honey warmed by the sun, but the lovely line of her lips gave nothing away.

He directed his gaze back to the smithy. Everything seemed to be of good quality, and had been well maintained. The firepot was set in a stone hearth. It too was hollowed from stone. A pipe of fired clay led from its side through the wall of the hearth and out to connect to the wind channel and the two bellows bags.

"Deerskin on bellows is old—" He pointed to the stiff leather. "Need make new."

"I will see about getting you appropriate hides. The hunters of the Lake Village can kill a doe, and their women sew leather well."

He nodded, deliberately not meeting her eyes. Had Medea looked like that, he wondered—small and pale, with a mass of dark hair whose tendrils escaped the braids wound around her head as if their power was too great for such bindings? What would that hair look like unconfined?

He thrust the image away and counted the fire tools, neatly racked in a wooden stand. The space in his chest had barely been enough for his hammers and other tools. And there too were a stout oaken bucket for water, a quenching tank, and a tightly woven basket for ashes, lined with clay. The charcoal would be kept in the shed outside. He hoped the shed might also contain clay for making molds.

Between the hearth and the workbench stood the anvil, a block of granite set into a section cut from the trunk of a mighty oak. He had brought with him a selection of smaller anvils made of bronze that he used for fine work, but for large pieces, the granite would do well.

"What will you make first?" asked Anderle.

"Spearheads," grunted the smith. "Galid steals mine." That memory burned in his belly, though not as badly as his brief return to slavery must trouble Mikantor.

Velantos still shuddered when he remembered how close the younger man had come to snapping. If Mikantor had fought, Galid's minions would have brought him down. *And me, as well,* he thought grimly, *for no amount of sense would have kept me from trying to defend him.* Which would at least have solved the problem of how he could survive without Mikantor in this strange land. *Or whether I would even want to . . .* he thought wistfully. Already Galid's threat was forcing them apart, he to the smithy and Mikantor to the training field, but at least here he would have work to do.

"Galid . . ." echoed the priestess. Her voice thinned, and Velantos felt that thrill of danger once more. He grimaced. She was half his size and weight—he could *break* her—so why did tension stiffen his limbs? *All* of his limbs, he realized, turning abruptly so she would not see how his body had responded. He set a piece of scrap bronze on the anvil and picked up the square-headed hammer, channeling his arousal into a blow that made the metal ring.

If this is what the woman's presence does to me, he thought ruefully, *I predict I will be working long and hard. . . .* And that was just as well, for Mikantor's men would need arms.

"Galid needs killing," he growled. "You find me bronze and I make spears."

"You will make swords . . ." she corrected softly. She had come so close he could smell her scent, like warm earth and flowers. "You will make *the* Sword, for Mikantor."

He jerked as Anderle's small hand gripped the hard muscle of his forearm, and turned despite his resolve, falling into the darkness of her eyes.

"A sword for a king . . ." she whispered, "and you are destined to make it. I have *seen* the Sword, Velantos, forged in fire!"

He could feel that fire blazing between them. With an oath he pulled away, breathing hard.

"Go!" he said harshly. "Send me workmen; I say what I need. But you go now—this is not your Mystery!" He twitched to the breath of air as she went by.

"Is it not?" The light flickered as she passed through the door. As her footsteps faded, he heard her laugh.

NOW THAT IS A MAN! Anderle laughed again as she sped down the path. She had forgotten what it was like to respond to a man's power. When Tirilan was mooning over Mikantor, she should have shown more sympathy, though how could she have known? Even when she was besotted with Tiri's father, Anderle had never felt such a fire in the blood.

It was clear that Velantos felt it too. Her lips twitched as she recalled his reaction. She had known he would work hard for Mikantor, but now, she thought, he would labor with all the passion he possessed to prove himself her equal in power.

Sexual attraction was a mighty force. The traditions of Avalon had a great deal to say about the ways in which it could be used to raise and channel energy. In the most esoteric teachings it was the female who was the awakener, whose energy aroused the male to purpose and power. And the power was greatest when it was channeled into labor of body or spirit rather than being grounded in the act of love.

Which was rather a pity, she reflected, remembering the hard muscle beneath the taut skin. If the rest of his body was as powerful . . .

It doesn't matter, she told herself firmly as she crossed the bridge that covered the low ground between the isles. His body had to be capable of the work he was needed to do. He could have been as ugly as the son of the Chiding One and she would still have put forth her power to attract him. Her business was his soul. That she might find denying the body's claims as painful as he did was not relevant. She was the Lady of Avalon, and her life belonged to the land. To bring the Son of a Hundred Kings to power, all sacrifices were justified.

By the time Anderle reached the courtyard where the community gathered on sunny days, she trusted that her flushed cheeks could be put down to exercise. Mikantor was waiting for her there. A healthy young animal, she thought, appreciating the picture he made with the sunlight glinting on his hair. Velantos was too rugged, too dark, to be beautiful. Why did the younger man not stir her blood? But of course, Mikantor was like a son to her. Surely that was reason enough—she thrust all other thoughts away.

"Did you get Velantos settled in the smithy?" Mikantor asked as she sat down beside him. "Does he have everything he needs?"

As opposed to everything he might want? Anderle smiled. "He will need supplies," she said aloud. "When you go over to the Lake Village, you can make the arrangements."

"I am going to the village? Of course I want to see them all, but I thought there were things—"

"This is one of them," said Anderle. "You cannot achieve the task to which you are called alone. You will need Companions. Ganath and Beniharen follow you already, but they are not warriors. The people of the Lake have fine scouts and hunters. Your foster brother Grebe is of an age to be useful. Talk to him, see if you want him in your band."

"Yes, of course," Mikantor said thoughtfully. "Now that Velantos has his forge I need to get started on the rest of it. But you have to understand, it is very important that he should be happy here—"

No, thought the priestess, *it is very important that he be* productive. *A little unhappiness is often a goad, where content would only sap the will to achieve.*

"We had to leave Bhagodheunon because of me, and then I dragged him with me across the sea—" Mikantor went on. "I can still remember how strange his country seemed to me, and I am sure he is feeling just as unsettled in mine."

"Leave him to me . . . though if I am to be . . . helpful . . . perhaps you had best tell me a bit more about him," Anderle replied. "I suspect he is not very forthcoming at the best of times—is that not so?" If things went as she expected between them, she might be the *last* person to whom the smith would want to open his heart. But it made sense to gather as much information as possible about someone who was so important to their cause.

Mikantor began to laugh. "He says himself that he can be like a bear with a sore head, but he never turned his temper on me—well, almost never, and then it was because he was in pain . . ."

Anderle gave him a quick look. "If you were his slave, I'd have thought you would be glad to see the last of him."

Mikantor frowned. "By their law he owned me, but he treated me as another human being from the first day. Not an equal, for I was only an ignorant boy, no better with his language than he is with ours now, but a fellow creature. He never demanded more of me than he did of himself. For Velantos, it is the work that matters above all."

"That, I can understand . . ." Anderle found herself smiling. *And I will give you work, man of the south, and until it is done spare neither you nor myself, whatever the pain!*

Tirilan lay on her bed, still wakeful, though midnight had come and gone. Through the narrow window she could see the waxing moon. Did Mikantor, who slept in the priests' dormitory with Ganath and Beniharen, watch the moon as well, or did he enjoy the sleep that was the normal reward of healthy exercise? He had spent the afternoon on the playing field, testing his archery against that of Grebe. They could not know that she had watched them, feasting her eyes on the graceful flex and release of his body as he bent the bow.

Since that morning when he first arrived, they had not spoken. Her memory of those moments seemed a part of the dream that had sent her to meet him on the shore of Avalon.

I gave him the blessing of a priestess, she thought sadly, *when what I wanted was to kiss him like a lover. And he looked at me like a man who sees the Goddess, not one who welcomes the woman he desires.*

She had thought that when they met again that would change, that he would realize she was a human woman, and they could begin to reclaim the friendship they had shared so long ago. When they parted he had been a boy, and she had been a dreaming girl, and neither had any concept of the body's needs.

If he had stayed, we might have made those discoveries together. From the appreciation with which he had looked at the priestesses, she thought he was not without experience. But she had been taught the theory and forbidden the practice.

When Mikantor encountered her at meals, or on one of the paths, his gaze flew to her face and then flicked away. Was he still seeing her as the Goddess, or had he learned that she had taken her vows and was not for any man? She could not even blame her mother this time. It was the Goddess Herself, or whoever had sent that dream in which she was the one who must make Mikantor a king, who had sent her to give him that blessing.

But her mother seemed to have taken charge of the king-making as well, she thought resentfully, sending word to the other priestesses of the sisterhood, summoning men to a conference at the Tor.

It is my own fault . . . she admitted, *for thinking that the Goddess gave me a destiny.* But short of stripping naked and surprising Mikantor when he went down to the Lake to bathe, she did not see how she could get him to think of her as a woman now.

Lady, help me, she prayed. *Because seven years have made him a man, and beautiful, and I do not know if the boy I loved is still there at all.*

But the moon did not reply.

EIGHTEEN

*S*ummer had come to Avalon, with more days of sun, or at least cloud, than rain. Only a few sections of the playing field squished underfoot, for which the young men who had come to join Mikantor's band were grateful. He stood watching them now as they used practice blades to go through the stylized sword moves.

"I wish my uncle had come with us," said Aelfrix, who was standing beside him with a waterskin filled with tea made from the hips of the wild rose. Anderle had sent it down to refresh them.

"Bodovos would have made you work harder," observed Mikantor.

"I know, but at least we wouldn't spend so much time standing around . . ."

Mikantor could only agree. He wished he had paid better attention during the endless drills Bodovos had imposed on the City of Circles Guard. But it had never occurred to him that he might need to pass on the knowledge imprinted by constant practice in his muscles and nerves. He knew how to *do* these things, but not to how to explain them. Far too often, drill would come to a halt while the instructor tried to remember the next step in an exercise.

The one advantage was that he himself had recovered all his old form. He might even have improved, although without a skilled swordsman with whom to spar there was no way to know. Possibly the lack of a convenient inn at which to drink with his companions had something to do with it. With two pure springs to draw from, fermented drinks were only for ritual use at Avalon.

"Crack! Clack!" The men worked their way back and forth, swinging the wooden blades Velantos had carved to have the general weight and shape of the swords he would be casting as more metal came in. In the meantime, the bronze stored in the old smithy had already been made into spearheads, so the men were not completely unarmed. Perhaps this afternoon they should switch to practice with the spears.

What Mikantor was going to *do* with these young warriors once he had trained them was still something of a question. Some of them, he suspected, simply craved the excitement of battle, but most came from places that had suffered from Galid's depredations. They assumed he would be going after the usurper to avenge his parents. But if he succeeded, what then? His aunt, the rightful queen of the Ai-Zir, had died while he was away. Anderle said that his cousin Cimara led a sad, circumscribed life on her farmstead, with the title of queen but no power. Galid had killed every man who dared to court her, so she had no children either. He thought he had seen her once at a festival, but she did not know him. If he got rid of Galid, would she even want him?

And was king of the Ai-Zir what he wanted to be? He had been born in Azan, but Galid had kept him from growing up there. He thought of the Lake Village or Avalon as home. He agreed that Galid needed killing, but how could he help the other tribes if they thought of him as a man of Azan?

They had taken a break to share the tea when Aelfrix came running back with the news that two more recruits had reached the isle. Mikantor looked around at the young men who were lounging or lying exhausted on the grass. He had tried to be honest with them, making no promises except for the training itself. One day he would want an army, but for now the number of his Companions must be limited to a group that could move swiftly and that he could afford to feed.

His foster brother Grebe had been the first to join him here. He was already a good field archer, but knew nothing of the sword. Acaimor and Romen were almost as dark and slim as Lake Folk, strong and fast. They had come up from the Ai-Utu lands, because Romen remembered Mikantor from his time in Belerion. Pelicar, as tall as Beniharen but fair, like him was from the People of the Boar. He was a son of their queen, accustomed to rule, and was proving an able commander. Dun-haired Tegues had been a boyhood friend of Ganath and followed him. Adjonar was the first of the Ai-Zir to find the courage to join the man they hoped would deliver them from Galid.

If we can watch over each other, we shall not do so badly, thought Mikantor.

As the newcomers approached, those who had been relaxing sat up, not yet hostile, but watchful as sheepdogs. The young man in the lead was of middle height and as black bearded as Velantos. In fact he had very much the look of the smith. As he neared, Mikantor held up a hand in greeting, "Be welcome, man of the south," he said in the Akhaean tongue.

The fellow stopped short, a white grin appearing in the midst of the short beard. "'Tis true then, you dwelt at the Middle Sea!" The accent was odd, but clearly the man had understood him. "Ach, I don't know the old speech well enough," he added in the language of the tribes. "I am called Lysandros son of Ardanos. My grandfather came here with Brutus after Troia fell. We took land in the southeast, where the white cliffs are."

Relieved to have guessed right, Mikantor clasped Lysandros' hand. "You will have to talk with Velantos of Tiryns, our smith."

"An Akhaean?" Lysandros grimaced, and Mikantor guessed he had been raised on tales of the rape of Troia.

"Troia has been avenged," said Mikantor. "Tiryns has fallen to the Children of Erakles, and Mykenae and Korinthos as well. Your people and Velantos are equally exiles now."

Lysandros shrugged and then grinned. "Very well, but do not tell my grandfather I have sat down in peace with an Akhaean!"

"And who is your companion?" Mikantor nodded toward the other man, a wiry fellow with reddish hair who hung back as if unsure of his welcome.

"His name is Ulansi," began Lysandros—

"And he is a filthy traitor, come to spy on us for Galid!" Adjonar interrupted him.

Mikantor raised an eyebrow. "Then we should at least grant him credit for courage. You, Ulansi, come here if you please. Is what Adji saying true?"

"If you mean did I serve in Galid's band, yes, it's so—" the newcomer said slowly. "He came to our steading looking for men. If my father had refused to let me go, he would have burned us out. To agree was the only way I could save my home. But as for the other accusation—never! Even before the next year, when the Ai-Ushen wiped out my family—and Galid did nothing to avenge them—I would have done all in my power to bring him down."

"I see . . ." Mikantor said slowly. It was a plausible story, but then it would be, if Galid had sent a spy. And yet there was little damage the man could do here at Avalon. Anderle would see into his heart and know if he was true. "Serving with Galid, you would know how he likes to fight, and how he trains his men . . ."

"Yes, lord." Ulansi's eyes brightened. "That is why I have come. If I must bear the name of traitor"—he glared at Adjonar—"it will not be for betraying *you!*"

Mikantor nodded. "You will be tested, of course, but I am inclined to trust you. My own teacher always said that a wise man knows his enemy, and I have been out of the country for a long time. To most of us Galid is as evil as Guayota, loathed for what he does, but we do not know *why.* I need to know how he thinks, what he wants . . ."

Ulansi looked taken aback by Mikantor's intensity, but he answered with a bow. "Lord, I was not in his counsels, but he has grown proud, and did not always watch his tongue before the men. I will try to remember what I heard, and help you in every way I can."

THE BRONZE BLADE FLEXED as Velantos laid it on the anvil, picked up one of his round stone hammers, and began to tap the edge. "By strength and skill the sword is made—hammer hit and harden blade!" he whispered, timing his strokes to the spell until he had established and internalized the rhythm, moving back and forth along the blade. Being hammered made the bronze harder—as the troubles he had endured had done for Mikantor. He looked back at the younger man, who leaned against the frame of the open door of the smithy watching him.

"The metal we got from Belerion was good, then?"

"Very good. Your friend the merchant chose well," Velantos replied. This was the second of the leaf-shaped swords he had cast since his arrival at Avalon, but the first with the new bronze.

Mikantor laughed. "I think Master Anaterve still feels guilty for letting me be snapped up by Galid's men under his very nose. He seemed quite happy to support the cause."

"You gave the first sword to Pelicar?" Velantos asked.

"He is a queen's son and had some training already. The others are working their hearts out to win the second blade! They've taken to practicing the hero feats as well. It will be a long time before we can do anything with chariots, but the playing field is large enough for races and the long jump, and the grass soft enough for tumbling and wrestling."

Velantos turned the sword and began to work down the other edge. Once he had crafted ornaments in gold for queens. If Mikantor was victorious, there might be time for such things once more. In the meantime, the blade had its own deadly beauty. And so, he thought as he looked at the young man again, did Mikantor.

There was a clarity to his features that had not been there before, as if the responsibility he now carried had stripped away the last of his boyhood. Mikantor might still doubt his ability to bear that weight, but despite his ambivalence, returning here had clearly been the right thing for him to do. Whether it was the right thing for Velantos remained to be seen.

It was inevitable that they should grow apart now that Mikantor was a man. It would have been wrong for him to try to hold the lad to their old companionship. But how he missed the days when they had shared everything. Moments when they could talk quietly were becoming increasingly rare, and if—when—the fighting was done they would be rarer still. When Mikantor was safe in his rightful place, the smith would leave, though where on this earth he might find a home he could not say.

"The men are shaping well," Mikantor said thoughtfully, "but they are still thinking of themselves as Boars or Rams or Frogs or Hares instead of as members of my band. Except for Adjonar, that is," he added, "who seems unwilling to breathe the same air as Ulansi, much less claim kinship. It was different in the guard, where everyone was born to the City or had come in from the countryside."

"That will change when they face the enemy," said Velantos. "When I was young, there was an old man at Tiryns who had been with Agamemnon at Troia and was always ready with a tale. He said that when the Akhaeans were stuck at Aulis waiting for a wind, the men of the different cities were ready to cut each other's throats, but they were all one people when they lay before the walls of Troia."

"Goddess, don't say that to Lysandros!" exclaimed Mikantor. "He learned to hate Akhaeans at his grandda's knee, though to him both Troia and Tiryns are as legendary as the Blessed Isles."

"I know." The smith smiled. "He looks at me as if I'm about to turn into a gorgon. It is a pity. I would enjoy talking to someone other than you with whom I don't have to speak like a child."

"It will come—you are much more fluent already," Mikantor said earnestly. "Would it help if I sent one of the men here each day to help you?"

Velantos' reply died on his lips as a sound or a scent or some sense beyond either turned him toward the doorway. Anderle stood there. As always, she seemed limned in light, and as always, her presence sent a flash of heat through his core.

"A man whose daughter serves in Galid's hall has arrived with news. The usurper knows that you are here." The priestess had clearly come in a hurry, dressed in an old gown and without her veil. Velantos noted the sparkle of perspiration at her brow and the pulse at her throat and looked quickly away.

"He's coming?" Mikantor straightened.

"That's a reasonable assumption," Anderle said dryly.

"We will have to leave. We cannot risk an attack on Avalon. This is not unexpected. Grebe and I have discussed what to do. There are places in these marshes that only the Lake Folk know. We can disappear like mist in the reeds and live on the land."

"That helps bind your men," said Velantos with a wry smile. "I pack tools. . . ."

"But you cannot go with them!" exclaimed the priestess. "You must stay at the smithy to forge the Sword!"

"*Swords*—" corrected Velantos, glaring. This was becoming an old argument between them. The blade Mikantor already bore was the best he had been able to make when they were in the City of Circles. He saw no point in trying to improve on it when what was needed was more blades for Mikantor's men.

"And be taken by Galid?" objected Mikantor.

"I can hide one," Anderle answered, "but not a whole band." She turned to Velantos, and her gaze was like the heat of the forge. "Swords, then. How many will you be able to make when you are skulking in the marshes?"

"But you cannot—" He looked at Mikantor and his voice failed. *Cannot go without me . . . cannot leave me alone with* her . . . He did not know which he feared more. But he could not say so, could not cling, could not even look at Mikantor lest the younger man see the desolation in his eyes. "Yes," he said, keeping his voice from wavering with an effort of will. "Is true I need the forge. I stay here."

The new moon was sliding toward the distant sea. Soon she would sleep beneath the waves, but on Avalon, there was no rest. Some were busy at the ovens, baking trailbread and stuffing into lengths of cured gut the mixture of pounded dried meat and berries that would stay good for moons if it was kept dry. Others were putting the last stitches into garments for Mikantor's men. Tirilan had snatched up several lengths of felted and oiled wool and the cords and wooden toggles that would turn them into rain capes and carried them off to her cubicle, afraid that if she worked alongside the others she would start weeping and they would ask her why.

She stabbed the bone needle through the cloth to bind the cut end of the wool and felt a tear splash hot upon her hand. Would her tears add protection? If so, let them fall. Let each tear be a blessing to keep the wearer of this cape from harm. And if the tears were not sufficient, an embroidered sigil of protection would be a more visible reminder. As she finished the last of the capes, she took up another needle and threaded it with yellow wool.

In another part of the complex of buildings that housed the community someone was singing a silly song about the adventures of a cuckoo bird. Tirilan smiled through her tears. Mikantor had been the cuckoo thrust into the Lake Village nest, but he had grown up beautiful, powerful, and fierce as a swan.

She looked down, and realized that the stitches she had just put in made the beginning of the shape of the bird. Let this one be for Mikantor, then. If she could not be there to protect him with magic, let her love be bound into the cloth. Stitching more swiftly now she finished the figure and began to add more—a lightning bolt, a tree, a bull, all the symbols of strength and power she could think of, intertwining across the shoulders of the cape in a frieze of protection. Finally, she added the winged sun that their ancestors had brought from the Drowned Lands and the triple moon of Avalon.

The young moon had already set, and the air was taking on the fresh damp scent that preceded the dawn. At this season the sun would rise early, and Mikantor wanted to move out with the break of day. Tirilan gathered up the capes and made her way down the passage that would let her take the shortcut across the garden. She stopped short as she realized that someone was sitting on the bench by the sundial, and in the next moment realized that it was Mikantor.

Goddess, my thanks for this blessing! She took another step.

"Tirilan, is that you?"

She nodded. Her heart was thumping so madly she did not know if she could form words.

"Do you have a moment to talk to me?" The uncertainty in his tone wrenched her heart. Slowly she moved toward him.

"Do you remember that argument we had here about our ages? When I found out I was not who I thought I was? Now that I know, it still seems unreal. I have learned to face my own dangers, but what gives me the right to risk the lives of others?" He peered at her through the darkness, and when she did not answer, moved over and patted the bench. "Will you sit with me, or is that not permitted by your vows?"

At his words a surge of warmth freed her and she took the steps that would bring her to his side. *It is discouraged,* she thought, *lest we fall into temptation—* Temptations like the solid warmth of him, that made her want to clasp him in her arms. All the men had scrubbed themselves thoroughly that afternoon— the last chance they might have to get really clean for some time—and she could smell the scent of the bath herbs on his hair.

"What are you carrying?" he asked.

"Rain capes, for you and your men." She found her voice at last. "This one is for you—" She lifted the topmost from the pile. "If you will feel along the top you will find the sigils of protection I have embroidered there. And the images of the powers. I have put a swan on it for the emblem of your band."

"Oh Goddess, yes—" He laughed. "Do you remember the time that Ai-Akhsi boy—I can't remember his name—tried to rob a swan's nest and the male broke his arm with a sweep of one wing?"

"He went home soon after," Tirilan recalled. If she kept talking, she might be able to resist the urge to take his hand. What was wrong with her? In the stories it was always the man who made the advances. But Mikantor had clearly gotten it into his head that she was as sacrosanct as Anderle herself.

"This place seems so peaceful and secure," he said slowly, "but it has its own dangers for those who are not meant to be here. Or at least that is what I keep telling myself," he added, "when I think about Galid coming to Avalon."

"My mother faced him down before," said Tirilan. "I believe in her magic."

"If he finds us here we will fight, and blood must not be shed on Avalon. And so I am right to go, though it feels like deserting in the face of the enemy."

"You are right to go—" She echoed as the silence deepened.

"And they will all look to me, once we are out in the marshes. Here at least I can turn to Velantos or Anderle, but what will I do if they ask questions I cannot answer?"

"What you do already," she answered, knowing he did not realize how often she had watched him unseen. "Call the others to council. You are beginning to know already the strengths of each man. Living in the wilds will confirm that knowledge."

"Of course—I have done that—and knowing I value their opinions seems to please the men . . ." He sighed. "Thank you. To talk to you is like giving my own soul a voice to answer me, Tirilan."

She repressed her own sigh, realizing that was true. He *was* talking to himself, not to a living, breathing human being with needs like his own. And yet if this was all she could do for him, she should count herself blessed.

"My spirit will go with you, Mikantor," she said softly. "Every day and every night, my prayers will shelter you. Talk to me whenever you have need, and in the silence of your heart I will answer you."

"And so I will have my very own protecting goddess? It is you who will be the swan, Tirilan, sheltering us beneath your wings . . ."

"Be it so—" she murmured, though her heart was crying out to him to take her with him. But what use would she be in the wilds? Better by far to let his belief in her give him strength than to weaken him with her fallible reality.

"Mikantor—" came a call from within. "Mikantor, where are you, man? The sun will be rising soon and we must go!" It sounded like Ganath.

Looking up, Tirilan saw that the sky was fading to gray. She could see Mikantor's face. Better that she should go now, before he got a good look at hers and realized that her cheeks were wet with tears. She rose quickly and stepped behind him, spreading the cape across his shoulders as if she were indeed shielding him with wings. He sighed again, and let his head rest back against her breast. For a moment she allowed herself to hold him, breathing in the scent of his hair. Then she kissed the top of his head and let him go.

"May Manoah light your way," she whispered, "and may Ni-Terat support you, and may all the gods and goddesses of this land grant you guidance and aid until we meet once more."

Before he could turn, she gathered up the other capes and sped back across the garden. Ganath called him again, and the sky grew bright with the coming of the day.

————

"Earth and water spread below,
Light and air above,
Food to eat, a place to sleep,
And a good woman's love!"

From somewhere back down the line, Romen, as usual, was singing.

"That's all I need for wandering,
That's all I need to go,
That's all I need to carry on,
That's all I need to know!"

"Hush up there, man, d'ye want Galid to hear ye?" called Pelicar.

"Water we've got in plenty, and food, if this sack I'm bearing does not lie, but places to sleep look less numerous, and as for women, where we're going, the marsh wives are all we're likely to see, and their beds are too damp for me!" Adjonar added cheerfully.

They all seemed cheerful, thought Mikantor. They sounded like a band of boys heading out on an adventure, as blithe as he and Beaver and Grebe had been when they explored the marshes so long ago.

"And speaking of love, that's a fine cape you're wearing," added Adjonar. "All prettied up with embroidery—"

Mikantor flushed. Even though it was not raining, he had worn the cape when they left. He had not seen Tirilan among those who waved good-bye, but he hoped that she had been watching from somewhere. He had felt her presence, and wondered if it was imagination that made him feel her near him still.

"The lady Tirilan made it," he said repressively, "and I'll thank you to respect her name."

"Oh, aye," Adji answered, sobering, "and we all are grateful for the capes, even without the fancy stitchery. A good and fair lady is that one, and we are glad of her blessing."

"We have it," said Mikantor through a throat that had gone oddly tight. That predawn conversation had left him shaken. Why had he never found time to talk to her? It occurred to him now that she had said very little to him during the time he had been at Avalon, though she had always greeted him with a smile. Perhaps her vows forbade it, he thought with an unexpected flicker of resentment. But absorbed in work with his men, he had not even tried to meet her, and now the chance was gone.

"But I suppose sleeping places are fair game for discussion," Adji said then. "D'ye have a plan for tonight, or are we to splash about until we trip over solid ground?"

"That is not fair—" objected Grebe, pointing to the wooden trackway that led to the higher ground to the south and west and the path around the edge of the lake. "Are you not still dry shod?"

"Aye well, that'll not last for long. . . ." mourned Adji, but he was grinning.

"The boats had better be waiting where your people hid them," added Pelicar. "I have never learned to swim."

"*You* don't need a boat, tall one," grunted Grebe. "You go like the heron, stalking through the reeds!"

Mikantor released a breath he had not realized he was holding as others joined in the joking and they continued on.

THREE CROWS HAD SETTLED on the oak tree at the corner of the garden. Every so often one of them cawed in a demanding, minatory tone.

"Galid is coming," muttered Velantos. "Yes. Thank you. We know." The Lake Village scouts who had been watching the roads for the past moon had brought word that the Ai-Zir were on their way, and the people of Avalon were waiting. Velantos hitched up the robe of undyed wool in which they had dressed him and wondered if Galid would recognize him. When he had looked into the waters of the reflecting pool, he had scarcely recognized himself. With his beard shaved and hair trimmed short enough to release its curl, the face that looked back at him was one he had not seen since his beard began to grow. Only the silver streaks that Anderle had painted into his hair belied that youthfulness. His lips twitched in amusement as he remembered that the priests at the healing shrine in Korinthos had worn their hair this way.

The only priesthood to which he had ever aspired was that of the Lady of the Forge. But if Galid's men searched, they would see the smithy on the Maiden's Isle, and to find him there would have identified him as the smith from whom the usurper had stolen those spearheads. Galid would not have left him free to make more for his enemies. And so here he was on his knees in the garden, hoping that he had not pulled up the sprouting lettuce instead of the weeds. Anderle had chosen to pretend that they had had no warning, as well as nothing to hide, and everyone had a task. With any luck, their foe would pay no attention to him at all.

From the passage between the dormitory of the priestesses and the Hall of the Sun came the sound of voices and then the scrape of footsteps. Velantos dug his fingers into the soil, waiting. The clouds left from yesterday's rain passed overhead, sending patterns of light and shadow among the leaves.

"As you can see, I have no army hidden here—" That was Anderle's most astringent tone. Velantos felt a sour satisfaction to hear it directed at someone else for a change.

"That is quite apparent. But why this demure hospitality? At the least I expected shrouding mists or lightning! I mistrust this face of innocence, my lady, even more than the defiance with which you usually greet me."

It was the gravelly voice of the man Velantos had met on the road. Surely it would be in character to turn and stare as the priestess and her unwelcome guest followed the path into the garden. This was certainly the same man, but he seemed older. Though his tunic was dyed a rich red, it bore old stains, and he had a nervous twitch Velantos had not noticed before. Or perhaps it was simply a response to Anderle. Galid sat down on the bench, and after a moment's hesitation the priestess joined him.

"The sooner you look at everything the sooner you and your bullies will be gone," the priestess said tartly.

"Who is that fellow?" Galid asked then. "I do not recall seeing him before."

"Do you not?" Anderle's tone was offhand and Velantos forced himself to turn to the lettuce again. "He is a minor priest, left with speech and wits impaired by a fever, but very strong in body, as you can see."

"Is he now? Perhaps I should take him off your hands—" Galid said pleasantly.

"That would be unkind, since as you have seen we are mostly a community of women and old men, and need someone who can carry heavy burdens. Besides, his illness has left him subject to fits when no strength of men will hold him. At other times he babbles nonsense, and can only be calmed when I speak a Word of Power."

Was that a sudden inspiration, my lady? wondered Velantos, moving from the lettuce to the climbing beans, through whose screen he could watch the bench, *or did you have that explanation planned? Babbling like a barbarian indeed!*

"Enough of the fool—" Galid's scabbard scraped the stone as he turned. "I can see that your young cousin is not here, but it is also obvious that you sheltered him. This will not happen again."

"*Will* not?" asked Anderle. "You forget that *I* am the mistress here."

"Only so long as I allow it. Be grateful that I do not burn your temple to the ground and take your priestesses to grind my corn! As for you"—his voice deepened—"you are still young enough to serve me in my bed . . ."

Velantos' fingers closed convulsively on some plant and wrenched it from the soil. He told himself that the priestess was in no danger. Whatever happened to the others, surely she could summon a dragon chariot like Medea and fly away.

"Or your lovely daughter might do—" From Anderle came a sharp hiss and Galid laughed. "Though she is rather too sweet for my taste."

"Galid—" Anderle's voice shook with wrath, not fear. "What in the name of all that's holy do you *want*? Have you dedicated yourself to evil for amusement or revenge? Who could have hurt you so badly that you must make the rest of the world suffer? Do you not fear the gods?"

The hair rose on the back of Velantos' neck at the usurper's laugh, and the crows began to caw once more. He parted the leaves. Galid was staring at Anderle. Still grinning, he reached out and took up a lock of her curling hair. "Lady," Galid said with bleak assurance, "do you think the world would be dying around us if there were gods? There is only this life, and the sensations we can force it to yield. Your calm is death in life. I could pierce that detachment . . ." His grip tightened on her hair. "They say that your bed has been empty since I killed that fool Durrin all those years ago. Have you found no man to be your match, or your master?"

His voice grew harsh, and Velantos saw that he was looking at Anderle as a woman, not as an opponent. Now, thought the smith, might be a good time to summon those dragons. Anderle's eyes blazed. Velantos felt a familiar stirring in his own flesh, knowing exactly what the other man must feel. And Galid had no inhibitions, no honor, no fear.

One of the crows flapped down to the trellis where the bean vines twined, head cocked as if to ask what Velantos was waiting for. Would a lunge reach Galid before he could draw that sword?

"Let me go!" snapped Anderle, and Galid reached for her with his other hand.

Help me, holy gods! Velantos started to rise.

"Paion!" squawked the crow.

Velantos opened his lips to shout, but what came from his lips was "Paion! Paion!" More words followed as he fell back to his knees again, but though they sounded like babble to the others, he recognized the hymn to Apollon that he had heard at the temple in Korinthos each day, its words already ancient when the Children of Erakles were exiled from their southern home. He barely understood them, but as his lips moved, meaning blossomed within.

"Paean, Lord of Light! Wind and fire and the lifting of darkness! Paean, light that banishes all shadow, light in which no evil can endure! Paean, Apollon, strong to save!" The heart-shaped leaves of the young bean plants fluttered to a sudden blast of wind. The clouds parted and suddenly the garden was filled with light as the crows swirled upward in a cacophony of black wings.

"Now see what you have done!" Anderle sprang to her feet as Galid, looking dazed, released her hair. "And he was doing so well!" Shaking her head, she hurried toward Velantos, muttering something that sounded like a spell. "My poor boy, be calm—he will not hurt me—all is well . . ."

Velantos looked up at her, seeing for once beyond the womanly body that had dazzled him to the brave spirit within. "Potnia . . ." he whispered, the fire in his soul leaping to touch hers, and saw in her eyes a spark of laughter.

Galid grunted. "Is the idiot your lover? I wish you joy of him. But this I promise you—when I have dealt with your bull calf I will return, and no power will keep you from me, neither man nor god!" He lurched to his feet. As he strode off down the passageway, cloud dimmed the light once more.

"Will it not?" Anderle hissed. Her grip tightened on Velantos' shoulder. "Could you not tell that a god was here just now?"

Velantos blinked, trying to understand what had just occurred. Like an echo he heard within his soul the Voice that had spoken in his temple dream. *"Indeed. . . did I not say you would find me in the north as well? Be strong. Your work here is not yet done . . ."*

NINETEEN

*T*he gray geese were gathering on the Lake, gleaning the last of the summer food. For weeks the skies had echoed with the cries of migrating fowl. The geese would be the last to go. There were still leaves on some of the trees, but Anderle did not need the birds to tell her that autumn was passing. The wind that blew across the water was cold. When the boat reached the village, Badger was waiting to help her up the ladder. Shivering, she followed him into his hut and set her cold hands gratefully around the clay beaker of hot herb tea.

"We are in health here, as you in Avalon," said the headman, facing her across the fire.

"I thank the gods for it," said Anderle. "It is the men in the marshes I fear for. I dare not bring them back to Avalon, and they cannot spend winter in the wilds."

"True. Damp is worse when it's cold. Many islets will be underwater soon." Badger added another brand to the hearth fire. His hair was all brindle now. One could scarcely distinguish the white streaks that had given him his name. "You cannot send them to the tribes?"

"In a settlement they could not be hidden. In the mountains there are other peoples like yours, descended from those who were here before the tribes. Can you contact them?"

"Ah . . ." The headman sat back, frowning. "It is so. They know places Galid's spies would not come, but the men of the tribes have not been kind to them. They will not welcome Mikantor's band."

"Is there no way to persuade them?" asked Anderle. "Mikantor cares for more than the Ai-Zir. Given the chance, he will do what he can to bring peace to all the land."

Badger leaned forward again to poke at the fire. "There is one way—" he said at last. "Very old ritual. Long ago we who now live on the edges used it to test our chieftains. If he can do it—if he survives it—all those of the old blood will follow him."

Anderle's skin prickled with apprehension, but the destiny to which Mikantor had been born was one of danger. It would be foolish to think she could protect him now. "Tell me—"

"You are priests of the Light on the holy isle, and this is a rite of blood, a mystery from the times when our people did not herd or plant, but lived from the breast of Earth our Mother. I tell you this because you are also of the old blood, and because Woodpecker was our fosterling." His voice grew softer and she leaned toward him across the fire. "The red deer is holy animal. The stag dies so that we live. But sometimes the Mother wants blood for blood, and the hunter is the offering. When we take life we know we owe our lives."

Anderle nodded. That blood debt was one reason they so rarely ate meat on Avalon. "But it is different for a king?" she asked then.

Badger nodded. "Hunters kill from a distance, with spear and bow, but the king must be brave to fight as the beasts do, face to face. The Virgin Huntress calls him, calls the Horned Lord into him, sends him to run with the deer." His voice was a whisper now. "He catches the King Stag, uses his tooth of flint to shed his blood—or the Stag's horns find his heart. Either way Earth is fed."

"And if the hunter lives?"

"He is given to the priestess who carries the power of the Mistress of the Beasts," the headman replied. "She gives virgin blood. He makes her the Mother. She makes him King. They renew the land."

He straightened, perspiration beading his brow. Had he ever seen this rite done? Clearly he believed in its power. And if Badger, whose people lived so close to Avalon that they had absorbed many of their ways, believed, then those others, the dark secret people of the hills, would surely believe as well.

"Do you have a suitable priestess?" she asked then. "If not, there is a maiden at Avalon who can carry the power."

She did not think Tirilan would refuse this opportunity. And when she had known the ecstasy of the Great Rite, Goddess joined with God, she would forget her childish fantasies.

MIKANTOR'S SKIN TWITCHED AS Badger drew the woad-soaked leather swab across his skin, leaving a broad streak of blue. It was mixed with other herbs, and had an odd, acrid scent. Whatever the deer smelled, it would not be man. After three days of preparation, Mikantor was no longer certain if he *was* still a man.

The flame of the torch flapped as the dawn wind blew more strongly, alternately dazzling and dark. The Lake Folk had brought him to a natural clearing in the hills to the north of the marshes, though he had had no chance to look around. He had been kept in a hut for the past three days. The part of his mind that still stood apart put his sense of dissociation down to the effects of a vegetarian diet and isolation. But his deep mind was increasingly ascendant, increasingly sensitive to the scent of forest mold beneath his feet and the sound the bare branches of the oak tree made as they rubbed together in the wind. He wore only a belt that held a flint knife, but he did not feel cold. They said that sometimes the hunter lost his life in this ritual. He wondered if the hunter ever lost his humanity.

"But why do they have to paint him *blue?*" asked Pelicar, still rubbing the sleep from his eyes. He had been the most protective, but also the most understanding. In his country, he said, there were special rites of test and consecration when a war leader was chosen by the queen. Though not, Mikantor gathered, quite like this one.

"I suppose because they don't have a dye that will turn him green," Ganath replied. "I believe that to the deer it is much the same."

"Well, I hope the priestess likes blue, because that stuff *stains!*"

"Maybe she will be blue as well," laughed Tegues, who could be depended on to join any conversation about women. "Blue titties and blue buttocks and blue—"

"Hold your tongue!" snarled Romen, for the old blood ran strong in the folk of Belerion. "This is a sacred thing. By rights we should not be here at all."

"Do you think we would give our lord into the power of the magic people unguarded?" retorted Pelican.

Mikantor's lips quirked in mingled exasperation and pride. He supposed their attitude was a tribute to the bond that the past few months had created among the members of his band, but it would not do to insult their allies.

From somewhere beyond the thicket came the throb of drums and a murmur of many voices. The elder folk were awake as well, gathering to see him triumph or die. Either way, the blood of a king would feed the soil. His heart raced even as he twitched in apprehension, the man in him responding, the beast wanting to flee.

"My lord, how is it with you?" Ganath's voice was low.

Mikantor's head jerked around, seeing his friend with doubled vision—a thickset, brown-haired young man in a threadbare woolen tunic, and a sturdy brown bear. Now that he was looking, he could see the animal shapes that followed all of them.

"Head's . . .fuzzy . . ." with an effort he formed the human words, though that did not quite describe the sensation, not exactly a headache, but a pressure within his skull. It had been increasing since the day before.

"It is expected," muttered Badger, swabbing color down his arms. "It will pass."

Mikantor hoped so. If he didn't fall over as soon as he began to run, perhaps action would burn it away. He twitched again, turning his head uneasily, and subsided as he met Badger's calm gaze. He told himself there was no reason to fear. He had been one of these people until he was seven years old. They would not intentionally do him harm.

Wild geese called above and he took an involuntary step forward. A mist had risen from the damp ground, clinging among the trees. But as his vision focused he saw their line unfurling across the paling sky.

"You want to follow them?" Badger laughed softly. "You have another race to run, my king. The stag waits for your challenge. Save your fire for him."

The headman made way for an old woman who wore a wolf's pelt over her garment of deerhide. Her white hair was pulled through a circlet of bone, and a little wooden bowl filled with some dark liquid was in her hand. She reminded him of Anderle. The necklace of amber and jet that marked her as a priestess thumped her flat breast as she bent, dipped a finger into the black stuff, and drew a lightning track up the muscle of his calf. It sent a pulse of sensation through his leg and he pawed the ground. When she did his other leg, only Badger's hand on his shoulder kept him still. Working swiftly, she daubed symbols on breast and arms and back, the sigils of all the clans. Fine tremors passed through every limb.

"When?" he whispered, fighting the ecstasy.

"Soon," answered Badger, "very soon."

The priestess straightened and stepped back, for the first time meeting his eyes. "Soon—" she echoed. "You run for all of us!"

His Companions fell in behind as Badger led him through the trees. He flinched again as he caught sight of the people waiting, but the headman's grip as he led him into the circle was firm.

A group of women stood on the other side of a fire whose flames were growing pale with the approach of day. The tallest wore a mask made from the head of a doe. She was swathed in a deerskin cloak; a garland of berries nodded above her brow. From the way she stood he thought she must be young. His nostrils flared, seeking her scent, but he could catch only the reek of herbs and wood smoke.

He sensed someone behind him, began to turn, and shuddered at the sudden weight of antlers. *That* was what his head had been missing! He stilled to let them lace the leather helmet that held the horns firmly under his chin, then swung his head back and forth, learning how to shift his shoulders to balance the weight.

Badger was speaking—"Osprey has found the trail of the King Stag and his wives. When you sight them, run and bring him down—"

He scarcely heard. The priestess was approaching, a voice like music intoned a blessing. His gaze moved from her to the forest and back again, striving to pierce the mists that veiled the trees. Beyond the trees lay the Otherworld.

The priestess anointed him with the musk of a stag, and that last scent drove out awareness of the human identity. One of the old humans beckoned and the strong hand that had held him let go at last. Powerful muscles launched him into a harmony of motion. The forest was waiting. The King Stag was waiting, his rival, his destiny.

THE HORNED HUNTER RUNS, fleet footed, sure of step, touching earth only to spring forward once more. Supple and strong, he weaves among the trees, head lowered to keep from tangling his antler crown. Dim in the distance the other hunters bay like hounds. Only two of the elder folk keep pace with him now, and all run silently, but the deer they have startled into motion crash through the trees.

The trail opens before him. The growing sunlight blazes in drops of mist collected on bare branches, coating fallen leaves and sere grass. Everything glows with a radiance beyond that of the human world. He breathes light, is one with winged ones that flutter among the branches, with burrowers snuggling beneath the soil, with the beasts that go on all fours, pounding over the leaf-strewn ground. He runs with the deer.

He does not know how long he runs. The world is bright now, though a glimmer of mist still hangs in the air. And gradually the air grows golden, charged with expectation. His steps slow. Beyond a screen of beeches brown shapes are moving. A sudden roaring shatters the silence. The King Stag is there.

The lips of the Hunter open and his own cry echoes against the trees. *"I come . . . I come. . . ."*

The deer are gathered in a clearing. Some twenty does, still fat from the summer's grazing, mill at the edge of the trees. In the center stands their master, neck ruff bristling, winter coat the color of oak bark. His body, longer than the hunter is tall, is heavy with muscle. The Stag huffs and lowers his crowned head, sharp hooves scoring lines in the fallen leaves.

The Horned Hunter steps forward, arms out, head a little bent. It is a wrestler's stance, though he no longer remembers where he has used it before.

"I am the King . . ." roars the Stag. *"Who comes to challenge Me?"*

"I am the Son of a Hundred Kings!" comes the reply.

"I have seen you before . . ."

Into the mind of the Hunter comes an image of the clearing atop the isle of the Wild God. He remembers does in red-brown summer coats, and the Stag with his antlers in velvet, and a golden-haired child who danced with the sunbeams.

"I have grown . . ."

"Now, you are worthy of my horns!" The Stag huffs again, with a sound that is very like laughter.

"Are you the same one I saw?"

"We are always the same," comes the reply. *"Always in our prime, always the King."*

"Then I challenge you."

The Hunter springs forward, dances aside as the antlers swing, darts in again. The Stag rears, striking out with sharp forehooves and driving the Hunter to one side. Back and forth they weave, attacking and defending in a deadly dance. An unexpected twitch of the antlered head lets a sharp tine score the thigh of the Hunter. Blood spots the fallen leaves.

Around once more, the Hunter leaps in, grapples, and is flung away. His blood continues to flow; he is growing a little dizzy now.

"Generation follows generation, and each time we fight, the weaker one must fall. The blood of the old king feeds the ground, and the young king gives his seed so that our Mother may bear anew."

The Hunter's time is running out. He crouches, breath sobbing in his breast, waiting as the Stag swerves back and forth, waiting. The crown of knives plunges toward him, at the last moment he swivels on his haunches, uncoiling as the antlers pass. Powerful hands grip the antlers at their base and force the great head down; he hooks a foot around a foreleg so the Stag cannot strike, and holds. For a long moment they strain, neither giving way, until at long last the Hunter feels the force that opposes him falter.

In some other lifetime, someone had asked if he was willing to die for the land.

"Do you go consenting?" He asks the question now.

The Stag heaves, loses balance and goes down on one knee. *"I am the Offering. . . ."*

"As one day I myself shall be—" The Hunter's grip tightens. Muscles flex and ripple as he wrenches sideways. Bone cracks. He holds as the mighty body of the Stag convulses, holds until the last twitchings have ceased, and the light fades from the dark eyes, and time begins once more.

"CUT HIS THROAT, MY king. His blood must feed the ground—"

He blinked, turning, and saw beside him a man with dark eyes and grizzled hair. Presently memory supplied the name, *Badger.* He realized that the flint knife was still hanging at his side, and drew the blade. The wooden hilt and bindings were new, but the stone was darkened by use and age. He wondered how many times that knife had tasted the blood of a king.

It was very silent. He pulled back the stag's heavy head to stretch the throat and stabbed just beneath the angle of the jaw. Another wrench pulled the knife through skin and veins and the rubbery windpipe and feeding tube. The air filled with a hot metallic tang as blood flowed in a red tide. Senses still attuned to the Otherworld noted the shimmer of energy above it, dissipating gradually into the forest as the blood soaked into the ground, and from the forest itself, a grateful sigh. The golden light of late afternoon shafted through the trees. The mist had gone.

"Go in peace, my lord," he whispered, "and leave your blessing on this land."

Badger dipped a finger into the blood and drew a red line between Mikantor's brows, more across his cheekbones and another upon his breast. When the flow of blood had almost ceased, the other men came forward, heaving the stag over onto its back and making a careful slit in the belly. He had seen the gralloching of a deer a hundred times before, but never had each movement held such solemnity.

One man pulled away the skin so that another could reach in and draw out the offal to leave for the scavengers of the wild. While the hunters bound the stag's legs and passed spears between them for transport, Badger sluiced and bound up the gash on Mikantor's thigh. He could feel it aching, but as a distant thing. Some of the power that had borne him through the hunt remained. One of the hunters unslung a cow's horn and blew three long blasts. In a moment the call of another horn echoed from the distance. From hill to hill his triumph was proclaimed— *"The king is dead. . . the king returns. . . ."*

That same serenity bore Mikantor back along paths he did not remember having seen before, back to the clearing where the people waited to hail a new king. There the women set the King Stag's head upon a pole and swiftly stripped off the hide. The heart and other choice portions were grilled above the coals while the rest was disjointed and cast into cauldrons to boil.

The king feeds his people, thought Mikantor as they draped the wet hide across his shoulders and led him to a seat before the fire. The priestess was waiting to crown his antlers with a wreath of red berries like her own. They brought her a platter with the roasted meat and she cut off pieces to feed him, beginning with the heart. With it came a beaker of honey mead.

Mikantor felt dizzy and did not know whether it was the drink, or the shock of eating meat after so long, or the presence of the woman beside him that made his head swim. Most of her body was hidden by her own deerskin robe. He could see one bare leg and a round arm. Her hair was done into a multiplicity of tiny braids. His flesh stirred at the thought that beneath the deerskin she must be as naked as he. Through the eyeslits he caught the gleam of eyes. Her hand brushed his as she handed him another piece of meat and he felt the pulse of power between them.

This was not quite like the morning's dissociation, when the spirit of the deer had overwhelmed his humanity. Once more his consciousness was being pushed into the background, but this time what was replacing it was a power at once fierce and benign, the power of a god. As his awareness shifted, his perception of the woman by his side was changing as well. Overlaid upon her mask he saw a multiplicity of images, human and animal, fresh maiden and opulent mother. He desired them all. Even the deathly hag called to him to pour out his life in her embrace.

As folk finished eating, the drumming began once more, supporting a bone flute whose shrilling touched the nerves with sweet pain. The hunters circled the fire, the deer hooves strung around their ankles clicking out the rhythm as they danced the story of the running of the deer. More drums added to the thunder as others joined the dancing. Women bent and swayed before him, loosening their garments to reveal a round breast or a flash of bare thigh. On this night he could have any woman he asked for. He was the king.

But Mikantor had eyes only for the one who sat beside him. The need to possess her was becoming a torment. He grasped her wrist and stood, pulling her against him.

Around him, the people were laughing. "This way," said someone. "A bed has been prepared for you."

He found his balance again as he followed the priestess along a path where the bones of the earth reared up through the soil. Beside a dark gash in the hillside a torch was burning. The priestess slipped from his grasp and disappeared into the opening. His escort unlaced the antler crown. Light-headed, he let the stag's hide slip from his shoulders and followed her.

In the flickering light of an oil lamp set on a ledge he had an impression of a womblike space just large enough for two. A bed of hides and furs covered most of the floor. The priestess had paused at the edge, as if for the first time uncertain. A step brought him up behind her, gripping her shoulders, pressing his body against hers. Her deerskin robe was in the way; he reached around to pull out the pin and drag it aside, hands closing upon her breasts before she could move. He strained against her, felt her nipples harden beneath his fingers, heard her sigh.

She twisted within his arms and slid free to face him, her swift breathing an echo of his own. She had pulled off her mask, but the lamp was behind her, and her face was in shadow. His eyes fed on a landscape of rounded white breast and swelling hips, painted as he was painted, with sacred signs. Seeing her beauty, the frantic lust that had consumed him a moment before vanished though his whole body was still one ache of desire, and he remembered that he had been trained at Avalon.

"Blessed be your lips, that speak Her holy words." he whispered, and leaning forward, gently set his lips to hers. They were soft, and sweet, with the taste of honey. He could spend an hour worshipping her lips alone. But the ritual carried him on. "Blessed be your hands, that do Her work . . ." He took first one, then the other, and set a kiss upon each palm. "Blessed be your breasts, that feed Her children . . ." He cradled them in his hands, felt her shiver at the touch of his lips. He kept his hands upon her, sliding them down her silken sides and legs as he knelt to bless her feet that walked in the Lady's ways. He remained kneeling, reaching up again to clasp her hips. "Blessed be your womb, the source of Life . . ." he whispered, drawing her against him. "You are the Goddess," he said hoarsely. "Let me serve You."

Her hands closed hard on his shoulders. He felt a tremor pass through the warm flesh between his hands.

"You are my Beloved . . ." Her voice held more than mortal sweetness. "Be welcome to my arms!"

TIRILAN WOKE FROM A dream in which she had fallen asleep with Mikantor cradled against her breast. For a moment she thought she was still dreaming, for the furs on which she lay had never covered any bed in Avalon. A little gray light flitered through what must be a doorway, and from outside she could hear a bird's first tentative morning song. From somewhere closer came a snort and a sigh. She jerked upright, reached out to touch tousled hair, and then the smoothly muscled shoulder of a man, stilled as he muttered and then subsided into sleep again.

A flood of images overwhelmed memory. A knowledge deeper than thought told her that this was indeed Mikantor. She had held him in her arms and more, to judge from the unaccustomed soreness between her thighs. And yet it was not she, but the Goddess, who had given herself to the God. As a priestess she rejoiced in the success of the ritual. As a woman she could weep that she recalled so little of its joy. How much, she wondered, would Mikantor remember of their joining? Anderle had told her whose rite she would be blessing, but he would not have known she was to be his priestess.

Soon someone would come to escort her back to her mother, who waited to return with her to Avalon. She fought the temptation to throw herself on Mikantor and cling so that they could not pry her away—she would not so profane the rite. And yet she refused to let this become no more than a shining memory. The Goddess had Her due, but what was there for Tirilan?

This was a gift, and a great one . . . but it is not enough, she thought, bending to breathe in the scent of the man, mingled with the scent of the herbs. *I can expect no more help from others. Tirilan herself will have to act to achieve her desire.*

From outside came the sound of a footstep on stone. She began to feel around for her deerskin cloak. Her hand brushed stiff fur, and then something harder, a knife in a leather sheath. That was all Mikantor had been wearing when he entered the cave.

"My lady—" came a soft whisper, "my lady, you must wake—it is time for you to go. . . ."

Tirilan pulled the deerskin cloak around her and fastened it with the bone pin, then reached down once more to draw the flint knife and take the sheath. Holding the cloak closed with her other hand she got to her feet and eased out through the passageway.

ANDERLE WAS WAITING BY the fire outside the hut where Tirilan had undergone her preparation. The girl still shivered from the scrubbing that had washed away most of the ritual paint as well as the scent Mikantor had left on her body, for at this season the water of the sacred spring was bitter cold. They had taken away her deerhide cape and restored her thick cloak of natural gray wool and her robe of priestess blue. But she had managed to retain the sheath of the knife, hanging from a thong between her breasts beneath the gown.

"You are glowing, my child—I take it that you passed a pleasant night?"

Tirilan's gaze flicked to her mother's face and then back to the fire, showing, she hoped, a confusion that was at least modest if no longer maidenly.

"I have reason to believe that the Goddess was pleased," Tirilan said softly. "As for me, I feel like the slave who carries the steaming meat to the master. He can smell its savor, but his belly is still empty."

"Do not try to tell me that your body still aches for the man," Anderle said tartly. "I know the effects of such rituals. The power rushes through mind and body and leaves a great peace behind."

"And what of my heart?" asked Tirilan. "I want to hear Mikantor's voice and see his face. I want to make sure that he has enough to eat and clean clothes to wear. And I want him to take me in his arms and know that it is me he holds."

The two women had kept their voices low, but one of the clanswomen, coming back to the fire, received a glare from Anderle that sent her scuttling away. The priestess turned back to her daughter.

"He has a band of men to take care of him! As for your heart—the Goddess has first claim on that. At Avalon we are spared the burdens that make a woman of the tribes old before her time. In return we give up the daily companionship over which you are sighing. What makes you think that he would want you? I don't recall him seeking you out when he was at Avalon. You will come home with me and be grateful for what you have had."

Tirilan felt herself flush and then go pale as her mother's words hit home.

"You may be right—" she said in a low voice. She had always believed that her mother knew everything. Anderle had ruled Avalon for twenty years, after all. "You usually are. But I don't believe you know anything about love."

Anderle shook her head in exasperation. "I arranged this for Mikantor, but also for you, knowing that you were lusting for him like a doe in season. I gave you this opportunity to get it out of your system and be done."

"Is that all the act of love means to you?" Tirilan exclaimed. "You scratch the itch, and then you both go your ways until next year? Was my father no more than a means to get you with child?"

"Of course not—" said Anderle, but her rejoinder lacked conviction.

"I don't believe you," Tirilan said flatly. "I am not going back to Avalon." *And if I am making a mistake, at least it will be my own . . .*

"And your vows?"

"I will not tell him any temple secrets," she said sweetly. "As for my other vows, I gave myself to the king as the Goddess required. If he desires me, I

will lie with him again. If he does not, still I will serve him, and unless you
have been lying about Mikantor's destiny for all these years, thus I will serve
the gods."

"You will serve as a drudge, in camp with all those men—" Anderle
began, but Tirilan interrupted her.

"If you try to stop me you will put the validity of the rite in question,
and I think you want to secure Mikantor's future even more than you want
to impose your will on me. There have been many who were called Lady
of Avalon, after all, but there is only one Son of a Hundred Kings."

Others were gathering now. Tirilan faced her mother defiantly and saw
the other woman shut her mouth with a snap, eyes glittering.

"Do not ask my blessing. You are my child no longer."

"My Lady, I have not been a child since you sent me out from the chamber of initiation to climb the holy Tor," Tirilan said softly. As her mother
turned away, she bent in the full obeisance due to the Lady of Avalon, wondering whether she would ever do so again.

"MIKANTOR, YOU NEED TO go back into the hut. Someone is waiting
for you."

Hearing an odd tone in Ganath's voice, Mikantor turned. His friend's
expression was strange as well, a mingling of consternation and amusement.
But at least it was not the superstitious awe with which everyone, even his
Companions, had looked at him yesterday.

All around them, the folk of the old blood who had gathered for the
ritual were packing to return to their homes. The space beside the firepit
was heaped with gifts they had left for him. Mikantor was still trying to
understand what their allegiance would mean. Three clansmen were packing the gifts onto the sturdy ponies that roamed the moors. They had promised guides and supplies and a dry place to shelter over the winter for him
and his band.

He started to say that he had no time, but the look in his friend's eyes
deterred him. Yesterday he had been limp with exhaustion from the hunt
and the night that followed. But he could afford no more self-indulgence,

and especially no more time trying to remember exactly what had happened in the cave. Few men received such a blessing even once, much less remembered or repeated it. The cure was to keep busy until the longing went away.

"All right, but you will have to keep at the men to get ready. Our guides must not be kept waiting."

Limping a little from the wound in his thigh, he crossed the clearing and ducked through the door of the hut they had built for him. A woman was sitting beside the fire, wrapped in a cloak with a woolen scarf over her hair. He stopped short, eyes widening, as she rose to her feet and the scarf fell away to reveal a pale face and curling golden hair.

"Tirilan? What are you doing here? Did you come to see the ceremony? I did not see you there. . . ." His babble failed as she unwrapped the thing she had been holding and held it out to him.

"I came to return something to you. . . ."

A leather sheath. *The* sheath for the flint knife that they had not been able to find when the elders came to take him from the cave. He took a step toward her and staggered as his stiffened leg lagged.

"Does the wound trouble you?" she said swiftly. "Have they tended it properly? Let me see—"

"No, no. It's fine, just stiff—*Tirilan!*" He caught her hands and held them, trying to sense truth through the contact of skin to skin as he was trying to hear in her voice the sweetness that he half remembered. "Does Anderle know you are here?"

"She knows. . . ."

"Did she *send* you?"

"She did not send me *here.*" said Tirilan.

"It was you, in the cave?" he breathed, beginning to understand, though he was not yet quite ready to believe.

"In the cave it was the Goddess and Her Chosen," Tirilan said softly. "I believe that it is Her will that I stay with you. You said I might pray for your protection. I will do that better where I can see you."

Mikantor shook his head, exasperation, pity, and an odd excitement struggling for mastery.

"You don't understand. I am only a man."

She shrugged. "I know that—I remember when you were a snot-nosed brat. But I also remember how you called the thunder. When you do not believe in yourself, I will believe for you. When I look at you, I still see the god."

An unwelcome thought came to him. "Has your mother cast you out?"

Tiri grimaced. "She was not pleased. You do not have to take me—" she went on, "but I promise I can walk as far and sleep as rough as any of your men. And I am trained as a healer."

He looked down at her and did not know what he felt, except that despite her brave words, just now she needed his protection.

"So . . . so . . ." He put an arm around her and drew her against him, simultaneously disappointed and relieved that at this moment his chief response was a rueful affection. "You shall come with me, then, and may the gods help any who would stand against us!"

TWENTY

$\mathcal{T}$irilan had turned her back on Avalon, but the lee of another tor had become her new home. She still found that strange. The moors northeast of Belerion were studded with rounded granite outcrops that thrust up from the soil. Best of all, they were solid ground, unlike so much of the moorland, which was a mix of peat bog and mire that could suck down a sheep, or a man. Today the land was covered with the white of last night's snowfall. Tirilan squinted against the blaze of sunlight on that glistening white blanket, and pulled her faithful gray cloak tightly around her to keep out the wind.

Mikantor was out there somewhere, on his way back from the next village, where he had taken some of their extra food. Winter had bit deeply on the moors, and while some of the men muttered that the supplies they had brought with them were for their own survival, Mikantor stood firm. The moor clans had welcomed them and helped them to rebuild their dwellings. The only way for all of them to prosper was to share.

Tirilan did not begrudge the food, but the moors were doubly treacherous when covered with snow. She took a deep breath and closed her eyes, taking the shape of a swan to send her spirit out in protection. This, at least, was something she could do for him. Their blankets were laid on the raised platform to the right of the hearth, but they did not share them. She had not expected to do so when they were traveling, but by the time they reached the moors the habit of separation had become a barrier that he apparently did not wish to break. He never touched her. Did he know how she longed for some small sign of affection? She would never have believed that two people could live side by side in such silence. If nothing had changed by spring, she might just as well admit that her mother was right and go home to Avalon.

The wind had come up, swirling the light snow as if to give form to the spirits she sensed dancing across the land. Once, these highlands had been a patchwork of field and pasture, with many villages built from the abundant native stone. But the place where the moor folk had settled Mikantor and his Companions had been long abandoned. They had rebuilt some of the house circles and called it Gorsefield, from the amount of prickly brush they had to clear. From the tor she could see the shimmer of smoke that filtered through their thatched roofs. When the climate worsened, most of the people had been driven down to the coasts. Now, only a few clans of the elder folk stayed here, herding their sheep across the hills.

"Goddess," she whispered. "Enjoy your lovely white garment, but send our men home safely, and soon."

It was a bitter truth that from their danger came their safety, for if travel on the moors was hazardous even with the clansman Curlew for their guide, it was certain that no enemy could attack them. And this corner of the country was rich in ancestral spirits, who haunted the standing stones they had left behind them, each capped now with its own helmet of snow. A league to the north stood the barrow of the Three Queens—the ancient Mothers who still watched over the land. It was a place where the power of the Goddess was strong. And it lay beside the current of power that ran from the tip of Belerion all the way through Avalon and across the land.

Another gust of wind sent a cold draft up her back. It was time to go home.

MIKANTOR SAID FAREWELL TO Pelicar and ducked into the angled entry of the house he shared with Tirilan, silently praising the ingenuity of the original builders, who had put all their entrances facing downhill to help with drainage, away from the prevailing wind. Behind him he heard the shouts as those who had stayed welcomed the others. He paused, gathering his resolution to face her. Living with her over these past months had made him acutely aware of her as a physical being, and his body responded accordingly, and yet he could never forget that she was a priestess, bound by her vows. He stamped the snow from his feet and hung his cape of tightly woven natural wool on a hook beneath the overhang before pushing past the hide that curtained the door.

"Did the meeting go well?" Tirilan looked up as he came in. She was mending one of his tunics. His breath caught as he saw how the flicker of the fire burnished the smooth planes of her face and her shining hair.

He shrugged off his sheepskin coat and hung it up. Fingers and feet were beginning to throb in the warmth of the room.

"Lycoren seems to be reliable, and he hates Galid. When we come down from the moors in the spring he has promised to join us with his band."

The Ai-Akhsi leader was the third chieftain who had made his way to this wilderness to pledge his support. The queens and their war leaders were still preserving an official neutrality, but word of the Running of the Deer had spread among the people. By spring, Mikantor might find himself leading a small army.

"I expect you could use something hot right now. I have a bag of yarrow tea steeping in the cooking hole—I'll just put in another rock to bring it to a boil." She set the tunic aside and with a deft flick slid the tines of an antler under the round piece of granite that had been heating among the coals. Another practiced twist dropped it hissing into the water that filled the stone-lined depression by the hearth, one of the amenities the long-dead builders of this place had left behind.

"I went up to the tor this morning," she observed, dipping up tea and filling one of the clay beakers they had brought with them. "The view was wonderful. This land is hard, but there is beauty here."

"Beauty, and fear," he agreed. "On the way back, Curlew was telling us about the spirits of the moors. I'm not sure whether he meant to warn or frighten us. He says there's a monstrous black dog that can run a man down."

"That sounds like the demon Guayota about whom they have such tales among the tribes," she replied. "Old Kiri used to tell us some truly scary stories—"

As Tirilan continued to talk, he took the beaker and sat down on the sleeping ledge, casting a surreptitious glance behind him. The sheepskins and blankets in which they slept were arranged, as always, in two neat piles. He sighed and stretched out his feet toward the fire. The men all assumed that he was sleeping with her, and the best way to protect her seemed to be to let them think so. But she took such pains to avoid any show of flesh that might arouse him, he had no reason to believe she would welcome his advances. Living with her day by day, he had finally come to understand that he loved her as much as he did Velantos. But he understood the smith. Tirilan was still a mystery. They had left Anderle behind, he thought bitterly, but her daughter was still bound by Avalon's rules.

TIRILAN SHIVERED AS THE roof beams flexed to another gust of wind. The houses were sturdy, with a rubble filling between two shells of stone slabs and a lining of wooden planks or sheepskins to insulate them within. The walls had been easy to repair. It was only the roofs that were a problem, for poles long enough to attain the proper pitch were hard to come by on the moors. There were spirits in that wind, she thought grimly, whose icy fingers plucked at the bindings to spin the thatch away.

The moon that followed Midwinter had brought one storm after another, swirling drifts man-high in one place, while others were swept bare, hiding the shape of the land even from those who knew it well. Stocks of food and fuel were getting low. Some of the men muttered that they should have stayed in the marshes, where they might be wet, but at least they would not freeze. She broke off a corner from the slab of peat and eased it into the fire, then picked up her spindle once more. Her fingers were almost too cold to grasp the wool, though she was already wearing every garment she owned, but she would not use more fuel while she sat here alone.

Mikantor and most of the other men were out there somewhere, searching for Pelicar and Romen, who had gone out to hunt that morning and had not returned. One could hope that the freezing weather had also hardened the surface of the bogs, but there were a hundred other ways a man could die in this land. They had been gone for so long! She yanked more wool from her basket and loosely joined it to the end of the fiber that dangled from her spindle.

She felt her fingers warm as she wound the thread around the shaft and hooked the rest over the end, pulled out the wool with one hand and with the other gave it a spin, letting the spindle's weight pull the loose mass of fiber through her fingers into a twisting strand until it neared the floor and she repeated the process once more.

As she worked she began to hum, shutting out everything but the hypnotic twirl of the spindle, the flicker of the fire. Twirling and winding, feeding in new wool and beginning again, vision blurred until it seemed to her that she was spinning flame. The Three Queens were sometimes called spinners. What did they spin? The image of the barrow formed among the coals, and she glimpsed three shapes that bent and hummed, spinning glistening threads from the flowing streams of light that swirled across the land.

"I spin out all the deeds that have been . . ." sang one.

"I spin what is happening . . ." sang the next, *"my thread has no end . . ."*

"From your threads I twist what shall be," came the voice of the third queen.

"And I break it, and twine it into the past once more," the first replied.

"Each life a strand, across the land, I take in hand . . ." together they sang. *"If you would see, whatever must be, hark unto me . . ."*

Lives . . . thought Tirilan, watching those clever fingers. *"Whose lives are you spinning now?"* her spirit cried.

"Would you join us?" called the third queen. *"Can you see the lifelines of those who struggle through the storm?"*

As she stared, Tirilan realized that lines of light were twisting through the glowing landscape before her. Some were bright, some fading. Some of them flickered away as she touched them while others came easily to her hand. One by one she gathered them, smoothing and straightening, drawing them in. "Come—" she whispered. "This is the way home—"

She never knew how much time had passed when the sound of shouting broke through the howling of the wind. A gust set the ashes swirling as the door flap was unpegged and thrust aside. She rose to her feet, shocked back to the present with a suddenness that set her temples to pounding. Mikantor stood in the doorway, eyes as wide as her own. She looked down and saw her spindle abandoned on the floor. But her fingers were still moving, still twining the lines of light that streamed into her hands from the remains of the fire.

Only the discipline of long training kept her from falling. She drew a deep breath. "Are all returned?"

Mikantor nodded.

Tirilan let out her breath in a long sigh, then bent and very carefully released the fire.

"We found them," Mikantor said hoarsely. "Romen had stepped in a hole and broken his leg, and Pelicar was trying to carry him. He kept falling. By the time Beniharen stumbled over them, he couldn't get up again. . . . He's a long lad to carry, is Pelicar, but we managed. Banur's bones, it was cold!"

"Get those clothes off. You're wet through—" Tirilan interrupted him. Except for two spots of red on his cheekbones his skin was corpse pale. She tugged off his cape and the sheepskin coat, wrapped a blanket around him, and pushed him down on the edge of the sleeping ledge, resisting the compulsion to throw her arms around him and force her warmth into him. She had to keep moving or she would faint with the relief of having him safe and be no use to anyone at all.

"We made a litter with our spears, but the snow—" He shook his head. "It was blowing from every direction. No stars, no paths, no shelter. . . . And we could hear a howling that was not the wind. Curlew said the Hound was on our track—I swear Guayota was out in that storm." He shuddered and winced as he took the beaker of ale she had kept warming by the fire. "Oh gods, I can feel my feet again—" he exclaimed as she pulled off the hide boots stuffed with straw, and the woolen leg wrappings that held them.

They felt like ice. She pulled a sheepskin with the fleece still on from the bed and set it beneath them. Only now could she allow herself to admit how deeply she had been afraid. Was this weakness what came of love? Was this why her mother had denied her own feelings so long and well?

"We were lost. I thought I would never see you again—" He took another gulp of ale and his shudders began to ease. "And then I felt a heat at my breast . . . I felt you calling me. . . ." His eyes moved from the fire to her face in desperate question.

"Ssh . . . ssh . . . you must thank the Three Queens, not me. . . ." Refusing to meet his gaze, she turned away to build up the fire. "Where are Pelicar and Romen now?"

"In Ganath's hut." He moved his feet on the fleece, wincing as returning circulation began to turn them from white to red.

"I will go to them—" She reached for her cloak, fighting back the hysterical laughter. *Yes, I found you. I think I saved you. Yes, I love you* . . . her heart cried, but if once she gave way she would be undone. "Get the rest of your clothes off and into bed. I will be back soon." She dared to drop a kiss on the top of his head, then slipped through the door.

Ganath's hut was warmer, rank with the smells of male bodies and wet wool. Most of the men had crowded into it, but they stepped back to give her room. The two rescued men lay on the sleeping ledge, wrapped in blankets. Ganath had set and splinted Romen's leg. She ought not to have worried—he had received the same training as she. She nodded as he described what he had done for them, passing her hands above the men to sense their energy.

"Romen is doing well," she murmured when she was done. "He is weak from pain, but Pelicar seems more depleted."

"That makes sense. He was using more energy—" said Ganath.

"Do we have any broth left? Get some into him," she answered. She turned back to Pelicar, held her hands over his head and breast, willing power out through her palms. In a few moments he seemed to breathe more easily and she stood back, flushing as she realized that the rest of them were staring at her.

"Did your prayers save us, Lady?" asked Acaimor.

"Thank the gods," she said quickly, "and the spirits of this land." She put on her cloak once more. "Ganath has done well. Go to bed, all of you, and stay warm. I must get back now. I left Mikantor sitting by the fire—I'd best make sure he has not fallen into it."

She made her escape then, but could not ignore the gestures of reverence they made as she went by. Had she saved them? If so, the way of it was like nothing she had learned at Avalon. What else might she learn from the spirits of this land?

When she got back to the house she shared with Mikantor, she found that he had crawled into his blankets still half dressed, and the fire had died down. She set in two more slabs of peat, angling them to burn more efficiently, and banked ash around them. Then she knelt on the sleeping ledge and shook Mikantor by the shoulder.

"Wake up—we've got to get these wet things off you—just for a moment, my love—please!"

He mumbled something and half sat without really waking. It was enough for her to pull the tunic over his head and snug the blanket around him as he subsided again, half curled on his side. His flesh was very white, and still cold, despite the blankets and the warmth of the hut. Too cold, she thought, chafing his long limbs. She could call for some of the other men to come and lie beside him, or she could share her own warmth, skin to skin.

Just until he was warmer . . . Tirilan shook her head as she realized that even now she was trying to deny her desire to hold him in her arms. But whatever came after, she had been too frightened by his danger to let this opportunity go by. Swiftly she laid her own sheepskins next to his, then stripped off her garments and slid into the bed behind him, pulling the blankets over them both and tucking them in.

I spun fire, she thought, feeling how chill his skin was against hers, *surely I can call fire to warm him now. . . .* She tightened her arms around him and sought inward for the core of light, with each breath willing the fire to rise within her, through her, and enclose them both in a cocoon of warmth. And it was working. . . . That deathly chill was fading from his skin, the shivers easing. The strong muscles of his back moved against her breast as he breathed. His arms lay loose beneath hers. He was warm now, warm and safe at last. With a sigh she turned her cheek against his shoulder and slid into sleep.

TIRILAN KNEW THAT SHE was dreaming of the night in the cave, for her body was flushed and throbbing. She sighed, striving to remember past the moment when the Goddess had overwhelmed consciousness, and heard Mikantor whisper her name. *That* had never been in her dream. She opened her eyes and saw his features half lit by the glow of the fire. He had turned to face her, and she could feel his body trembling against hers.

"Tirilan—" he said again, "I love you. I always have, I think, even when you were a wretched little brat teasing me. Will you let me love you? I swore I would never trouble you, but—"

"I am not the Goddess . . ." she whispered.

"You are a goddess to me. You carry light. I have always seen you that way. And you are a priestess, which is almost the same thing." He shook his head with a groan.

"Priestesses are women . . ."

"I can feel that—" he said wryly, trying to laugh. "That's why I dared— Tirilan, finding you in my arms, I thought I had died out there in the snow and gone to the Blessed Isles. But this is real, isn't it?" His grip tightened. "You could not still be lying here if you did not mean to be merciful . . ." His voice failed.

"Merciful!" She tipped back her head, trying to make out his features. "Is that what you think this is? Why in the name of all the gods would I have followed you into this wilderness if not that I love—"

Her words were cut off by his kiss. Her arm went around his neck, and she laid her leg across his and welcomed him to her fire.

THE CHARCOAL IN THE firebox pulsed with a fitful light that flickered across the smithy and the wicker screen Velantos had pulled across its open end. With strips of hide covering the gaps at the edges, it held the heat well enough so that beneath his broad apron of bullhide the smith was wearing only two woolen tunics instead of a mantle over three. Anderle wore a shawl over her long-sleeved tunic of fine blue wool.

With winter, the tension between them had eased, perhaps because with cold weather the woman kept her clothes on. A shapeless mass of wrappings was less disturbing than the glimpse of arm or breast the pinned garments of summer revealed. Since Mikantor had taken Tirilan with him to the moors the priestess had visited Velantos more often. At first he had thought it was to bedevil him, but lately he was beginning to suspect that she was lonely.

Velantos tightened the thongs that bound the pipe from the firebox to the hoses for the bellows, frowning as Anderle paced past him, and sat back to pump them once more.

"If you cannot be still, woman, take a turn at the bellows and be useful!" he snapped.

Anderle stopped, as if surprised to find she had been moving. "That is right, the boy Aelfrix usually helps you. Ellet told me that she has confined him to the healer's house until he recovers from his cough. What must I do?"

Velantos stood up, surprised in turn to hear her agree. "Sit there and take the handles for each bag. Alternate pushing them up and down, letting the sticks separate a little as you lift them again. You have seen me do it often enough. Force air through the tube. Air makes coals burn hotter, and melts the bronze."

The crucible that nestled among the coals in the firebox was filled with pieces of scrap metal from the bin. They had already begun to lose their outlines when Anderle arrived. Now they looked like blurred lumps in a molten stew. He grinned as she took a rather tentative grip on the handles and the bellows gave an asthmatic wheeze.

"Did Mikantor do this for you?" she asked, panting.

"How do you think he got those shoulders?" Velantos grinned. "He learns quick, that lad. I think he's good at any craft he tries, but metal does not sing to him . . ."

"He was born to be a king. . . . Do you miss him?" she asked then.

Do you miss your daughter? He did not say those words aloud.

She paused, wiped her forehead, then unwound her shawl. As she settled back into the rhythm, he saw how the movement alternately tightened and released the fabric across her breasts, and felt his flesh stir.

Work was the solution, for both him and her. He fixed his gaze on the coals whose brightness pulsed with each wheeze of the bellows. It was good oak charcoal, well able to reach a temperature that would melt the metal, although that also depended on the proportion of copper to tin.

"I miss him . . ." he said at last, still watching the fire. "I was the son of the king of Tiryns, but not of the queen. They apprenticed me early. I was never one of the warriors, and most folk find smiths uncanny anyway." He paused to bank the coals more securely around the crucible. The bronze had been heating since noon, and the sun was now descending. It would be ready soon. "I had no companion, until the boy . . ."

"But he was a slave—"

"Maybe at first, but then—" He shook his head, unable to explain the link between them. "When they enslaved me after my city fell, I thought death better than to be some man's property. Woodpecker made me live, treated me the same as ever, until I knew who I was again. When the king of Korinthos set us free, I felt no different. Some men are slaves to fear, or to love, some to the will of the gods. We choose our chains."

"Am I the slave of the goddess, then?" She shook her head. "It must make a difference that I willingly took oath to serve Her. That is why I could not understand when Tirilan—" She broke off, glaring as if he had forced her to that revelation.

"You were brought up to it. I think you could not choose different any more than I could choose not to defend my city. But Tirilan and Mikantor make their own path, and can you be sure that she does not also do the will of the gods?"

Anderle frowned and began to work furiously at the bellows, sending fountains of sparks toward the soot-stained ceiling. As the bronze melted, perspiration ran down her face and made damp patches on her gown.

"Let me do that for a time," he said when he thought she had worked off some of her anger. She winced a little as she straightened, and tottered to the bench to sit down. He took her place on the stool, working the bellows with strong, efficient strokes. He could feel her gaze upon him, hotter than the fire, and was glad its glow hid his flush of response.

"And are you free now?" she asked softly.

"Are *you*?"

"For twenty years I have served my vision," she said slowly. "I saw Azan-Ylir in flames, and that happened, so I must believe that it was a true fore-seeing of what might be."

"Tell me—" he said quietly. All the bronze seemed to be molten now, the color gradually brightening until it was hard to look at. Best to give it a little longer, he thought, retying the thong that bound back his hair and reaching for the leather wrappings that would protect hands and forearms.

"I saw enemies landing here, men of another language who will destroy all we are, because our warring tribes will not unite. But I saw the child dead, too, and yet I saved him, so I believe that future can be changed as well."

"Then Galid is only the beginning—" Velantos said thoughtfully, "for Mikantor. For me, to wipe that smirk off his lying face is enough. To meet the man two times is enough to hate him. A third time, if the boy does not kill him, I will."

"With the sword you are making now?"

"Not a sword—I sent a dozen blades to the moors for Mikantor's men. I make my own weapons now. This will be the first of a pair of axes, like the ones I had in the City of Circles. Ax or hammer"— he grinned whitely— "either one fits a smith's hand. I make the original in wax and cover it in clay; the wax runs out when I fire it. The bronze goes in at the open end." He lifted the roughly ax-shaped clay mold from the hearth where it had stayed warm next to the firebox and smiled at the clear "tink" he heard when he gave it an experimental tap with the small bronze hammer. Care-fully he positioned it, open end up, against the stone rim of the hearth.

Velantos peered at the crucible again. "The bronze is ready to pour. You must be quiet now." He took a deep breath, damping his awareness of ev-erything except the task at hand. He turned, lifting his hands to the two goddesses above the hearth.

"Potnia," he murmured in his own tongue, "Spirit upwelling, Lady of all Craft. By fire and by water, grant this work your blessing!"

Thrusting his hands into rough leather mitts, he poked the coals away from the stone crucible, gripped it with the tongs, and lifted. It was only about as big as a large beaker, but heavy for its size. At the top of the vessel a gray skin covered a red glow, but the lower part was as bright as the coals. His arm trembled just a little as he used a bronze disk to skim off the dross; then, holding the tongs with both hands now, he slowly and steadily tipped the crucible over the open end of the mold.

Sun-bright bronze ran out in a glowing stream, blazing up in a spurt of flame as it hit the clay. When it overflowed the mold, Velantos tipped the rest into a corner of the hearth and set the crucible down.

"What happens now?" asked Anderle as he began to strip off his leather wrappings.

"Now we wait—" he said wryly. "Like a woman with child. The mold is a womb. You have to wait to find out what you have. But this does not take so long."

After a few moments he took the tongs again, lifted the mold, and dropped it hissing into the quenching tub. The water bubbled like a cauldron, releasing gouts of evil-smelling steam. When it eased, he plucked the mold forth and set it on the stone slab on his workbench.

He nodded to Anderle. "If you wish, come see—" She leaned over the table as he steadied the mold with the tongs, for it was still quite warm despite its bath, and took up a small bronze hammer, the antler handle curved to fit his hand. Then, with a sudden grin, he offered it to Anderle, his excitement masking all other reactions.

"I won't hurt it?" she asked.

"If casting is good, you cannot," he replied, "and if not, it does not matter what you do." She looked suddenly much younger as, biting her lip in concentration, she gave the mold a tap. "You are Lady of Avalon—" He found himself grinning. "Hit hard!" Without thinking, he set his hand over hers, and together they struck the clay.

At the contact, energy shocked through him. *Like the lightning,* he thought in confusion, dropping her hand and taking a swift step away. She swayed, holding on to the table, then turned to him with a cry of delight.

"Surely we have worked a great magic—look!"

Head still pounding, he stepped forward and smiled at the gleaming arc of straw-colored metal visible where the clay had split away. A few more taps released the rest of the ax head, straight along the top and curved below,

with a pierced knob at the end to receive the haft and a blunt hammer head
beyond.

"How can a thing meant to deal death be so beautiful?" she murmured
as he turned it in his hands.

"The striking falcon is beautiful, and that lynx that Mikantor killed in
the great mountains," he replied. "Anything where form and action match—"
As you and I would be matched, he thought, *if ever we should come together
in love.*

He turned away rather quickly, found a piece of soft leather to wrap the
ax head and set it in the chest. "It must be ground and polished," he mumbled, back still turned. "It is not done." He remained where he was as the
silence lengthened.

"Thank you for an educational afternoon," she said finally, her tone gone
as cool as the water in the quenching tub. He could hear the rustle of cloth
and knew that she was putting on her shawl and the cloak she had hung by
the door.

"But you never answered my question," she said then. "What chains have
you chosen, master smith?"

"My craft . . ." he answered slowly. "Always I can trust metal to follow
its own law. If I fail, it is because I do not understand."

"And do you understand how to forge the sword that Mikantor will
need, the Sword from the Stars?"

At that, he turned to face her. "All that man can do for him, I do. What
you want, Lady, must come from the gods!"

TWENTY-ONE

*M*y lady is brighter than the sun . . . where she walks, she leaves a trail of flowers. My lady is the light of spring, and the world's sweet joy. . . ." Mikantor caught sight of Ganath's smile and stopped singing, aware that he was blushing like a maid, except that no maiden of either gender could have comprehended the mixture of sensation and memory that had prompted his song. Spring had come to the moors at long last, and though a light wind was still chasing last night's rain clouds across the sky, the elder folk had joined with Mikantor's band at the barrow of the Three Queens to make their offerings. Their hide tents clustered at the base of the hill. The rich odor of roasting lamb was already scenting the breeze.

"Never be ashamed of loving her, my friend," said the priest. "The joy that you and she have found blesses us all."

For a moment a throat gone suddenly tight prevented Mikantor from responding. He took a deep breath of the sweet air. With the Turning of Spring, the bitter storms had passed, and the moorland meadows were a vivid green. "The men are not jealous?" he managed when he could speak again.

"Of you and Tirilan?" Ganath shook his head. "They knew you had lain with her when she *was* the Goddess, in the ritual. Is this so different? You are the king. Your continued union with a priestess of the Lady of Life brings healing to the land."

In the first rapture of his love, Mikantor had not thought of it in quite that way. Making love to Tirilan was glorious, but he thought that even if he were forbidden to touch her, the bond between them had become so strong their relationship would remain the same. Once, he had loved her as a playmate and friend. Now he was her lover. When he was with her, he sensed a different kind of connection, even stronger than his link to Velantos had been. Wherever he lived, he had felt himself a stranger. Even when he thought he was one of the Lake Folk, he had never truly belonged. In Tirilan's heart he had found a home.

"Is that what it is?" he asked. "I kept wondering how I could lead men from so many different tribes, but Avalon serves them all, and so do I through my union with Tirilan."

"Do not undervalue yourself as a leader." Ganath grinned suddenly. "But it is true that Tirilan gives them a living symbol to fight for, and I think this is something that even the Lady of Avalon did not include in her plan. No one who sees your lady can doubt she brings the grace of the Goddess to us here."

Both men looked up the slope, where the gorse was coming into golden bloom. Was it the shifting clouds or some inner radiance that made it seem that Tirilan walked in a pool of light, that her hair shone brighter than the flowers? She was leading the women of the clans up the west side of the hill, with jugs of sheep's milk and bannocks for the offering at the barrow. She had defied the spring breezes in a wrap of pale blue, caught at the shoulders with bronze pins, that left her white arms bare.

She reached the top, paused to speak to one of the women, then turned and gestured. Mikantor stilled, listening with his heart. "I think she is calling me . . ."

"I will go with you." Ganath smiled. "For this, the man you need at your back is a priest, not a warrior."

"YOUR MAN IS A stag on the hillside—" As the old woman spoke, Tirilan realized that her gaze had been fixed on Mikantor since she sent the mental call. "A war chief for the clans too, not just the tribes."

Not a stag, thought Tirilan as he strode up the slope, but something fiercer, for in honor of the occasion he had thrown across his broad shoulders the lynx skin he had won in the great mountains. He walked with the feral grace of some great cat, poised to leap upon his prey. . . . Her body responded as she imagined him bearing her down on her back in the new grass. With an effort she composed her features.

"My ladies—" He addressed the women with a wary bow. "Do you have need of me?"

"The Mothers need you—" the woman replied. She was a wisewoman among these people, for all that she was no taller than a child of ten among the tribes, weathered as one of the stones that studded the moors.

He glanced uneasily at the barrow behind her, a long mound covered with green turf a little more than the height of a man, showing just a rim of stone where the earth had washed away, and under it a dark opening.

"What must I do?"

"Nothing too hard for such a great warrior—" The old woman gave a wheeze of laughter. From the bag slung over her shoulder she drew a black bowl and gestured toward the water that gleamed beyond the cluster of oak trees. Tirilan's eyes widened as she realized it was carved from jet, incised with a meander pattern around the rim. The gods alone knew how old it might be. "Take this bowl to the sacred pool, fill it with water and return."

"Very well—" His eyes flickered to Tirilan, and she smiled encouragingly, though she had no more idea what the woman wanted than he.

"And you," said the wisewoman as he started off, "must sit upon the mound."

Tirilan had already touched the powers to which this place belonged. She could feel them now, waking in response to their descendants' summoning.

"You don't need to fear." The woman cackled once more. "What harm, on such a fine spring day?"

Tirilan considered her with a frown, then turned to face the barrow. *"Mothers,"* she prayed, *"you helped me before. Is this your desire?"* The answer came not in words, but in the cry of a merlin that circled three times above the mound before sliding off across the sky.

"Kneel there, just above the stone—"

One of the younger women gave her a hand and she clambered to the top, and knelt. After a moment she realized it was one of the poses in which the Goddess is portrayed, and began to understand. She loosened the pins that held her wrap at the shoulders so that the garment was held up only by her sash and her breasts were bare. Another girl climbed up with a wreath of hawthorn from the hedge below the hill, and set it on her hair.

None too soon, for Mikantor was returning, walking with careful steps as if all the waters of the world brimmed in that black bowl. Intent on his task, he did not look up until he reached the mound. His eyes widened as he saw her sitting there and he straightened, holding up the bowl in offering.

"Life comes from the womb . . ." The wisewoman's voice seemed very far away. "Life comes back to the tomb. The Mothers give, receive, give back again. What will you give, Stag King?"

Tirilan held his gaze, hands rising to cup her breasts as he took another step forward.

"My blood and my seed—" he answered, "for You, Lady, for this land!"

"Then make your offering," she whispered, indicating the dark opening below her thighs. Her hands touched his head in blessing as he lifted the bowl and poured. At the touch, power flared between them, through them, and into the earth of the mound.

"Now the Mothers know you!" the wisewoman cried triumphantly. "You fight with their blessing. And soon—"

Above the pounding of her heart Tirilan heard shouting. Wrenching her gaze from Mikantor's, she looked up, saw a group of his men coming up the hill. As he turned, she began to pin up her garment, shivering with reaction as the moment of unity was replaced by a different kind of excitement. Pelicar was in the lead.

"My lord—my lord—a messenger has come—gods know how they found us—a man from Galid's band. He's brought a challenge, my lord, an invitation to battle in the vale below the White Horse downs!"

"Guess he got tired of chasing us around the marshes—" Tegues said into the silence.

Tirilan got her feet under her and began to work her way down from the mound. Mikantor faced the men who were crowding around him. By now the original dozen Companions had grown to a band nearly a hundred strong.

"Some we can hide, but not all," said Curlew, "or you can go to our brothers in the south. . . ."

"We've done enough hiding!" Pelicar exclaimed. "If I send to my mother, more men of my tribe will come. Galid has stolen too many of our sheep!"

"And mine," said Romen, as others began to echo him.

"Will you accept the challenge? Are we ready?" murmured Tirilan, taking Mikantor's arm.

"The men will go stale if we wait too long—" He glanced at the mound and then down at her. "But you—"

"I will go with you, of course," she said firmly. "Ganath cannot tend your scrapes all alone."

For a moment, Mikantor looked into her eyes, the desire to keep her safe clearly warring with the realization that if he left her here she would follow on her own. Then he nodded, and scrambled to the top of the mound.

"Men of the moors, and men of the vales and hills and plains, I call you!" he cried. "Galid has challenged me! The land itself cries out against him— will you follow me to put an end to his evil?" The cheering of the men around them seemed to echo against the sky. "Then let us feast tonight, and tomorrow we will be on our way!"

BENEATH GRAY SKIES THE downs glowed a vivid green. Soon the red of blood would add another note of color to the scene. But standing here with his warriors around him, hard-bodied men who had tested themselves against him and each other for nearly a year, Mikantor could not believe it would be his own. Who could defeat them? Certainly not men who had spent the winter lazing by Galid's fire.

"Clack, clack, clack!" The Vale resounded as enemy spearshafts struck wooden shields. Their swords were still sheathed. Mikantor knew his own men had better blades. He suppressed the inner whisper that those swords had not been tested in battle, whereas Galid's warriors were scarred and grizzled veterans. He had had a winter to think about battle, to play out strategies with stones and sticks for men. But there was only one cure for inexperience, and Galid had the medicine.

He adjusted the set of his helmet, of hardened leather over a bronze frame, wishing he had one of the bronze-plated helms he had seen in Tiryns. Most of his men made do with simple leather caps. They had insisted he wear a vest of boiled leather as well, though they did not have enough metal to reinforce it. Most of his men had some kind of protection, and he could see that Galid's force did as well, though the clansmen and men of the tribes had none. Some had stripped for action and would go into battle bare.

Mikantor had placed his men on a grassy pasture where the downs fell in wooded folds to the rolling ground of the Vale, his Companions in the middle and his allies to either side. Above them, the stylized outlines of the White Horse showed stark against the green. Mikantor had thought of the woods beneath it as a refuge. They might also be a trap, he realized, but it was too late to change his dispositions now. From the trees a crow was calling. Others answered from the air or settled with their brethren among the trees.

Tell your Lady to be patient, he thought grimly. *She will have her offering.*

Through the clamor as his men moved into their positions came an oath in the language of the Middle Sea. The voice was too deep to be Lysandros'. Heart pounding, Mikantor turned and glimpsed a familiar burly form.

"Velantos!" he called. "What are you doing out in such weather?" The skies were releasing a mizzling drift of moisture that could not decide whether to be rain or cloud.

"The gods know I nearly went back to bed when I saw the sky," grumbled the smith, pushing through the crowd, "but I thought you might be able to use another pair of arms."

Mikantor slid his shield off his arm and gripped the older man's shoulders, only at that moment realizing how deeply he had hoped the smith would be there to fight at his side. The muscles moved like rock beneath his hands.

"Now we are unbeatable!" He grinned.

"Clack, clack . . ." replied the enemy spears.

"They look strong—" said Velantos.

They looked *experienced,* thought Mikantor as they drew closer, opposing a steady confidence, or maybe it was contempt, to the enthusiasm of Mikantor's men.

"Well, so are we—" he said brightly. "But where is your shield?"

"Castor and Pollux here will ward me," said Velantos, loosening the two wickedly gleaming axes thrust through loops in his belt.

"Those are new," Mikantor said appreciatively.

The smith shrugged. "I got tired of making swords, and thought it was time to make use of Bodovos' training."

"We both owe him a great deal. I wish he was here." Mikantor sighed. "Speaking of which, what have you done with Aelfrix?"

"Left him at Avalon with orders to tie him up if he tried to follow me."

"And Anderle?"

Velantos looked uncomfortable. "That one has no need to travel. She can ride the wind."

"That might not make any difference. So can Tirilan, but she is up on that hill—" He nodded toward the cluster of trees that hid the old tomb. "She said she could watch from afar, but not bind up our wounds unless she was with us. The men all promised her they would survive the battle unscathed, but she came anyway." He and Velantos exchanged looks.

"We must do our best not to need her skills," said the smith. "Where do you wish me to stand?"

"I've placed the tribal bands on my right and the men of the old blood on the left, with my Companions in the center. We have trained to fight in threes, so Pelicar and Acaimor will stand to either side of me. But you might watch my back, and take on anything that gets through their guard."

"I expect there will be enough work for all of us," Velantos remarked, his gaze on the enemy.

Mikantor glimpsed the russet cloaks of Galid's personal guard and felt hatred flare through his veins like the fire in which Galid had allowed his mother to burn. In waking life he did not remember her, but he still had nightmares about fire. At least the warlord had not had the gall to assume the royal horns of the bull. Galid's men wore fox pelts around their shoulders. He hoped that would prove a prediction—foxes were sly thieves, as ready to flee as to steal. Perhaps he should have worn his lynx skin, he thought then. He was going to need the wiry strength of the big cat today.

He tensed at a ripple of movement along the enemy line. Spearmen peeled away to either side to reveal Galid's guard in the center, facing his own. Galid himself stayed in the midst of them, next to a man even taller than Pelicar, and heavier. This must be Muddazakh, the warrior from some northern land whom Galid had made his champion. The big man leaned on the young tree he used for a spear shaft as a smaller, slighter figure emerged from the enemy ranks to dance toward them, the beast tails fastened to his hide cloak fluttering with every move.

"That is Hino, the usurper's fool," muttered Ulansi from behind him. "Get ready for insults—that's the only kind of humor the idiot knows."

"Ho there, hill hares—you ready for the foxes? Hares run good. You ready to run?"

"Kick good too. We'll kick your butts," muttered the men of the moors.

"Our butts? Do you have moss to wipe your own? You'll be fouling yourselves soon—a bunch o' brown butts, that's all we'll see of you. A bunch of baby butts, running for your mothers."

"Galid killed my mother," Mikantor replied. "I don't leave this field till his blood feeds the ground."

"Poor little boy!" retorted the fool. "Traded from pillar to post, herding the sheep and sweeping the store. Even those holy bitches on Avalon threw him out. Don't you wonder why no one would keep him? Poor little bumboy—how many masters did you serve?"

"Steady!" cried Mikantor as the growl of outrage behind him swelled to a roar, Velantos' loudest of all. "Better to serve honest men than to batten off a pack of murdering thieves!" Now there was anger in the murmurs behind him. Even those who had not suffered themselves had friends or family with reason to hate Galid's men.

"Clack! Clack! Clack!"

"Galid, come forth!" Mikantor's shout rose above the beating spears. "Will you hide behind this fool? We summon you to answer for the men you have murdered, the women you have raped, the farms you have destroyed! The land itself cries out against you! The Goddess rejects you—"

His voice cracked on the final shout as the clacking ceased and the spearmen dropped to one knee. There were archers behind them. Mikantor was still lifting his shield when the arrows came.

He staggered as three bolts thunked into the wood. Acaimor cried out and sagged against him, a black-feathered shaft standing out from his breast. Mikantor took a quick step to stand over his body as Ulansi dashed forward to take his place.

The men of the moors and marshes got their bows up and began to reply, but their bows were lighter than those of the enemy, and they could not match the concentrated power of that first, unexpected flight. A few of Galid's men fell, but the rest were filling in the gap before Galid's guard and advancing, shields up, spears poised. For a pack of robbers, they showed surprising discipline.

Mikantor had the higher ground, but that would make no difference if they did not use it. "Companions, up spears!" he cried, lifting his own as the enemy came into range. "Cast!" This was a move his men had practiced. A dozen arms swept back, a dozen lithe bodies flexed, and the spears flew.

Now it was the enemy who were staggering and going down. "Charge!" cried Mikantor, seeing holes appear in their line. Drawing their swords, the Companions lengthened stride, using the slope to propel them toward the foe, as the allies fell in to either side to form the flanges of the spearhead. "Choose your man!" his screamed, fixing his own gaze on a scruffy fellow with a brindled beard. Then suddenly the man was before him; he smashed his shield against the enemy's, spinning the man around, arm swinging to slash his unprotected side.

The sword sprayed crimson as he recovered; for a moment it was the King Stag Mikantor saw, understanding dawning in his widening eyes. He had a moment to be surprised that it should be no different to kill a man. Then he whirled, angling the shield to knock an oncoming spear aside, blade rising to counter another, passing beneath the shaft to pierce leather and cloth and flesh. He jerked the blade free, dodging, striking. There was no more time for thought, only reaction, as responses trained by endless practice directed sword and shield. Pelicar and Ulansi moved in rhythm beside him. Behind him he heard a meaty thunk and a scream as Velantos' ax clove flesh and bone.

A chaos of bloody, struggling forms surrounded him, in which his Companions formed islands of disciplined violence. Too few, he thought, when for a moment no enemy confronted him. A flicker in the light brought his gaze upward, and for a moment he glimpsed the shining shape of a swan. He could feel Tirilan's love strengthening him, but his allies were being driven off the field. He had to get to Galid. The usurper would be hiding behind his champion, whose tall form rose above the fray. Even with the sword the man would have the reach on him, but at least the giant had lost his spear. Mikantor began to work his way toward him.

"Ho, big man!" he cried. "Is that a sword or a club you're wielding? D'ye know what to do with that blade?"

"Stick it up your arse, bumboy!" grunted the giant, swerving to face him.

"Give us space!" Mikantor called to the others, springing forward, ducking under Muddazakh's swing to slash at his calves. His foe was more nimble than he had expected; the sharp tip of his blade barely scored the flesh before the man had moved, blade whirling around in a blow that would have taken Mikantor's head off if he had not gotten his shield up in time. The heavy blade smashed into the top of his shield, cracking the bronze rim and shattering the wood a handbreadth down.

He could feel the wooden slats begin to give as the next blow fell, but it held his enemy's blade as he stabbed upward, felt the point go in. A spray of blood followed as he danced back, but Muddazakh took no notice. Was the man made of stone? Mikantor glimpsed faces, leering or cheering, in a ring around them. He ducked aside as the sword came down, slipped on wet grass, rolled, and came up again, but the shield had cracked as he hit the ground. When he caught the next blow, it split, and all he could do was cast the pieces away.

At this point, in practice, an honorable opponent would step back and drop his own shield. That was not going to happen here. All Mikantor could do now was dodge and parry, feeling the shock ripple through his arm with each clang of the blades. But he thought that Muddazakh might finally be slowing. . . . He straightened, breathing hard. The giant strode forward with lifted blade, blood streaming down his breast, not even trying to guard.

I have him now, thought Mikantor. As the enemy sword came down he stepped under the swing, bringing up his own blade to deflect the other and pierce that bull-like neck in a stroke the giant would not be able to ignore. Muddazakh's blade blurred toward him, struck with a clang. A sound Mikantor had never heard from a sword split the air as the leaf-shaped blade cracked across and the top half wheeled away.

What was left barely reached the giant's belly. Knocked off balance, Mikantor rolled as Muddazakh's sword bit into the ground where he had been, grasped the shaft of a shattered spear, and came up swinging. The ring had disintegrated into a chaos of struggling men, half of whom seemed to be surging toward him. Beyond them, his allies were beginning to flee. He batted an enemy sword away, slashed with the stump of his own, too busy trying to stay alive to wonder whether he should follow them.

Something hit him from behind; he went down once more, limbs still responding even when thought was gone. "Tirilan!" he cried as what remained of his sword was knocked from his hand.

"POTNIAAAA!" VELANTOS SCREAMED, THE twin axes scything a circle of death around him. In ages past, the Kouretes had taught men to shape bronze into weapons, and then how to use them in this deadly dance. Beyond the gathering of russet cloaks he could see Galid's gilded helmet. While Mikantor kept the giant occupied, the members of his guard were making a barrier around him. But like everyone else here, they had trained with sword and spear and shield. The smith laughed as he realized that no one knew how to defend against the double-ax technique that Bodovos had taught him. Forge-hardened muscles flexed and flowed as he struck, the sharp blades shearing through leather and muscle and bone.

This is the third time, you bastard, he thought as he plowed into them, and for a moment instead of Galid, it was King Kresfontes of the Eraklidae whose face he saw.

Like a voice from another world he heard Mikantor's cry.

Men who are winning do not cry out a woman's name . . .

Velantos' right-hand ax lopped off an arm as he whirled and saw Mikantor on the ground, foes gathering around him like wolves on a fallen deer. A sideways leap brought him into the midst of them, Castor and Pollux jumping in his hands. Blood sprayed as one ax sheared through someone's throat. The hammer end of the other slammed into a head, and suddenly the ground was clear before him. He bestrode Mikantor's body, arms swinging, and laughed again as he saw them cower.

He dared a glance downward. Was the boy dead? But no, he had got a grip on a piece of spear and was trying to rise, though his helmet was gone and blood from a head blow was streaming into his eyes.

"Woodpecker—get up, lad—" Velantos said in the Akhaean tongue, in case the boy should think him an enemy. "It's time to go. Get up, boy, and hold on to me."

Groaning, Mikantor made it to his knees, got a grip on the smith's belt and pulled himself upright, swaying as Velantos struck at a foe who had thought this would make him vulnerable, but not falling down. More by instinct than design the boy batted away the next weapon that came at them.

Velantos grinned. "Forward now—we're a three-handed monster, and no one will oppose us—" They lurched toward the hillside. The surviving Companions battled toward them, the less scathed protecting those with more serious wounds. Not all of their allies had panicked. From the woods a flight of arrows discouraged their enemies.

"I'll take him, sir—" said Ulansi as they reached the trees. "You're the best one to guard our backs now."

Velantos nodded, and turned as the Ai-Zir boy and Lysandros got Mikantor's arms across their necks and dragged him away. Galid was yelling from across the field, but the enemy warriors recoiled at the sight of the smith standing there. They gestured and shouted like figures in a dream. Velantos looked again and realized that neither blood loss nor darkness was affecting his vision. A mist was rolling down the hillside, shrouding those who still lived in a ghostly veil.

"Follow us if you dare!" he cried. "Land fights for us! Come and I cut you down!" He took a step backward and then another, until he was hidden by the trees.

Velantos could hear men moving nearby, but he could see nothing but branches. Still, it was a safe bet that to move upward would be better than down. Slipping one of his axes through its loop and holding the other ready, he began to work his way among the tree trunks. The battle fever had receded enough for him to start limping on the leg that had been injured at Tiryns when a voice brought him to a halt, ax poised.

"Sir—don't hit! I'm friend!"

A slim form appeared before him and he let out a long breath as he recognized the man as one of the dark folk of the moors.

"Come, sir, I take you to the others—we gather at the old tomb on the hill."

At least, thought Velantos as he followed the twisting path his guide found through the forest, *in this weather I am unlikely to be hit by lightning.*

By the time they reached the road at the top of the downs, the stresses of the fight were catching up with him. He did not seem to have any serious wounds, but his cuts were aching and muscles had stiffened enough to make him wince with every move. But as they came into the campsite among the trees, any tendancy to self-pity disappeared.

The air was heavy with the scent of blood, the ground crowded with wounded men. Tirilan moved among them, with Ganath and Beniharen. As she bent to give water to one of the Lake Folk, in her fine features Velantos recognized for the first time Anderle's disciplined severity. He gazed around him, searching for Mikantor, and felt something unclench within him as he saw the younger man sitting up, a bloodstained bandage around his brow.

It was only then, as the moment when he realized that Mikantor had fallen came back to him, that Velantos remembered that on the ground beside him he had seen the broken half of the leaf-shaped sword. He swayed where he stood, unable to suppress a groan.

"It is the smith!" someone cried.

"Sir, are you hurt? Let me help you—"

Velantos shook his head, pushing aside Ganath's supporting hand. Mikantor had heard and was gazing at him, his face brightening in joy. The smith closed his eyes. The sword had broken. *His* sword.

"Come and sit down—we have hot soup—come now . . ."

He could not resist the hands that led him toward the fire, could not evade Mikantor's welcome.

"Once more you saved me! I thought I was dead, and then I heard you calling me, and I thought I was back in Tiryns and had overslept after some evil dream!"

"Saved you!" Velantos forced himself to meet the boy's eyes, his face contorting in pain. "After my sword betrayed you! The sword *I made!*" The sword Anderle had sworn was not good enough. She had been right, after all. . . .

"Velantos—" Mikantor laid his hand on the smith's arm. "It was only bronze . . . and the giant had an arm like a tree. Against that blow, no blade could stand."

"You don't understand," Velantos whispered. That sword had been the best he could fashion, made with all the skills he had learned in the City of Circles. It should not have broken. He should have been able to shape a blade that would endure. "But I am glad that I reached you in time . . ."

"You are mourning a broken sword," said Mikantor, the light leaving his eyes. "I am mourning my men. Acaimor is dead, and Rouikhed, and far too many of the Ai-Akhsi and the men of the moors. There are other swords, but I can never replace those men. . . ."

Hearing the pain in his voice, Tirilan came up behind him and bent, the folds of her cloak falling around him like the wings of some great bird. Mikantor sighed and leaned against her, the anguish in his face beginning to ease.

Adjonar patted his shoulder. "We will always honor them. The miracle is that so many of us survived. Our discipline held. We learned."

Pelicar, who had settled down beside them, gave a nod. "If the men of the tribes will let us teach them, we will do better another day. And we gave them a savaging. The scouts who have gone back to spy on Galid's men say that the giant is coughing blood, so that sword of yours did not entirely fail!"

It broke . . . Velantos gave him a dark look. He drank the soup they gave him, though the spreading warmth did nothing to ease his aching heart. *They do not understand. I fought well, but Mikantor has many warriors. I am a smith. Only I can craft the weapon that will protect him, and I failed.*

He did not protest when Ganath washed his wounds and bound up the worst of them, and presently, for there were many who had far more need for the services of the healers, they left him alone.

And so it was Velantos, distracted neither by the body's pain nor by the need to treat it, who first noticed when the old men arrived. Or perhaps, he thought later, it was some other sense that had brought him upright and staring as they came into the circle of firelight, dressed in kilts and capes of deerskin, and carrying a burden wrapped in yellowed cloth.

At first he thought them scouts, for they clearly belonged to the people of the elder race who had been helping Mikantor, but he had never seen any of that folk who were so old, their black hair gone silver, the brown skin hanging loose on the fine bones. They were old, he thought as they looked about, both in years and in wisdom, so old there was not much in this world left for them to fear. They did not seem overly impressed by the tall warriors, and though they nodded respectfully to Mikantor, they continued to examine the company.

Velantos felt his skin chill as one by one those dark faces turned toward him. One of them said something to Grebe in the elder tongue. Mikantor's foster brother pointed, and they came to where he sat on the other side of the fire.

"He asks are you the one who shapes metal—" said Grebe. "The one from a far land."

If Velantos stood, he would tower over them, though he was not the tallest man there. Still sitting, he nodded. Grebe said something more and turned back to him.

"I tell them that you made all the swords for our king's Companions."

And the one that mattered most, thought Velantos, *failed.* But he did not say that aloud. His gaze kept turning toward the bundle the strongest of the old men was holding. What was it? He could feel the throb of power. The elder gestured and the burdened man came forward. He spoke again.

"He says . . . this is for you." Grebe paused, seeking for words. "Long time ago, light came in the sky. Hit earth, set it on fire. The fathers of his fathers find this stone—but they know now it is not stone. It is metal from the stars—"

The old man spoke again, and Velantos understood, not with his ears but with his soul.

"Some of our people saw when you bore the lightning. Our fathers hammered this with stone and made a club, but the god will give you the power to shape it. You take it now, make a sword such as your people use—"

The old man put back the wrappings and held out a rough pillar of dully glinting dark metal half the length of his arm. *Iron* . . . thought Velantos, bracing against the weight as the elder set it in his arms, a mass of iron such as he had never seen.

"A Sword from the Stars . . ." he whispered, remembering what the god had promised. He saw Mikantor watching him, eyes wide and dazzled as his own must be. He lifted the iron. "I will forge a new sword for you—a Sword from the Stars for the hand of a king . . ."

TWENTY-TWO

"Lady of flame,
Praise to thy name,
Endless thy fame—be with me . . ."

*W*ith each verse Velantos heaved at the bellows, watching the light pulse through the coals as the fire fed on the blast. With each push the warm glow flared on the walls of the smithy, for he had waited until darkness so he could gauge heat by the color of the flames. Outside, the rain had started up once more, the drip of water from the eaves blending with the whisper of the fire, but in the smithy, thank the gods, it was dry.

"Fire in the heart,
Fire be my art,
Fire every part of my working . . ."

In the midst of the coals the crucible was beginning to glow. The mass of iron lay at an angle within it. It was too big, really, but he had broken two of his hammers and shattered the surface trying to crack it cold. Perhaps it would melt from the bottom—that worked sometimes with scrap bronze.

"Do you want me to ply the bellows, sir?"

Velantos looked up and saw Aelfrix, who was polishing a bronze spearhead. He had forgotten the boy was there. He shook his head.

"Keep on with the bronze," he said. *I wish I could.* He glanced at the worktable, where he had left the wooden bowl filled with crumbled bits that had flaked off when he tried to hammer the star metal cold.

The euphoria with which he had received the gift from the elder folk had lasted for barely a day. Long before he got the iron back to the smithy on the Maiden's Isle he had begun to realize that no one he knew of had ever worked with so large a piece of iron. His experiments with Katuerix had taught him only that it would not behave like bronze. The smith of Bhagodheunon had not been able to melt bog iron, but perhaps this star stuff would be different.

> *"Lady of skill,*
> *Wisdom, and will,*
> *Guide me and fill me with learning."*

Fine words, he thought bitterly. But his whole prayer could have been expressed in a single phrase—*Please, Goddess, don't let me fail.* . . . If he was unsuccessful with a bronze sword—and when he was learning to shape the leaf-shaped blades he had ruined several—he could melt down the metal. If he destroyed this piece of iron, the gods were not likely to send him another meteor.

He straightened, sweating in the waves of heat the came off the forge. The charcoal blazed with the radiance of the rising sun in his own land, not the pallid, mist-shrouded orb that he saw in this chill northern isle. That was hot enough to melt bronze. Was it the right heat to soften the iron? He did not know, but he had to try *something.*

"Now you can work the bellows," he told the boy. "Keep the coals at just that color."

He glared at the crucible as if the heat of his gaze could ignite it. Some of the priests said that the stars were balls of fire. If so, how hot must they be? Could this metal be melted by any fire made by men? The crucible was white-hot now. He peered at it and swore—the shape of the iron had not changed so far as he could see.

A breath of air lifted the hair on his neck and teased a spurt of flame from the coals. He looked over his shoulder and stiffened, seeing Anderle in the doorway. She let the leather rain cape slide from her shoulders, shaking off the water before hanging it on a post by the door.

His instinct was to order her out, but she had been right about the need for a special sword. Perhaps she was supposed to be here. She lifted an eyebrow as she met his glare, and took Aelfrix's place on the log.

"Does the work go well?" she asked pleasantly.

"The work does *not* go well—" He grasped one end of the bar with the tongs and lifted it. It was glowing a soft red, but the surface was unchanged. He scowled, resenting the compulsion to try to explain. It was hard enough to talk about his work when he knew what he was doing.

"Are the coals hotter than the crucible? Could you perhaps get it started if you put the iron directly into the fire?" she asked.

It was even worse when the person you were talking to started to offer suggestions, especially when you had no better ideas.

"Maybe . . ." he said aloud. "Maybe I can break it if it's hotter. Smaller pieces will melt, I think . . ." He took a deep breath to focus his energies, checked the color of the coals, and reached for the tongs once more.

"Lady, bless the work—" he whispered. Gripping the iron at both ends, he lowered it carefully into the forge. Then he set the largest of his granite hammers in the warm ashes at the edge. Hammers had been known to break when hot metal met cold stone.

He banked the coals around the bar and turned to face her. "I told you, I never worked with iron like this before. If I succeed it is mercy of the goddess, not my skill."

"Then I will pray to Her—"

"You do that," he snarled. "You are the one with visions. You want your king to have an iron sword, you ask your gods how I make it!"

"It is the gods who want that, not I—" she replied, flushing in turn. "I never asked for a vision. It cost the life of a man I loved."

Velantos winced. Anyone who looked at Tirilan could see how fair a man her father must have been. Of course Anderle would have no interest in a soot-stained, muscle-bound smith who barely spoke her tongue . . . and thank the gods for that. The woman was a sly, managing bitch, even worse than Queen Naxomene. But he must not say so. He saw Aelfrix watching them wide-eyed as he continued to work the bellows, and took a deep breath.

"Then blame the gods, not me! I never ask to be carried from my home to this wretched cold country for a cause not even my own!"

"Not even for Mikantor?" she asked softly.

"If not for Mikantor I would be dead," he replied. *And maybe better so.*

"And he would be dead, if not for you—" she retorted. "In this, the gods command us all."

He closed his eyes, shaken even by the memory of terror he had felt when he saw the boy struck down.

"Should the iron be doing that?" Aelfrix asked.

Velantos whirled. The coals were white-hot, and sparks were spitting from the lump of metal in the forge. He grabbed for the tongs, tried to grip the iron, missed, caught and swung it across to the anvil, trailing fire as it had when it first fell from the stars. The iron itself was burning—he had to put out those sparks—he dared not lose any more! Shifting the tongs to his left hand, he took up the hammer. It seemed to rise of itself, propelled by his fear.

Before he could plan the stroke the hammer was descending. Sparks fountained upward as it hit, and the iron seemed to explode. There must have been an air pocket within. Velantos yelled as a flying shard seared his shoulder. Another came to rest sizzling at the hem of Anderle's gown. Aelfrix had ducked the one that was now smoldering by the wall. The boy leaped up to sweep it back with the broom.

Shaking with fear and fury, Velantos turned on Anderle, the hammer still swinging in his hand.

"Out!" His roar shook the smithy. "This is not your magic!"

"I am the Lady of Avalon and I go where I will!" She rose, drawing her skirts away from the smoking shard.

The hammer whipped around. With the last of his control he changed its direction and sent it crashing through the smithy wall. As a final bit of plaster fell, they stood staring, their harsh breathing the only sound.

"Then I leave! Before *I* kill you." His voice hissed with the effort it took to form the words. "I will make another forge. The elder folk will help. If the gods will, I make the Sword, but I want no help from you!"

Her face went white, then red, but he had silenced her. Skirts flaring, she grabbed her cape and strode through the door.

Still shaking, Velantos began to search for the scattered pieces of iron.

IT WAS STILL RAINING. Mikantor wiped away the water that had crept in beneath his hood and peered at the track they were following. Beyond the edging of trees the meadows were flooded by the brown waters of the Sabren. By now he had hoped to be safe with Pelicar's people in Ilifen, but on such muddy roads no one could travel fast. It had been a risk to take this route, so close to the eastern Ai-Ushen clanholds, but with the river running this strongly, surely King Eltan's men would keep close to their own hearths.

He turned as Pelicar came splashing back down the line.

"There's a village a little ways up the road. I think we should make for it. It's early to stop, but this will be our best chance to sleep dry."

Mikantor nodded. "Send someone ahead to ask their hospitality. We all need hot food. We can share our supplies if they will share their fires."

At the beginning of this journey he would have begged shelter for the women, but it had become clear that despite her apparent fragility, Tirilan could outmarch *him*. She was at the end of the line now with the men who were carrying Tegues, whose wounded leg was going bad. Pelicar had his arm in a sling, and Mikantor himself was still limping. There was not a man among them who was not marked somewhere, and they were the ones who could still march. He had been forced to leave four of his Companions and nearly a quarter of those who had fought for him at the White Horse Vale. And they were better off than those who had been burned in the great pyre on the battlefield.

He slid on a patch of mud and forced his attention back to the road. Pelicar was approaching again, followed by an old fellow who must be from the village. He began to chatter in the local dialect before they had even reached the column.

"He says they are a small place," translated Pelicar. "They will help as they can, but it has rained so much their stocks of wood are low."

"Then we will go into the woods and gather more," said Mikantor. *When I have rested a little,* he admitted as they forded a swollen stream and trudged up the track, his leg muscles trembling from the effort of slogging through mud all day. The rain had started up again.

The village was called Three Alders, a cluster of roundhouses and outbuildings built along a ridge of higher ground above the flood plain where another river joined the Sabren. It was a flooded plain now. To one who had grown up in the Lake Village the expanse of gleaming water broken by clumps of trees seemed almost like home. Mikantor found himself missing Grebe, sent home to recover from a slash across the shoulder.

Despite their guide's warning, the villagers found shelter for everyone, for the junction of the rivers brought trade, and they often had visitors. Mikantor found himself being treated with a mixture of anxiety and respect that would have concerned him if hot food and warmth of the house had left him with the energy to do anything but doze by the fire. Tirilan was still on her feet, conferring with the chieftain's wife about herbs to treat a sick child. He only realized that he had fallen asleep when he was roused by shouting at the door.

"We're not the only travelers caught by this storm—" Pelicar squatted by his side. "Men are stranded between the rivers. Their boat capsized crossing the Sabren. The waters are rising, and the second stream is too rapid for them to get through. The chieftain here is organizing the men to try a rescue."

"Do they need our help?" Mikantor rubbed his eyes, momentarily dizzied as the prickle of danger warred with his fatigue.

"They mean to send men into the river. I think they can use everyone who is fit."

"All right then—give me your shoulder—" He gripped Pelicar's arm and heaved himself upright.

"Are *you* fit, my lord?" Pelicar steadied him.

"I will be," grunted Mikantor, avoiding Tirilan's anxious gaze. As Pelicar went to find his leather cape, he took a deep breath and then another, drawing on the disciplines he had learned at Avalon. By the time the other man returned, his head was clear, and his warmed limbs seemed willing to obey him again.

The first blast of rain as they emerged from the roundhouse nearly sent him back inside again. But the others were slogging down the village street and he was ashamed not to follow them. And then he saw the surging waters glinting in the light of the torches, and in the need of the moment all other awareness fell aside. A line of trees showed him the other bank of the river, though most of it was already underwater. Several men were clinging to the lower branches. They waved as they saw the light.

"They cannot try a boat—the river runs too fast—but a line of men on a rope may be able to cross without being swept away," Pelicar shouted in his ear. The villagers were already fastening a heavy length of braided hemp around a tree a little way upstream.

"Our warriors are heavier than most of these folk," said Mikantor. "We had better help them." Pelicar and Ulansi and the others fell in behind him as he made his way toward the tree. An inner voice questioned why he should take this risk for people he did not even know, but if his combat with the King Stag meant anything, it was that whether they knew it or not, these *were* his people.

The villagers began to uncoil the rope and the men got into line. The stranded travelers had seen them and answered the chieftain's hail. At the words, Ulansi hissed suddenly and gripped Pelicar's arm. "Ask them where these people are from!"

"From the hills to the west, the chieftain says—" Pelicar's voice faded as Ulansi dropped the rope and stepped away.

"Ai-Ushen!" exclaimed the Ai-Zir man. "I thought I recognized their lying tongues."

He should have known, thought Mikantor, his own grip loosening. If they were coming from the other side of the river, what else could they be? Ai-Ushen, who with Galid had made him an orphan and a wanderer, wild folk from the hills, always at war with the other tribes. Most of his own men had as much reason to hate the Ai-Ushen as he did. One by one they dropped the rope and stepped aside. The village men stopped in confusion, looking at Mikantor.

He peered across the heaving waters at the wretched figures clinging to the trees. They did not look like enemies.

"They are men—" he said at last. "And death by water is as evil as death by fire. If I need to kill them, I will do it when they can face me with a sword in hand. I am going to pick up the rope, follow me who will."

One by one all except Ulansi took up the rope once more.

The shock of the cold water sent a shudder through his limbs as he edged in, one arm wrapped around the rope while the other gripped it. Two of the local men were ahead of him, his own men mixed with the villagers behind him. He felt for footing, swaying as the current slammed against him. Inevitably they were carried downstream, but that had been expected, and even at an angle the rope was long enough to reach the trees. As they reached the bank the first man fell to his knees, clinging to an outthrust root, then pulled himself upright and worked his way back again, taking up the slack by getting the end around one of the sturdier trunks, and making a riverman's knot that would hold.

Mikantor began to believe they could actually bring it off as the tree allowed them to put some of their weight on the rope instead of having to support it against the current. The stranded travelers were working their way down through the tangled trunks. One by one they reached their rescuers, who braced themselves against the current and passed them along the upstream side of the rope to the other side. Eight men in all were saved. Three had been carried away earlier, and during the rescue a fourth lost his grip and was washed away.

It was not until morning that Mikantor learned that one of the survivors was Tanecar, son of the Ai-Ushen queen and King Eltan's nephew and heir.

"IF YOU KNEW WHO I was, would you have gone in the river to help me?"

Mikantor considered the young man who had hunkered down beside him, cradling a beaker of steaming tea. Tanecar looked to be a few years younger than himself, shorter, but sturdily built, with a shock of dark brown hair.

"If I had known that this morning I was going to feel like a clout that the laundress has been beating against rocks in the stream, I would not have left this fire," he replied.

"Prince of the Ai-Zir, that does not answer my question . . ." Tanecar smiled carefully. At some point he had hit his head against a tree and the side of his face was bruised.

Mikantor sighed. "I knew you were Ai-Ushen, but you looked pretty pitiful, hanging on to those trees. I would not leave any man to drown."

"My uncle was Galid's ally . . ." The Ai-Ushen prince sipped some tea and set the beaker down. "But my mother says it is time for that to end. She says that the other tribes have turned against us because of him."

"Your mother is a wise woman . . ." With an effort, Mikantor kept his tone even.

"I was on my way to visit Pelicar's people in hopes of a marriage alliance," Tanecar went on. "That's off for now, of course—all the gifts were lost in the stream. I'll have to go back home once the floods go down. Come with me, Mikantor. I think it is time for the Wolf and the Bull to be friends."

"I am not the Bull of the Ai-Zir," Mikantor said soberly. "That title belongs to whoever my cousin, if she ever has her rights, may choose. I started out to bring Galid to justice, but now— I have run with the deer, if that means anything to you . . ."

"I had heard a rumor of it." Tanecar drank again. "Perhaps you are meant to be a Defender, such as we hear of in the old tales, who in times of danger unites the tribes. This is a matter for the queens to decide."

"Will he be safe?" asked Pelicar, who had joined them when he heard his name.

"I owe him a life," said the queen's son. "Mine will be his surety."

THE SCENT OF THE boar, pit-roasted since early morning, mingled pleasantly with the resinous smoke of the fire. Tirilan took a bite of the generous slice on her wooden platter, blessing the hospitality that had seated her beside the Ai-Ushen queen. The beast was still lean from the winter, but they had packed it with herbs while it was roasting, and she had not tasted anything so good for a long time.

Ketaneket was a solid woman in her middle years, silver threading the hair that had once been the same seal brown as that of her son. Her daughter Tamar, who sat on Tirilan's other side, was enough like him to be a twin. The queen's household were behind them. Among them Tirilan recognized Saarin, the Sacred Sister who served the Ai-Ushen, but she had not yet had a chance to speak with her.

Certainly Tirilan could not complain of their welcome. The storms that had led to their meeting with Tanecar had finally passed, and the feast had been spread in a clearing surrounded by pine trees. Their sharply etched needles framed a sky whose fiery glow was just now giving way to a luminous blue. Perhaps this year would have a summer after all.

Mikantor, his lynx skin draped across his broad shoulders, sat with the men on the other side of the fire with his Companions behind him, except for Ulansi, who had been left at Three Alders with the excuse that someone had to stay with Tegues. The truth, of course, was that the Ai-Zir warrior could not be trusted to control his desire for revenge. There were many like him. The Wolves of Ushan had raided widely, and now that they wanted peace—if indeed they did—they could hardly expect the other tribes to welcome them with open arms.

A rumble of drums brought everyone upright as a dozen young warriors danced into the space between the men's and women's sides of the fire. They wore only loincloths and the skins of wolves, forelegs crossed over their chests and snarling heads drawn over their own. From their hands came the brown flash of knives. In a whirl of feigned attack and retreat they danced, adding their own howls to the music.

Was it their land that made them so fierce? The moors of Utun had been high and rugged, but Ushan was a country where rearing mountains brooded above deeply cut valleys. Forests clung to the slopes, and men carved out holdings wherever there was a little level ground. The mountain pastures and cold winters made it a good country for sheep. As evening cooled the air, Tirilan was grateful for the mantle of woad-dyed wool the queen had given her.

Mikantor watched the dancers as if he were evaluating them for a place in his band. That might even be true. He sat next to Tanecar, who himself had the place of honor next to the king. Eltan was not much like Ketaneket, being lean as an old wolf himself, his hair silver gray. It was said that they had different fathers. But whatever King Eltan might do on the war trail, he apparently deferred to his sister on their home ground.

"You are Mikantor's cousin, they say," said Tamar when the dancers had gone. As the member of the queen's family closest in age, she seemed to have been assigned to question Tirilan. Or perhaps she was simply curious.

"My mother and his were cousins," answered Tirilan. She did not feel quite ready to explain what else she was to Mikantor. When they arrived she had not objected when they gave her a bed in the Women's House, but that might have happened even if she had arrived as his wife. "We grew up together at Avalon."

"Then he must be like your brother!" the girl said brightly. Tirilan suppressed a glare. Could Tamar possibly be as ingenuous as she seemed? "He is very handsome."

"Yes, he is . . ." Tirilan agreed. Royal women had a great deal of freedom in the tribes, but she doubted the girl would be allowed to sleep with a guest whose status was still uncertain. If they made a formal alliance, it might be a different story.

But for now, Tamar's interest seemed no more than that of any young girl introduced to a handsome stranger. It was her brother who appeared to have fallen in love with Mikantor in the way of a boy for a slightly older man. His head was close to Mikantor's now, eyes alight as he pointed to one of the warriors or whispered a comment that sparked Mikantor's swift smile.

"He does not yet have a wife?" asked Tamar.

"He does not yet have a *home!*" she snapped. "Time enough to think of marriage when he has dealt with Galid," she added more gently.

So far no one had questioned her presence with Mikantor's band. Priestesses of Avalon, like the Sacred Sisters who served the tribes, traveled freely throughout the land. His men, whom she had healed and fed, whose clothing she had mended and whose troubles she had heard, honored her for her own sake. But she was beginning to feel the need for some more formal recognition of her relationship to Mikantor, whatever that might be. The role of wife did not quite seem to describe what she had become.

"I suppose that must be so. Perhaps they will arrange something for him at the festival . . . At Midsummer," added Tamar in response to Tirilan's questioning look, "when the queens meet at Carn Ava."

Tirilan nodded. With so much rain, she had forgotten that the season was advancing. The Lady of Avalon attended every year, and she had gone with her mother several times when she was younger. It was a time of truce, and a time to make alliances.

"Will you be there this year?"

"Oh yes . . ." answered Tirilan. Mikantor must go to seek support against Galid, and she must fight for her right to stay with him.

"There—" Velantos pointed to the excavation they had made in the packed dirt floor of his new smithy. "Put the stone next to the hearth."

Grebe nodded and said something in the old dialect to the other men. Mikantor's foster brother had been at the Lake Village, recovering from his wounds, when the smith had sent to ask for help in moving. He had organized everything, including the building of a new smithy. Only a moon had passed, but once the rain stopped the work had gone swiftly, and the mud plaster and limewash were drying on the interlacing of willow that made up the walls. Only the roof remained to build. Beyond the walls the beech trees whispered in the breeze.

Velantos took a deep breath, smelling dust and ripening grass from the downs beyond the grove. Through the open door he could see the great stones that fronted the old tomb near the White Horse. The downs were farther than he had expected to go, but when the elders suggested he build his smithy there, he had that sense of rightness that comes when the hammer hits true. They believed that the lightning stroke he had survived was a mark of favor from the gods, and the place where that happened clearly held power. Perhaps they were right, for the gods knew he needed help. The elder folk had given him the metal, but the one thing he needed most—the knowledge of how to craft it—they could not supply.

He turned at the sound of something very heavy being dragged across the ground. Half his height, the sarsen the men had on the ropes might once have been part of the tomb, but over the centuries it had rolled aside, and it was just the right shape for an anvil. If the ancestors approved him, surely they would not mind if he made use of one of their stones. Aelfrix and the other boys ran ahead of them, laying down dry grass over which the stone would slide smoothly until they heaved it upright and tipped it into the hole.

"Thank you!" he exclaimed, bending a little to pass his hands across the flat top. "This does very well indeed! Rest now, friends, and have some ale!"

His gut knotted with the knowledge that soon the smithy would be ready, and he would have to begin work on the metal shards. Before they exploded under his hammer the fire had changed them. The surfaces were smoother now, and in the broken edges he could see layering. He knew that he must somehow meld them together. But how much should he heat the iron? How hard should he make each blow?

Frowning, he sat down on the stone, staring unseeing at the rectangular hearth, long enough to hold a sword. The rim had been built up with boulders and clay. The charcoal to fill it was coming soon.

"Tomorrow we bring thatching and give you a roof against the rain, and put the hides beneath, so your sparks will not set it on fire—" Grebe smiled. The past few days had been fair, almost warm enough for comfort, but that would not last.

When he had installed his image of the Lady of the Forge in her niche, he would make her an offering and ask for inspiration. He had some bronze with him. Perhaps he could hammer out plates to armor a leather sark for Mikantor while he waited for the goddess to tell him what to do.

TWENTY-THREE

*T*he stepped cone of the Wombhill rose white above the green grass as if one of the great clouds that still hung above the horizon had settled there. But beyond a few sprinkles that morning there had been no rain today. It was a good omen, thought Anderle. The surviving emmer wheat and barley were forming heads. If the Goddess was good to them, there would be no more floods until after the harvest, but even so it would be another lean year.

She cast an experienced glance over the women who had gathered on the green. Between them and the Henge of Carn Ava sprouted a flock of tents and bothies, their inhabitants clamorous as the waterfowl that covered the Lake each spring—but not as numerous. Once this had been a time of bountiful feasting, but in recent years the Midsummer Festival had grown smaller. No one could afford to feed a large gathering. A few more years of this and the system would break down entirely. Something had to be done.

Still, all the queens and clanmothers who were expected had arrived, even Ketaneket of the Ai-Ushen and her daughter Tamar. They must have come in the night before. Anderle nodded to the other priestesses and they took their places at the head of the procession. To the soft beat of the drums and the hiss of rattles they began to move. Soon the Wombhill rose before them, the chalk surface dazzling white in the light of noon. The drums fell silent as they moved sunwise to circle the mound. Anderle lifted her hands.

"We salute you, Great Mother, and ask Your blessings. Renew Your promise that life will go on. Grant us sunshine to ripen the grain. Keep our beasts and our babies healthy. And grant that our quarrels be no more than the spats of children—" Her voice strengthened at the murmur of agreement behind her.

She stepped aside and one by one the seven priestesses ascended the steps that made a winding path up the mound to lay their offerings at its summit. When the last of the Sacred Sisters had completed her task and returned, they turned to face the assembly.

"Children of the Goddess, hear Her promise—" she cried. As the priestesses joined hands she could feel the energy of the mound behind her as a child feels the protecting presence of her mother. She took a deep breath, letting awareness of the Lady of Avalon flow out and the Lady of Life flow in, sharing it with the others through their linked hands, for here at the mound the power was too great to be borne by any single soul.

"Listen, my children, to the promise I give you; hear, oh my beloved, the words that I say." Eight voices resonated as one. "I see you more clearly than you can see yourselves, and I chastise your evils only that your good may grow. Know that there is nothing but your own wills that can separate you from My love, and even when you turn from Me, I sustain you still."

Ni-Terat, bountiful Mother, hear us, called that part of her awareness that still belonged to Anderle. A multitude of faces glimmered before her like light on water; her ears sang with myriad names. Each one was different, and yet they all were One, as she and the Sacred Sisters and the women they were blessing were once individuals and components of a greater identity. Their linked hands lifted as the words of the promise rolled forth once more.

"Come to Me all you who are hungry and I will feed you from My own flesh, for My body is eternal. Come to Me all you who are thirsty and I will nurse you at My own breasts, for they are never dry. As you have brought these offerings to Me, so I give Myself to you. You have turned to Me at last, and behold, I welcome you to My arms."

Power surged through their linked hands, burst free, and blazed outward to bless those who waited, and through them, outward through the land.

And then it was done.

Anderle swayed as the power departed and she was only herself once more. *I hope they remember.* If the queens and clanmothers could reach agreement, the men who were spending this day testing their strength against each other in warrior games would have to listen. And Velantos would have time to forge the iron sword. Her task now was to make sure that when Mikantor had a weapon that would command the respect of the warriors, the men would follow him.

As if the thought had evoked its own answer, Ellet fell into step beside her. "My lady, Mikantor is here! He and his band rode in with the Ai-Ushen!"

Anderle stopped short, staring. The last she heard, the boy had been on his way to Ilifen. How in the Lady's sweet name had he pulled off this miracle? And if Mikantor was here . . . She turned, seeking the Ai-Ushen group amid the crowd, and saw among the dark heads the bright hair of her daughter, Tirilan.

SUNSET HAD KINDLED FESTIVAL fires among the clouds, outshining the bonfires on the earth below. The ruddy light reddened Mikantor's hair and warmed the faces of his men, squatting by the Ai-Zir bonfire in attitudes of conscious relaxation. As Tirilan followed him into the queen's tent, she blessed them with her best smile. The festival was under truce-bond, so they should have been safe even if Galid's men had been there. But Galid never attended the festival. Beneath the banner of the Bull, Queen Cimara offered a meager hospitality to the clanmothers who had joined her here while most of their sons and husbands prudently stayed home.

As Mikantor looked from one to another of the women who awaited him, Tirilan realized that he had never seen the queen before. She eased past him and bent before a faded woman who looked nearly Anderle's age in a headdress of amber beads with lappets hanging to either side.

"Mother of Azan, we greet you. May your way be blessed—"

"That is a hope I lost years ago," said Cimara, "but you are kind to say so. I welcome you to my fire. . . ."

"Hope is what I have come to discuss with you," came Mikantor's deep voice as he eased down beside Tirilan.

For a moment the queen looked at him with tired eyes. "Hope is a luxury. I am content to survive."

"And your people?" Tirilan found herself speaking more sharply than she had intended.

"They too. Time will pass, and one day we will all die whatever we do."

"Then you will die without having truly lived, and leave nothing behind you!" exclaimed Mikantor.

"That is a choice you can make for yourself, but you are a queen." Tirilan echoed him. "You have no right to doom your people."

Cimara gave her a pitying smile. "When I was your age I believed as you do. But I saw my mother's life worn away by long years as a captive. I saw men killed for loving me. I perform the ceremonies, but I am a barren stock. My household has one small farm for its support. Galid does not quite dare to kill me, and I have refused to give him the name of king. That is the best I can do. Do not ask me to make you my king. He will kill you."

"He has already tried—" said Mikantor dryly. "But that is between him and me. I was born to the Ai-Zir. By blood, you are my kinswoman and my queen. But I was not raised in Azan, I was not fed by its earth, I do not know its ways. I will lead your warriors, but I am not the right man to be your king."

That, at least, had pierced Cimara's despair. The beads of her headdress clicked as she shook her head. "But what do you want, then?"

"To be your protector, lady."

Tirilan reached out to take his hand. They had spoken of this through the hours of darkness when they lay twined together after making love, seeking to find a way through the demands and dangers that surrounded them. "They tell me that I was born to be a king, but it is not king of Azan that I would be. Something more . . . or less . . ." He shrugged. "The shape of it is still unclear. But the calling I feel is to serve all in this Isle."

"We come to you first because you are his rightful queen," added Tirilan.

"Do you wish my blessing?" Cimara looked bemused. "It is more likely to prove a curse instead."

"And yet that is what I ask."

"Then it is yours, and though it is little enough support that the wretch allows me, I can at least offer you a beaker of beer. . . ."

Anderle settled into her place between the men's and women's sides of the council fire. She surveyed the array of faces dappled by sunlight where there were holes in the canopy of oiled wool, queens and clanmothers facing war chieftains and kings. A ring of lesser folk surrounded them. In all the years it had been her privilege, and sometimes her penance, to mediate the negotiations of the tribes at the Midsummer Festival, never, she thought with a flutter of apprehension, had she faced them with such hope and such fear.

As always, they began with the awarding of prizes for the warrior games, an event that was ostensibly neutral, although one could tell a great deal from the tribal affiliations of the winners and the strength of the cheers. A fair number of those prizes, she was pleased to note, had been won by Mikantor's men. They were identified by the tribes from which they had come, but the buzz as one after another returned to stand with him was encouraging. At least the tribes could see that he knew how to train warriors.

Mikantor himself was called forth to receive the prize for swordplay. There was a gratifying clamor of approval as men beat upon their thighs and women ullulated behind their hands. *And when he has the Sword from the Stars, they will know he can use it. . . .* The gods had ordained that Mikantor should have that sword. *But even the gods,* came the traitorous thought, *cannot always compensate for the weakness of men. . . .*

The women continued to cheer as Mikantor bent to receive his crown of oak leaves from Queen Cimara. The gathering buzzed with comment. Was the queen granting him the kingship of the Ai-Zir? Surely he was a sight to gladden any woman's heart, tall and strong as a young oak himself, with a graceful stride and that sudden sweet smile. The buzz of speculation grew even louder as Mikantor returned to his place with the onlookers instead of seating himself among the kings.

On her visits to the queens Anderle had been amused to learn how often Mikantor had been before her. She was gratified by how thoroughly he had charmed the women, although the presence of Tirilan made it difficult to broach the possibility of a marriage alliance. What did the girl think she was doing? Her vows prohibited her from marrying Mikantor herself, so why did she stand in the way of an alliance that might bring him warriors? They needed to talk, but Tirilan had been remakably elusive throughout the festival.

The goodwill generated by the prize giving was somewhat tattered by the time they had finished hearing the tally of complaints regarding thefts of stock and violations of borders. Some could be settled with compensation, but not all. The wounds were too deep, the needs too great. They were like starving cattle fighting each other for the last wisps of grass. Anderle drew a deep breath. Now, if ever, the time for change had come. She took up the wand hung with disks of silver and began to shake it, overcoming the dissonant voices with a shimmer of sweet sound.

"Mothers of the people, this cannot go on!" Her stern glance swept the assembly. "We can no longer afford to fight each other. Wind and rain are a sufficient enemy."

"And will you appoint yourself to judge us, Lady of Avalon?" came a voice from among the men.

"A judge must be able to enforce his rulings. My powers are of the spirit. I can bless or curse, but we have had enough of the latter already. Would you have me curse your seed?" As the uneasy laughter ceased, Anderle shook her head. "We need a judge who is also a Defender, who can enforce his decisions with a precise stroke of the sword, who serves all the tribes while belonging to none."

"And where, oh great priestess, will you find this paragon?"

"Your children have already found him," she replied. "He is the Son of a Hundred Kings, descendant of kings from across the sea, but born and bred in this land. He has lived in the moors and marshes and on the plains.

He has run with the deer and gained the blessing of the elder folk who were here first of all. He is Mikantor, nephew of Zamara of the Ai-Zir and son of Irnana of Avalon."

It was not hard to find him. Heads were turning that way like flowers to the sun. From across the circle Mikantor's gaze flicked to her and then away. Anderle's lips twitched. If he did not wish to be surprised, he should have made a point of visiting her when he was making his rounds among the queens.

"Let us see him!" came the cry. "Come here where we can look at you!"

Eyes bright with apprehension, excitement, and something suspiciously like amusement, Mikantor came forward, Tirilan at his side. Whatever he expected, he had dressed for the occasion, Anderle observed sourly, in a white short tunic with colored braid at neck and hem. Tirilan wore white as well. Her mother did not know whether to be relieved or angry that she was not wearing the blue of Avalon.

"The Ai-Giru speak for him," said their queen.

"And the Ai-Utu," Urtaya, the slender dark woman who was their lady, echoed her.

"Oh, he is a fair young man—" The king of the Ai-Ilf got to his feet. "But there is a difference between borrowing a stud bull and allowing ourselves to be yoked like oxen while he takes over the herd. I serve my queen, but I will bow to no man!" A hubbub of approval from the men's side echoed him. Mikantor opened his lips as if to speak, but Tirilan squeezed his arm and he remained silent.

"But such a leader has been chosen before, in times of great need." The voice of Queen Ketaneket rose easily above the noise. "A Defender was named, who protected all the tribes."

Another murmur swept the assembly as they realized that the queen of Ushan was supporting Mikantor. Eyes flicked to their grizzled king, who responded with a frown. How, wondered Anderle, could they convince the men?

"That's all very well," said Menguellet of the Ai-Akhsi, "but the king's authority comes from the queen, and the queen's from the Goddess for her land."

"He have the blessing of the Goddess," observed an old woman of the elder race who sat among the clanmothers. "When he kills the King Stag, he gives himself to the Lady. Her priestess is there—the one who carried the power." She pointed to Tirilan. "Let her come to each one of you, learn your lands, be your voice to him."

Anderle glared at her daughter as the queens began to argue. This was not part of her plan! To be sure, at first Tirilan had looked as surprised as she was, but her expression was changing.

"Will the girl do it?" asked someone. "She is a priestess of Avalon."

"And bound by vows—" Anderle began, but no one was listening. Tirilan had stepped forward so that light from one of the tears in the canopy made a radiance of her hair. Even for those who did not have the inner Sight, she *shone*. A cheap trick, thought her mother, if the girl had been aware of it, but Tirilan seemed unconscious of the effect as she turned to face the queens.

"I have sworn to serve the goddess . . ." Tirilan's soft voice, pitched as she had been trained at Avalon, carried easily. "She is One and many, the source and the streams. At Avalon I studied the eternal truths, but on the sacred isle one forgets the needs of those who struggle to live from day to day." She glanced toward her mother in what might have been apology; then she went on. "I have learned that while we live in bodies, we must honor Spirit as it manifests through each thing—each spring, each field, each tree. To serve Her in the great things, I must pay attention to those that are small."

Anderle started to speak, but she could feel the mood of the assembly shifting. To make any objection might weaken Mikantor. She seethed silently, recognizing that she was being forced to choose between her plans for Mikantor and for Tirilan.

"Let her come first to me." Queen Cimara spoke softly, but a buzz of repetition carried her words through the crowd. "I will teach her my Mysteries."

"And will you give Mikantor the name of king?" asked King Eltan.

"And make him your equal?" responded Cimara with a flash of spirit that reminded Anderle of the girl she once had been. "No. I will choose my king when I rule my land again." She turned to Mikantor. "Yesterday when we spoke, I had no hope, but last night I dreamed of a dragon and a swan who flew above Azan. You were right, cousin. I have stayed alive, but I have not lived. It is time to change that. I accept your service and I give you a command. Destroy Galid. He is the poison that is killing my land."

Mikantor went down on one knee before her. "Mother of Azan, I will . . ."

He rose and turned to face the men. "In the Games, you saw that I am blessed by the fellowship of heroes. We are not many, but we can make Galid's life a misery. Yet that will not destroy him. If you will have me as your leader, you must fight beside me. To take out Galid's forces will require an army drawn from all the tribes."

"You are a strong warrior," King Eltan agreed. "But you must prove you have the favor, not only of the queens but of the gods. Let them give us a Sign that you are their Chosen."

"In our land we remember that such a Defender bore on each forearm a dragon," said Queen Urtaya, "pricked into his flesh with thorns, so that he could never forget. If Mikantor will endure that ordeal, Utun will accept his service."

"He will have something more." Anderle found her voice at last. "He will have a Sword from the Stars against which no earthly weapon can stand!" *If Velantos is able to forge the blade. . .* Her gaze found Mikantor's, and she saw the same question in his eyes.

The shortest night had fallen. There was a certain release in having made a public commitment, thought Mikantor as he followed the Ai-Utu queen to her fire. At least it relieved him from having to make any more decisions. Sparks whirled up to mingle with the stars as more wood was tossed on. It reminded him of the forge fire, and abruptly he wished Velantos could be with him now. Perhaps his decision to save the smith was the choice that had brought him to this day. If he had not done so, he might still be a slave in the lands of the Middle Sea.

But if he did not have Velantos, at least he had Tirilan. Instinctively he reached out to her and found her hand waiting to slip into his own. Word of what had happened at the conclave had spread throughout the encampment, and people were already gathering. He supposed it was too much to ask that he be allowed to endure his ordeal in privacy. That was another choice he had forgone by committing himself to serve them all.

He had assumed it would take time to find someone who knew how to prick the pattern, but after the meeting an old man of the elder folk had appeared with a basket full of bags containing powdered colors and a piece of rolled leather full of thorns. Mikantor told himself he should be grateful that all the symbols with which he had been covered for the running of the deer had only been painted on. Going into a battle was different. You knew you might be wounded, but never really believed it. He thought about being pricked by thorns, like the stings of a thousand bees, and realized with bitter amusement that he was not sure how well he would endure the pain.

"It will be all right," said Tirilan. "They have said that you may lie with your head in my lap while the old man is working."

"That will certainly distract me—" he said with a smile.

"I thought it might—" She squeezed his hand.

"Better lay a piece of heavy cloth across my loins, lest I embarrass us all," he added, and saw her blush, and laughed.

They had laid out a straw mattress near the bonfire. The old man was there already, mixing a dark blue liquid in a bowl made from the bottom half of a gourd. The Sacred Sisters were there as well, with Anderle. He ought to have expected they would come to bear witness for their tribes, reflected Mikantor as he bowed.

"The boy has good manners," said one of them. He thought it was Linne of the Ai-Giru. "You taught him well—"

"I have tried . . ." Anderle's tone was even, but Mikantor felt Tirilan's fingers tighten on his. The priestess got to her feet, draperies as blue as the stuff in the pot swirling around her.

"Mikantor, son of Irnana, you are summoned here to confirm your commitment to all the tribes. Know that in the ancient lands across the sea, these dragons marked those of the royal line who dedicated themselves to serve. Is that your true will?"

My true will . . . His head whirled. How could you ever really tell? He knew only that he had set his feet upon a path from which he could not turn back now.

"I serve my Lady. I am ready to do Her will . . ." he said aloud, not adding that ever since he returned to Avalon he had seen the Goddess with the face of Tirilan.

His tunic had short sleeves, so he need not disrobe. He pulled at the lacing on his leather bracers, slid them off, and handed them to Ganath, who had entered with the rest of the Companions behind him. With their eyes upon him he would not dare to groan. The skin that the bracers had covered was pale, the skin tight across the hard muscle, threaded by blue veins. The tattooing should show up well.

Tirilan took her place at the head of the pallet, and Mikantor eased down before her, suppressing his response. He had not been entirely joking about the cloth. *When I no longer rise to your touch, my beloved,* he thought wryly, *you will know I am dead and gone.* They gave him a piece of wood to grip with his other hand.

"I am Fox," said the old man in the elder tongue. "You will please lie very still."

"I thank you, honored one," Mikantor answered in the same language, stretching out his arm. He twitched at the first touch, but it was only a narrow brush with which Fox was drawing the sinuous shape around his arm.

"Breathe slowly," came Anderle's voice from the other side of the fire when the design had been drawn on both arms. "Ride the drumming. Ride the song . . ."

He closed his eyes and Tirilan set her hands on either side of his head, stroking back his hair. *This is not so bad,* he thought at the first prick of the thorn. He breathed in to the drumbeat and out again. Tap, tap, tap, the little hammer pecked the thorn into his skin with a rhythm like the beat when Velantos was hammering out some golden ornament in the forge. *If beating on me would help you to master that lump of metal,* he thought distractedly, *I would set my arm on the anvil.* It was beginning to hurt more now, a throbbing ache that radiated out from the actual wounds. He tried to make his pain an offering, but it was getting hard to think about anything but his arm.

"Breathe slowly," whispered Tirilan as he gasped. "I am here . . ." Mikantor let out his breath, forcing himself to relax against her. "Do not resist the pain, let it flow through you . . ."

"You are flowing in the river, you are blowing through the grass, you are glowing in the fire, you are here and you shall pass," the women sang.

Mikantor fixed his mind on the images, and for a moment he rode the agony. Did a woman in childbed feel like this, striving to bring new life into the world? He took another breath, let it out, clinging to the beat of the drum.

"You are here and you shall pass . . ." they sang once more. Who were the men who had worn these dragons before? His mind reeled and for a moment he was standing on a terrace of reddish stone, looking down at a sea whose color was a brighter blue than any that ever washed his own Isle's shores.

"From life to life still learning, to joy transmute your pain. From death's dark sleep returning, walk in light again," came the singing. It was one of the sacred chants of Avalon. If he could sink into that sleep, where would he awaken? His awareness flickered with memories that were not his own.

And then the singing stopped. He lay, breathing carefully, a part of his mind wondering at the throbbing ache in his arm while the rest grasped at the images that had come with that pain. There was movement around him. The old man was switching to his other side.

No—he thought dimly at the first prick of the thorn. *I can't do this again. Not yet. Not now!* But his will did not reach his limbs. The drumming caught his breath, and as the anguish in his right arm began to match that in his left he let it carry him away. The rush of images began to focus to the memories of one lifetime, the one he needed to remember now.

He was rocking in a boat as the world exploded in fire and thunder, seeking something unimaginably precious that he had lost . . . He was standing in the ring of a great henge, singing to the stones . . . He was standing atop the Tor at Avalon, a bright-haired woman in his arms . . .

He opened his eyes, saw her gazing down at him. "Eilantha . . ." he whispered. Her expression changed as confusion gave way to a dawning joy.

"Osinarmen . . ." she replied. "At last, we have returned."

He could feel the dragons on his arms outlined in fire. His gaze met that of the old man, who faltered for a moment, then bent back to his work. He gazed around the circle of faces, sensing that if he looked long enough at some of them he would know their names. His gaze met that of the slight, dark woman on the other side of the fire, and he remembered that she had been a mother to him, though never the woman who bore him. Nor had this earth borne him, though it had cradled his bones.

"When I was Micail, I tried to rule this land with magic, and repented it," he whispered. "This time what is needed is a warrior with a sword."

"You shall have the Sword," said the dark woman, rising and coming around the fire to gaze down at him, speculation and wonder warring in her eyes.

"It is done," said Fox. The wounds stung as the old man poured clear water over them and blotted the blood away.

The sensation divided his memories and sent him whirling back to awareness of his body once more. He blinked, and knew that he was Mikantor, but that other was still awake within him, just as he still saw the woman he had loved as Tiriki looking out of Tirilan's eyes. He lifted his arms and saw the dragons outlined in drops of blood darkened by the dye.

"I give you herbs to put on it. They will help to heal, take pain away." The old man spilled the remaining dye into the fire and began to pack up his gear.

"Can you sit up?" asked Tirilan.

"I think so," he replied, flexing stiffened muscles and rejoicing in the strength of a young man's body as he came upright. Micail, he remembered, had died old.

His men set up a cheer as he got to his feet, but the sound faltered as they met his eyes, sensing that the man who now bore the dragons was not entirely the same as the one who had lain down by the fire. He reassured them with Mikantor's crooked grin. The queens returned his smile with appreciation, their kings, more warily.

They too know that something has changed, thought Mikantor. Was this why Anderle had never suggested giving him the dragons? Had she known the ordeal would waken knowledge that would transform him from the boy she had raised to a man?

The only thing that had not changed, he realized, was his love for Tirilan. To the accompaniment of more cheers, he turned, though at each movement the wounds on his arms throbbed and stung, gripped her shoulders and kissed her, long and hard.

ANDERLE LOOKED BACK OVER her shoulder at the southern circle of stones within the Carn Ava Henge, where the long shadow of the great central standing stone lay across the green grass. When the sun came up at dawn, that shadow had pointed at Mikantor. He still blazed in her memory, standing like a young god in the first light of the longest day with the royal dragons coiling around his arms. The people had seen that as an omen and hailed him as Defender of the land. The gods had given her what she had worked for, and if things had not worked out precisely as she had planned, she would be a fool to complain. But she was finding it hard to enjoy her victory.

"Mother—"

She allowed herself a sour smile as she saw Tirilan standing there.

"Mother, I thought we would have time to talk at the festival, but they tell me you are planning to leave this morning . . ." Her voice trailed off uncertainly.

"I was not aware that there was anything to say," answered Anderle as they continued across the grass toward the causeway. "You have what you wanted. You get to be with Mikantor and still be some kind of priestess, though it is not clear whether you will end up as high queen or the servant of them all."

"I will not be with Mikantor while I am finding out which it is to be, and he will be fighting a war of raids and ambushes until he can command the kings with the iron sword," Tirilan said unhappily. "They tell me that Velantos has built a smithy near the old tomb in the White Horse Vale. I thought you would be helping him."

Anderle glared, but Tirilan did not appear to realize what a shrewd blow she had struck just now. They were nearing the ditch that surrounded the Henge, with the white chalk of the bank bright in the sun beyond it.

"He is not a man to be driven," she said at last, "and I do not understand his craft. The best thing I can do for now is to leave him alone, and pray that the Lady of the Forge will inspire him."

"I will pray as well," said Tirilan. "Mikantor has impressed the kings, but without the Sword it will be hard to gather the force we need to strike Galid down. And we cannot even begin to address all the other things we need to do until he is gone."

Anderle looked at her daughter, young and strong and hopeful, and her anger went out of her in a long sigh. She had been that eager, long ago, and what had she been striving for, if not for the day when her children would fly free?

They crossed the ditch and started back to the camp.

"Good-bye, Tirilan. May the Goddess shelter you in Her mighty wings." Anderle lifted her hands in blessing. As she went down the path she looked back once more and saw Tirilan still standing there, bright as a primrose in the morning sun. But she kept walking.

TWENTY-FOUR

*T*his is the heart of Azan," said Cimara, pausing as they topped a small rise. Tirilan nodded, eyes widening as she took in the undulating expanse of green. They had left Carn Ava the day before, matching their pace to that of the old pony that drew the cart with their gear, and picked up the track that ran beside the Aman river. Here it turned south across the plain.

"It is beautiful," she replied. "The sky seems huge above all this open land." She had heard that this was the greatest expanse of grassland in the Island of the Mighty. It was certainly the largest she had ever seen. Winding bands of darker green and the occasional silver gleam of water showed where rivers had cut through the chalk to the clay. Here and there she could make out a pond, or a dark mass of foliage, or a spiral of smoke that marked a farmstead amid its fields. But for the most part the plain was pasture for the red cattle that had given the tribe its name. Fescues and oat grass trembled in the wind that stroked across the plain, with here and there a patch of golden or purple flowers. And unlike most places in the island, it was good country for wheeled vehicles, which was why Cimara had a pony cart, which Tirilan had rarely seen in use before.

"Have you never been here?"

Tirilan shook her head. "I have only been to Carn Ava a few times, and we took the road from the west."

"It is shorter, and these days, safer for you as well." Cimara sighed. "When I was a girl the people of Avalon usually traveled to the festival by way of Azan-Ylir. They would rest and break their journey, and we would finish the trip together. Our families were close in those days. There have been many marriages between our lines, and we have sent many to train at the Tor."

"When Mikantor has dealt with Galid, those days will come again," said Tirilan stoutly.

"May the gods grant it be so—" Cimara started walking again and her servant tugged on the rein of the pony to set the cart creaking forward, with the rest of her people coming along behind.

Tirilan followed, still thinking about Mikantor. The motion stretched sore muscles and she felt her face heat as she remembered the vigor of their farewell. Carn Ava at festival time did not offer much privacy, but he had found a clearing within a thicket of hawthorn that could be reached at the cost of a few scratches, and proceeded to make sure she would not forget him with an afternoon of lovemaking intensified by several weeks of deprivation and the anticipation of several more.

As if I ever could forget him . . . she thought fondly. *If the memory of a boy's smile was enough to hold my heart throughout those years when he was gone, I will not forget now, when his touch burns in my flesh as vividly, if not as visibly, as the dragons mark his.*

She smiled, remembering how he had lain, taut and quivering, while she had kissed every part of his body, as if thus she could armor him against all harm. And then he had made love to her with a focused passion that she had not known in him before. It seemed to her that everything he had done since receiving the dragon tattoos had an extra measure of authority, as if by remembering that other life he had reclaimed a part of himself that had been missing until now. By the time she saw him again, what other qualities might that new knowledge reveal?

And could she recapture the memories of the woman he had loved then, and match him?

It was a little past noon when they heard the drumming of hooves upon the plain. Tirilan wondered if wild ponies roamed the grasslands as they did the moors and turned to ask the queen, but the words died on her lips as she saw the other woman stop short in the road, her face suddenly aged by despair.

"What is it? Is something wrong?"

"Chariots—" said Cimara. "Get back among my servants and pull your shawl over your hair. Perhaps he will not notice—oh Goddess, I never thought—Go, Tirilan! Go!"

None of this made sense, but the queen's urgency was clear. As the hoof-beats grew louder, Tirilan hurried back to take her place with the two women who waited on the queen.

"What is the matter?" she whispered. "Why should chariots make her so afraid?"

"Are you stupid, child?" the woman replied. "Only one man in Azan keeps chariots. It is Galid who is coming up the road so swiftly, and you had better pray he does not know you are here."

Tirilan felt suddenly ill. They had not hurried their departure. There would have been time for a runner to tell Galid what the queens were plan-ning. But did he know that she would be staying with Cimara? The usurper had seen her at Avalon, but now she was wearing a linen tunic and a brown-striped skirt kirtled up for walking, not the blue robes of a priestess. She pulled down her veil to hide the blue crescent tattooed on her brow. If this was a chance meeting, he might not recognize the daughter of the Lady of Avalon.

Goddess be with me! She drew up strength from the earth and forced her breathing to slow, wondering if this was how Mikantor felt before a battle began. *Whatever happens, I must not let him know I am afraid.*

She could see the horses now, with the men standing in the chariots behind them, swaying easily as the carts bounced along the road. One pair of horses swung out to each side while the third pair galloped straight toward them. Mikantor had told her of the terrifying charge of the chariots at Tiryns, and now she began to understand. To face them must be like try-ing to stand against an avalanche.

Just when she thought the leader was going to run the queen's party down, the charioteer reined his pair to one side and brought them to a halt with the chariot blocking the road. A quick glance identified the warrior who stood behind the charioteer as Galid.

"Midsummer greetings, Lady of Azan—" Galid's smile did not reach his eyes. "They say you have had a busy festival, you and the queens. But you should not have made so many decisions without my counsel, my dear."

"What business of it is yours? You are not my king—" Cimara's voice had a slight tremor, but she had not moved.

"I am something more important," Galid said softly. "I am your master. Every bite you eat, every breath you take, is by my mercy."

"You do not dare to kill me! The land itself would turn against you!"

"I do not have to. Clearly I have been too generous—a horse and cart, and all these servants . . . what need has a beggar queen for these? Soumer, Keddam"—he motioned to the warriors in one of the other chariots—"cut the pony loose and bring it along. And the men—" He pointed to the two male servants. "I need more labor for the Little Down farm. Take them too."

"What are you doing?" exclaimed the queen. "My women cannot manage the heavy work of the farm! If you take the horse, how shall we get our belongings home!"

"You should have thought of that before you started plotting against me." Galid sneered. "If your Goddess is so powerful, let Her help you!"

Well, that answered the question of whether Galid had had a spy at the festival. The oldest of Cimara's female servants had sunk sobbing to the road. Tirilan bent to put her arms around her.

"Be grateful I leave you your women—"

Tirilan heard the creak of wood and then footsteps as Galid descended from the chariot and came toward them. She tried to spin mist around her, but she had waited too long.

"The old ones, anyhow. I've no use for them . . . but this one has good legs; she might brighten things up at home. What do you say, lads—shall we take her along?"

Tirilan squeaked as a hard hand closed on her arm and hauled her upright.

"What are you good for, eh, girl?" He pulled her close, eyes glinting with amusement. His breath was foul. "Can you grind grain? Can you spin? Are you good for anything but to spread your legs for Uldan's brat?" he added more softly. "You should never have left your bitch of a mother, little girl."

Tirilan glared at him, clutching at her shawl. "I am a priestess of the Lady, and if you hurt me, you will feel Her wrath."

"But you gave all that up when you ran away, did you not? Still, I've no intent to harm you. In fact, I think you may be very valuable indeed. . . ."

The color left her cheeks at the thought of what Mikantor would risk to reclaim her. She tried to pull away, and cried out as Galid's fingers dug into her arm. His warriors stood grinning, leaning on their spears.

"Come along then, little bitch—"

As he dragged Tirilan toward the chariot, Cimara stepped into his path, and for the first time since they had met, she looked like a queen.

"The girl is under my protection. Let her go—"

"And your protection is worth what? You should have accepted my service when I offered it all those years ago." With one blow of his free hand Galid knocked the older woman to the ground. "But I'll not leave you entirely without attendance. Keddam—stay with them. Escort the queen to her farm. And make sure they all *remain* there—I'll have no tales told of this day's work until I choose!"

Then he grabbed Tirilan's waist and swung her into the chariot. The lurch as the charioteer started the horses threw her to her knees. All she could do was to hang on to the rail while Cimara's curses faded and Galid laughed.

THE CENTRAL ROUNDHOUSE AT Azan-Ylir was a place of half-light and flickering shadow. The meager fire in the center of the great hearth did little to dispel the chill, or the gloom. Tirilan stood with her back to the fire and her shawl wrapped tightly around her, legs locked as if by refusing to let her body yield she could armor her soul.

"You take after your father—" She twitched as Galid walked around her and tipped up her chin. "I only knew him briefly, but you might say we made a powerful connection—"

Tirilan stared past him, nostrils flaring. Was this the scent of evil, or simply the odor of the refuse that she could see beneath the benches? As they drove in she had seen a dog gnawing what looked like a human hand.

She doubted that the depressed-looking slatterns she glimpsed peering through the door felt much motivation to keep the place clean.

Once, if her mother could be believed, this had been a handsome hall. Galid had rebuilt it after the burning, and filled it with the spoil of a thousand raids. But twenty years of soot had dimmed the colored carvings on its pillars and the moth-eaten rugs that kept drafts from the walls. There might well be twenty years of dirt on the floor.

"Aren't you going to question me?" Galid's teeth were bad as well. "Don't you want to know how your father died?"

"He sacrificed himself so my mother could escape you. That is all I need to know about him, or about you." Everyone said that Durrin had been handsome, and her mother must have loved him, for she had never chosen another man, although Tirilan sometimes wondered whether Anderle had sacrificed her capacity for love to her need for the strength she must have to lead Avalon.

"So cold!" Galid rasped. "So cold and fair. I struck your father down with a sword of bronze. Shall I find a warmer weapon for you?"

This time the tone of his laughter left her in no doubt about his meaning. The thought of his hands upon her in obscene parody of Mikantor's lovemaking made her skin crawl. She closed her eyes, drawing up earth power for protection.

"I am a priestess of Avalon. I give myself as the Goddess wills."

"Was it the Goddess who sent you like a bitch in heat to Mikantor's bed?" Galid grinned. "I think not, little slut. If you moaned for him, I will make you scream."

"I suppose you do not care what men would say if you raped a priestess," she said defiantly, "but you might fear what the Goddess will do . . . Will your men still follow a leader whose prong has become a rotting reed?"

"Why should I bother with a pallid slug of a girl?" he replied after a pause. "Your mother, now—there is a woman with fire in her belly. If I threw her down she would claw and scream!"

"That's what you need, isn't it?" Tirilan frowned thoughtfully. "You can't get it up unless a woman fights you. I'm safe then! Do what you will, I won't oppose you, won't respond, unless it is to vomit at your stench. Speaking of which, do you enjoy living like a pig in a wallow, or do your servants have no idea how to clean a hall?"

"Perhaps"—his voice overrode hers—"I'll give you to my men—"

Tirilan forced a shrug. "Will they obey you? They may still value their manhood, especially when I tell them you are not taking me yourself because I have already blasted yours . . ." Living with Mikantor and his Companions, she had come to understand that for some men that was a very real fear.

"Cleanliness, eh?" His gaze shifted away from hers to survey the room. "If that's what concerns you, go ahead and clean. If you can get those sluts in the cookshed to help you, use them with my goodwill. If you earn your keep I may even feed you. When your back is aching and your fingers are raw, you may prefer to earn your dinner on your back instead."

"I am not afraid of honest work," she said quietly, suspecting that her fragile looks had deceived him. She was surprised to realize that though she had many fears, just at this moment anxiety for herself was not among them.

That night, a messenger came, and Galid drove off with his warriors in the morning. He had left three hard-eyed men to guard her, and when she found they could not be bribed to let her go she turned to cleaning the hall. She grew accustomed to the smell, but the spiritual miasma of Galid's hold could only be endured by strengthening her mental shielding. She dared not let down her guard enough to ride the spirit road to her mother or Mikantor.

When her guards commented on the improvement, she began to nag them to help. By the time Galid returned, a fortnight had passed. By then they were ready to beg him to take her away. That, it would appear, had already been his intention. Several of his men had come back with wounds, so they must have been fighting somewhere. Had they encountered Mikantor? No one would say. But Azan-Ylir was clearly no longer a secure location. On the second morning after his return, Galid hustled Tirilan into the chariot once more and bore her off across the plain. This time she was able to stand, although by the time they came to a stone shepherd's hut by a dewpond, her legs were trembling with the strain.

As the chariot came to a halt she jumped down, stumbling as she tried to force her legs to run. Foolish hope, for in three steps he had her. She saw his fist blur toward her; then pain exploded in her head. Half conscious, she was thrust into the dark interior. A bag of bread and a skin of water came after her.

"I understand that you holy fools sometimes feel the need to retreat from the world," said Galid, slamming the door. "Enjoy your solitude!" She heard the sound of a bar being dragged across, leaving her in the dark.

THE FIRST NIGHT SEEMED endless. Tirilan tried to send her spirit in search of Mikantor, but Galid's blow had left her too concussed to focus her will. She jerked awake at every squeak and rustle, her head throbbing so badly that by the time dawn lent a faint light she could no longer distinguish nightmare from reality. The ground seemed to rock beneath her . . . her stomach roiled but there was nothing in her belly to cast out. Cold and damp set her shivering, but far worse than any physical pain was the knowledge that she had lost Mikantor . . . no, it was Micail. The man he was then had been taller, with hair like a new-kindled flame.

But I found him again, she thought, fighting her way back to awareness. *I'm remembering the Sinking.* She trembled as her mind filled with the image of a great mountain exploding in flames. *We lost our world then, too, and yet we survived!* Was that why Eilantha and Osinarmen had been born together once more?

She slept at last, and when she woke once more the glimmer through the thatch had the golden glow of afternoon. The air smelled of damp earth and moldy straw, and a rustle of movement in the corner indicated she was not entirely alone. Her head still hurt, but it was becoming possible to think again. On her hands and knees she set herself to learn the limits of her prison. A faint illumination came through the thatching, but the stone walls were too high for her to claw her way out through the straw. She forced herself to eat the bread the mice had left her, and drink from the waterskin, wondering how long it would be before someone brought her food again.

As the light faded Tirilan found herself weeping, afraid to endure another night like the one before. To her surprise, it was a memory of one of her mother's scoldings that enabled her to regain control. There was no human experience, Anderle had told her once when she had skinned her knee, that could not serve as either a lesson or an opportunity. She had not appreciated the advice at the time, and she was sure that by calling this prison a retreat Galid had meant to mock her, but perhaps she could make it true. Then she would not be ashamed to face her mother and Mikantor when she saw them again.

After casting a circle to discourage any vermin who might misinterpret her immobility, Tirilan settled herself cross-legged on the damp ground and began the counted breathing that would carry her into trance. From somewhere nearby came an intermittent rustling. Probably a mouse, she thought, and let the awareness fade away. The wind that always seemed to blow across this open country whispered and moaned in the thatching. This too she noted before letting the awareness go.

Cimara had promised to teach her the secrets of this land, and one way or another, she was determined to learn. As darkness fell outside, she closed down her awareness of her surroundings in order to open and extend her perceptions of their inner reality. She sensed the life among the dense root systems of the grasses that covered the well-drained dry soil. Below the earth a porous layer of chalk allowed water to seep through to the clay beneath. Water carried energy, but the power in the land followed other paths as well, surfacing at the barrows and standing stones. She reached out to the spirits of the ancestors, remembering how her mother had called on them for help when she and Ellet fled the destruction of Azan-Ylir.

When her body's needs at last called her back to consciousness, a little light was filtering through the straw. She dozed then, and woke only when she heard the clattering approach of a chariot. She found herself almost disappointed when it was not Galid but Keddam who opened the door of her prison and tossed in another bag of supplies.

The days that followed passed in much the same way. Between visits from her captors, Tirilan's spirit sought refuge in trance. On one of those journeys it seemed to her that she was in Avalon, in her mother's garden.

"Where are you? Are you in danger?" asked Anderle, but Tirilan did not know where she was anymore, and could not reply. She tried to take swan shape to fly to Mikantor, but he was fighting, and she dared not distract him. In her waking hours she was aware that she was getting weaker, and tried to force her body to exercise, but increasingly, it was easier to walk in her dreams.

"TINK, TINK, TINK, TAP . . ." Velantos worked the hammer around the bit of bronze, drawing it out to form a flat half-circle, then setting it on the workbench to start a new row of scales. It was simple work, but it eased his mind. "Tink, tink, tink," and then a tap on the small bronze anvil to maintain the rhythm as he shifted the position of the bronze he was working on. He had completed a goodly number already. In the firelight they glinted like sunlight on the sea. The women of the old race were preparing the tunic of boar's hide to which those scales would be riveted. When Mikantor put it on, he would look as if he were wearing a dragon's skin.

And what weapon will this great warrior hold in his hand? The unwelcome thought intruded once more, breaking the rhythm of the hammer. Velantos suppressed the impulse to cast it across the room. He wondered if Anderle had repaired the wall of the smithy at Avalon.

The men of the elder race had worked well, and the smithy on the ridge was complete, with space for all his tools and straw mattresses at each end for him and the boy, where Aelfrix was snoring now. Beyond the beech grove an encampment of the elder folk had sprung up. The women brought food to the smithy each day. The weight of their expectation had been added to Anderle's vision and Mikantor's hope. Velantos had everything he needed, except, he thought grimly, the courage to begin again with the sword.

The hilt, at least, could be made of bronze. He had done that already, as an affirmation that one day there would be a blade for it to hold. He took it from the doeskin bag and hefted it, running his fingers across the grooved grip wound with gold wire.

Setting the bronze aside, he drew back the leather he had wrapped around the iron shards and picked up one of them, rubbing his thumb across the place where the metal had begun to curdle and run. Clearly it *could* soften, and if so, it could be worked. But what if his hammer hit another hidden flaw? He took up the tongs and set the piece in the fire, then bent to the bellows to pump up the flames.

They leaped as the deep orange of the coals began to brighten, and presently a shimmer of silvery lavender swirled above. Brighter and brighter they glowed; he snatched out the iron as the first bright flickers sparked from its surface, laid it on the stone anvil, and tapped, swearing as scales of metal began to fall away. Even a few strokes had begun to shape the iron, but at this rate, by the time he flattened it, half of its substance would have flaked away.

Shaking his head in frustration, he plunged the glowing end of the shard into the quenching brine. The only way to learn was to try and fail and try again, but he dared not risk the iron.

"Lady!" He turned to the image of the goddess. "This work is not for my own glory, but for Yours, and only You can teach me how it must be done!" Carefully he set the piece of iron at her feet. It was the only thing he could think of to do. If the gods wanted this sword made, they would have to take a hand.

He worked his shoulders back and forth, only now realizing how tense they had become, then thrust a chunk of oak wood into the center of the hearth, banking the live coals around it to smolder through the night.

"Sleep . . ." he whispered, "as I shall sleep. Send me good counsel . . ." He stripped off his tunic and crawled beneath the blankets, and somewhat to his surprise, slid into slumber almost immediately.

VELANTOS DREAMED AND KNEW that he was dreaming.

He walked through a landscape like one of the fire mountains in the lands of the Middle Sea, and with another part of his mind understood that this was a forge. Around him glowed boulders of every shape and size, stretching away to the rim of the caldera, or perhaps it was the wall of the hearth. With the logic of the dream it did not seem strange that he should wander here. This was his element.

The path led him toward the center where the fire was hottest; with each gust of wind the red and orange shapes around him pulsed to a white-hot glow. But each step was harder, the waves of heat a palpable pressure against which he must force his way.

What was he seeking? A lightning prickle of power passed through him as he realized that he faced a Presence, and in the next moment his vision shifted, and he perceived the form of a woman within the column of flame. Seeing Her, he recognized the Lady he had served for so long. Her flesh was shaped from white fire; Her hair streamed with flame borne up by the blast. He could not meet Her eyes.

"So, beloved, you have come. . . . Why do you seek Me here?" Her voice both warmed and burned.

"I seek Your aid to shape a sword," he replied.

"A sword of iron," she echoed, "as you are iron. Are you ready to submit yourself to My fire?"

"What must I do?"

In answer, She opened Her arms.

This was death, he thought, but for a smith, what better death could there be? He stepped toward Her and the fire enfolded him.

Consciousness split. He was standing in the smithy, staring down at the glowing human shape upon the anvil, and knew that it was his own.

"You are the smith and you are the iron . . ." came the Voice of the Fire. "You shall forge yourself into a weapon for the one you love!"

"But how will I remember?" he cried.

"Look at Me. . . ." She whispered, "Look at Me . . ."

The Lady still stood among the flames. Her color had deepened. Her body glowed with the rich orange of the setting sun, but Her hair and eyes were now the color of the charcoal before it meets the fire. Slender, intense, it was Anderle's face and form he was looking at, Anderle's voice that had spoken those final words.

Velantos woke, ears still ringing with Her final "Remember . . ." and on his lips the name *Anderle*. He untangled himself from the bedclothes and knelt by the fire, half afraid of what he might see. The coals were veiled by a thin layer of ash, but a shimmer of heat in the air above them told him that they waited only for a breath to wake to glowing life once more.

His muscles ached with the memory of labor. The knowledge he needed lay within them, waiting for the word that would set them to work once more. But who would say that word? He only remembered that he must surrender himself to the fire.

Or to Anderle—he thought grimly. He had seen the Goddess speak through her at rituals on Avalon. If she could surrender her own will to the Lady of the Forge, he would face Her fire. He heard Aelfrix whistling outside and clambered to his feet.

"Summon Grebe," he said as the boy came through the door. "I must send a message to Avalon."

BY THE TIME GALID came back, Tirilan had lost track of how long she had been a prisoner. She stumbled as he led her blinking into the sunlight, amazed at the solid vividness of the world.

"Have you enjoyed your retreat?"

"Yes . . ." she said slowly. "I thank you. I have learned many things . . ." From his expression, this was not what he had expected to hear. The skin beneath his eyes was dark and pouchy, as if he had not been sleeping well. She took a deep breath and felt her focus return. "What do you intend to do with me? I am no use to anyone rotting here. . . ."

"It is true that it would be simpler to slit your throat and be done with it. But that's so final." There was a bench by the old sheep pen. As she stumbled again, Galid shoved her toward it and she sat down. "Much as I'd enjoy seeing Mikantor's face when I tell him how you died, it will be much more entertaining to tell him how I plan to kill you. To save you, I fancy he will give up everything. Perhaps I'll tie you where you can watch what I do to *him* . . ."

Tirilan lowered her eyes to hide the terror that threat awakened. It was harder to keep her voice steady this time.

"What good will that do? You control the plain, but you are not the king. You make nothing grow, nothing prosper. The powers in the land do not speak to you. What were you seeking when you betrayed Uldan all those years ago?"

Galid frowned as he realized that she really did want to know. And she realized that he had no answers.

"I think you are a hollow man," she said softly. "The wind blows through you, and soon it will blow you away. The ancestors will not welcome you—it will be as if you never lived at all."

"And if I am," he said through gritted teeth, "how am I different from all the rest of you, clinging to life in a dying land? What is the use of being an ancestor if there are none to follow?"

After so many days of silence, every sound was layered with meaning. He meant his voice to hold menace, but what she heard in it was pain. She bit back a cry as he gripped her wrist.

"There is only *now,* my dear, and while I am alive I will wring from life everything I can. If I cannot feel pleasure, I will feel pain, and if I cannot *give* pleasure, I can surely make you feel agony!" Suddenly his dagger was in his hand. "Shall I begin by cutting off one of these pretty fingers as a gift for Mikantor?"

He slammed her hand against the wood of the bench and set the blade of his dagger against the crease where her little finger met the palm.

"Just a little more pressure and it will be off," he whispered. He pressed and she winced as the sharp edge split her skin. "But I will wait until I find your beloved—the finger should be fresh enough for him to recognize it as yours." Laughing, he lifted the blade and let her go. "That moves you, does it?" She drew a shuddering breath and he grinned. "This opens up all sorts of possibilities—your pretty nose, for instance . . . how if I leave you alive, but spoil your beauty. Will your fine warrior still want you then?"

"Will *you?*" she whispered.

Her vision had adjusted and she saw him clearly—the lines cut by cruelty and rage, the flesh that sagged from too much food and drink, and deep within those pale glinting eyes, desolation. *He knows his time is over,* she thought, *and fears . . . what?* Sharper than his knife was his need, and her heart, opened by those endless nights, responded.

"Will my blood ease your thirst? Then drink—" She held out her hand, where red drops were beading along the line his knife had made. As he recoiled, she sighed, and then opened her arms. "If I will love you, freely and without force, will you let Azan go?"

For a moment Galid simply stared, all expression gone; then his fist swung up and he struck her to the ground.

"Whore!" he hissed. "All of you, stinking, deceiving whores!" He staggered toward the chariot. "Drive!"

"What about her?" asked the charioteer.

"Throw her back in her hole. She can rot there. . . ."

TWENTY-FIVE

*T*he setting sun that bathed the downs in a fiery glow sent Anderle's shadow into the smithy before her. She paused in the doorway to let her vision adjust, waiting until she could see the man who stood by the hearth. Velantos had dressed carefully to meet her. His sleeveless tunic of saffron wool had patterned banding at neck and hem, but he seemed thinner, as if he had been fasting. She remembered him wearing that garment at the Midwinter Festival. He had not prepared himself for *her,* she realized then, but for the goddess he served. The smithy had been swept, the hearth was clean and empty, but the shelf on which he had placed his clay image of the goddess bore a bunch of early summer flowers.

"You came . . ." he breathed.

"You called."

After the way that they had parted, for him to send for her argued great need. At Avalon she had no purpose but struggle to make sense out of her dreams. Here at least there might be something she could *do.*

"Lady—be welcome here. I see now that I dreamed true," he added. "When you stand in the sunlight your skin is the color of the coals, the color of *Her* skin. This is why I sent to you. I ask you now, will you let Her speak through you to tell me how to forge the Sword? Will you trust me? Will you trust *Her?*"

"Will *you?*" she replied.

"I must. I am sorry for what happened at the smithy on Avalon." He coughed, and she realized what that admission had cost him. "I ran away from you—I cannot run from myself. I was proud of my skill. I rage because

I know nothing. But in my dream the Lady of the Forge speaks. She said I must surrender to the Fire . . . If you give the fire a voice, then I will know what to do."

Anderle believed him. She had seen that look before, when an initiate prepared to take the herbs that would break down the barriers between the worlds. Sometimes death came with the illumination. One must be willing to accept either outcome. For the first time she understood that smiths were also a priesthood.

Her own heart beat heavy and slow. "Priestess to priest, I will work with you, and if your Lady wills it, as goddess to smith as well."

"WHY IS THE HEARTH EMPTY?" asked Anderle. Night had fallen. A dozen flickering rush lights made the smithy a temple of the Mysteries.

"That is always the first task, to make the fire . . ." His voice rasped with suppressed emotion. "The fire is the goddess with us, the power of transformation that hardens what was soft, and make soft things hard. Fire is *change*. Lady, will you bless the hearth?"

A shiver of memory passed through her as she remembered the frozen Lake where she had invoked the Fire. Had that been the moment when the balance tipped and the changes that had brought them both here began? She took a deep breath and stretched out her hands above the rock-rimmed oval on the floor.

"Be thou the womb, burn with desire, transmute and transform, Lady of Fire!"

He lifted the basket and tipped the glistening black chunks of charcoal into the hearth, cascading onto the packed earth with a curiously musical sound. Carefully he spread and banked them, with a depression in the middle opposite the point where the bellows pipe fit through the hearth wall.

"Sit, while I make a flame," he told her, picking up the fire drill and the piece of soft punkwood that had been laid ready. She sensed that the energy he put into this action was also part of the ritual. As he looped the bowstring around the shaft of the drill and settled its head into the groove in the wood, she took her seat on the bench at the head of the hearth.

Surely, to kindle fire with a bow and drill was a kind of magic, she thought as he steadied the wood between his knees and began to spin the shaft with regular thrusts of the bow. To keep the drill at the correct angle and maintain the spin required considerable skill. Fascinated, she watched as he swayed to the motion.

"Spin the shaft and chant the spell . . ." she whispered. "Work the bow and wind it well. Harden shaft and swiftly spin, heat release the flame within. . . ."

He looked up, something kindling in his gaze that awakened an answering heat between her thighs. Startled, she stood, and found her hands lifting in the same pose as that of the clay goddess who watched over the hearth. Had he intended this? *"The symbol is nothing, the reality is all,"* was a watchword of the Mysteries. The bend and sway of the man's body, the steady penetration of the drill, the friction that was even now beginning to kindle a faint thread of smoke from the wood, were both symbol and reality.

They had not discussed how he was to call the goddess into her, but Anderle realized that she herself had pronounced the spell. Her body moved in instinctive response to his motion, her breathing altered to match his. The smoke was a blue swirl; the scent of pine filled the forge.

"Lady of Fire, hear me . . ." Velantos whispered. "Lady of the Forge, be with me! I offer you my strength, I kindle your flame, in my need I call you! Lady, come to me now!"

Anderle could have called fire, but he had kindled a fire in her instead. She strained for completion, but it was her spirit that opened to receive the Power. Fire blazed suddenly as Velantos nudged dry reed and then thin shavings into the smoldering groove, and heat surged from Anderle's sex to fill her whole body, leaving her consciousness no more than a corner from which to share the ecstasy. In a single swift movement he tipped the flaming kindling into the nest of charcoal and blew.

"Make Me a bed of coals—" she told him, and the vestige of Anderle that remained within noted that she was speaking in the tongue of the Middle Sea. His startled gaze turned to wonder. The charcoal was catching quickly. As the temperature in the smithy rose, she loosened the pins that held her garment and cast it aside. At the naked lust in the smith's gaze, the fire within her grew. Smiling, the Lady gestured toward the workbench where he had laid the iron shards.

"Come, beloved, we have work to do—"

VELANTOS BENT TO THE bellows, pushing with strong, steady strokes to force air through the coals. At each blast, flames spurted upward, and each time they sank the coals retained a brighter glow. It seemed to him that the same glow pulsed from the body of the woman who stood on the other side of the hearth. The firelight burnished breasts still round and firm, gleamed on the curve of her waist and the sweet joining of her thighs. His own flesh ached with desire, but he had expected that. Now he had another use for that energy.

How swiftly the coals were heating! Sweating, he pulled off his own tunic and tossed it on a bench, then thrust at the bellows once more. Fire kindled the pieces of charcoal to a brightening sunrise glow.

"Take the first of the shards and set it among the coals," the Lady said. "Heave at the bellows until it glows like the sun."

He cast her a doubtful look, for a white heat was far too great for working bronze, but her face remained calm. In any case, the time for calculation was past. He could only go forward, and trust that the goddess he served understood iron as well as she knew bronze. The coals pulsed white-hot, and far more quickly than he would have believed, the piece of iron glowed white as well.

"Now you must take it from the fire," said the Lady. "Set it on your anvil and take up your midsized hammer. Stroke from one end to the other to compress and beat out the iron, gently but firmly, as you would caress a lover. . . ."

With his left hand Velantos reached for the tongs and used them to grip the dull end of the shard, swung it over to the anvil in a shower of sparks, and essayed a tentative tap. More sparks flared, but there were no explosions. Had he not heated the iron *enough* before? The ductile metal yielded to his hammer, stretching, extending. As it cooled, the color deepened. He felt the moment when it began to resist him, thrust it once more into the coals, and began to work the bellows again.

"You are the hammer," she said softly, "and I am the forge. The Sword is the child we are making together, by your will, from my womb." He looked up from the bellows, and could not tell if her eyes shone or only reflected the flames.

Once more the metal was glowing. Once more he returned it to the anvil and began to shape it, always tapping down its length in the same direction, teasing out pockets of air, driving out impurities. Again and again the iron made the journey from fire to anvil, until he had forged the rough metal into a single solid bar.

And then it was done. Velantos looked down at the cooling metal, watching the glow fade until it was a dull black. No longer the unformed meteor, it held now the shape that he had given it. He heard a step and looked up. The Lady stood before him, a beaker of clear water in her hands.

"Drink and be restored, and then take up the next piece and begin."

Three times more, Velantos set tongs to a raw shard of meteor and thrust it into that fiery womb. Three times more he stroked and shaped the glowing metal. And when he had finished, the Lady directed him back to the first length, and he began again. Three more times each piece was heated and hammered, heated and shaped, until he had four black strips a little less than the length of a sword. He laid them out on his workbench, running his fingers along the gray-black surfaces with a dull wonder. The lamps had all burned out, and the only light was the glow from the forge. From the stillness and the feel of damp in the air, it must be close to dawn. His neck was stiff, the muscles of his upper back and shoulders were aching, and his right arm trembled from strain. He shook his right hand to loosen fingers cramped to the shape of the hammer's shaft.

He heard a sigh and turned. The Lady had sunk down upon the bench—no, it was Anderle, blinking in confusion and wrapping her garment around her.

"Is it done?" she asked.

"By the Lady's grace it is begun," he answered her. "Now we need rest . . . and food." On a chest beside the door he saw a wooden platter with meat and cheese, and wondered who had put it there, and when.

Velantos carried it over to the priestess, but she had eaten no more than a few mouthfuls when her eyes closed and she slumped against his shoulder. He still had the strength to lift her, a little surprised to find that tenderness was his only response to the lissom body in his arms. All his desire was spent, as if he had been making love to her all this time, and in a way he supposed that was true.

He laid her down upon the bed and pulled the blanket over her, and with that, exhaustion took him and he sank down beside her and knew no more.

VELANTOS LAY CRADLED IN warmth, as if he had been laid in the forge. Then he tried to move. Suddenly all the muscles of his back and shoulders were screaming. He had thought himself inured to the labor of the forge, but forging was a small part of bronze work, and in the past moon he had not even been doing much of that.

I must get up . . . he told himself. *The iron is waiting . . . and the goddess. . . .* He opened his eyes and tensed with alarm as he realized the other side of the bed was empty. Then someone touched his shoulder and he turned to see Anderle kneeling beside him, a clay beaker of steaming soup in her other hand. Or rather it was the goddess, for she was once more naked, and the flesh that touched his burned from within. Obediently he drank, feeling the heat spread through his core. When he set the beaker down, she began to knead his shoulders, and the same heat suffused his muscles, driving out the pain. He closed his eyes. *This is how the iron feels, when I hammer it out, hot from the forge.*

She took his face between her hands and kissed him, and from lips to groin he burned with her fire. When he could think again, she was standing by the forge. They had slept through the day. On the workbench a lamp flickered brightly. More charcoal had been added to the hearth, and the new coals were already beginning to glow.

"Arise, oh my hammer," she told him, "and thrust the iron into the fire!"

When he worked with Katuerix they had heated bits of bog iron and hammered them together. Could he weld the iron strips he had forged the day before? It must be possible, for the goddess had stacked them together and was clasping them against her breast. When she held them out to him, they were already hot, as if they had been in the fire.

Reverent as if he were touching a woman's body, Velantos drew the poker toward him to open a way through the coals. He gripped the stack of iron bars with the tongs and gently slid them into the glowing valley, then moved to the bellows.

Again and again the fire flared and fell. The iron was beginning to glow. Velantos looked at the Lady and saw her smiling, watching the fire. Not until the metal glowed sun bright did she gesture to him to take up the tongs. He gripped the duller end of the pile tightly and swung it over to the great stone anvil, grasped the large stone hammer, and swung. Sparks flew, but he could feel the iron yield.

"Strike with strength and weld it well—hammer's heft beats out the spell. Many melding, four to one, hammer till the work is done!"

He did not know if the chant came from his lips or hers. Now he must put forth all his strength, heating and beating, brushing off loose scale and hammering again. The iron strips gave way beneath his blows, softened and lengthened, flowing, clinging, melding until a single glowing shape lay in the fire. Obedient to her soft suggestions, Velantos brought it to white heat once more, hammering it wide and flat, twisting and folding and beating it out again.

As the stars wheeled across the night sky and the sparks flew about the forge, the Lady stood beside him, murmuring spells, and he beat their magic into the iron. Courage and command were in that chanting, endurance and honor, certainty and skill. He hammered in the virtue to strike surely and to cleave clean, to find the right target with each blow.

When dawn came, the smith drew from the fire a dully glimmering iron bar. The patterns that all that folding and twisting had melded within it were sensed, rather than seen, but he could feel the power within. He set the iron upon the workbench and found that food and drink had been provided, and the priestess was herself once more. They ate and drank and lay down together, sharing their warmth, emptied of desire.

ANDERLE WOKE AS THE last light of sunset was shafting through the doorway, bathing everything in a warm glow as if the smithy had become part of the hearth. Velantos still slept beside her, curled on his side with one arm laid protectively across her thigh. In sleep his face had a curious innocence, the lines carved by purpose and passion that sometimes gave him such a ferocious aspect smoothed away. She understood now that this was a man who would sacrifice everything, even himself, for a worthy goal. No wonder they had struck sparks—they were far too alike, she thought with an inner smile. He was thinner than he had been when she arrived. So, she supposed, was she. To carry a god took energy, but she had only to let the power of the Lady flow through her. He was burning from within, consumed by the power he was putting into the work as the fire consumed the coals.

Contemplating those rugged features, she felt her heart wrenched by an unexpected surge of tenderness. She lifted a hand to touch him and then stopped, trembling. *One day,* she promised herself, *we shall lie like this and make love, but if I touch him now, we will waste in bed the power that should be spent in the forge.* . . . Even the thought of embracing him was enough to send a pulse of sensation through her flesh. Gently she moved his hand and eased from beneath the covers, wrapped a cloak around her, and stepped outside.

When she returned, she found that a wooden bowl full of steaming stew had been set beside the smithy door. Though she had not seen them, it was clear that the elder folk were keeping watch and anticipating their needs, as they had taken Aelfrix into their keeping when she arrived. She brought in the food and set it on the workbench. The rich scent awakened her hunger and she ate eagerly.

The bar of iron lay where Velantos had left it. The metal was cold, but to eyes trained to see the spirit within, it held a subtle glow. The raw energy she had sensed within the shards had altered to a contained blaze of power.

But it was not yet focused. That, she thought, would come when it had been given the shape of a sword.

It was dark now. She lit more rush lights and fixed them in their holders of stone, and tipped new charcoal into the hearth. On the bed, Velantos sighed and stirred. It was time to work once more.

Anderle hung the cloak from its hook and combed out her hair. She could feel the presence of the goddess as a pressure behind her, patient and a little amused. "Lady of Fire," she whispered, "naked I stand before you. May both preoccupation and passion depart from me. For the cause of Life and the good of this land, I offer myself as a vessel for your will. . . ." She let out her breath in a long sigh.

For a moment she hovered on the edge of awareness, and then, softly, smoothly as the metal absorbs the heat of the coals, the goddess came in.

"NOW! TAKE THE IRON from the fire—"

Velantos looked at the Lady in surprise, for coals and iron alike glowed with the rich orange of the setting sun on a hazy day.

"It is hot enough. The welding is done . . . now you must shape the blade."

He nodded, and with swift efficiency lifted the iron bar from the forge, holding in his mind the image of the finished weapon. Now he would need not only his great strength, but all of his skill, and everything he had learned when he struggled to create such swords from bronze. Then, the casting had accomplished half of the labor. Now he would have to forge the metal into the shape he desired. It would be difficult and demanding work, but he had spent enough time tapping around the edges to straighten and harden bronze blades to imprint that shape in his muscles and bones.

He laid the glowing end upon the anvil and began to flatten and shape the base and tang to which he would rivet the hilt. It was a simple form, and would give him a place to grip the iron while he worked on the rest of the blade. The metal cooled and he laid it once more in the forge, pumping the bellows until it began to glow.

Back to the anvil came the iron. The hammer swung down. "Tap, tap, tap, ting"— he found the rhythm, drawing the softened metal out and working it away from the center toward the sides. Muscles loosened, flexing and releasing as he swung. To weld the iron bar had forced a singular focusing of will. This part of the work was different, requiring a flexible coordination of hand and eye, of heart and will. Turning and tapping, he persuaded each glowing section of metal to take its new form. With each stroke of the hammer, he felt the substance of the metal changing, as the flesh of a woman changes beneath the arousing fingers of her lover. And as making love also changes the lover, his soul flowed into the hot iron.

And presently, as he bore the evolving blade from the forge to the anvil and back again, he became aware that the ringing of bronze hammer on iron had become the foundation for a song. From the lips of the Lady came a sweet descant to the rhythm of the hammer, an answer to the wheeze of the bellows and the whistling of the flames in the coals.

Sometimes it was pure music, and sometimes words surfaced from the song. She sang of the dark spaces of the heavens in which the iron had floated, cold and alone, of the searing flight that had ended as it buried itself in the soil. The elder folk had told him how their fathers had dug it out, still smoking, and tried to hammer it into some useful form, and that too was in the song. She sang of the trees that had captured the light of the sun in the forest, and the long slow smolder in a womb of turf that transformed them into charcoal. She sang of their delight as they were at last allowed to blossom into flame. A forge song she sang, a song of fire and iron, a song of the sword, writhing beneath the hammer as it sought its destiny.

When he glanced up, he could see the Lady, shining and singing in the light of the fire, and found himself striving to incorporate the long sleek curve of waist and thigh into the shape of the sword. Thinning from the center on one side and then on the other, drawing the iron from the narrower neck downward to the swell of the blade and then inward once more, he persuaded the metal to take the form he envisioned so vividly. He had believed that when he cast bronze he poured part of his spirit into the mold, but this intense, extended forging was an altogether more active and intimate creation, like the grapplings of love when a man strives to give his seed. But what he was forging into this sword was his soul.

Throughout that night the smithy rang. In the encampment of the elder folk they heard the forge music, and drummed and prayed. And when dawn spread the sky with glowing banners, Velantos lifted the black sword he had shaped and carried it outside to salute the coming day.

Then he turned back to the smithy, blinking as the shadows of the forge replaced the light. Now that the night's labor was over, he could feel the ache in every limb. The sword was not finished—beneath his caressing fingers the metal was smooth, but the marks of the hammer would have to be ground out and the edges honed. As he crossed the threshold, the leg that had been wounded in Tiryns betrayed him and he stumbled, instinctively thrusting out the iron blade to break his fall.

He felt it give beneath him. When he straightened, recovering vision showed him that his lovely blade had bent like a bow. He whirled to face the Lady.

"What is this?" he cried, fury displacing his fatigue. "It bends like an old man's pizzle! Better a bronze sword that breaks—at least you can stab your enemy with the ragged end. What have I done wrong?"

The iron had passed a handbreadth from the Lady's face as he swung it up, but she did not move.

"You have done nothing wrong—but you are not yet done . . ." She sounded amused. "Put it on the anvil and hammer it flat again. Do not fear to mar it. The metal is quite tough and will not be harmed."

Velantos realized that he was shaking. He did not begrudge the labor, but after so much effort, and hope, to fail now would destroy him as well as the sword. He laid it on the anvil and took up the smaller stone hammer. A few well-placed blows straightened the blade. He turned to the Lady.

"Very well—it looks almost the same. But I will not sleep easy, wondering how this weakness may be healed . . ."

"This day we will not sleep at all," said the Lady, "though we may rest. The sword is formed, but not yet finished. For that, it must be cradled in the heat of my womb." At his look of confusion She smiled once more. "Put more charcoal into the hearth and pile it high. Heave at the bellows until it glows like the rising sun. We shall place the sword within and pack the coals tightly around it. There it will grow an armored skin like a dragon's hide.

But we must be vigilant to keep the coals at the same heat until the sun outside glows red once more. For three nights you have put forth all your power. What is needed now is the patience to endure."

"Patience has never been one of my virtues, Lady," he muttered, and she laughed.

"Do you think I did not know?"

As Velantos brought more charcoal from the storage shed, he felt the pounding of his heart begin to ease. He had never heard of the technique the Lady was describing, and could not imagine what use it might be. But so far her directions had been good. To trust that she knew how to complete the task was all the hope he had.

By the time all was ready the sun was climbing up the sky. Once more, Velantos used the poker to open a way. Slowly, reverently, he slid the black blade into the hot depths of the forge, then adjusted the piled coals until no part of it could be seen.

"Should I ply the bellows now?" he asked.

"Net yet. You can estimate the intervals, for you know how this charcoal behaves. From time to time you will need to check the color and give the fire more air, but the iron will melt if it grows too hot, just as it will weaken if it is too cool."

He nodded, swaying. For three days the desire to complete the work had driven him. Now he did not know what to do. He looked down at his strong hands, blinking. They were blackened by the work and bore a few scrapes he had not noticed at the time.

"First, we should eat . . ."

Velantos looked up as he heard her voice alter. The goddess had departed and she was only Anderle once more, shivering in the morning breeze that came through the open door. He forced his limbs to motion, took down her cloak and wrapped it around her, then guided her to a bench and made her sit down. Now he too felt the cold, and pulled on the tunic he had cast aside three days ago.

"This time they have brought us soup," he said, picking up the bowls set by the door. "With marrow," he added, breathing in the rich aromas, "and some kind of roots, and barley." He handed one of the bowls to Anderle, then took his own and sank down beside her. She cradled it gratefully between her hands.

"We had a dish something like this when I was growing up," he said as the rich soup began to restore him, "though they cooked it with more herbs."

"At Avalon, this was festival fare," Anderle replied. "Our food is healthy, and plentiful except when we are fasting, but we rarely eat meat, and strong flavors make us think too much about the body when we are trying to focus on spiritual things."

That explained a lot, thought Velantos. "Just now our bodies need feeding," he said instead. She nodded, and he heard her spoon scrape the bottom of the bowl.

"What was it like, growing up by the Middle Sea?" she asked.

His chuckle rumbled in his chest. "What I remember most just now," he answered, "is that in the summer, it was *warm*." He got up and poked the fire, saw that the coals still glowed orange, and sat down again.

"Will the goddess tell you when it is time to take the sword out?" he asked.

"I believe so," the priestess replied. "I can feel Her presence like a pressure within my skull, perhaps in the same place I was lurking when She was here. I think that when you need more direction, She will come in again."

"Then you remember what we have done?"

"I retain images, though I do not always understand." She sighed and set down her bowl. A companionable silence fell between them. He could hear the sweet song of a warbler from the trees outside. It was a winter bird in the lands from which he came.

It was the first time, he thought, that he had been in Anderle's presence and felt at ease. But truly, he was too tired to feel either lust or irritation, and so, he supposed, was she. For the first time they could see each other as they truly were. Without thinking, he had put his arm around her, and she leaned against him gratefully.

They continued so, sharing stories or sitting in silence, as the sun passed its zenith and journeyed westward, rising every so often to feed more air or fuel to the fire. At some point during the day Velantos slid from the bench to sit with legs outstretched and his back against it. He only realized that he had slept when he heard the wheeze of the bellows and started awake to see Anderle kneeling to work them on the other side of the hearth.

"I am sorry—" he began, but she shook her head.

"You have done your work. It is the part of the man to labor to plant the seed in the womb, but after that, all he can do is to take care of the mother and wait while it grows."

"Are you saying that this sword is our child?" His lips quirked in unexpected amusement.

"After three nights of forging, do you have to ask? Rest. When the blade comes from the forge, you will have to polish and sharpen it and give it a hilt, as the father raises the child. But I think that watching over it is my task now."

When Velantos opened his eyes he found himself surrounded by fiery light. For a moment this seemed quite natural, as if it was he, not the sword, that lay in the hearth. Then his vision cleared, and he realized that the light was coming through the doorway. Through the trees he could see a flicker of orange light that must be the setting sun.

Panic jerked him upright, casting the blanket that had been drawn over him aside. His pulse slowed as he saw Anderle—no, it was the Lady of the Forge—standing beside the hearth.

"My Lady, is it time?" His heart begin to pound once more.

"This is the hour when the Sword from the Stars must come forth from the womb of fire." Her voice was measured and slow. "Take up the tongs and draw it out. Lay it on the anvil to make sure it is straight, but only for a moment. Before it can cool, you must put it into the tub of brine."

"But that will soften it again—" the smith exclaimed.

"Fool! This is not bronze! A quick quench will soften copper, but like the slap that wakes the child to life, the shock of the water hardens iron. Move, man! The time to bring forth has come!"

She stretched out her hand, and fire seared his veins. With a single swift movement Velantos took up the tongs in one hand and in the other a shovel with which he lifted the coals. Parts of the sword had glowed while he was forging it, but now what he saw in the depths of the forge was a sword made of fire. Swiftly he gripped it, carried it in a swirl of smoke to the anvil. A practiced eye saw that it was still straight and true. He lifted it again, poised it over the brine tub, and with one last frantic glance at the goddess, plunged the blade straight down.

It hissed like a serpent, and he began to believe that it might have grown a dragon's hide. The water bubbled around it and released a cloud of evil-smelling steam. Velantos held it steady until the water stilled, and then, hardly daring to breathe, lifted it free.

"From fire and water it is born . . ." said the Lady. "After passion, peace. . . ."

The blade was already cool enough to hold in his bare hands. The dark surface seemed opaque, but along the thin edges ran a rippling border of paler gray.

"Bend it—" the Lady said then. He looked at her in alarm. "Bend it, for if you do not test it now, you will always fear—"

She was right, he thought grimly. And if it failed, he could plunge what was left of it into his own heart. He swung the blade down, set the point in the earth, and leaned. His heart stopped as he felt it give. He jerked back, his cry of anguish cut short as the sword quivered in his grip like a live thing and flexed back to its original shape once more.

Velantos fell to his knees, holding the sword in both hands, examining it as closely as ever a father examined his newborn child. But there were no tiny cracks along the edges, no distortion in the blade. The sword was without flaw.

Weeping, he cradled the blade against his breast. When he could see again, he found Anderle beside him. Her eyes were shining with the same exultant light that he knew must blaze in his own. From somewhere outside he could hear cheering.

"We have done it," she said softly. "Drink to your triumph, my dear—" She held out a clay cup. "The elder folk have sent us mead."

He needed the support of her arm to get upright again. He took the cup, turned, and tipped it hissing onto the coals. "To You, my Lady, with all my heart," he whispered. "This is Your miracle. . . . And *yours*," he added, turning to Anderle. She poured more mead into his cup and he drank it down.

Then, very carefully, he set the sword on the workbench and his cup beside it, took Anderle's from her hand, and pulled her against him. She stiffened in surprise, but not, he sensed, in rejection. Kissing her, he felt the heat grow between them. He stroked down her back, waiting for the yielding that was like the moment when the metal ceases to resist the hammer. It came swiftly—they had had three nights of foreplay, after all. The bed was before them. All thought ceased as he lifted her in his powerful arms.

TWENTY-SIX

*M*y Lady . . ."

Anderle stirred unwillingly as the soft voice broke through her dreaming. And they had been such lovely dreams too. . . .

"Lady, you must waken! There is a messenger!"

She started to turn, realized that Velantos' arm was lying across her breast and smiled, understanding that it had not been a dream after all. Carefully she moved his hand and sat up, rubbing her eyes and blinking at the pale light of dawn. It seemed strange to have slept through the night, but she could see the sword lying on the workbench. All her dreams, she thought with a surge of joy, had come true.

Velantos murmured her name and reached for her as she eased out from beside him. Even in sleep he looked happy. She supposed the smile on her own face was the same. Her skin was still sensitized by the touch of his work-roughened hands. She dropped a kiss on his palm and tucked it beneath the blanket as she drew it back over him, then rose, found her cloak and pulled it around her, and went to the door.

"What is it that cannot wait until we are properly awake?" she asked the woman who waited by the door.

"A man comes from Avalon. He says he must see you now!"

Anderle looked past her. The messenger might have come from the Tor, but he was no man of Avalon. Her throat tightened as she recognized the gray cloak with a swan's feather tucked into the pin that marked him as one of Mikantor's men. She pushed past the woman and joined him under the trees.

"You are Ulansi, are you not? What has happened?"

"I am sorry, my Lady—" he babbled. "I thought I would find you at Avalon, but they said you were here. I came as quickly as I could, but I have been nearly half a moon on the trail."

"Never mind that!" she exclaimed. "Has harm come to Mikantor?"

"My lord is well in body, so far as I know—" He swallowed. "It is your daughter, Holy One. Galid holds her prisoner. . . ."

She staggered and he put out an arm to steady her. The muscle was like oak beneath the taut skin. Velantos' whole body had been like that, hard against her own.

Galid! Her heart raced as she remembered his threats. What would he do to her child? If she offered to take Tirilan's place, would he let the girl go? Could she make such a sacrifice without abandoning her own duty?

"My lord marched off with most of the Companions to help the Ai-Akhsi king deal with some brigands who've been troubling him. The lady Tirilan went away with Queen Cimara to learn the ways of the land. I was still in Carn Ava—one of my cousins was there—I hadn't known he was still alive, and Mikantor said I might stay. So I was there when Soumer—he who's now Galid's right-hand man—came driving up in his chariot and demanded to see the lady Nuya. When the priestess came out, he dropped Tirilan's shawl in the mud before her, said that he had Tirilan prisoner, and if Mikantor wanted his whore back he should come to Azan-Ylir.

"But we have spies in his household—she is not there, and no one knows where he has hidden her now. We sent our best runner north to fetch Mikantor, and they sent me to you because I knew the way to Avalon. The Sacred Sister has asked all the tribes to gather on the Plain of Azan."

At least, the priestess thought with a bitter relief, this news had not come while they were still forging the sword. Now the conflict was not between duty and duty, but only between duty and desire. From what Velantos had told her, the steps that remained to complete work on the sword were all things he understood. He no longer needed the goddess to hold his hand. Her heart ached at the pain he would feel when he found her gone, because that pain was her own. But better he should think she had abandoned him than that he should follow her and fail to complete the sword. She thanked the goddess for the miracle She had wrought in the forge—she had no right to expect happiness as well.

She gestured to the woman. "I must go with this messenger. When the smith awakens, give him food, and tell him that when he has completed the sword he must take it to Mikantor at the Plain of Azan." Because, by the time the weapon was completed, that was where he would surely be.

"I have to return to the war band—" said Ulansi when the woman had gone, "as swiftly as I may."

Anderle gave a short laugh. "Go ahead, if you think you can go faster, and never fear for me. I have ways to pass unseen, and I know Azan. I will search for my daughter. Tell Mikantor to gather an army that will destroy Galid once and for all."

VELANTOS SAT IN THE doorway of the smithy, grinding the sandstone down the length of the sword. Beside him was a bowl of half-eaten porridge. The elder folk were still feeding him, but where before they had feared to distract him, now they feared his wrath. The smith scarcely noticed that he had not spoken to another human being for three days. Even Aelfrix was gone. First on one side, then on the other, but always in the same direction, he pushed the stone outward to smooth the surface from the swelling center to the honed edge. Already it gleamed like the wing of the gray goose in the sun.

The labor required coordination and judgment, lest one grind too much of the metal away and unbalance the blade, but compared with the forging, it was a simple, repetitive task. Once, he had welcomed this part of the making, a time to sit and think and work his own magic into the blade. Now, thought was his enemy.

Why had Anderle left him?

He had assumed they would take the sword to Mikantor together. He was sure she had told him that she had the materials with her to make the scabbard when the sword was done. And yet she had scurried off without a word to put out whatever brush fire was burning at Avalon. She had been in charge there for too long, he thought angrily. She had left a dozen full priests and priestesses on the holy isle—why did she think she was the only one who could fix the world? Grimacing, he ground out his anger and his frustration into the sword.

Sunlight flared as he lifted it. The shape he had forged had been true, but it had veiled the sharply drawn form he was revealing now, as a caul veils a newborn child. At least, he thought grimly, he could still trust his craft.

He put down the sandstone grinder and picked up the fine-grained greenstone, working it carefully down the blade to smooth away the faint lines that were like the vanes of the feathers on a bird's wing. Even the most highly polished bronze gleamed no more brightly than the reflection of the setting sun in a pool. But the meteor sword was beginning to shine like the sun at noon.

"Blaze like the white-hot coals from which you were born! May your light blind the wicked, your fire sear all evil away!"

That radiance illuminated his spirit, but his heart still ached with un-comprehending anguish for the loss of what he had so briefly known.

ANDERLE'S NOSTRILS TWITCHED AS she carried the pitcher of ale into the central hall of Azan-Ylir. The hide that had covered the carved bull's head on the wall was moth-eaten, and none of the rich hangings and gilded or-naments with which Galid tried to disguise his spirit's poverty could dispell the pungent aroma of urine and spilled beer. It had been worse, the other women assured her, before the half of a moon that Tirilan had been a cap-tive here.

At least Galid kept his other prisoners outside. Between the gate and the roundhouse stood a row of cages. When Anderle arrived she had feared to find Tirilan in one of them, but the captives were all men, starved creatures confined for the gods alone knew what offenses, who were released some-times to run about while the warriors cast spears.

She walked with bent head and curved spine, rags obscuring her body and a dirty cloth covering her hair. That, and the aura she had cast around herself, had kept her from unwelcome attention. She had always known how to cast the glamour that made her appear more beautiful. This was a simple reversal of the spell.

It was not something that Tirilan had ever needed to learn, but from what the women said, the men had respected her. Her mother was simultaneously amused and amazed that the girl had filled her time here with housework. At Avalon the students were all trained to help, of course, but it was not the kind of labor expected of a priestess. But if her daughter could do it, so could Anderle, and so for the past four days she had been Galid's servant. There had been no difficulty in getting them to take her on. The usurper was calling in all his men, and needed all the help he could get to keep them housed and fed. The only problem was that Tirilan was no longer here, and none of the servants seemed to know what had become of her after he carried her away.

Anderle approached carefully, for Galid himself was sitting on a bench covered by a bearskin at the head of the hearth. Two men from the war band were with him, a renegade from Belerion and a younger man of his own clan called Keddam whom she had not seen here before. The men held out their beakers to be refilled without really looking at her, any more than they would have noticed one of the dogs.

"Is the bitch still alive, then?" Galid's speech was slurred, and Anderle wondered how much he had drunk before she brought her pitcher in. "And mad—is she not mad by now?" She paused, realizing that he was not talking about a dog, then slid behind one of the great posts that held up the roof of the hall

"She eats the food I bring . . ." said Keddam with a shrug. "When I arrive I hear her singing sometimes. She sings very well. And she thanks me."

"Nay, 'tis her lover who must be mad," the man from Belerion replied with an evil laugh. "Will he try and kill you with a stone knife as they say he did the deer? I suppose not—by the time he gets here he'll be too tired."

Anderle's heart was wrenched by pity when she thought of what Mikantor must feel. Even if Nuya had not been able to send the message to Lady Leka on the wind, the runner must have gotten there by now.

And is Velantos worrying about me? she wondered then. She hoped he thought she was at Avalon, for he would never have believed that she could pass through Azan far more safely than he. She tried not to think about him. Such memories would only distract her now.

"Just remember that if you want to force Uldan's cub to give battle soon, you must keep the girl alive," observed Keddam. "If she dies, he can take the time to gather all the tribes. They have closed their eyes to what you do with folk here, but I don't think they will be happy if you starve a priestess."

Anderle gripped the pitcher so hard she wondered later why she had not broken it. *They will tear you limb from limb,* her heart cried, *and if they do not, I will!* With an effort she managed to hold still as Keddam went on.

"Why not let me bring the lady back here?"

"Never . . ." muttered Galid. "She is a witch and a whore. Do not listen to her singing—she will offer you her love and steal your soul. Love is the last trap . . . and the worst one." He took another gulp of beer. "*This*"—a knife with a gilded hilt appeared suddenly in his hand—"is the only thing that's real!" Both warriors flinched as Galid struck the blade into the bench and left it quivering there.

What, wondered Anderle, had her gentle Tirilan done to this man? He looked sick, and old, and more than a little mad. Unfortunately, whatever was wrong with him seemed to be catching. In recent years his example had been followed by bandit chieftains across the land.

The dogs began to bark as more warriors came into the hall. She slipped from behind her pillar and scurried back to the kitchen, knowing she would overhear no more useful conversation today. But clearly Keddam was the man to watch. And at least he seemed to want to keep Tirilan alive, wherever she might be.

VELANTOS TAPPED THE LAST rivet into place at the base of the hilt, and laid the hammer down. The bright bronze and gold shone in the lamplight, but theirs was a soft and friendly glow in comparison with the radiance of the Sword. In the pommel he had set a piece of rounded crystal the size of a pigeon's egg that caught the light as if moonfire burned within. He gripped the hilt and lifted the sword, savoring the way hilt and blade balanced so that it seemed to swing up of its own will. The hilt shone with the light of sun and moon, but the blade blazed like a star.

As he turned it, he contemplated the depths within that blaze. The edges gleamed with a pale, wavering line where he had honed them until they would cut a hair upon the wind. When he had wiped down the blade with a little vinegar to remove any oils his hands might have left upon it, a pattern of light and shadow glimmered within, subtle and lovely, like a memory of the many foldings from which he had forged the blade. He set the sword down suddenly as that image transmuted to a memory of his body and Anderle's folded together in love.

She had left him.

Velantos told himself that he must lay his heart in the fire until it grew a hard skin like the sword. The work was done, and since Anderle was not here to share his triumph, he could only salute the Lady of the Forge. And perhaps that was just as well. *She,* at least, had never betrayed him.

That night his sleep was troubled, as he woke, reaching for Anderle, and sank back when he realized she was not there. But just before dawn he dreamed as he had dreamed when the goddess wore Anderle's face, the kind of dream that even while it is going on imprints itself upon the memory.

He was walking over a field of red earth, and he was carrying the Sword. With every step the blade thrummed in his hands.

"I am alone," it sang. "I am deadly and beautiful, but I am alone . . ."

"So am I," Velantos replied. "I cannot help myself. How do you expect me to help you?"

"Thrust me into the earth and I will beget offspring—" sang the Sword, and although the part of Velantos that knew he was dreaming winced at the thought of scratching that shining blade, the dreamer found it quite natural to plunge it into the ruddy soil.

Velantos felt the earth shudder, and stared in horror as from the place he had stabbed blood began to flow. He retreated from that red tide, nostrils flaring at the scent that was the same as that of the iron, and then it grew brighter, and he realized that it *was* iron, flowing sun bright as the metal he heated in the forge.

The red stuff in the ground must be iron ore, thought the detached observer in Velantos' mind, just as copper ore was green. With sufficient heat, perhaps it could be smelted, even cast like bronze. He had seen such red earth in many places . . . Copper and tin were rare, but he realized that those who knew the secret of extracting it from the ore could make iron almost anywhere.

The river of iron sank back into the soil, but the vision was not finished. Once more the earth shook. Bright points poked through its surface, sprouting an army of swords. The blade he held thrummed a greeting as they grew taller, raised by human shapes whose armor had the same bright sheen. Velantos pointed the sword and the army began to march. Where they passed they left a swathe of destruction, but structures greater and devices more complex sprang up in their wake, all of them made from iron. Iron saws and axes cut down forests; iron wagons tore up fields. Iron creatures roamed the land and the oceans and the heavens, and the smoke of their furnaces stained the sky.

"This is your doing!" cried Velantos, shaking the Sword.

"I am a sword," came the stark reply. "I cut what you place before me. If you bleed, blame the mind behind the blade."

I have meddled in matters beyond my understanding, thought the smith, struggling to awaken. Knowledge could not be suppressed forever. What one man had discovered, others would learn. But at least he could delay that day. *Let men think this sword a miracle of the gods. If the gods wish men to use iron, they can teach the secret to others,* he vowed, *but it will not come to them from me!*

With the thought, he opened his eyes.

Moving like an old man, the smith got himself out of the bed and limped to the workbench. Carefully, he unwrapped the Sword. It gleamed in the morning light.

It is neither good nor evil—he thought then. Or at least there had been no evil in the work he and Anderle had done to forge it, but what had he ground into it after she had gone? He remembered what she had said about the parent's effect on the child. Had he imprinted his own anguish in this blade? He lifted the sword and turned to the image of the Lady of the Forge.

"*Astra Chalybe*—Star Iron—" he whispered. "By my own heart's blood this doom I lay upon you, that you shall be the death of anyone who tries to use you for evil ends, and you shall be drowned in the Lake of Avalon rather than remain in any unworthy hand."

MORNING LIGHT SHOWED THE tracks of the chariot clearly in the dew-wet grass. Anderle walked quickly, despite the heavy sack of pilfered supplies she bore. For three days she had watched Keddam, fearing that Galid would decide he was too sympathetic to the prisoner and give the duty of feeding her to another man. He had several chariots, and they were likely to go off in any direction at any time. But Keddam had also been carrying a bag when he drove out this morning, and the gods had given her an easy trail. Indeed, it seemed to be leading in the direction of the great henge, not so far from the route she had taken when she fled with Mikantor all those years ago.

Anderle tried not to think about what she might find at the end of that road. Fear sapped strength, and she was going to need all she had. At least this time she was not pregnant, and no one was pursuing her. On the other hand, she was no longer eighteen years old. And now the child she strove to save was her own.

Why did that seem so strange? Had her labors for Mikantor and for Avalon deprived her daughter of the love she deserved? If Anderle had been better at mothering, would her child be in danger today?

Preoccupied by her thoughts, she did not hear the chariot returning until it was already coming over the rise. For a moment she froze. Then she pulled off the headcloth and shook out her dark hair, straightened, and strode off at right angles to the track. Would an innocent traveler pause to see who was coming? She thought so, turned, and felt fear shock through her again as the driver pulled back on the reins and the chariot slowed.

"And where would such a fine-looking woman be going on such a fair morning?" Keddam called, with what he clearly thought was an inviting smile.

Anderle's lips twitched. Apparently her transformation from an old woman to a young one had been effective. "I go . . . see *Achimaiek*—grandmother—

lord," she replied in the heaviest accent she could manage. "She very sick. I help her long time now . . ."

"Oh—" His tone cooled. "Well, go on then. And don't bring your diseases to Azan-Ylir—" He shook the reins and the ponies tossed their heads and trotted on.

Azan-Ylir is already sick, thought Anderle. *You just don't recognize the symptoms.* When the sound of the chariot had faded, she turned westward once more. The dew had dried, but Keddam had driven this way often enough to leave grooves in the grass. Over the rise and down again she made her way, and as she crested the next one she saw to her right the stark shape of the great henge.

But it was the lump of piled stone in the distance beyond it that riveted Anderle's attention. As she drew closer, she saw that it was a shepherd's hut with a roof of moldy thatching. The track of the chariot led directly there. Her steps quickened, despite the weight of the bag she bore.

The hut was silent. Anderle fought to control the pounding of her heart. Keddam had looked cheerful enough. Surely if Tirilan had been dead, fear of his master's anger, if nothing else, would have caused some concern. She set down her bag and approached the door.

"Tirilan—" she called softly. "Tirilan, are you there?" She stilled as she heard a sob, quickly stifled, from within. "Tirilan—" she called again, but there was no reply.

Anderle was a small woman, but desperation lent power to her arms as she dragged the heavy bar aside. The door swung open, releasing a wave of foul air that reminded her of Galid's hall. She recoiled, then took a deep breath and stepped inside. Near the open door she could see a bag of bread and two waterskins, a pile of earth surrounded by buzzing flies in the far corner, and between them, Tirilan, hiding her eyes from the light. She was emaciated and filthy, but she was alive.

"Sweet Goddess, help us," murmured Anderle, bending to grip the thin shoulders. "Can you walk, my darling? Yes, it's me, you're not dreaming— I'm so sorry, my dearest, that it took me so long to come."

"I didn't think I was dreaming," said Tirilan as her mother got her upright and assisted her out into the light. "I thought I was going mad . . . I'd heard your voice inside my head so often, you see. I thought I'd forgotten how to tell what was real."

"Well, this surely qualifies as a nightmare," said Anderle. She felt Tirilan's recoil as she drew her toward the bench, and laid her down on the clean grass instead. "You need feeding, and you're weak," she said briskly, though she was weeping inside. "Is there anything else wrong?"

"I'm dirty—" whispered Tirilan. "The hunger was not so bad. Avalon taught me how to fast. Not being able to get clean was the worst of all. . . . You *are* real, aren't you?" She clutched at Anderle's arm. "Although if you are not, still I like this dream." She sank back again.

"We can deal with that immediately," said Anderle. She returned to the hut and brought out the waterskins and food bag. "I'll sponge you clean with this. We can get more from the pond I saw nearby."

She winced again when she got Tirilan's clothes off and saw how the bones poked against her skin. Galid had kept her alive, but only barely. Her clothes were hopeless, but Anderle had brought others. After a moment's thought, she took the soiled garments back to the hut, and the emptied waterskins and food bag as well. Then she carefully replaced the wooden bar. Let Keddam try to make sense of *that* when he came again!

Velantos had told tales of a sorceress from his own land who summoned dragons to carry her away. Anderle wished she had them now, or even one of Galid's chariots, though that would have been hard to explain to Keddam when she met him on the road. If the schedule remained the same, Tirilan's keeper should not be back for two or three days, but things could always change, and they should not stay here. Tirilan was looking a little better already, but it was equally clear that she could not walk far. They would have to take it in slow stages, thought Anderle, returning to kneel by her child.

"Up now, my darling—I am sure you want to be away from here as much as I do!"

"Yes, Mother—" Tirilan did her best to help, though she was trembling by the time Anderle had her on her feet. "Where are we going?" she asked as they began their slow progress across the grass.

Anderle got her shoulder more firmly under Tirilan's and shifted the strap of her bag. Above the next rise she could just see the crisp line of great gray stones.

"Until you are stronger we will take refuge at the Henge. If anyone thinks to look there, I can draw upon its powers."

"Galid will be sorry he tangled with the Lady of Avalon—" Tirilan managed a smile.

"Hush, child, and save your strength for walking," said Anderle, but she was bitterly sure that when Mikantor, and Velantos, and the folk of the tribes learned what Galid had done to Tirilan, she was not the only one who would make that vow. And Tirilan was not the only one who needed avenging, she thought with a stab of guilt, only the one that Anderle had been able to rescue.

It was time to make an end.

VELANTOS LOOKED AT THE huts the elder folk of the White Horse Vale had built to live in while they served him and felt ashamed that it had never occurred to him to visit them before. They were rude dwellings, nothing like so well made as the smithy they had built for him.

He cleared his throat, looking at the apprehensive faces around him— old men and women, mostly, with a few younger ones and a child or two clinging between their elders. He supposed that Grebe and the other young men had already left to join Mikantor. Had he really been so frightening? Perhaps so. Serving him this past week must have been like trying to tend a wounded bear.

"I come to thank you—" he said slowly. "I finished the Sword. I want you to see it. It belongs to you too. Without your help I could not do it." He shrugged off his pack and untied the long bundle that held the Sword, laid it on the ground and lifted the folds of linen away. There was a whisper of indrawn breath as they saw it shining in the sun.

"Do not touch," another voice cautioned as they bent over it. "Is a thing of power."

Velantos looked up at the old woman who sometimes brought his food.

From the ornaments around her neck and the tattooing on her brow he realized that she must be one of their wisewomen. He was ashamed not to have noticed that before. But his dream of the Age of Iron had lanced something that had been festering in his soul, or perhaps simply put his own problems into perspective. In any case, his mind was clear once more.

"Yes," he answered. "The metal was powerful when you gave it to me, and the goddess gives it more."

"What do you do with it now?" they asked.

"I will take it to Mikantor, to the king. I ask that someone takes that word to the Lady at Avalon."

"Oh, she is not there—" said the old woman. "She and the warrior were going to Azan. He comes to say that Galid has her daughter. Mikantor brings an army and the man goes to join him, but the Lady said she looks for the girl."

Velantos blinked, wondering why his vision had darkened so suddenly. How could Galid have gotten his hands on Tirilan? It made no sense—And it made no difference. Despite their quarrels, or perhaps because of them, Anderle would do anything to save her child. Even, he thought in anguish, if it meant sacrificing herself. She was like a queen, and he did not want to watch a third queen die.

Why didn't she tell me? wailed his heart, and his head supplied the answer. *Because she didn't want me to follow her. . . .* But the Sword was finished now. He bent swiftly to wrap the blade and sling his pack again.

"I ask one thing more—" he said harshly. "A guide to show me the fastest road to Azan!"

TWENTY-SEVEN

A mizzling rain had been falling since early that morning, not hard enough to slow the march, but sufficient to make it thoroughly uncomfortable. Mikantor would have gone forward through a howling snowstorm, and his men were as eager as he. Since they heard of Tirilan's capture they had averaged seven leagues a day. But an army, however motivated, could not move as swiftly as a single man. The journey had seemed endless, and with every step his heart cried, *Tirilan!*

For two days they had been following the road along the ridge above the White Horse Vale. When the drifting mists revealed the land below, he could almost believe he was the same lad who had walked this way two years before, still fearing his destiny. But the dragons on his forearms seemed to writhe as he lifted his spear. His road was clear at last. He would kill Galid, and he would bring order to the land.

He knew his people now. He might not be able to stop the rain from drowning the crops, but if the tribes would follow him, he could redistribute the resources they had. The dragons were a symbol, but even if he had had no personal reason to oppose him, destroying Galid would demonstrate his power.

"It's not much like the last time." Ganath echoed his thought as he came up beside him. Mikantor looked back along the line of marching men. Pelicar's fair head and Beniharen's dark one bobbed above the others. Ulansi, who had met them on the road, was close behind him. From somewhere farther back he could hear Romen's voice lifted in song. His only regret was that Velantos was not at his side. His Companions had grown dear to him, but his bond with the smith went deeper. Velantos had shaped him as surely as he had shaped the Sword. But he would see both soon.

Adjonar and Lysandros and Ulansi followed with the new lads who aspired to join the Companions, including the Ai-Ushen prince Tanecar, leading his mother's men. Grebe and Aelfrix had reached them three days before. Behind them strode the men he had recruited in the north. Fighting beside them had given his own recruits some necessary seasoning and healed the shame of their defeat in the Vale three moons ago. His men were now a more fit fighting force altogether, and those who had been with him the preceding winter were motivated by a concern for Tirilan that almost matched Mikantor's own. He suspected that his allies were simply looking forward to a good fight on somebody else's ground.

"I wonder how Velantos is doing now?"

"We'll find out soon," said Mikantor. "I think the smithy Grebe told us about is by the tomb, just beyond those trees." He pointed at a clump of beeches whose tops showed above the next rise.

"That must be it," said Ganath as a thatched roof appeared among the trees. "Velantos' quarrel with Lady Anderle must have been like a battle of the gods. I wish I could have been a fly upon the wall!"

"I don't see any smoke," said Mikantor. His gut tightened with mingled apprehension and excitement. Had Velantos finished the sword? "Aelfrix—run ahead and tell the smith that we are coming!"

What was he expecting? The vision of the Sword from the Stars had come to Anderle and Velantos, not to him. When his bronze blade broke, he had grieved for the smith's pain, not the loss of a weapon. A sword was only a sword, and only as good as the hand that wielded it.

Except that if the old men who had given that hunk of metal to Velantos were to be believed, this one might be something more. Mikantor would value it, if only because it meant so much to those he loved, but even as he tried to maintain his detachment, the man he had been when he was called Micail was awakening within him, a man who had known how to wield the kind of power such a sword might hold.

As they turned up the path to the old tomb, Aelfrix came running back.

"He's gone!" exclaimed the boy. "Most of the elder folk are gone as well. Old Squirrel says that the Lady of Avalon went when Ulansi came to tell her that Lady Tirilan had been taken, seven days ago. It is three days since Velantos went away, after he finished the sword!"

"He's done it?" breathed Mikantor.

"Squirrel says it was beautiful, shining like a star," the boy replied.

"But where did he go?" asked Ganath.

"He went after the Lady," said the boy. "They both went to Azan."

Mikantor exchanged a worried glance with his friend. He still resented the sensible advisors who had kept him from heading south alone when he heard the news. What kind of trouble could the priestess and the smith get into, wandering in enemy territory alone?

VELANTOS SANK DOWN IN the lee of the barrow, unslung his bag and the swathed length of the sword, and pulled his cloak over his head against the wind. In the past year, he reflected, he had become quite familiar with tombs. The grave mounds of the Island of the Mighty, if not as elaborate as the great tholos tombs of his own land, were more numerous by far, and older. Where the earth had fallen away to reveal a shadowed entry, the stones that framed the door of this one were as large as any of those in Mykenae's Cyclopean walls. He wondered if the Cyclopes had come from these isles.

The Plain of Azan was fading into gray distances as the sun went down. It was the beginning of the season of harvest, and here and there he could see a ripening field or a rough-cut meadow where they had already scythed the hay. The barrow where he had settled was one of a line that stretched northward. Somewhere in that direction the great henge must lie.

The sky was darkening. He glimpsed a flicker of firelight as a door was opened in one of the scattered farmsteads on the plain. Smoke from their cookfires drifted on the air. But he dared not ask for shelter, not so close to Azan-Ylir. At the farm where he had slept the night before they said that the steadings closest to Azan-Ylir were all held by Galid's men. The rain seemed to be stopping, and he did not feel cold. Was he finally becoming accustomed to the climate in this country? That was a disturbing thought, as if he were losing part of his identity.

A single stranger at a farm would be conspicuous, but Azan-Ylir was full of people coming and going, swelling Galid's army, or seeking the scraps that fell from his table like crows around a carcass brought down by wolves. As if the thought had been a summons, a large crow settled on the mound.

"Nay, I did not mean you—" Velantos said genially, remembering Paion, whose bird this was. "And now that I think about it, I was probably being unfair to the wolves, at least the ones who have now allied with Mikantor. I should have called Galid's followers maggots, battening on the body of this land."

He pulled open his bag and tossed a piece of cheese to the bird. "Take that in honor of your master. He told me that he sometimes visits these lands. Ask him to watch over me," he added, although he might do better to call on Erelas, god of travelers and thieves—and beggars. Odikeos had passed unknown when he came as a beggar to his own hall. When Galid saw Velantos in Avalon he had not recognized him as the bronze trader he had met on the road two years ago. After sleeping under hedges for several days he looked a proper vagabond. There was no reason his enemy should recognize him now.

As for his present location, Velantos did not fear the dead. It was the living who had succumbed to Galid's contagion. Once, this had been a well-populated and fertile countryside, but today's march had taken Velantos past more than one deserted farmstead. Elsewhere men still fought to wrest a living from the land. Here, too many had given up the struggle and preyed on others, taking no thought for those who would come after. This was the evil that Mikantor was born to battle. It was for this that Velantos had forged the Sword.

The smith ate the rest of the cheese and drank from his waterskin. The opening in this barrow was too small for him to crawl inside, but at least it kept off the wind. He wrapped his cloak around him and despite his discomfort fell into a troubled sleep.

Surprisingly, his dreams were fair. He found himself walking across some

Otherworldly analogue of the Plain of Azan, for all the fields here were well tilled, the heads of barley hanging heavy on their stalks, fat red cattle grazing in meadows where the grass was knee high. He had never seen this country so richly bountiful, and began to understand why Mikantor loved it.

"It is beautiful, is it not?" Someone spoke behind him. As Velantos turned, a crow glided past him, its feathers flashing white as they caught the sunlight, to perch on the outstretched hand of a young man in a white tunic and red mantle ornamented in the style of this land. But the dark curls and lambent gaze belonged to the god he had met when he dreamed in Korinthos, in Paion's shrine.

"I told you that I had another home here in the Hyperborean lands," said the god, "and that you would meet me here."

"We have met here already," answered Velantos, "when Galid came to Avalon. You helped me then. Will you hide me from him now?"

"You are going into the bear's den, and you ask me to protect you from the bear?" Apollon laughed. "If you want to be safe, you are traveling in the wrong direction. Turn around, and you will find your beloved with an army at his back, hot for revenge. You will be well guarded then."

"Lord, it is not for my own sake that I ask, but for a woman who may be in danger."

"And what is this woman to you?"

Velantos gazed at him for a long moment, seeking a reply. "My lady," he whispered at last.

"She is not the Lady of the Forge, though the Lady spoke through her—" warned the god.

"I know it. She is an opinionated bitch of a woman, and a witch as well, and yet in her I see the goddess I have served. I am a man of my hands," he exclaimed, "not of words. I do not know how to explain what has grown between us. I only know it is there."

"Are you a hero, I wonder, or a fool?" asked the god.

"I wonder that sometimes myself—" Velantos tried to smile. "I am compelled to make sure she is safe, just as I was compelled to craft the Sword."

Apollon sighed. "Even the lord of Olympos cannot fight fate."

"Is that what drives me?" Velantos asked.

"If you must go forward, leave the Sword in the barrow," the god said then. "The ancestors will guard it well."

"If I have served you by forging it, I ask whatever aid you *can* give."

"I cannot change your fate, only give you the power to recognize it. But I will give you an oracle. If you go to Azan-Ylir, you will pay with your heart's blood for your heart's desire."

"If that is the price, I accept it," Velantos replied.

The figure of the god grew brighter, so radiant Velantos had to hide his eyes. When he opened them again, he was looking at the golden light of a new day.

"WHAT WAS THAT?" TIRILAN jerked upright, staring.

"It was the wind, my darling," Anderle replied, "only the wind on the plain."

"No, I heard hoofbeats—" She ran her hands through her tangled hair, looking wildly around her.

"Breathe, child, it is only the pounding of your heart," her mother replied. She had hoped to be gone from here today, but Tirilan was not yet strong enough to walk far. She needed hot food. Perhaps for a little while they could dare to light a fire. The last time she had been here, the Henge had been a gateway for the dead, but it would restore life to Tirilan.

"You can laugh—" the girl said bitterly. "You are the one Galid lusts after. Me, he only kept as a weapon against Mikantor!"

"Be still!" Anderle felt her patience snap. "I've half a mind—" *To let him have you if you cannot act like a priestess of Avalon*— her thought ran on.

"Do you remember what I taught you about these stones?" she said instead, indicating the four tall trilithons still standing within the Henge. The uprights and lintel of the fifth were fallen. She and Tirilan had slept in their lee the night before. The smooth surfaces were slightly concave, a solid gray in the morning light that slanted across the toppled stones on the eastern side. It was said that they had been felled in a magical battle between two factions of the priests who had founded Avalon. But power still flowed through the stones.

"The Henge lies on one of the rivers of force that flow through the land. Whether the power rises here because of the Henge, or they built the Henge to mark an intersection of forces I do not know. But those who have been trained as *we* are trained can draw that power up into the stones. Try it now—breathe out and let your awareness sink into the soil . . . reach out, sense the power . . ." She saw Tirilan's eyes widen as she felt it, and smiled. "Now breathe in and draw that force upward. That's it," she added as the energy began to move.

Tirilan gazed around her, her thin face flushing in wonder. "I can see them glow!"

"That also is part of our training," said Anderle. "But someone outside the circle would see only a distortion in the air. It is the same with sound. We cannot hear much from outside, nor can others hear what passes within."

"So we are safe . . ." Tirilan let out her breath in a long sigh and the glow began to fade.

Anderle looked up as a shadow flickered across the stones. It was a swan, not a usual sight on the plain. No doubt the bird had paused at the nearby dewpond. It reminded her of Avalon. Her daughter saw it too, and for a moment looked like her old self once more.

"She flies so high and free," murmured the girl. "After so long in the dark I forgot the beauty of the sky."

"Did Galid abuse you?" Anderle dared to ask.

"Do you mean, did he rape me? No—" Tirilan gave an odd laugh. "He threatened to, but that last time he came, his pain was so great, like a hole in the world, I would have given myself to him just to ease him. But he ran away and left me in the dark. . . ."

Anderle gathered her daughter against her, crooning as she had not done since Tiri was a little child. She had hated Galid because of the blood he had shed and the homes he had destroyed, but the man she had seen at Azan-Ylir was suffering from a sickness of the soul. A despair so great it could cloud Tirilan's bright spirit was a danger to the world.

"By now Mikantor knows you were taken. He will be burning up the leagues to rescue you."

"But *you* rescued me—" Tirilan hugged her and laughed. "I weep to think how he must be suffering now, but I suppose that to know he is not the only one who can do heroic deeds will be good for him."

"We are all heroes, my dear, when danger threatens those we love. . . . And I do love you, even though we do not always agree—" she added unwillingly as she let the girl go. There could only be truth between them here.

And how could she apologize to Velantos for running off without a word? She should have trusted him, but for so long she had been accountable to none save the Goddess. What would their relationship be when this war with Galid came to an end? Had he and she been no more than tools for the gods to wield, or could they forge a life together somehow?

"If we did not love I suppose we would not care enough to quarrel—" Tirilan said softly, stretching out her arms. "Oh, how thin I have become! I must try to eat more. Mikantor will not want a bundle of sticks in his bed!"

Anderle repressed a smile. The girl was definitely on the mend. But she must have some occupation, or she would begin to fret once more.

"When Velantos brings the Star Sword, it will need a sheath." She pulled a long bundle from her pack. "This was made for the bronze swords. Velantos forged the iron blade to the same pattern. It is two slats of wood hollowed to receive the blade and covered with rawhide sewn and shrunk."

"It is not . . . very pretty . . ." Tirilan said dubiously.

"Just so," her mother agreed. "And so we have this—" She unrolled a piece of doeskin dyed red with madder. "Cover the rawhide with this, and paint on the symbols that will ward the man who bears the blade." She realized now that she had already made her contribution to the forging of the Sword. It was Mikantor's mate who must make the sheath for this blade.

And when, Anderle wondered, had she accepted that Tirilan would not be returning to Avalon? *When I feared that I had lost her forever,* the answer came.

———

VELANTOS HEARD A HEAVY step behind him and dodged the fist, remembering just in time to cower instead of using the power of his forge-trained arm to knock the man across the yard.

"Make way for a warrior, slave!" The man lurched past. He wore a blade, though to call that length of pitted bronze a sword was as questionable as to call the oaf a warrior. Velantos picked up the firewood he had dropped, cursing his own inattention. He looked the part of a drudge, but even when he really *was* a slave he had found it hard to act like one. Fortunately the men who were most likely to greet a newcomer with a blow were those who had been vagabonds themselves not so long ago. There were a lot of them. Mikantor was not the only one who was recruiting men. The roundhouses within the palisade were full of them, and more were camped in the fields outside. The dirt and the stink were becoming overpowering. If Mikantor did not come quickly, sickness would do his work for him.

There were almost as many rumors as there were men. The best information came from the women who labored to feed the growing horde. They were grateful for Velantos' strength, and happy to talk to a man who did not confuse a smile with an invitation. When he said he was looking for his cousin and described Anderle, they told him she had been there, but three days ago she had gone.

He was chopping wood outside the palisade when a chariot came rattling in with sweated horses and a wild-eyed driver. "And what was that all about?" he asked the cook when he brought in the next load.

"Oh, it is a great secret—" The woman sniffed. "So of course the whole camp knows. Keddam has had the chore of taking food to the fair-haired girl that Galid captured a moon ago, the one who made us clean the hall. They had her in a shepherd's hut out beyond the Henge. Anyhow, this afternoon he found the door of the hut barred as always, and the girl's clothes within, but the girl herself was gone. Everyone is saying now that she was a witch, though when she was here she seemed a sweet girl, even if she did have a bee in her bonnet about keeping things clean."

Velantos turned away heart pounding as he realized that this was the information for which he had come. If there was a witch involved, it was not Tirilan. Anderle was safe, but where were she and Tirilan now? Galid had scouts out scouring the plain. Two had returned with the news that a great force was coming down from the north. Already men were gathering their weapons. Commanders strode through the crowd with orders to form up outside the palisade. He had best be gone before he found himself in the middle of a battle—on the wrong side.

"My lord!" Another scout was pushing through the throng. For a moment the crowd parted and Velantos caught sight of Galid coming out of the roundhouse. The warlord had put on weight since his last visit to Avalon, but he moved with a nervous energy that reminded the smith of a rabid wolf he had once seen.

"Lord Galid," stammered the scout, "I saw smoke coming from the great henge. I could not go too close without being seen, but a woman with yellow hair was looking out from between the stones—"

"Was she now?" Gaild replied. "Keddam, harness the horses. While Dammen gets the men in motion, let us go and see if the bitch has been found . . ."

"He saw a spirit, lord," said the warrior who had followed Galid through the door. "If it is she, she is a sorceress, and best left alone."

"I will kill her before Mikantor's eyes, or she will kill me—" snarled Galid in reply. "And I don't much care which it is just now. It is time to make an end—"

And time for me to go— thought Velantos.

"SOMETHING IS MOVING DOWN there," said Ulansi. "Men are marching. I think the bastard knows we are coming." They had crossed a fold in the land and found a slight vantage point as they came over the rise beyond.

"Good," muttered Mikantor. "It will give him more time to be afraid—" He bent his head so that Aelfrix could finish lacing up the coat of bronze scales they had found at the smithy. The boy said that Velantos had made it while he was waiting to forge the Star Sword.

"Ah, in this coat you will blind your foes." The boy stepped back. "In the sunlight you shine like a god."

"A god of vengeance," said Ulansi. In the last two days contingents from the Ai-Utu and Ai-Giru had joined them. The force that marched behind Mikantor now included men from all the tribes.

He held out his hands for shield and spear. He felt an inner stillness now that the time for action had come. His mood seemed to have communicated itself to his army.

"For the Lady Tirilan!" he cried, shaking his spear, and five hundred voices echoed him.

VELANTOS SPLASHED THROUGH THE Aman and climbed up the bank, straightening his shoulders and shedding the servile hunch along with the water. When he left the barrow he had noted the landmarks carefully. As the line of humps came into view along the skyline he veered to the right, casting a quick glance to the west where the Henge was coming into view. He could see no smoke there now, but dust was rising to the north—that could only be Mikantor and his men. His lips drew back in a feral grin and he hurried on.

Sunlight showed full on the face of the barrow, but the opening was as secret as before. Was it imagination that made Velantos sense a pulse of power from the Sword, as if it knew its destined master was near? He drew out the bundle and started north.

He had just crossed the processional way that led to the Henge when he heard hoofbeats and the rattle of wheels behind him. A quick glance showed him five chariots driving toward him across the plain. Behind them was a dark moving mass that must be the army. The chariots were coming fast, and there was no cover anywhere. He should have stayed hidden by the barrow, he should— There was no time to think what he should have done. What could he do now? Cursing, he pulled his threadbare mantle over all and forced his shoulders to slump once more.

The hoofbeats were too close now to pretend he did not hear. Velantos did not have to feign his recoil as the first pair of horses plunged to a halt beside him.

"What have we here?" said the warlord.

"My home burned, lord—" Velantos muttered, head bowed. "Now I wander . . ."

"You've chosen a bad time and place to go wandering," Galid replied.

"He's no vagrant, lord," said the chariot's driver. "I've seen him carrying wood at Azan-Ylir."

"A deserter, then? Why aren't you carrying a spear in my army? You look strong—" His tone sharpened. "Hold up your head, lout, and look at me!" He gestured, and one of the others approached with leveled spear. Velantos gathered himself to run, but the spearpoint was already at his throat.

"No wanderer indeed . . ." Galid said in a different tone. "I know this man! He is a bronze dealer I met on the road two years ago."

"I've seen him too—" Keddam said suddenly. "He fought with axes at the battle in the Vale!"

"My lord—" said the driver, "the enemy—"

"—is on foot," snapped Galid, "and cannot reach us until noon. Let's have the pack off and see this merchant's wares . . ."

Velantos dodged the spearpoint; the shaft caught him on the neck and he went to his knees, grabbing the spearman's leg to pull him down. But they were too close, and too many.

"Take him alive!" cried Galid as Velantos snapped a spearshaft with his next swing. Then something hit him from behind.

He continued to fight, though his head was ringing and he could hardly see. But in moments, his hands were bound and the contents of his pack were strewn across the grass. His vision was just returning when they found the Sword.

For an endless moment no one said a word.

"Are there gods after all?" Galid said in a shaken whisper as the blade came blazing into his hand.

There are gods, and they have betrayed me, thought Velantos, ceasing his struggles at last.

———

"MOTHER, I HEAR CHARIOTS—" Tirilan looked up, the stick with whose frayed end she was painting symbols on the leather sheath poised in her hand. Her eyes were wide with fear.

Anderle's heart sank. Tirilan had been so much better. She had been working on the sheath steadily since the day before, gaining the same strength from the sigils she was painting that she was infusing into the leather she held. Today, she might even be strong enough for them to leave the Henge.

Then she heard the hoofbeats too. "Your ears are better than mine." She forced her voice to calm. "You know what to do. . . ." She stood up and the two women clasped hands. "Reach down, tap into the power and send it through the stones . . . " Her skin prickled as the air pressure within the circle changed. Even if the intruders could see them, they would find it very hard to enter here. Humming softly to maintain the energy, she positioned herself behind one of the uprights at the edge of the circle where she could see eastward across the plain.

There were five of them. A flare of hatred shook her concentration as she recognized Galid's grizzled head. After him came Soumer and Keddam and two others she had seen at Azan-Ylir. She took a deep breath, forcing herself to calm. Beyond the chariots a dark mass moved upon the horizon, as if instead of wheat the fields had sprouted warriors. Even when the chariots halted, the earth trembled beneath the feet of marching men.

"If Galid is sending out his rabble, Mikantor must be near. We will have a good view of the fighting."

"You will forgive me, Mother, if I am less than eager to see." Tirilan made a brave attempt to match her mother's tone.

Galid had dismounted from his chariot. He seemed to be shouting, but a murmur of sound was all they could hear. Then he gestured, and the men in the second chariot heaved a body out onto the grass—a burly man with black hair. His hands and feet were bound.

It was Velantos. But how changed! He had always had a certain polish even when stripped for work, clothing mended and beard trimmed, as one might expect of a man raised in a king's hold. Now he looked as if he had been sleeping in ditches. And even at the height of his frustration over the

Star Sword every movement had radiated tension. Now she saw him emptied by despair. Instinctively she thinned the barrier so that she could hear as well as see.

"Tirilan!" Galid cried. "This man's blood will be on your head if you do not come out to me!"

But it was Anderle who stepped out from between the stones.

"Lady Anderle!" Lust and loathing were contained in those syllables, fear and a desperate need.

"Myself—" she replied. "Did you think you could take my child captive and I not know?" She cast a quick glance at Velantos, who had raised himself on one elbow. She flinched from the anguish in his gaze. "This is between you and me, Galid. Let the man go."

"No, Anderle!" Velantos cried. "Get back behind the stones!"

"Do you know him?" Galid favored them both with a nasty smile. "He seems to know you. Do you care if he keeps his head?" He giggled suddenly and reached back into to the chariot for a long bundle. "That stiff neck might take some cutting, but look! He himself has provided me with a sword!" Radiance flickered across the stones as he drew what looked like a bar of light from the wrappings and swung it high.

"Pretty, is it not?"

Velantos' eyes closed as Anderle stifled a cry.

"What do you *want*, Galid?" Anderle said evenly.

"Does that matter?" He spoke with a frenetic gaiety. "Your gods have given this island into my hand. No one will resist the man who wields this sword."

And that, Anderle thought numbly, was no more than the truth. That was the power that she and Velantos had forged into the blade. But not for *him*—

She wondered that the Star Sword did not leap in disgust from his hand.

"I suppose I should test it," Galid went on. He stood over Velantos, twirling the blade with a wrist that had clearly lost none of its skill, though his belly hung over the belt of his kilt. "A slash, or a stab? Which would be the best way?"

"Oh that will be a brave deed," Anderle said scornfully. "To slay a bound man!" She turned her gaze on the men in the chariots. "Surely the bards will sing scorn of the men who follow him!"

Galid looked sidelong at his men, who were beginning to grin as they scented a fight.

"Not that it will prove much of a contest, if the sword is as good as you believe . . ."

"Let the wretch up, my lord—" called Soumer. "There's no sport in sticking him like a hog!"

The others were leaning forward, avid as she had often seen them when the yard rang to the snarls of fighting dogs. They had no honor to appeal to, but if she could challenge Galid's manhood, he would have to respond.

"Prove it, Galid!" she cried. "Your tame giant is dead. Prove that you have the stones to face a man with a weapon in his hand." To stand against the Star Sword might be hopeless, but she could at least give Velantos a chance.

The earth was still shaking, and another dark line had appeared on the northern horizon. Mikantor was coming, and from the length of that line, half the Island must have joined him. She took a deep breath. Great powers were converging, and if she did not yet dare to hope, she sensed that perhaps the gods had not quite abandoned them after all.

"Very well," Galid said at last. "Cut his bonds and give him a spear."

As Velantos stood, rubbing his wrists where the ropes had scraped them raw, resolve began to harden the lines of his body once more. There was no hope in the dark eyes that met her own, but that leashed tension was something she recognized from the forge. Still holding her gaze, he bent in formal salutation, as if she had been a queen.

Her throat ached as she bit back all of the things she had never had a chance to tell him, but she responded with a smile.

She felt Tirilan's fingers close hard on her shoulder. "Mikantor is coming," she told her. "Velantos can buy us time."

"Mikantor would fight as hard for Velantos as he would for me," her daughter replied. "If I thought it would change anything, I would give myself up to Galid now. But we can only watch and pray."

And send energy to our champion, thought Anderle. She reached out to Velantos with her mind.

"Fight hard, my beloved . . . fight well. . . ."

Velantos bent to stretch the muscles of his legs, trying to remember everything he had heard about fighting with a spear. The left ached a little from the old wound, but he was used to that. He straightened, working his shoulders back and forth to ease them, and flexed his arms. No doubt tomorrow they would complain about the wrenching they had received bouncing around on the floor of the chariot—if tomorrow he was still alive to feel anything at all. But his muscles were moving smoothly enough for now.

He was surprised to find himself so calm. This was not the first time he had faced a foe who meant to destroy all he loved. He could even die content, if it were not for the Sword. *Lady, why did you give me the craft to forge that blade if you did not mean to set it in Mikantor's hand?*

One of Galid's men tossed his spear rattling across the grass. The bronze head glinted in the morning sunlight. Velantos grimaced as he picked it up, recognizing it as one of his own.

The shaft was of sturdy ash wood, a little over his own height, quite long enough to keep an enemy out of range—until the first time it was hit by the Sword. Velantos got a good grip on the spear, planted his feet in the grass, and took a deep breath, surprised to feel energy flowing up from the earth on which he stood. Did the land itself fight for him, or was it Anderle? Perhaps just now they were the same.

He gripped the shaft and jabbed, getting a feel for the heft of the spear. Galid swung; Velantos gauged the angle and batted at the blade. The sword rang, turning in Galid's hand, and a splinter flew from the shaft of the spear. Velantos feinted and thrust once more, grinning as Galid lurched backward. If he could lame his foe . . . He jabbed toward Galid's head. As the sword swung to deflect it, he flicked the spearpoint around the blade and plunged it downward.

But Galid was learning. The Star Sword came around in a whirl of light.

Velantos tried to drop the spear, but the blade caught it halfway down the shaft. As the shock reverberated up Velantos' arms, the blade slashed through. Unbalanced, he went over and kept rolling. He came upright with the stock of the spear in his hand, batting wildly at the Sword. The other half had fallen near the stones. He ducked Galid's next blow and dove toward it.

Galid was laughing, peal upon peal of bitter glee. Velantos' fingers closed upon the other half of the spear; he rolled again, came up with a piece in each hand and danced to one side, whirling both sticks to distract his foe. The Sword flared toward him and took another handbreadth off the end of the one in his left hand.

My greatest work will kill me . . . I wrought too well.

He had no defense. The Star Sword could shear through bronze; it would reduce wood to splinters. That knowledge brought an unexpected peace. If Velantos no longer had to worry about survival, he could focus on saving the Sword.

He dodged another slash, that strange clarity allowing him to foresee his opponent's movements even while his own seemed to slow. He had all the time he needed to bend, feigning a jab at Galid's feet with the spearpoint. As Galid reversed his hands on the hilt and stabbed downward Velantos rose, head tipped back, arms opening as if to embrace his foe.

The point of the Star Sword entered his breast just above the collarbone, stabbing down through the lung and scraping along the underside of his ribs, his body a living sheath for two-thirds of the blade. His momentum brought him the rest of the way up, wrenching the hilt from Galid's hand. Velantos felt the impact, but his body did not yet understand what had happened, and there was no pain. As he reeled toward the stones, he saw Galid fall back, eyes white rimmed, and the other warriors standing beyoned him, too startled to move.

"Anderle!" he cried in a great voice, as once he had cried out on their bed in the smithy. "Anderle, let me in!"

She came suddenly into focus, standing by the stone, and he knew the barrier was down. The world dimmed and brightened as shock began to take hold, but Velantos was still on his feet. He took one step and then another, put out a hand to support himself and felt the gritty surface of the stone. Then Anderle's arms were around him and she and Tirilan were pulling him into the circle. Everything beyond was lost in a distorted shimmer as Anderle snapped the warding into place once more.

The first wave of pain hammered Velantos to his knees, but it did not matter now. He had brought the Sword to Anderle. She would give it to Mikantor. The world was a whirl of light around him as he fell.

TWENTY-EIGHT

*T*he bronze disks sewn to Mikantor's leather shirt chimed faintly as he trotted forward, his spear resting on his shoulder and his Companions running to either side. To begin the last stage of their race they had risen before the sun. The skin of the lynx he killed in the great mountains was draped across his shoulders, for in this battle he would need all his allies. Galid's forces were taking up position on the plain before the great henge even now. Mikantor ran with grim exultation. Soon he would kill Galid and find Tirilan.

Several chariots were drawn up before the Henge. As the Companions approached, the drivers whipped up the horses and sped away. What were they doing there? Whatever it was, men on foot could not catch them— Mikantor took a deep breath and slowed. Now that they had sighted the enemy, they had better save their strength to fight them.

As they drew near, the Henge seemed to shimmer as he had seen stones shimmer in heat haze in the southern lands. But this was a typical cool summer day in the Isle. No one else seemed to notice anything unusual, but Mikantor's senses prickled, and after a moment Micail's memories identified that wavering in the air as the aura of power.

"That way—" He pointed with his spear. "Galid will wait for us. First we must go to the Henge . . ." He met the uncertainty in the Companions' eyes with a frown, and by now, they had followed him long enough not to question. Presently the others began to see the shimmer too, but as they neared, it faded away.

The buzz along Mikantor's nerves eased as well. As the stones came into clear focus, he saw waiting beside the heel stone a woman, wand slim, with shining, sun-bright hair. His heartbeat faltered, then began to race as he recognized Tirilan. His Companions set up a cheer.

"Take command—" he told Pelicar. "Form them up in a crescent as we planned, facing Galid's line."

"I understand, my lord," said the tall man, "but do not take too long."

Mikantor dropped his spear by the stone. Then Tirilan was in his arms and he was kissing away the tears that mingled with his own. It was only when he felt her shaking that he realized she was weeping with grief, not joy.

"What is it, love? Did he hurt you?"

"Not me—not me—" whispered Tirilan. "It is Velantos. My mother is with him. You must come."

Mikantor could not imagine what chance had brought all three of them to the battlefield, but that did not matter now. His heart skipped once more as he saw Velantos lying on one of the fallen stones, Anderle at his side. The blood on his lips was a shocking red against skin the color of whey. Even when his leg had gone bad on the way to Korinthos, he had not looked so ill. It was only when Mikantor knelt beside him that he saw the handbreadth of blade and hilt of the Sword.

"Velantos—" Anderle spoke in the tone Mikantor remembered from his training in meditation, and he understood that the priestess had been keeping the wounded man in trance. "Come up from your sleep. Wake now, my beloved. Mikantor has come. . . ."

"Velantos . . ." The older man did not stir, and no wonder, for even in his own ears Mikantor's voice did not sound like his own. He took Velantos' hand, feeling the calluses rough against his skin, hoping that flesh might speak to flesh where words failed, as it had before. The smith's hand was cold, though Mikantor could see beads of perspiration on his brow. The squeeze that responded to his own had no strength to it. But at least that faint pressure had been there.

"Velantos—" he tried again. "It's Woodpecker. I'm here at last. My lord, what has happened to you?"

Velantos grimaced as he drew the first perceptible breath Mikantor had seen. "You mean, how did I become a sheath for my own sword?" The dark eyes opened. He tried to smile, but it was clear that every movement caused pain.

Mikantor made a little helpless gesture as Velantos took another careful breath and went on. "It was the only way . . . to get it out of Galid's hand . . ." As his eyes closed once more, Tirilan's quick murmur filled Mikantor in on the unequal fight.

"This is *your* Sword," said Anderle, "the Sword from the Stars."

"I was not so clever . . . as I thought," muttered the smith. "Galid caught me, found the Sword. Broke the spear . . ." He stopped, becoming a shade more pale.

Mikantor looked at the angle at which the hilt protruded and felt sick. He had been in enough battles by now to have a pretty good idea of the internal arrangements of the human body. The blade had clearly gone through the smith's lung.

"Why have you left him like this?" He touched the hilt, saw Velantos twitch, and jerked his hand away.

"He insisted." Anderle spoke in an unnaturally even tone. "He said that *you* must draw the Sword."

Mikantor looked from her to Tirilan. "And what will happen if I do?"

"He will die. . . . We think that he is still alive only because of the pressure of the blade," Tirilan continued as Mikantor recoiled. "When it is withdrawn, he will bleed . . . more. . . ."

"And if you leave it in?"

"I will die . . ." gritted Velantos, "but slowly, and in greater pain . . . Take the Sword, lad. My blood . . . has washed Galid's taint away."

"You cannot die." Mikantor shook his head helplessly. "You cannot leave me."

"You saved me at Tiryns . . . You cannot save me now. . . . My death was only . . . delayed. . . ." Velantos paused until the ripple of pain that twisted his features passed. "What work of my craft . . . could surpass this one? It is what the gods . . . sent me here to do."

The hand Mikantor held had grown so cold— As he cradled it against his breast, he met Anderle's eyes and saw in them an anguish that matched his own.

"The god . . . said that my blood would be the price . . ." Velantos tried to smile. "I do not think it too high . . . for you. . . ."

I do! thought Mikantor helplessly.

"Even Diwaz . . . cannot change what the Fates have spun. . . ." Velantos' skin was like wax, the pauses growing longer between his words. He was bleeding to death within. "Take . . . my gift. Claim . . . your destiny, and . . . grant me mine . . ." The next breath caught on a new wave of pain.

Stay with me! Mikantor's heart cried. But in Velantos' gaze he read a love, and a resolve, that overmatched his own.

Must I beg you? came the silent appeal. *Let me go!*

"Before you came he told me how it must be," Anderle said in that same even tone, as if grief had already extinguished all emotion. "Kneel by his shoulder and draw it out, smoothly, and slow."

And then you will heal him? thought Mikantor, but there was no hope in her eyes. His body seemed to move of itself as he obeyed her command. He had killed men, knew the feel as the sword goes in, the shock as a man realizes his death. He had given the mercy stroke to wounded comrades, and felt the life slip away under his hand. But never like this. . . .

And even as the thoughts passed through his mind, he gripped the gold-wound hilt and began to pull, until the Sword was freed from its sheath of flesh and came sheened red with blood and shining into the day. Blood bubbling from his lips, Velantos gave a long sigh, and the last tension in his strong features eased.

"Is he dead?"

"He still bleeds," answered Tirilan as Anderle bound a folded linen pad over the oozing wound. "But I do not think he will speak to us again."

Anderle straightened, and spoke as a priestess once more.

"Velantos and I created the Sword, but you are its master. The time has come to use it. Destroy Galid, and then heal this land."

For the first time, Mikantor really looked at the weapon he held. Through Velantos' blood he could see its silvery gleam. It felt light and eager in his hand. He got to his feet, swaying on legs that hardly seemed his own.

"Go," echoed Tirilan, "my spirit will ward you . . ."

Mikantor nodded. He walked out of the circle to the plain where two armies waited for the decision of destiny, and the Sword from the Stars shone red beneath the sun of noon.

TIRILAN SANK DOWN WITH her back against one of the stones that supported the southeastern trilithon and began the sequence of breaths that would set her spirit free. Through a gap in the outer ring she could see the battlefield. Her mother remained beside Velantos, murmuring the spells that guide the spirit to the Otherworld. To death or victory, neither of the men they loved would journey alone.

Surface awareness faded away. Tirilan drew power from the earth and felt heat rush up her spine. Consciousness rode with it, for she knew herself strong enough now to launch her spirit outward and still return. Swiftly she assumed the swan shape she had used before, beating upward on shining wings, the last fears that had kept her from offering her full power falling away. Velantos had given everything. She could do no less now. The green plain whirled and dipped below her, then leveled as she caught the thermal power that flowed through the Henge and began to glide, effortless as if she floated on the stream.

To the east she saw the shining serpent that was the river and the round thatched roofs of Azan-Ylir. Below her, the precise circles of stones in the Henge pulsed with their own light. Between them the forces of despair and hope faced off against each other, preparing to do battle for the future of humans in this land.

The battle was not, she realized from this vantage, for the earth itself. The life streams of the land flowed strongly, any areas of weakness local, and already adjusting to the challenges the changing climate would bring. It was only humanity that believed things should always stay the same. She must remember that—it was something that Mikantor would need to know.

Galid had divided his forces into three groups, with his chariots in a line before them. Mikantor's Companions formed the center of a crescent whose wings curved forward. The golden scales of his armor gleamed in the sunlight, but to her eyes his spirit blazed even more brightly. She realized then that the light around him had two sources—Mikantor's own golden aura and a white radiance that must be the Sword.

As her glide carried her across the line of marching men, she saw the glow expanding, kindling the life-lights of Mikantor's Companions and spreading to the bands of allies that had joined them. She had seen a group soul form in this way in ritual, when trained adepts linked their spirits to work magic, but she had never imagined that so many untrained minds could be bound. But of course this was not a binding at all, but an offering made freely, as Velantos had poured his soul into the Sword.

Was the same thing happening to the enemy? She willed herself eastward, circling, and recoiled from the miasma that rose from Galid's men. The darkness was not universal—some sparks burned brightly even among that crew of cutthroats, just as not all of Mikantor's warriors had blazed with equal light. But Galid's infection of soul seemed to be contagious. At least, she thought grimly, it would be easy to tell friend from foe.

She soared in a long glide back to Mikantor's men. Ganath looked up as she passed, and touched Mikantor's arm. One or two of the others who had the Sight saw and saluted. Someone called out, "A swan, a swan!" But it was the radiance that eased the grim lines of Mikantor's face that warmed her spirit, and the connection that flared between them as she added her power to his. He lifted the Sword.

"The Sword from the Stars!" cried Beniharen. "The Sword from the Stars and the Lady Tirilan," Ganath echoed him, and the host behind them took up the cry.

From the other side Tirilan felt a cold wind of opposing power. It bore a cloud of arrows. She beat upward on strong wings. In the wake of the arrows, Galid's chariots lurched into motion, a warrior with a bucket full of javelins behind each charioteer. Mikantor's front line locked shields against them as they charged. Javelins arced outward like a flight of serpents as the chariots swung past. Most glanced off the hardened hide of the shields, but a few found targets and men fell. Their friends lifted shields and straddled their bodies, waiting as the chariots wheeled around for another pass. Mikantor whistled, and his own archers sent a cloud of arrows after them. Two of Galid's warriors fell screaming, and a maddened horse stampeded back into his own line.

Before the enemy could recover, Mikantor whistled twice more. The men in his center began to jog forward, increasing their pace until their crescent had become a wedge. Their allies fell back to either side to guard their flanks, while the Companions, better armed, trained, and armored, drove forward. The enemy were closing ranks, making a bristling hedge of their spears.

Tirilan swooped lower, tracking Mikantor's glow. Light was all around her. She drew it in, sent it through their link, and saw him grow brighter still. A great cry rose from the running men. Shields locked, they crashed into the enemy line.

MIKANTOR GLIMPSED THE BLUR of a spear coming toward him, struck upward through the shaft and saw the top third wheel away. The same stroke continued around to take off the head of the man who had wielded it. The Sword cut even better through flesh and bone. In the first moments of the battle, that had disturbed him, remembering Velantos. But trained reflexes carried him forward, striking left and right as he sought for Galid among his foes.

Another warrior came at him with a bronze blade that broke as he tried to parry Mikantor's first blow. The Sword drove onward through his corselet of hardened leather, through ribs and lung and heart and out again. He jerked it free in a splatter of red, looking for a new foe. Enemy gore had washed Velantos' blood away some time ago.

"The Sword!" cried a man whose leather shirt was sewn with plates of horn, trying to scramble out of the way.

"The Sword from the Stars!" The Companions' war cry rose above the clatter of metal and the screams of dying men. Each time he fought, Mikantor was astonished anew by the sheer *noise* of a battlefield.

He was getting closer, he thought, leaping foward. This must be one of Galid's guard, who knew what the Sword could do. His enemy had not been in the center of his line, but he must be somewhere in the battle. Mikantor had only to keep killing until Galid had no place left to hide. He felt another surge of power from Tirilan and drove the blade through the back of a fleeing enemy, lips moving in the song the Sword was singing in his soul—

> *I am the blade that bathes in blood,*
> *The edge that eats the enemy,*
> *I slice and slash, I am the Sword*
> *That deals out doom and destiny.*

His shield had been hacked to bits, but the Sword itself was teaching him how to use it to defend as well as to kill. Lighter, sharper, more flexible than any bronze blade, it struck with the joyous precision of a tool perfectly suited to its task. If it had a spirit, it was that of Velantos in those moments when he had seen the smith perfectly centered and focused on the work at hand.

Two spearmen who had not heard of the Sword rushed toward him and Mikantor broke the first shaft, feinted to avoid the second and dove under it, bringing the blade around in a long slash that sliced through the man's throat.

"Galid!" he shouted, straightening. "Come face me! Come face the blade you used to spit a disarmed man!"

They were trampling someone's wheat field. The dry stalks scratched Mikantor's ankles. As he turned, the Sword flared crimson in the light of the sinking sun. Men gave way before him. There were not so many now. Here and there knots of men still struggled, but a bloody harvest of the dead lay on the field. Of those still standing, most seemed to be his own.

They had beaten the foe back almost to the riverbank. At the edge, he saw a concentration of enemies. In his mind the Sword was whispering—

Dividing lives, deciding death,
I am the force to face the foe,
I am the Sword, but you, the soul
Defining where that force shall go.

To Galid—he replied. *Find him and avenge your maker. Find him and free this land!*

His Companions fell in behind him as he strode forward, and seeing their grim faces, the heart went out of what remained of Galid's guard, and they melted away to either side.

Galid was standing there, a bronze blade in his hand. A lucky slice had left part of his corselet hanging, but he seemed otherwise unhurt. Mikantor himself could feel a few scratches, and the stress of an afternoon of furious activity ached in his shoulders and arms, but he too was essentially unharmed.

Good . . . no one will be able to say I killed a wounded man. Mikantor wondered why he should care about giving justice to a man who had denied it to so many others. Galid watched him approach with a sour smile. But though he knew better than anyone what the Star Sword could do, he did not seem to be afraid.

"Galid, I summon you to single combat," Mikantor said evenly. "In the name of the people of this land—"

"So, it is the bumboy at last," his enemy interrupted him. "I pronged your master, but now you have the bigger weapon, and I suppose you intend to skewer *me*. Do you think that will make you happy? You can kill and kill, and it will not bring back those you've lost. I know." Galid gestured at the allied chieftains who had brought their men to circle the killing ground. "Do you think your victory will make them love you? They cheer you now, but the first time you try to make them share their wealth they will turn on you. Men think with their cocks and their bellies. I know. . . ."

Mikantor met that bleak gaze without flinching. He had certainly seen enough when he was a slave to realize—that for some men at least—that was true. But he had also known Velantos, and his Companions, and Anderle and Tirilan.

"You know . . ." he echoed. "And what do you know of hope, or love, or sacrifice?"

Galid shook his head with something very like pity in his gaze. "I know that they are illusions," he said softly, "that vanish when confronted by Necessity. . . . To escape it, your own woman offered to be my whore."

Mikantor would not have blamed Tirilan, for he had his own memories, but their spirits were still linked, and she was sharing images of that afternoon.

"Galid, she offered herself to ease your pain—" he replied with the same implacable compassion Tirilan had shown.

"Lies—all lies—" Galid said hoarsely. His pupils had expanded as if he were looking into some immensity of darkness. "There is only life . . . and death. And life is what I can make you *feel!*" He settled into a fighter's crouch. "Come, little bumboy, come feel my blade!"

Mikantor centered himself on the earth he loved, balanced in the stance for fighting with sword alone that Bodovos had beaten into him, right shoulder forward, sword held two-handed at an angle from which he could strike high or low. For a long moment they stood without moving. Galid broke first, moving surprisingly fast for a man of his girth. Mikantor shifted his own blade just enough to catch the other and saw a chunk fly from the edge of the bronze sword. Galid reeled back, face flushed.

"That's a good sword, isn't it?" He laughed. "Went into the smith's chest sweet as pronging a girl—"

Mikantor started forward, fury darkening his vision as Galid had intended. And the Sword from the Stars sang to him once more—

> *You hold the power in your hand—*
> *Defend the weak, direct the strong,*
> *Sever sickness from what's well,*
> *Good from evil, right from wrong.*

He stopped, took a deep breath, and felt Tirilan's spirit steady his trembling arm. "No . . ." he whispered. "You come to me. . . ."

Galid's shout could have been exultation or agony. He charged, swinging wildly. Mikantor took one step to the side. With a crack like thunder, the Sword shattered Galid's blade. As the severed half spun sunward, Mikantor struck at last, and Galid turned with a movement that if Mikantor had known it was very like the one with which Velantos had faced him, and opened his arms to be set free.

ANDERLE AND VELANTOS STOOD at the edge of a field full of fire. For her the vision wavered, so that sometimes she saw wind rippling through the grass on the plain, but that happened less and less often as the afternoon drew on. When she had come here to guide the spirits of the dead to the Otherworld, she had remained firmly rooted in this one, but as internal bleeding slowly released Velantos from his body, the smith's mind had proved stronger, drawing her into his world. That was a danger she had been taught to fear, but she no longer cared if she returned.

Here, they could speak of all those things for which there had never been time, and admit what pride would never have allowed them to say.

"You will watch over the boy?" said Velantos, then shook his head. "No—you must tell him to watch over *you*—he is a man now, and a king. Tell him that I loved him, as well as I knew how."

"My dear, I think he knows."

In the silence that fell between them the sound of cheering came faint from the other world. "Mikantor!" they heard. "The Sword from the Stars and the Lady Tirilan . . ."

"Is it over?" Velantos asked.

"He is safe," she answered as the exultation grew. "I believe that we have won. . . ."

"Then it is time for me to go." He gathered her into his arms, surrounding her with a gentle fire. "They are waiting for me—do you see?" He pointed, and she saw bright figures beckoning. "The god who brought me here, and the Lady of the Forge. She has your face. . . ."

Anderle looked away, unable to bear the beauty that blazed from the

Lady's countenance. She had always thought Velantos mad, she remembered now. But for a little time his faith had enabled her to bear a tithe of the Lady's power—was that indeed what she could become?

"*Yes* . . ." came the answer, "*you may.* . . ."

Velantos' fire blazed up around her. When it faded, she was sitting in the circle of stones. The light of the setting sun sent their long shadows toward the men who were coming toward her, and touched each blade of grass with flame.

Velantos's body lay beside her. He was already cold. How long had it been since that great heart had ceased to beat? *After passion, peace,* she remembered, wondering how long this serenity would remain. But for now, there were things that must be done. She saw Mikantor coming. As Tirilan woke from her own trance, he began to run.

EPILOGUE

*A*s the first stars lit the heavens, the funeral pyres were kindled upon the Plain of Azan. Three days had passed since the battle, time enough to search the field and identify the slain. In the fighting, Adjonar had fallen, and Romen, and Beniharen, felled by a stray arrow as he tried to drag a wounded man off the field. Those too badly hurt to recover had received the last mercy from friend or foe. The prisoners had been put to work carrying bodies and gathering wood for the pyres.

Much of the labor of organizing the funerals had fallen to Tirilan. Anderle had scarcely spoken since Velantos died. She sat now upon the grass beside Velantos' pyre. The loot of Azan-Ylir had yielded a length of linen of intricate weave from some southern land to wrap his body. He looked like a carven image, lying there.

The authority which the queens had given Tirilan included the duty of leading the rites for the slain. Her function here was, she realized, the complement to the power the people had granted to Mikantor. And so, one by one, she had blessed the pyres. This was the last, and the chief men of all the tribes had gathered to bear witness as Mikantor said farewell to the man who had forged the Sword about which so many tales were already being told.

Tirilan heard a murmur from the crowd and turned. Mikantor was approaching, with Ganath and Grebe, Lysandros and Pelicar and Ulansi behind him. He was carrying the Sword. It was not only the gold headband and the gold that pinned the white mantle that made him look like a king. His dark eyes seemed set more deeply, the line of jaw and cheekbone more clearly defined. Her heart gave a little skip, as it always did when she saw him after an absence, opening her soul to his. He looked up as if she had called his name, and his fixed expression eased. She stooped at her mother's side and helped her to stand. Their roles, she thought wryly, were reversed from those of a few days before. Now it was she, newly clad in a crimson robe, who was strong, and Anderle who wore the black rags of grief. She seemed to speak to them from a distance, as if a part of her had gone with Velantos to the Otherworld.

Mikantor came to a halt, gazing at the pyre. A muscle twitched in his jaw. Then he turned, forcing his own features back to stillness as he faced the warriors and chieftains who had gathered around it.

"We are gathered here to honor the passing of Velantos son of Phorkaon, a prince of Tiryns by the Middle Sea. You know that he crafted this Sword. Know also that Velantos faced Galid weaponless and alone, allowing his foe to sheathe the blade in his body in order to wrest it from his hand."

He waited as a murmur of appreciation rose from men who remembered vividly the terror of battle even when they fought with comrades at their sides.

"We must be worthy of his sacrifice," Mikantor went on. "With your help a great evil has been cleansed from this land. But there is much left to do. The times our fathers knew will not return. If we cease to fight each other we can learn to live in a world that will be as fair, even if it is different, than it was before. Let us save our swords for those who share Galid's sickness, meet greed with generosity, and bring hope to counter despair."

"Easy for you to say," came a voice from the crowd, "armed with that sorcerous blade."

"The magic was in the making, not the metal—" Anderle spoke suddenly. "And the making was directed by the gods. But you are right to fear the power of the Sword from the Stars. The smith himself set a curse upon it, that the blade shall turn on its wielder if ever it is used to conquer instead of to defend."

"Then put the thing away," came a mutter. "It hurts the eyes." There was an uneasy murmur from the crowd, and Mikantor held out the Sword as if wondering whether he should lay it on the pyre. Tirilan stepped forward.

Her mother and Velantos had not labored so hard to forge the thing for one battle alone. Now was the moment she had been waiting for.

"The Sword was made to defend you, and it will be needed again." She spoke clearly. "Galid sheathed the Sword in Velantos' body, but I will give you something better, a scabbard to keep the Sword in peace instead of war." She held out the red leather sheath she had kept hidden among the folds of her gown.

Mikantor's eyes widened. "You speak for the land, my lady." He took the sheath and carefully slid the sword inside. For a moment he held it so, hilt and crystal gleaming; then he handed it back to Tirilan. "My Lady, I entrust you with this power. You will tell me when it is right to draw the Sword."

She could feel the energy in the blade, but the sheath contained it. Mikantor held out his hand. "I defend you," he added softly, "but you sustain me."

"Mikantor!" shouted Ganath, and hundreds of voices took up the cry. "Mikantor and the Lady Tirilan!"

The earth trembled to that shout, or perhaps it was she and Mikantor who resonated to the waves of exultation coming from the people who surrounded them. She opened her awareness to respond, and realized that she was also sensing the flow of power through the earth.

This is what the Lady of the Hidden Folk promised, she realized then, *the thing my mother could not understand. I am still a priestess—but just as Mikantor has become the Defender, I am Lady of this land.*

Still holding her hand, Mikantor turned to the pyre once more. "My lord Velantos," he said softly, "I owe you more than you could ever understand. I had lost myself, and you gave me back my soul. For me, you transcended the limits of your craft. At the last your sacrifice gave me this victory. All that I can give you now is the fire. When it is finished, we will build a great mound for you among the kings on the plain."

"No," Anderle spoke suddenly. "Let his ashes lie in the old tomb by his smithy above the White Horse Vale."

"She is right," said Grebe. "The elder folk would ask it. He should rest there."

"Very well—" For a moment Mikantor's attention went inward. His posture changed, and another man seemed to look out of his eyes. Then he spoke a *Word*. It was not in any human language, but Tirilan felt the hairs rise on her arms at the passage of power. Though no clouds hung in the heavens, thunder crackled across the sky, and a bolt of lightning flared to ignite Velantos' pyre. It caught quickly with a roar like the forge fire, gold and orange and around the edges a silvery blue.

"The smith has gone to the fire again . . ." said Anderle as those flames embraced the still form. "Lady, ward him well, until he is drawn forth from the forge, made new."

AFTERWORD

*A*s I complete this book, beside my computer is a small table that bears a hammer and an anvil, a bit of meteor iron, and a small wrought-iron Thor's hammer. There is also a clay reproduction of a Mykenaean goddess, a small bronze figure of Hephaistos, and a red candle. Leaning against it is a reproduction of a leaf-shaped sword. Together, they represent the sources and influences that shaped *Sword of Avalon*. There were times, during the writing, when I felt as if I were on the anvil myself, being hammered out like the sword.

The story of King Arthur remains one of the most enduring legends of the English-speaking peoples. One of the elements everyone remembers is his magical sword, Excalibur. But the medieval romancers refused to speculate on its origins. Marion Zimmer Bradley was scarcely more explicit in *Mists of Avalon*—

> Fallen to earth in a falling star, a clap of thunder, a great burst of light; dragged still smoking to be forged by the little dark smiths who dwelled on the chalk before the ring stones were raised; powerful, a weapon for a king, broken and reforged this time into the long leaf-shaped blade, tooled and annealed in blood and fire, hardened . . . *a sword three times forged, never ripped out of the earth's womb, and thus twice holy.* . . .

What was this sword whose possession gave Arthur both victory and authority? Where did it come from? How old might it be?

These are the questions I have tried to answer in *Sword of Avalon*.

Since Marion had established that the sword was both very old and had been remade more than once, I knew that I would have to begin well before the Romans came to the British Isles. The aborigines of Britain might have roughly hammered a piece of meteor iron, but the first point at which such a piece could have been turned into a sword would have been at the end of the Bronze Age.

Scholars agree that around 1200 BCE, the great cultures of the Mediterranean world fell. That is the only thing on which they *do* agree. Causes ranging from epidemics to ecological catastrophe to barbarian incursions with new weapons have been suggested. Those who have read *The End of the Bronze Age,* by Robert Drews, will recognize that I have drawn on his theory about the effectiveness of the leaf-shaped sword. For information on the Bronze Age in general, see *The Rise of Bronze Age Society,* by Kristian Kristiansen and Thomas B. Larsson, which includes material on that period in Northern Europe which is often ignored.

Archaeology tells us that in the south, the palaces of Tiryns and Mykenae burned, and in the north, the climate was growing colder and wetter. But the problems we have today teach us that disasters rarely have a single cause, and nothing happens in isolation. Perhaps a change in the climate set populations in motion and eventually impacted the Mediterranean. For both ends of Europe the twelfth century BCE was a time of transition, when people had to change or die. I was able to visit Greece while I was writing, and thought it would be fascinating to combine the story of a Mykenaean master smith, displaced by the destruction of his world, with the birth of a legend in a time when Britain was suffering as well, a story that turned out to be uncomfortably relevant as it became clear how very much we need to change, and to hope, today.

To TELL THIS STORY, I had to explore the world of the smith. What inspiration, divine or otherwise, led men to discover the secrets of making bronze and working iron? For some time now it has been popular to assume that the magical swords of mythology were made from meteor iron, which is tougher than pure iron because it includes nickel. Until smelting was mastered it was also the only source of large lumps of iron. The tools of smithcraft have not changed all that much since the Bronze Age. The technology is historical—but in the knowledge of how to apply it to iron—there lies the fantasy.

To understand the mystique, I drew on many sources. Published materials that were particularly inspiring or useful include *The Forge and the Crucible,* by Mircea Eliade, *Craft and the Kingly Ideal,* by Mary W. Helms, *Ukko,* by Unto Salo, and Jane Sibley's *The Divine Thunderbolt.* For methods, I drew on *The Complete Bladesmith,* by Jim Hrisoulas, *Iron for the Eagles,* by David Sim and Isabel Ridge, and the amazing wealth of the Internet, from debates on the properties of meteor iron to a YouTube video of bronze-casting at the experimental archaeology museum at Old Lejre in Denmark (in fact I should put in a word of praise for the burgeoning resources available online, which have added immeasureably to the accuracy of my information). I was delighted to find that other scholars have also speculated that the name "Excalibur" (or "Caliburn" as it is in some of the medieval romances) might come from *chalybe,* the old Greek word for steel, which itself comes from the name of the Anatolian tribe whom legend made the discoverers of ironsmithing. I am even more grateful to my correspondents from the SCA West e-list, to Scott Thomas, the blacksmith at the Ardenwood Historical Farm in Fremont, CA, who spent an afternoon demonstrating techniques, and to Loren Moyer, who let me come and hammer both bronze and iron at his forge.

MANY ELEMENTS OF LATE Bronze Age culture survived into the Iron Age and beyond. Language and mythology were evolving into those we know from history. A reference to a "Lady of the Forge" in Mykenaean documents suggests that the archetype of the goddess who is both the forge fire and the inspiration of the smith goes back a very long way, as does the archetype of the dour smith who strikes lightning with his hammer. We find him in gods from Ilmarinen to Ogun and Wayland Smith. We may find Her in the later relationship between Athena and Hephaistos (see Karl Kerenyi's monograph), and the identification of Brigid as a goddess of goldsmithing.

And so, in Brigid's season, I offer this book to Her. May she shape us well!

IMBOLC, 2009